"Come sit here by me, Angeline," Richard coaxed, patting the ground beside him.

Angeline hesitantly obliged, and he slipped his right arm around her shoulders and drew her up against him with such practiced agility that her breath caught in her throat. He was *very* experienced in consoling women, she thought.

"Come to Boston with me, when I'm sent home," he said.

"In what capacity?" she asked sharply. "As your servant?"

Richard was stung by her comment, but seeing the anguish in her eyes, he offered her a gentle smile. "No, Angeline, it is *I* who should be *your* servant, after all you've done for me." He pressed his lips to her neck, raining an ardent stream of kisses along her creamy skin.

Angeline felt paralyzed. She knew she should pull away, but something kept her in his embrace, a hidden desire that seemed too strong to fight.

"Your beauty, your kind, healing ways have bewitched me," he went on, loosening her collar and baring her flesh as he kissed it. "I so want to bring that same heavenly magic to you."

Angeline found she could do nothing more in response but surrender to his skillful caresses . . .

Autumn Angel

Ashland Price

ZEBRA BOOKS
KENSINGTON PUBLISHING CORP.

ZEBRA BOOKS

are published by

Kensington Publishing Corp.
475 Park Avenue South
New York, NY 10016

First printing: March, 1990

Printed in the United States of America

To Brad and to my in-laws,
Betty and Ernie, Peg and Herb,
and Jan Skraba, who have been
family to me when I've needed it most.

And to Brenda Hoffman, spiritual
counselor, for her courage and amazing
healing power.

Special thanks, too, to my editor,
Lydia—one of the best in the
business.

Waste are those pleasant farms,
and the farmers forever departed!
Scattered like dust and leaves,
when the mighty blasts of October
Seize them, and whirl them aloft,
and sprinkle them far o'er the ocean.
Naught but tradition remains of the
beautiful village of Grand-Pré.

— Longfellow
  from *"Evangeline — A Tale of Acadie"*

(Taken from THE POETICAL
WORKS OF LONGFELLOW,
Houghton Mifflin Company)

Chapter 1

*Late spring 1755 — the Acadian village
of Grand Pré*

Angeline DuBay's hands froze on the spinning
wheel, as she heard an odd sort of rustling sound
emanating from outside the cabin door. She sat
perfectly still and listened for the noise again.
Hearing only the distant fiddle music of that
evening's festivities coming from the heart of the
village, she gave her shoulders a perplexed shrug
and whispered, *"cauchemar."* That was always her
explanation for mysterious sounds about the
cabin. They were caused by the ghost of her dead
infant brother, she thought, come back to haunt
her in the night. The poor babe had died before
they had been able to fetch a priest to baptize
him, and every Acadian knew that such a soul
was destined to play the part of a lesser ghost,

lurking about the home from which it had arisen haunting the sleeping room of any of its brothers or sisters. In this case, however, there would be no more siblings, because Angeline's mother had died as well on that tragic evening some nine years earlier. She had suffered bleeding that even Angeline's remarkable healing powers could not stanch.

Angeline swallowed dryly, regretfully, and continued with her spinning. *Cauchemars* generally struck fear in the hearts of others, but Angeline felt nothing more than sadness at the presence of this one. There was really nothing for her to fear, after all. Its stirrings could not harm her when she considered that the pitiful creature had already caused her the greatest pain of all in having claimed the life of her mother with its birth.

Angeline had, of course, taken the usual measures to prevent the ghost from coming around, including regularly draining the cistern on the roof, so the *cauchemar* couldn't settle there. Her aunt, the village midwife, had been careful to sprinkle the infant with holy water upon its birth. But such precautions had obviously proven futile, and Angeline could do nothing more than resign herself to the spirit's presence over the past nine years, sadly reasoning that it simply wanted to keep her company during her father's long fishing trips and trading expeditions. It was better than being completely alone, she supposed.

With that melancholy thought, she sped up the

pace of her spinning, finding an inexplicable comfort in the rhythmic clicks of the spinning wheel's spokes, as she worked its treadle with her right foot. She began to hum a tune she felt she'd known since birth. It was a ditty that she believed dated back to the early 1600s, a song her ancestors had learned in the French coastal town they'd left in order to settle Acadia—this plentiful fishing and trapping land on the shores of maritime Canada. But as lilting as the tune was, it did little to take Angeline's mind off the matter that had been troubling her for weeks. Her father, Daniel DuBay, was, as far as Angeline knew, holed up at Fort Beauséjour, some fifty miles away across the forked waters at the end of the treacherous Bay of Fundy, and, if food and supplies were not smuggled to the fort's occupants soon, he and his cohorts were very likely to starve to death—if they hadn't already.

Angeline's father had traveled to Fort Beauséjour some six months earlier in order to show his support for the Acadians who were residing there, determined not to surrender the French stronghold to the British. Daniel DuBay had left Grand Pré that autumn, when the waters of the bay were still temperate enough to travel. For some reason, however, an entire winter had passed and he hadn't returned home. Angeline shuddered to think what the reason for this might be. An accident of some sort? An attack on the fort by the British? There was no way to say for sure, because the British had been polic-

11

ing the waters of the Bay of Fundy so vigilantly in the past few months that no one from Grand Pré or any of the other Acadian villages of Nova Scotia had been allowed to cross the bay and bring back news of what had been happening at Fort Beauséjour. The only thing that was clear was that the British intended to starve out the fort by intercepting any ship or vessel that they suspected of attempting to carry provisions to Beauséjour's occupants. For that reason, Angeline's repeated appeals to her fellow villagers for help in going to save her father had fallen on deaf ears.

It wasn't that anyone in Grand Pré wished to see Daniel DuBay or any other Frenchman at Beauséjour die; it was just that none of Angeline's fellow villagers seemed willing to put his life on the line in order to come to the rescue of his countrymen, and Angeline was growing very impatient with such sentiments. She had also had her fill of the continuous admonitions of her neighbors and friends that she simply bide her time and see if the warmer waters of spring and summer would bring her father safely back to her. Angeline doubted that they would. After all, the British had done nothing but cause trouble for the Acadians since they'd taken occupation of the area in 1710, and now, with their repeated demands that all French settlers take an oath of allegiance to their English king, matters seemed to have worsened to the point where no Acadian who fell into British hands was apt to make his way back home.

When Angeline was thirteen, some six years earlier, the Acadians had defeated the British troops when Charles Lawrence, the British acting governor of Acadia, had attempted to take over Fort Beauséjour. For quite some time after that, the Acadians had honestly thought that the British would ultimately abandon any hope of capturing the fort. Unfortunately, however, Charles Lawrence wasn't that easily dissuaded, and it was obvious that he was now carrying out a plan to keep the occupants of the fort from receiving the food and supplies they needed to survive.

Angeline didn't really blame her father for having gotten caught in the middle of the starve-out. She shared her father's anti-British views and was proud that he was displaying the courage to stand behind his convictions. It was just that, with her mother having been dead for so many years, her father was the only immediate family she had left in the world, and Angeline wished that he'd been thoughtful enough to leave the dangerous business of tilting with the British to men who would not be leaving only children behind to fend for themselves.

Again, Angeline heard some suspicious sounds from outside the cabin, and she stopped her spinning and sat bolt upright on her stool. There *was* someone out there. She was sure of it this time and, as she called out toward the cabin door, she felt her heart beginning to race with the hope that her father had finally returned. "Who's there?"

Before she could rise to answer the question for herself, the door swept open, bringing with it a gust of chilling evening air, and Angeline's cousin, Elise, stood in its threshold. "It's Luc," she announced breathlessly. "There's been an accident, Angeline. You must come!"

Angeline rose skeptically from her stool and slowly crossed her arms over her chest. "What *kind* of accident, pray tell? I warn you, Elise, if this is just another of his drunken stupors, I'll make *you* finish this spinning!"

Elise shook her head. "No, no. It's much worse this time. He fell near the east marshes and hit his head."

"*Sacrébleu,*" Angeline grumbled. But she was embarrassed at her utterance when she noticed that her cousin wasn't alone. Three young men who had apparently accompanied Elise to the DuBay's cabin stepped into the doorway, appearing a bit blushful at hearing such strong language from the mouth of their village's healer.

"It's true, Mademoiselle DuBay," one of them confirmed. He was Marcel Lagrange, one of Luc Léger's constant companions, Angeline noted — one of the silly wags whom she'd seen carousing with Luc on several occasions. "What your cousin tells you is the absolute truth. Luc fell near the east marshes and hit his head on the jagged edge of a log. His temple is bleeding terribly, and none of us can seem to get the bleeding to stop!"

14

Angeline immediately turned her gaze away from the young man's penetrating stare. She'd been afraid of men since her mother had died so horribly in childbirth, and she always did her best to avoid meeting their eyes. She crossed slowly to the dining table now, where her basket of healing herbs was resting beside a glowing lantern. Again she folded her arms over her chest. "I believe you," she replied after staring for several moments down at the rough-hewn table-top. She had waited weeks for an opportunity such as this, and she turned back to the callers with an exacting expression. "But . . . I'm afraid that, if I agree to come and help Luc now, I must ask a favor of all of you in return."

"What is it?" her cousin asked anxiously.

"You already know what it is . . . all of you. It's what I've been requesting for weeks."

"*Angeline!*" her cousin exclaimed. "I'm your first cousin, for heaven's sake, practically a sister to you, and Luc is my fiancé. How can you stand there and attempt to barter with us at a time like this?"

"*Oui,* you are my cousin," Angeline conceded, "but Daniel DuBay is my *father,* and he needs help now as desperately as Luc does."

"*Mon Dieu!* Can you possibly be such an extortionist?" Elise asked in amazement.

Angeline didn't flinch. She'd never asked for much in return for the healing services she'd rendered to her fellow villagers as their *sage femme,* but now she genuinely needed their help

15

and the opportunity to procure it had finally presented itself.

"Oh, very well. *Very well!*" one of the young men exclaimed. "Anything, mademoiselle, to save Luc."

Angeline was greatly relieved at having at last received an agreement from one of them, but she knew she couldn't let her satisfaction show just yet. She couldn't afford to let them think she was softening. "I'll be needing at least one more volunteer," she said coolly. "It's a long row to Beauséjour, and the bay is still hazardous this time of year, so I'll want enough hands to man a fishing boat. And," she added gingerly, "I guess that also means I'll be needing a *fishing boat* . . . your papa's will do very nicely, Marcel," she concluded firmly.

Marcel issued a plaintive moan. "Ah, but, mademoiselle, everyone knows that the British are confiscating any boats caught trying to cross the bay."

Angeline fixed her jaw determinedly. "Not if the occupants are only out fishing, which we will pretend to be. Besides, as my cousin said, do you really have the time to stand here arguing with me, when your friend Luc is lying out there in such a state?"

"No. I suppose not," he answered, continuing to groan at having to strike such a distasteful bargain with her. "We'll get you a boat then," he agreed. "And Philippe here will be your second volunteer for the journey," he said, sternly elbowing the tall young man who stood to his left.

"Very well, Angeline," Elise broke in, making no attempt to conceal her rage. "Are you satisfied now? Can my poor Luc have his life in exchange for your blasted boat and crew?"

"In exchange for my father's *life,* more specifically," Angeline corrected, finally unfolding her arms and turning back to the dining table to take up the lantern and her basket for the trip to the marshes.

Maintaining her righteous air, Angeline crossed to the door and hurriedly handed her cousin the implements. She turned around and took her black cape from the wall peg beside the door. She couldn't believe she'd finally succeeded in enlisting the help she'd needed for so long. She tried not to let her elation show, however, as her fingers raced to tie the cape's drawstring about her neck and she reached down to arrange her long black braids of hair out over the front bodice of her gray flaxen jumper dress. There seemed to her no advantage in gloating over the fact that she'd at last gotten some of her fellow villagers to agree to take part in her precarious mission of mercy to Beauséjour.

"You cold-blooded sorceress!" Elise snarled under her breath as Angeline reached out to take her lantern and basket.

"I'm no more a sorceress than you are, *angel-maker,*" Angeline replied in an even whisper. "We are both of the same half-breed blood, after all."

"Only you *give* life and I *take* it . . . right?"

17

Elise returned defensively.

"We both give it," Angeline answered in an amenable but detached tone as the five of them stepped out of the cabin and began the hurried walk to the marshes. "With so many dozens of children born at the hands of you and your mother each year, be assured that we *both* give it."

Elise fell silent as they rushed along, obviously allayed by Angeline's conciliatory words. She remained at Angeline's side as the men continued walking a deferential few paces behind them.

"But tell me the truth now, cousin," Angeline urged softly. "Luc *was* drinking when this accident occurred, was he not?"

Elise's tone was defensive as she replied. "Oh, what does it matter if he's taken a swig or two tonight?"

"It matters, because they bleed faster when they've been drinking."

Angeline heard a skeptical grunt from one of the young men and she froze in her tracks and turned back to face them. "It's *true,*" she declared, trying to determine, in the chastising glow of her lantern, just who the disparager was. "The alcohol thins one's blood and one bleeds faster."

The trio of males stood perfectly still now, all directing their gazes sheepishly downward, and it was clear to Angeline that she'd have no help in discovering who had uttered the challenging sound.

"*Dear God,* Angeline," Elise said pleadingly.

"Are you going to help Luc or are we going to have to spend the rest of the evening arguing with you while he bleeds to death?"

At this, Angeline turned about once more and resumed her rushed pace, feeling rather badly now that she hadn't been dedicating more of her energies toward the task of making her way to her patient's side. God only knew how serious his injury truly was, and her escorts had certainly conceded to all of her requests thus far. There was probably no point in continuing to spar with them.

"I wouldn't, in the end, have refused to help Luc, you know," she whispered to Elise, who continued racing along at her side. "I mean, even if Luc's friends here had turned my request down, I would have agreed to come with you to the marshes," she assured. She reached out the hand which bore her basket about its wrist and gave her cousin's left arm a consoling squeeze.

"I know that, I guess," Elise replied breathlessly. "I mean, you've never refused a request for help. I really couldn't believe you'd do so now."

"But tell me honestly, Elise . . . just how serious is it?" Angeline asked, still keeping her voice low. Even though her cousin was little more than a midwife's apprentice, Angeline felt certain her opinion was worth asking for now.

Elise shook her bonneted head discouragedly, and her voice cracked a bit as she answered. "Very bad. There's a gash the size of a plum pit in his temple, and he looked as though he might

19

swallow his tongue, when we left him . . . as though some evil spirit had gotten in through that hole in his head and begun to torment him!"

Angeline bit her lip with concern. "I am in agreement, dear cousin. That does sound very grave."

Angeline saw how true this was as she examined Luc Léger's wound a few minutes later. The crowd of villagers who had gathered around the injured young man had subsequently moved him to some higher ground to the south so that Angeline could work on him without having to kneel in the cold sogginess of the marsh. Nevertheless, Angeline could still feel the dampness and cold of the spring ground beneath her, as she took her place beside Luc's unconscious form.

The onlookers had had the good sense to turn the young man's head to the side, so that his gash faced upward and the bleeding was thereby slowed. They'd also been trying to stifle the blood flow with a long strip of cloth, which appeared to have been torn from the hem of one of the women's petticoats. But there was still enough bleeding to make Angeline feel quite apprehensive, as she began rummaging through her basket of herbs in search of just the right styptic.

She noticed that a hush had fallen over the crowd since she'd arrived and, though she knew it reflected their respect for her and her skills, she couldn't help feeling rather unnerved by it now. She'd never attempted to ply her craft in front of such a large audience, and it was definitely making her nervous. They were expecting some sort of miracle, after all, some kind of tribal hocus-pocus that was, undoubtedly, supposed to have been handed down to her by her maternal grandmother, an Abenaki Indian who'd possessed extraordinary healing powers. The crowd was sure to be disappointed if that was, indeed, what they expected, because Angeline's abilities had never been of the ostentatious variety. They simply consisted of an extensive knowledge of the local herbs and an odd sort of trancelike state that she induced in herself before going to work on her patients. This state usually allowed her an awareness of only two sensations. The first was an inexplicable calm, which seemed to wash over every inch of her, and the second was a strange kind of heat, which began at the crown of her head and ran all the way down her arms and hands to her fingertips.

She wondered whether or not Luc Léger was feeling that heat now as she pressed some wild alum root firmly to his wound and shut her eyes to recite the prayerlike incantation that her grandmother had taught her in order to stanch bleeding. The words weren't simply a plea for God's help, she reminded herself. They formed a deliberate, hypnotic chant meant to slow her heart's beating to nearly a standstill, and she was somewhat afraid that this process might cause her to lose consciousness now—as it had a few times before—and the others wouldn't know how to

21

revive her. But Elise was by her side, Angeline reminded herself, and she would probably know what to do if Angeline's trance state went too far. Elise had had to deal with it once before, when Angeline had been summoned to stop the bleeding of a man whose legs had been crushed under a pile of fallen logs. Angeline tried to assure herself that she could risk letting herself go . . . letting herself sink into a state in which her breathing and heartbeat seemed to slow almost to a halt.

She could feel the life pulsing in Luc's punctured vein as she continued to press the root to his temple. But she could also feel herself taking command of him, compelling his pulse to become one with hers . . . stiller, slower . . . merging, merging her quiet, flagging heartbeat with his. *Un, deux, trois, quatre . . . un . . . deux . . . trois . . . quatre . . .* until the feeling of throbbing in her fingers, *in his head,* was nearly gone.

Minutes later Angeline eased up on the styptic she was pressing to Luc's gash, and she slowly opened her eyes to see that the bleeding had almost stopped. The flow was little more than a trickle now.

"Do you see that?" someone in the crowd whispered from behind her, and another lantern's light was added to that which emanated from hers. "The bleeding has stopped! She simply stopped it with her fingers!"

"It's as though she pressed the blood right back into him," another onlooker noted with a gasp.

Angeline could hear the words around her, the amazed utterances of the crowd, but she didn't really comprehend them. She was still too united with her unconscious patient, still too concerned about the critical next steps—during which the bleeding could start up again—to pay much attention to what was happening about her.

"Holy water," she heard herself order in an odd monotone, and Elise, having become quite expert at assisting her mother in the craft of midwifery, had the tiny vial uncorked and closed within the fingers of Angeline's extended left hand within seconds.

This was the trickiest part, the moment of truth when Luc's wound would either be flushed out and purified by the blessed liquid, *or* the pressure of the water spilling over it would cause it to begin bleeding once more.

Angeline could hear her cousin draw in a tense breath, much in sync with her own, as Angeline slowly tilted the mouth of the vial downward toward the gash. She held herself completely still as the holy water splashed over Luc's temple. To her great relief, the lanterns' steady light revealed that it was only clear liquid that spilled from the wound and trickled down over her patient's face. There wasn't a trace of red in the water, and Angeline could feel Elise squeezing her left shoulder with obvious relief and gratitude.

All that was left was to suture the wound with some flaxen thread. Though she didn't know the

23

reason for the practice, Angeline had learned from her Indian grandmother to keep her threaded suturing needle in a small flask of strong ale. This was one of her most outlandish practices, so she wasn't surprised that the crowd of onlookers stepped back abruptly from her as she poured the flask's sharp-smelling contents out over her upturned hand and the unexpected needle and thread landed in her palm like a tiny coiled snake.

"Oooh . . . what is it?" one woman asked, sounding both intrigued and repulsed.

"Nothing more than a needle and thread. You see?" another observer replied. "She must be planning to sew him up."

"Back, back!" Angeline heard her cousin order sternly. "How can she see with all of you casting your shadows in her light?"

Angeline felt the crowd step back even farther from her, and she looked over at her cousin with a grateful expression. "Press your fingers there," she said to Elise a moment later, indicating a point just above Luc's temple. "You must keep him from starting to bleed again while I sew."

Elise drew up closer to her cousin and did as she was told. Angeline, in turn, began the grim task of suturing the gash. It was really too dim to tell whether or not the vein from which he'd been bleeding would be sewn shut as well, and Angeline was unsure of whether or not it *should* be. That was the most frustrating part of being a *sage femme,* as far as she was concerned; dealing with the portions of a body that confounded the naked eye with their minuteness and concealment. And this problem was only made worse in situations such as this, where the lighting was so poor. Yet nothing could be done about it, she concluded, about what went on inside of a patient. All of that had to be left to powers far greater than her own. All she could do was sew the poor young man shut, as though she were darning a sock. Then she'd say a few prayers over him and *go on praying* for the best.

"Will he live, mademoiselle?" Angeline heard Luc's distraught mother whisper down to her when the suturing was finished.

Angeline shrugged. "Probably. If I've managed to patch him up correctly. And only time will tell about that," she added guardedly. She'd already learned, during her relatively short career as the village healer, that there was nothing to be gained by giving anyone false hope. "It will be your task, though, to see to it the ill humors don't enter through the wound and take hold of him," she continued, looking up to meet Mme. Léger's tear-filled eyes. "Watch for too much redness or pus from the wound, and send for me if you should see either. In the meantime," she added more hearteningly, "you should prepare a salted meat broth for him and a juice of cranberries and honey for him to drink when he awakes."

"But what if he *doesn't* awake?" Mme. Léger asked in a voice filled with dread.

Angeline looked up with a knowing expression

and scanned the faces of those of Luc's friends who stood about her. "But he will awake, Madame, if what I suspect is true . . . that it is not so much the fall that has rendered your son senseless, but what he was drinking *before* the fall."

An uncomfortable silence ensued, especially among the men in the crowd, and Angeline couldn't help feeling rather amused by it. The Acadian men, for the most part, had always been given to imbibing more than she considered proper, and she took a certain pleasure in being afforded the opportunity to point this shortcoming out to them in so public a situation.

"And you send for *me* to remove the stitches when the time comes," Angeline continued firmly to Mme. Léger. "If they're cut out too soon, there's no telling what harm might come to your son."

"Bless you, Angeline DuBay!" Mme. Léger replied, as though inexpressibly grateful for her help. As she backed up, once again merging with the crowd of villagers who surrounded her unconscious son, she executed an odd series of demicurtsies, as though paying homage to Angeline. "You are truly a worker of miracles!"

"I do it only with God's help," Angeline replied, rising to her feet.

Luc's friends began gathering up his unconscious form in order to carry him to his parents' home.

"Let us just hope your 'God-given' miracles are

as helpful to us, mademoiselle, against the British on the bay," Marcel Lagrange whispered to her pointedly as he squatted down to wrap one of Luc's limp arms around his neck. When he rose again an instant later, he met Angeline's eyes squarely. "If not," he continued in an ominously low voice, "we are sure to find ourselves in far worse shape than *mon ami* here!"

It was clear to Angeline that he was already convinced their mission was doomed.

Chapter 2

Boston, Massachusetts

Richard Brenton was once again in the titillating, if potentially frustrating, position of trying to determine just how far a young lady would let him go before she called their love play to a halt. He knew that the voices of their Puritan consciences would soon begin cautioning them to stop this dangerous dalliance before it was too late. But so far the lady seemed more than willing, and surprisingly unaffected by his repeated warnings to her that he had every intention of culminating the act if she didn't attempt to stop him.

He glanced over at the corner chair near the door and took a mental inventory of all of the garments he'd managed to remove from his latest

28

conquest thus far. There was, of course, her embroidered gown at the bottom of the heap. Next was a billowing nest of kirtles, topped off with the young lady's hose and shoes. Even her ornate fan, which had served to signal to him her willingness to be pursued only half an hour before, now lay shut upon the mound of silken clothing.

All that was left to be removed from her were the flimsy essentials, the underpinnings. They were somewhat moist now, due to her obvious mix of apprehension and anticipation as he lay over her and she let his large, adept hands fondle the warm flesh beneath them with a passionate roughness.

"We're sinners *both,* if you let this go on much longer, dear lady," he warned again in a hot murmur near her ear. The tips of his fingers slipped in beneath her shift and sought the well-rounded flesh that had, only minutes before, been clinched down almost to flatness by the bosom knots of her gown's bodice.

The object of his heated attentions drew in a quick breath, apparently in shock at feeling his fingers entering so intimate a zone. "God help me then, Richard, for I'm thinking now only of paradise . . . and not of a sinner's hell." With that she arched her neck upward, bringing the perfumed hollow of her throat to his lips. "Lead me, then, to paradise, love, before we are both damned."

Richard, feeling almost unable to resist her

now, obligingly pressed his lips to her neck, letting the tip of his tongue trace a wet trail downward to a point just beneath the ruffled edge at the bustline of her shift. At this the young lady, a Miss Susanna Bromwell from the neighboring Bromwell family manse, let out a timorous gasp. It was much like what one might hear issue forth from a little girl, and Richard was again reminded that Susanna was over ten years his junior and trouble, indeed, if anyone should happen to notice their sudden absence from this evening's affair and come searching the wings of the Brenton estate for them.

It had been over two decades since Richard's twin sister had taunted him into a childhood game of "doctor" in the storage loft of the estate and he'd been subsequently punished for his participation in that relatively innocent bit of exhibitionism at the receiving end of his father's crop. Yet that was the day he invariably thought of at times like these, times when he snuck off to bed some wench who'd been all but *begging* him most of the evening to make love to her.

This time the temptress just happened to be the fair-haired Miss Bromwell, the white-blond girl-child who'd been an almost constant companion to his youngest sister, Amelia, in her youth. And though Susanna was nearly nineteen now and her wispy blond hair had turned a sophisticated and provocative honey color, Richard couldn't help being mindful of the fact that, if they were discovered like this — in such states of undress, lying upon one of his family's guest-room beds—the penalty would be essentially the same. Either he'd find himself at the end of Mr. Bromwell's horsewhip or at the end of one of his muskets, awaiting Susanna at the altar of the nearest Puritan church.

Both fates struck Richard as dreadful, and he couldn't help emitting a muffled groan. Yet he'd allowed himself to be drawn so far into this heated encounter that the desirous throbbing of his loins actually seemed to be drowning out the voice of reason in his head.

In his most unaffected moments, he honestly acknowledged that bedding virgins had become as much a sport to him as turf horse racing and fox hunts. He took great pride in the fact that his sisters' young girlfriends eyed him solicitously at social events, their fans conveying every invitation yet known to womankind and their sweet rouged lips whispering such irresistible praise to him as, "They say you're the gentlest, the finest behind closed doors, the man who can make that first time well . . . painless . . . nay, actually pleasure-ful for a lady. Pray you, sir, might you choose to take me, as well? If a maiden must learn, why not from one so adept? One so well known for not leaving a young lady with the burdensome evidence of such encounters?"

So, he told himself, he really wasn't to blame for his popularity with the ladies. He'd simply been fortunate enough to avoid impregnating any of his conquests thus far and had, therefore, unwittingly become the Romeo of Boston's upper crust. What man could be expected to refuse such solicitations, after all, delivered as they always were from the winning cherry-colored lips of one blushing maiden after another? The word had simply gotten around, as it did with all fine goods and services—be they licit or otherwise— that an hour's steal away with the ever-discreet Richard Brenton brought a young lady all of the pleasure she could want with a minimum of the usual pain. He was, he often rationalized, just performing a necessary function in Bostonian society, saving many a damsel from the sad fate of losing her chastity to some holier-than-thou Puritan lout of a husband, who would come to his wedding bed after one too many pints and end by mounting his virgin bride as though she were a heifer tied in the stall of a barn.

Who could blame the young ladies for wishing to avoid such a fate, especially that first, frightening time around? Who could blame them for baring themselves, as this one was now, to the irresistible stroking and reassuring whispers of a man who'd simply had more than his share of practice at performing pleasurable deflowerings? It was really, in the final analysis, not much different from their going to someone to have their ears pierced as expertly and painlessly as possible.

He tried not to show his amusement as he looked down the length of Susanna's body to see that she had already eased the last of her petti-

coats down to her ankles. She continued to lie
beneath him, anticipating his entry with her eyes
pressed tightly, fearfully shut, as though she was
awaiting some dreadful leechcraft from a physician.

"You'd be more comfortable, surely," he murmured, "if we dispensed with this altogether.
Don't you think?" he queried softly, reaching
down and pulling the garment free of her feet.

She only nodded, obviously too embarrassed to
open her eyes and again meet his, as he stared
down at her.

"I promise you nothing, then, my lady, if we
see this act through. Is that understood?" he
asked in an admonishing tone. "There is no
breach of promise where no promises have been
made."

She let her eyes fall open again, and she stared
up at him solemnly. "I understand," she replied
softly.

"Then you'll understand, too, my dear, why I
must rise now and, after having taken so much
off, put something on," he declared in a sportive
whisper.

As with most of the innocents he bedded, she
appeared to be quite puzzled now as to his
meaning. She simply looked on blankly, as he
lifted himself off of her and got out of the bed.
He rose to his feet and again saw the clothing he
had shed so far. It was piled up on the floor near
the foot of the bed, much like the young lady's
was on the corner chair. With due haste, Richard

walked over to his garments and began rummaging through the pockets of his outer coat for one of the sheaths he always made certain he had with him at such social gatherings.

Seconds later, he withdrew what he'd been looking for and, without thinking, turned back toward his guest, as he lowered his breeches and reached down to put on the sheath.

At this, Susanna gasped with shock and rolled over on the bed, so that her face was pointed away from him.

"I'm sorry, my dear," he said. "How indelicate of me. I should have guessed you weren't ready for such a sight. I'm frightfully sorry."

The young lady, continuing to keep her face averted, simply gave forth a shuddering whimper.

Richard, in response, stepped out of his breeches and crawled back in beneath the bed linens.

"I've changed my mind," she said suddenly, sounding very near tears. "I've changed my mind about all of this, Richard. I think I want to go home."

He moved closer to her and reached out to hug her shoulders and back to him. "You only *think* you want to go home?" he asked in a gentle whisper. "You're not sure?"

"I think I'm sure," she answered feebly.

He emitted a soft laugh and hugged her more tightly to him. "Oh, stay, Susanna," he urged in a provocatively low voice. "We were doing so nicely before I got up. Don't you agree?"

34

She nodded hesitantly after a moment.

"And things aren't always what they seem, love," he continued entreatingly. "Some things look far more large and fearsome than they feel."

He felt her shudder again slightly, as she apparently caught on to what he meant.

"Shall we give it a try? I give you my solemn vow that you can stop me at any time, if you still wish to change your mind."

She was silent for several seconds. Then, to Richard's great relief, she finally nodded. He moved away from her a bit, in response, and gently rolled her onto her back once more. Her eyes were again squeezed shut, and she was wearing an odd sort of grimace, as though some part of her believed she was about to be beheaded.

Richard drew up close to her once more and began stroking her neck and left shoulder with a whisper lightness. "Susanna, dearest, I'm a lover, not an executioner. Relax, for heaven's sake, girl . . . I'm nothing more than your best friend's brother. So think of Amelia now, if that will make this easier for you."

"Very well," she replied with a brave swallow. "I'll concentrate on Amelia."

Richard fought back a laugh as he saw her arms grow rigid at her sides. They were pressed as tightly to her torso as her legs were pressed to one another. "Think of Amelia, my dear," he whispered again waggishly, slowly rising up and moving to lie over her, "but hug *me*." With that, he reached down, gently clasped his hands about both of her wrists and brought her arms up to encircle his broad back. His legs succeeded in parting hers slightly, and his muscular thighs positioned themselves between hers and began moving them farther and farther apart. "Hug me," he urged once more in a seductive tone, and, in that same moment, he reached down and carefully drew each of her legs up and around so that they encircled him as well. He heard her issue another shocked gasp as he eased her into this precarious position.

He simply shushed her and bent down to press a hot, wet trail of kisses to her throat and the level of her collarbone. In those same seconds, his hands began kneading her tense shoulders and back with the adeptness of a masseur. "Let's take it a bit at a time."

He gradually stopped his massaging and moved his right hand slowly, surreptitiously downward, arching over her a bit more, so that he could slip it in between her legs. From there, his fingers reached upward and, without benefit of his vision, felt their way an inch or two into the soft moistness of her lower lips. She still wasn't objecting, so he opened her a bit more and began pushing the sheathed tip of himself slowly into her.

Again she gasped, this time followed by a few muffled whimpers as she tried to adjust to the strange, new sensations she was feeling below.

"You see," he said in an assuasive tone, up

near her ear, "it's not so bad, is it?"

"I guess . . . I guess not," she replied tentatively.

"Of course not. In fact, I'm willing to wager that, within the hour, you'll be asking to do it again."

She winced a bit as he seized the distraction provided by their conversation in order to ease a few more inches into her. "Umm, no I-I don't think so," she mumbled.

"I do," Richard replied confidently.

Her eyes opened widely, as though in wonder at his amazing certainty about this. And, with her attention amply diverted, he plunged the rest of the way into her.

In those same seconds, he lowered his lips to hover just above her left ear. " 'If it were done, when 'tis done, then t'were well it were done quickly,' " he said consolingly.

Susanna seemed capable of doing nothing more than simply moan. Richard's ear, however, was discerning enough in the realm of making love to virgins to know that it was more out of a sense of relief than out of any lingering discomfort.

"I hardly think this is what Shakespeare had in mind when he wrote those words," she said after a moment, in a tone which reflected both amusement and dissent.

"No matter, sweet Susanna, they apply."

"I . . . I don't think—"

"Shush . . . Susanna," he interrupted. "Just lie

back and be still, my dear." With that he began slowly, gingerly moving in and out of her.

She issued a long "oooh" after a moment, and he could feel her body growing compliantly limp beneath him. "I didn't realize there was so much to this," she declared. "I mean, that it would go on for a while."

"Shhh," Richard urged again. "Let it be like your fan talking to me earlier . . . silent . . . silent, as mine talks to you now."

He bit his lip and offered up a prayer, as he continued his thrusts, that she'd soon stop her attempts to converse. He'd learned through the years that there were generally two types of virgins; those too embarrassed by the love act to speak during it and those too embarrassed to stop speaking. Sorrily, Susanna Bromwell was turning out to be one of the latter, the sort who made it difficult for him to concentrate on the sweetly torturous sensation of holding back when he wanted to let himself give in to the warm depths of a young lady and erupt, like a raging bull, inside of her.

Over a minute had passed since he'd last requested that she be silent and, mercifully, she hadn't uttered anything but appreciative groans. "Thank God," Richard said under his breath. Thank God she wasn't going to go on talking. It appeared that he'd actually be allowed to transport both of them to the heavenly heights of a climax without any voices anchoring them to the annoying reality all about them. Just as he was starting to take comfort in this realization, however, he did, in fact, hear a voice from somewhere close by. It was a stern male voice which he knew all too well, and it was calling out his name in a tone that reflected absolute certainty that he was in that vicinity.

He felt the young lady's body stiffen apprehensively beneath him, and he couldn't help issuing an angry "damnation", as he realized who was summoning him.

"Your father!" Susanna exclaimed, reaching up to cover her gaping mouth. "Oh, Heaven help us, Richard, it's your father!"

"Shhh!" he scolded, glaring down at her. "Be still and perhaps he'll go away."

"*Richard,*" the ominous voice bellowed again, now accompanied by a thunderous pounding on the bolted door of the guest room they occupied. "Damn it all, son, I know you're in there, so there's no point in pretending you are not! I shan't go away until you come and answer this door!"

Richard gave forth a furious cluck and found himself withdrawing from the young lady. After achieving a rather inelegant uncoupling, he rushed to his feet and began fumbling about to get back into his breeches.

"Cover yourself, my dear, and turn your face away so he doesn't see you," he cautioned, turning back to Susanna with an apologetic expression.

The girl looked at him blankly, as though not

the slightest bit angered or offended by the interruption. Then she hurriedly took his advice. Drawing all of the linens up and about her, she rolled off the right side of the bed and came to rest, with a light thud, out of view on the floor beyond.

Richard was pleased at seeing this. He had chosen wisely in deciding to bed Susanna. She was a bit too talkative for his tastes, granted, but he'd always known her to be fairly discreet and, as was evident from her behavior now, she was admirably amenable.

Richard slipped into the shirt, which was lying on top of his mound of clothes. Then he smoothed back the strands of sandy-brown hair that had fallen free of the bagwig that bound his hair back at the nape of his neck. With that, he rushed over to the door, unbolted it, and cracked it open to greet his father.

Two disgust-filled dark eyes awaited him just beyond the threshold an instant later. "Visiting Miss *Laycock* again, I gather," his father acknowledged in a low voice.

Richard donned a shocked expression that, he should have known, would only serve to irritate his father all the more. "Such language, father! I'm surprised at you."

"No you're not," William Brenton replied, pushing his way into the room and scouting about, with raised eyebrows, to see what evidence of his accusation might be visible in the background. "Saying is far less a sin than doing will ever be, and you, Richard, have been doing for years . . . I would have thought you'd at least have had the decency to wait until after your sister's piano recital to sneak off with another of your wenches!"

"But I was just showing a friend about—"

"About the estate," his father finished for him, nodding his head wearily all the while, as if he'd heard the lie at least one hundred times before. "About your anatomy, more likely, and I'll thank you to save your damnable lies for your ladies. Now, do please get dressed and come to my study directly! We've some pressing business to discuss."

Richard furrowed his brow. "At eight o'clock on a Saturday evening?"

His father finally gave up scanning the room for Richard's partner and turned to leave. "You should know by now that there are some kinds of business that simply don't wait until the moment is convenient." With that he made a brusque exit and slammed the door behind him.

"Can I come out now?" Richard heard his guest whisper seconds later from where she still lay hidden on the other side of the bed.

"Yes, I think it's safe," Richard answered hesitantly, as he walked back to his pile of clothes and began rummaging about in search of his cravat. "But wait until I've gone to return to the festivities," he cautioned. "It will be far less suspicious if we don't reappear together."

The girl began struggling to her feet in her

41

shroudlike wrap of bedsheets. "I do hope your father doesn't intend to cane you or something because of our little . . ." she paused, obviously struggling to find a discreet way of putting it. "Our little encounter," she said finally.

Richard laughed as he arranged his cravat's ruffled ends neatly under his throat and hurried into his flared coat. "Caned by my father at the age of thirty, Susanna? I hardly think so."

"Well, it's just that he sounded so annoyed, and that bit about having to discuss business at this hour. Well, it must be something very grave to require attention tonight."

Richard smiled knowingly over at her, where she lay on her left side upon the bed once more. "Get dressed, you prying creature, and get on about *your* business. I'll have a page deliver a note to you as to where we might meet to take up where we left off."

At this, the young lady smiled as well, seeming very pleased to hear that he still wanted her. Richard, in turn, stepped into his buckle-topped shoes an instant later and quickly took his leave.

Chapter 3

A few minutes later, Richard Brenton was doing his best to sit back and relax in one of the hooped-back chairs before the desk in his father's study. Despite his attempts to make himself comfortable, however, there were two quite unnerving factors at work now. First of all, in his rush to get dressed and meet with his father, he had left himself hoseless, and he knew that his attempts to hide his legs from view under his chair were proving unsuccessful. Secondly, his father had invited a third party, a Mr. James Dolman, to be present for their meeting. Dolman, being a long-time and very important customer of the merchant and shipping business that Richard and his father owned and operated, had always inspired an odd mix of uneasiness and loathing in Richard. And those feelings were made even more intense this evening, because Richard didn't have the slightest idea what the man could want to discuss at such an hour. The only conclusions he could reach were the worst possible ones. Either Dolman was about to announce that he wanted to take his business elsewhere or that he intended to eliminate the cost of using the Brentons' services by establishing a merchandising company of his own. Both of these possibilities would deal the Brenton family business a critical blow, and Richard understood now why his father had been in such a foul mood when he'd come searching for him earlier in the guest-room wing of the estate.

Curiously, however, it was Richard's father who opened the discussion and not Dolman, as Richard had expected.

"Richard," William Brenton began, leaning forward at his desk. Richard saw a lot of himself in his father's face in that instant. Fortunately, he'd inherited the same princely features; the high-set cheekbones, the straight, aristocratic nose, the light-brown eyebrows that came to an elegant arch over dark-brown eyes. But Richard's greater fortune, he realized, was having inherited his mother's nonchalant personality, the free-and-easy manner that was the only possible match for his father's high-strung and demanding nature. In business, as in marriage, William Brenton had always needed a buffering personality to offset his own, and Richard had come, over the past six years, to fill that role for him as his partner in the family shipping and merchandising company. That business was part of what had come to be known as the "triangular trade," the thriving seagoing trafficking of rum, molasses, and black slaves. The Brentons, however, hadn't as yet become involved in the last of these three commodities because Richard and his father were adamantly opposed to taking part in the buying and selling of human beings.

"Richard," his father said again more firmly, as though aware that his son's thoughts had been straying. "Mr. Dolman has come to make us, or you, rather, a proposition," he explained, and the forced, diplomatic smile he wore as he did so warned that he expected Richard to accept this proposition whether he cared to or not.

Richard eyed Dolman cautiously, taking in the stout and sanguine features he'd always found so distasteful in the man. Dolman's double chin was less pronounced than usual as he leaned forward in his chair, and his steely blue eyes positively gleamed with enthusiasm. It was evident that he had no intention of taking "no" for an answer, either.

Richard had never trusted Dolman; not only because Dolman took part in the loathsome business of slave trading, but also because he had, on more than one occasion, shown himself to be extraordinarily ruthless. Over the years, Richard had come to believe that Dolman might actually be capable of selling his own mother into slavery, if the highest bid were high enough. Richard had, however, always kept such feelings to himself. He knew that his father liked Dolman, and there had never seemed to be any point in stirring up trouble. On this particular evening, however, with Dolman so busy employing what few winning ways he possessed in the hopes of persuading Richard to take him up on his mysterious proposition, Richard found that he could hardly stomach looking the man in the face, and he ended up directing his gaze at his father once more.

"Make *me* a proposition?" Richard asked blankly. "What manner of proposition could that be?"

William Brenton leaned even farther forward at his desk and locked eyes earnestly with his son. "Well, I'm hoping you will hear Mr. Dolman out, Richard. It really is quite a pressing matter and one that none of us colonists can afford to take lightly. It's—"

"Your father speaks of the threat to the north of us, Mr. Brenton," Dolman interrupted in a patronizing tone that made Richard want to grit his teeth. "It's the terrible threat posed by those lawless French and Indian communities in nearby Acadia."

Richard furrowed his brow in confusion. "Are they threatening our shipping operations in some way?"

"No. Not presently," Dolman answered. "But I imagine they could in the future, if something isn't done to remedy the problem soon."

Richard knew that his face was continuing to

reflect his perplexity. "I'm sorry, sir, but I'm not sure I understand what problem you speak of," he said finally.

"Why, the problem posed by their very *presence,* Mr. Brenton . . . their illegal smuggling of goods from one part of Acadia to another . . . that sort of thing," Dolman added, waving his hands as though he felt quite put-upon by having to explain himself further.

Richard directed his gaze at his father again and saw that he appeared to be almost equally annoyed with Richard's line of questioning.

Richard's focus instantly returned to their guest. "I'm told, Mr. Dolman, that petty smuggling has gone on for the last century among those little French settlements up there, under both British and French rule. Now, am I to understand that, after all this time, you believe it has somehow become a threat to us?"

"That's precisely what you are to understand, Mr. Brenton," Dolman replied emphatically, his face reddening.

Richard leaned back in his chair, making no effort now to hide his bare calves and ankles. "And what, pray tell, has all of this to do with me, gentlemen?" he asked with marked reluctance, knowing that he really didn't care to hear their answer.

"Mr. Dolman only asks that you consider putting your naval skills back into practice," Richard's father answered gingerly. "As with so many of our good patrons, Mr. Dolman is a longtime friend of Charles Lawrence, the acting governor of Acadia at present, and they simply wish to do you the honor of making you a captain of a British ship for a few months, while they attempt to put an end to these problems in the North."

Richard's mouth dropped open in disbelief. "Me? Captain a ship after all these years? You must be mad, both of you."

The two older men laughed uneasily, almost in unison, and then Dolman chimed in again. "Of course we're not mad. Who better to recruit for such temporary duty than a mature gentleman such as yourself . . . one who has already been trained as a naval officer under His Majesty and who is also enough of an entrepreneur to realize that he has vested interests in preventing any threats against these colonies from developing into an ungovernable state."

Richard met Dolman's eyes squarely. "Am I to assume then, sir, that the Acadians have threatened to attack our British officers there?"

"Threatened?" Dolman repeated huffily. "Indeed, they've done a great deal more than threaten! They did battle with Charles Lawrence himself, when he marched upon Fort Beauséjour five years ago."

Richard smiled wryly. "You mean they defended themselves when he attacked their fort?"

Again Dolman's face reddened, and the bluish veins in his temples appeared to distend. "But it isn't *their* fort, don't you see? That's British land now. It has been for over forty-five years, and it's high time those French peasants realized it! *We* rule those shores, and if we are to continue to do so, we must encourage more of our young men to take their turns at patrolling those waters."

"If it's young men we need, Mr. Dolman, I hardly think I'm much of a candidate. It's been over six years since I donned a naval uniform and, as I'm sure you know, I'm into my thirties now."

"That is young enough still for these purposes," Dolman countered with an aggravatingly resolute expression. "After all, we're not proposing that you serve as a second lieutenant or some lowly foot soldier in the front lines of battle. You would be a full-fledged captain with, of course, all of the attendant pay, honors, and creature comforts. And there's no arguing the fact that His Majesty's captains are very often in their thirties and beyond." With that, Dolman sat back imperiously in the chair he occupied to the right of William Brenton's desk. He folded his arms over his chest as though he'd said all there was to be said on the subject.

"Richard," William Brenton began again in a duly cajoling voice, "I've discussed this matter, not only with Mr. Dolman here, but several of our other most esteemed patrons, and I can honestly tell you that they have all assured me that there is little danger of your dying in battle with the Acadians—"

"How could he?" Dolman interrupted with a knowing laugh. "By the time he gets up there, all

49

of their weapons will have been confiscated by our men."

"So, you see," William Brenton continued, "there's really nothing to fear in agreeing to participate in this defense effort."

Richard gave forth an incredulous laugh and rolled his eyes disgustedly toward the ceiling. "I am not afraid, gentlemen! On the contrary, I think the Acadians have far more to fear from us than we ever shall from them. I'm simply skeptical about it all, you see, unsure what any of this has to do with me and what I stand to gain by agreeing to participate."

"Think not of what you stand to gain," William Brenton said in a low, cautionary voice, "but of what you stand to lose, if you don't agree to it."

"Yes, such as most of your highest-paying patrons," Dolman added pointedly. "Now, Richard," he continued after a moment, leaning forward once more with a placative smile, "let us be sensible about all of this, shall we? After all, Lawrence's present objective in Acadia is really such a modest and reasonable one."

Richard, beginning to seethe now at the fact that his father hadn't been courteous enough to warn him of Dolman's request before summoning him to this meeting, let an inordinate number of seconds pass before asking the obvious question. "And what objective might that be?" he inquired at last in as frosty a voice as he could muster.

Dolman was, of course, more than happy to

furnish an answer. "Well, you see, Fort Beauséjour is definitely a hotbed of rebel activity. There is a French priest living there by the name of Le Loutre, and he and that band of Indians, to whom he has been ministering since his arrival from France, have done nothing but stir the coals for our British governors in Acadia. Hence, it is time their troublemaking was stopped, and Lawrence thinks that the best means to that end is to starve out the fort's occupants, so they are compelled to surrender the place peacefully. It is nothing violent, you understand. It is simply a starve-out."

"Starve-out?" Richard echoed in confusion.

"Well, yes. Surely you know what that means," Dolman continued. "It means that no one has been permitted to transport food or goods to the fort for the past few weeks and no one shall be allowed to do so for a few months more . . . until such time as the occupants of the fort choose to recognize His Majesty's supremacy there and surrender the place to British hands."

"Therefore, you wish to have me sail to Acadia and help see to it that the French occupants of Fort Beauséjour starve to death?" Richard asked, his matter-of-fact tone now meant to underscore what he felt to be the atrociousness of the proposal.

"Richard," William Brenton said sternly, "you seem to be missing Mr. Dolman's point in all of this. Those people are free to surrender the fort to Lawrence at any time. It is they who have chosen to risk starving to death."

Richard leaned forward, rested his elbows on the edge of his father's desk, and began nodding his head thoughtfully. "Oh, I see. Yes. But, of course, you're right. They will be entirely to blame for their own deaths," he replied sarcastically.

At this, Dolman issued an exasperated cluck and rose abruptly from his chair. "I've had quite enough of this, William! I refuse to go on listening to one with such obviously treasonous sentiments! It is quite clear to me now that I have come to ask for assistance where none will be given, and we simply have nothing further to discuss," he concluded, crossing brusquely to retrieve his hat from the wall peg near the study door.

"On the contrary, James," William Brenton countered, rising hurriedly and rushing after him. "You brought your request to precisely the right parties, as shall be proven to you by Richard's presence on the next ship bound for Acadia. I'm sure he will be more than willing to serve in this endeavor, once he's had a bit more time to think it all through."

Richard glared at his father in disbelief. Before he could offer another word of protest, however, his father was setting his hand to the agreement by reaching out and shaking Dolman's.

"I assure you, James, that the last thing the Brenton family wishes to have said of it is that we are, in any way, disloyal to the wishes of His

Majesty," William Brenton continued, meeting Dolman's broad smile now with one of his own.

Richard was so frozen with shock that he continued to find himself unable to choke out even one word of objection, as Dolman took his leave and his father followed him out of the room—apparently with the intention of walking him to the estate's front door. By the time William Brenton returned to the study, however, Richard's outrage at having been drafted into such objectionable service began pouring out of him with an articulateness that surprised even himself. "How *dare* you agree to such a thing! I'm thirty years old, for God's sake, Father, eleven years past the age of manhood, and you simply had no right to give your word to that man that I would act in the service of Charles Lawrence or anyone else!"

To Richard's dismay, his father appeared quite unshaken by this outburst, as he sat down at his desk once more.

"Oh, do settle down," he replied, in a voice so placid that it only served to infuriate Richard all the more. "You know I would not have agreed to all of this if I didn't truly think it necessary. And it will only be for a few months, after all. It's not as though our business can't spare you for so short a time."

"I . . . I know that," Richard stammered, still finding himself somewhat tongue-tied with anger. "But the business is not the point here, Father! The point is that I don't care to take part in those absurd skirmishes between our British governors and the French and Indians up there, and I never shall! The Acadians left France for much the same reasons that your grandfather left England; in order to gain religious and political freedom, and you must know that it goes against everything I believe to be asked to travel up there and attempt to force *our* king and *our* ways upon them!"

His father let out a long, weary sigh and rolled his eyes. "Can't you, just this once, forget about those fanciful 'enlightenment' readings of yours? Surely, the welfare of your family means more to you than the ramblings of some silly philosophers!" William Brenton suddenly donned a beseeching expression as he spoke again. "You were such a fine naval officer, after all. Your commanders did nothing but sing your praises when you served under His Majesty. Don't you see the compliment paid you in Charles Lawrence's choice to have Dolman approach you with this request? Can't you simply view it all as the compliment it was intended to be?"

Richard leaned back in his chair and crossed his arms over his chest. "No! I'm not in the least bit flattered by it! I've come to see, since my callow days in the navy, Father, that playing at war is for children. That is why they send such young men off to fight them. There's no gain in it for grown men like ourselves. Why, I earn more in a fortnight in business with you than I would in three months in naval service."

"Damnation! Stop trifling with me, Richard! You know bloody well that there is a great deal more at stake here than your weekly earnings," William Brenton growled. "You heard Dolman. If you don't agree to serve in Acadia, he and our other patrons who share his views will see to it that we are put out of business. And, far more importantly, charges of treason may well be leveled against us! Now, I have warned you countless times that your promiscuous actions and beliefs are bound to get you hanged one day, but you know as well as I that you can't run the risk of letting them bring ruin upon the rest of this family! And a few months' inconvenience is truly a small price to pay in order to prevent such severe consequences from being brought down upon your loved ones. Don't you agree?"

Richard was silent for several seconds, and he stared solemnly down at his hoseless shins. His father was right, of course. No matter how much this request went against Richard's personal beliefs, he clearly had no right to cause his family hardship by choosing to be uncooperative now. And Dolman was precisely the sort of man who would resort to making public accusations of treason. After a moment, Richard felt his head nodding at the obvious truth in his father's words.

"Very well, then," William Brenton said in turn. "There's a good fellow. I really believe that, once you've had an hour or two to ponder the situation, you will come to see that you've made the wisest choice."

Richard glared at him in response to this final, patronizing bit of encouragement, but he saw that it was too late. His father wasn't looking at him. He was already up on his feet again and heading out of the room.

Richard sat in glum silence for a minute or two more before taking his leave as well. There would be no secret rendezvous with the lovely Susanna Bromwell now. For the next few months there would be no horse racing or fox hunting, no delicacies prepared by the chief cook of the family estate. Instead, Richard was bound for the icy waters of a forsaken land that was overrun with French smugglers and savages. God only knew what fate awaited him there, going as he was to enforce the rule of a king to whom he, himself, felt very few loyalties.

Chapter 4

Richard was beginning to realize that the only thing that could make his sudden expedition off to the ice-cold waters of Acadia an even worse prospect than it already was was the presence of his treacherous twin sister, Margaret, and her equally conniving husband, Nathaniel, at Richard's send-off breakfast. It seemed the two of them had risen earlier than usual this morning, expressly to make Richard's last few hours amid the comforts of civilization as miserable as possible. Richard was, nevertheless, doing his level best to ignore them, as he sat with the rest of the Brenton family awaiting the kitchen servants' entry with the morning meal.

Richard leaned back in the carved, cherry-wood dining-room chair he occupied and took in the sky-blue walls and ornate white trim of the dining chamber with a weary sigh. Life had been so much easier for him before Margaret had married and begun her covert campaign to snatch the inheritance rights to the Brenton family business and estate out from underneath him.

Richard had always been adored by his sisters in his youth, surrounded by their adulatory merriment and genuine amazement at his masculine feats. He had three sisters, including Margaret, and even this antagonistic fraternal twin had sung his praises on several occasions. But something had gone awry on the evening of their nineteenth birthday. Even though Margaret had been born a full three minutes before Richard—a fact that she rarely let a day go by without reiterating for all to hear—their father had decided that it was "more in keeping with the practices of the day" to name his son, Richard, the heir apparent of the Brenton family holdings. He proceeded to do so, publicly, at the party which celebrated the fact that the twins had reached the age of majority, and Margaret became Richard's archenemy from that day forward, taking full advantage of every opportunity to malign Richard in the presence of their parents and the upper-crust business community of Boston.

Richard couldn't help glancing across the huge cherry-wood table at her now, however stealthily. As always, he wondered at the conspicuous lack of color in her clothing. While most of the wealthy women of Boston insisted on having a brilliant range of hues in their Pierrot bodices and billowing skirts or gowns à la polonaise, Margaret tended toward colors more befitting a badger. And though she attributed this penchant for browns, grays and blacks to the influence of their conservative Puritan ancestors, Richard had come to suspect that it was simply Margaret's contempt for all things feminine that compelled her to dress so drably and severely.

It was all rather sad to Richard now, because he'd been so fond of Margaret in his youth. They had been almost inseparable and very much alike. In fact, Margaret had been such a tomboy that their mother had been tempted to breech her, along with Richard, when the two of them reached the age of five. As Richard took in Margaret's sour features now, her mousy brown hair and pallid complexion, he again realized how much he missed the constant companion of his childhood, that little girl who fancied herself a boy and who, in her futile hopes of somehow attaining the rights and privileges enjoyed by the male gender, never turned down a dare of any kind.

It had amused Richard in their youth; her incessant efforts to be like him, to deny the characteristics of her own sex and, in essence, transform herself into her father's firstborn son. But of course, no effort, no matter how well backed by will, could do that, and by the time they'd reached their twenties, Margaret had hardened into a stiff and critical matron who seemed to be growing more and more bitter with each passing year about the procreative cards Nature had dealt her. It was no surprise then that, when she did finally marry, at age twenty-five, the only bachelor she could snare was the impoverished son of a simple farmer, a fiancé who was clearly more interested in Margaret's sizable dowry and the Brenton family's wealth, than in her.

"Isn't one more entitled to a last supper than a last breakfast in such situations, good brother-in-law?" Richard heard Nathaniel ask teasingly as their meal was finally served.

Richard's gaze shifted from Margaret to her husband, who sat just to the right of her. He tried to summon his accustomed nonchalance as he issued a dry laugh at Nathaniel's comment. "I hardly think my fate is as certain as the Savior's was, Nathaniel. Do you? Though I must admit to having a Judas or two in my midst," Richard added, raising his goblet of orange juice to his brother-in-law with a biting wink.

"You godless lot," Mrs. Brenton scolded, bringing her folded hands down heavily upon the table and flashing her husband a glare that demanded he lead the family in saying grace. "We'll have no more comparisons drawn to the Lord Jesus this morning, will we, William."

"We certainly will not," William Brenton confirmed sternly, his glare seeming equally dispersed between his son and his son-in-law.

"Sorry, sir," Nathaniel Prentiss offered under his breath. "It was I who began it, and I do apologize now for the obvious irreverence of the analogy."

Ass-kisser, Richard thought, as he bent his

head in prayer with the others. That was the most irritating aspect of Nathaniel's paltry personality all in all; his incessant brown-nosing. Why, it had never even occurred to Richard to sweet-talk his father, until this dowry hunter had married into the Brenton family and made it almost a daily necessity for him.

". . . And, dear Lord, let our only son be returned to us with as sound a body and mind as he leaves us with today," Richard suddenly heard his father saying, as his thoughts returned to the moment at hand. "Let him fight the savages to the north, that their warring will not reach our peaceful shores, and let him return with a heart more appreciative of the bountiful blessings You've bestowed upon us, as we strive each day to live in the image of Your Son . . ." Again Mr. Brenton's pious words faded out of focus for Richard, as his eyes wandered from the hands he had folded before him on the breakfast table's lustrous surface to the despicable figures who sat across from him with their heads bowed so hypocritically in prayer.

Margaret and Nathaniel weren't praying for his safe return, that was for damn sure! On the contrary; Richard shuddered to think what wishful images of butchery filled their minds now, as they both sat with their eyes dutifully closed . . . *Richard Brenton served en brochette over the campfire of a band of Canadian Indians? Richard Brenton on the half shell, smothered in some bloody white sauce concocted by a French pirate?* It was simply too gruesome to continue

61

contemplating. However, contemplating what would go on here in Boston in Richard's absence wasn't much better. Nathaniel would, undoubtedly, persist in his efforts to persuade Mr. Brenton that involvement in black slave commerce was, given the competitive nature of the shipping business in the colonies, inevitable. And, without Richard around to support his father's opposition to slavery, Nathaniel might finally succeed in making William Brenton weaken.

Then there would be Margaret's attempts to undermine her brother. It was all sorrily predictable to Richard now. She'd begin taking over the estate's ledgers and, little by little, she and her husband would slither into the inner workings of the Brenton family holdings like two African constricting snakes and squeeze the life out of all of the modi operandi that Richard had worked so hard to establish. Worse yet, their ruthless and greedy enterprises would give rise to more of their kind, until the estate was teeming with their influence, as it teemed now with the flock of children they'd produced since their wedding some five years earlier. Richard had sorrily come to realize in the past few months that there was no greater weapon than productivity—both biological and vocational—when it came to inheriting family estates. And he knew that his obligation to marry and procreate couldn't be avoided much longer if he was going to continue to maintain his position as heir apparent.

Where were the little Prentiss brats this morning, anyway? Richard couldn't help wondering, as his eyes scanned the lawn through the window beyond where he sat, in search of the hooligans his mother and father prized so highly for being their "only grandchildren"? Asleep in the nursery in the west wing of the estate no doubt, he concluded. It was, after all, terribly early for them to be out antagonizing their poor nurse on the village green.

Margaret Brenton gazed across the table at her brother as her father finished saying grace. The tension in her lined forehead seemed to ease a bit, and her thinnish lips gave way to a clumsy, unaccustomed smile as she began to speak. "Do pass the lime marmalade, Richard, when you've finished with it," she said in as genteel a voice as she could muster. "We're going to miss you so awfully, you know, when you've gone. Especially the children. They shall be beside themselves at hearing that their good uncle has gone off on such a perilous mission."

Margaret bit her lower lip. She didn't know why she'd added that last part about the children. It was clear to everyone that Richard loathed her offspring, and that they weren't much fonder of him. But it sounded convincing, anyway, she supposed, and her parents seemed to like hearing anything that painted their grandchildren in a favorable light.

"Now, be sure to take some of those wonderful books of yours with you, dear brother," she continued. "Those volumes with all that high-flown talk about 'enlightenment' and the 'invalidity' of divine right to rule," she added with a derisive laugh. "I'm told the nights can be terribly chilly and dark up there, even this time of year, and you're sure to get lonesome without your books."

Richard simply dropped his gaze to his plate, deciding it was best to act as though he hadn't heard this biting second round of utterances from her. She was so predictable, always so quick to mention the Enlightenment studies he'd become such a devotee of at Balliol College in England. Their father usually referred to them, with great disapproval, as those "waste-of-time" courses at such dear cost to the family, and they always seemed particularly frivolous and self-indulgent when compared to what Margaret had been doing with her life in those same years. Forced by her gender to spend her young adulthood either attending an English finishing school or staying at home in Massachusetts, she had chosen the latter, and, in so doing, she had cultivated the more practical, parent-pleasing skills of running a household and entertaining business guests. This was, of course, yet another fact about which she never hesitated to remind the family.

"Thank you for your concern, Margaret," Richard said coolly after a moment. "But I'm not traveling to Acadia in order to pass the time reading. I am going to defend the colonies, something about which I'm afraid you and your husband know very little," he concluded with a composed smile.

Margaret pursed her lips, and her beady brown eyes flashed with her deep-seated resentment of him. She swallowed dryly and did her best to appear unruffled by the comment. She'd long since learned that her shows of anger were ineffective against her twin's aggravating nonchalance. "There are many ways, dear brother, to bolster Massachusetts in times such as these. She can be strengthened from within by the wealth brought by her commerce and by the prudent rearing of her next generation." *Well done, Margaret,* she silently congratulated herself, and her throat swelled with a warm, surging sense of triumph at having so smoothly delivered such a direct hit. Richard's greatest failing, after all, was his philandering. If he was ultimately to lose his position as heir apparent, it would be because of his unwillingness to marry and create an heir apparent of his own, and Margaret always took great pleasure in pointing this out to her parents.

"That's enough, daughter," she suddenly heard her father admonish in a low voice, and her sense of elation seemed to drain out of her immediately. "One doesn't belittle the actions of a man who is about to go off to battle on one's behalf," he continued, and as his dark exacting eyes met hers, Margaret found that all she could do was swallow dryly again and give a compliant nod. "Richard is a captain now, a full-fledged officer in His Majesty's navy. If I hear any of you addressing him with less than the respect he deserves for his courage, you will have to answer to *me* for it," William Brenton threatened.

"Indeed, Father. Yes," Margaret replied, flashing him an amenable smile that, she was sorry to see, seemed to do little to soften his chilly expression. She'd have to be more careful in the future, she told herself. With Richard off on what her father viewed as so valiant a mission, her efforts to acquire the holdings that should have been her birthright would have to be more covert than ever.

Several days had passed since Luc Léger's accident near the marshes and, because Luc insisted on taking his friend Philippe's place on the journey to Fort Beauséjour, Angeline's efforts to go to the aid of her father had been delayed. Angeline was happy, however, about this last-minute substitution because it was common knowledge in Grand Pré that no one knew the treacherous waters of the bay as well as Luc Léger and his fisherman father. What was more, Luc's wound had healed considerably by this time, and Angeline knew that Luc's feeling of personal obligation to her would make him a far more loyal companion on the trip than his friend Philippe might have proven. To Angeline's dismay, however, Luc was nowhere to be found when she came to collect him on the morning of their departure, and his disappearance necessitated a lengthy search of the Léger family farm, a search that ended in Luc being found asleep in the corn-loft of his father's barn.

To Angeline's further dismay, she chanced to see her cousin, Elise, sneaking out the back entrance of that same barn only seconds after

Luc emerged from its great door. And though Angeline was most anxious to leave for Beauséjour, she knew that it would be irresponsible of her not to confront her young cousin about such promiscuous and dangerous behavior—especially now, when she'd be catching Elise red-handed and her cousin couldn't deny Angeline's accusations.

"Go and put the provisions in the boat," Angeline said to Luc as he and his father headed back toward their cabin. "I'll be along in just a few minutes."

Luc, still looking terribly disheveled from sleep and finding himself busy fielding his father's questions about why he had chosen to sleep in the barn, appeared very apprehensive about Angeline's intentions to stay behind. As he met Angeline's eyes, it was clear that he wanted to prevent her from speaking to Elise about what had occurred the night before in the corn-loft. Angeline knew, however, that the angry flash in her eyes now warned him that, if he did anything to stop her, she'd relate what she'd seen to his father, and it appeared that Luc dreaded that possibility even more.

"Don't be long, mademoiselle," Luc said gingerly. "The waters may get rougher as the sun comes up. They have the past few mornings."

Angeline met his uneasiness with a knowing smile. "I won't be. Rest assured," she concluded, hurrying off in the direction in which she'd seen her cousin dash seconds earlier.

She had to run at full tilt for several minutes,

far into the evergreen woods behind the Léger barn, before she finally caught sight of the light-gray skirt of her cousin's jumper dress. Her throat and lungs burned now with her rapid inhalations of the cold morning air, but somehow she managed to choke out some words. "Elise, you stop at once and talk to me!" she ordered sternly, feeling certain that her cousin had been well aware of her pursuit before now.

Elise slowed her pace a bit and called back to Angeline breathlessly. "Just go, Cousin. Go while the men are still willing to accompany you."

"You stop at once!" Angeline shouted again, still pursuing her. "Stop or I shall tell your mother that I saw you coming out of the Léger's barn just now."

At this, Elise's gait ended in a staggering last few steps, and she turned back to face Angeline with her hands on her hips. For some reason she looked shorter than usual to Angeline in that early morning light, plumper and younger than Angeline generally thought of her as being. Though they shared the same maternal ancestry, the dark, sharply boned features of a mix of French and Indian blood, Elise's facial character-istics had always been less dramatic than Ange-line's, more obscured by baby fat. The snow-white Acadian bonnet and antique, gold earrings Elise habitually wore only served to emphasize this roundness, as they framed her face with a kind of cherubic glow.

The frosty morning air caused Elise's hurried breaths to rush up toward the dark treetops in white wisps, as she spoke again. "Is there . . . is there no end to your blackmail?" she asked, her chest heaving as she tried to catch her breath. "What do you care what Luc and I did on our last night together, our last night before *you* take him off to his death?"

Angeline, dressed for her journey in the mannish garb of an Acadian fisherman, now closed the distance between herself and her cousin with several angry strides. "He volunteered to take Philippe's place, you know. I didn't force this decision upon him."

"I know," Elise conceded, still trying to catch her breath. "But it's no business of yours what Luc and I were doing. And I'll thank you not to meddle."

Angeline reached out in those seconds and plucked up a fistful of her cousin's skirt. Then, with a snarl, she pulled her closer. "You listen to me, Elise Presnell," she said from behind clenched teeth. "I'm no fool, and I'm sure now that you've been compromising your virtue with that man for months. So, it is high time you realized that, just because your mother is the village angel-maker, doesn't give you the right to sleep with a man before you're wed! One day you're going to find yourself with child and you're going to discover that your mother won't be willing to abort one of her own grandchildren, no matter how you plead with her."

Elise jerked free of her cousin's grasp and folded her arms defiantly over her chest. "She's helped other young women, and she'll help me

69

too, if I request it."

"Maybe she will, and maybe she won't," Angeline countered, not taking her dark eyes from her cousin's, "but do you really want to run that sort of risk? Do you really want to find yourself a ruined woman at the age of seventeen?"

"You let *me* worry about that, and just be on your way to take food to your father and the rest . . . to that power-hungry priest, Le Loutre . . . who condemns the work that both of us do."

Angeline could feel her face beginning to glow with indignation. "I'm not going to Beauséjour for Le Loutre, Elise, and you know it as well as I do. The only *father* I care about at Beauséjour is my own."

"Then, by all means, go and rescue him, and leave me to look after my own affairs! You're only a couple years older than I, you know. Just because the others have named you *sage femme* doesn't give you license to think for me!"

"*Oui,* but I am old enough to know that what you've been doing is dangerous. Women can die from such folly, while their men simply live on to indulge in it again and again."

"Not every woman dies as your mother did, Angeline. I wish you would finally realize that. Not all of us want to spend our lives holed up in our fathers' cabins with nothing but a shepherd dog to keep us company!"

Angeline reflexively drew back from her cousin at this stinging remark.

"And who will you come to for help, Elise, if your mother refuses you?" she asked after several seconds.

Elise looked taken aback by the question, as though she'd never even considered such a chain of events. "I'd . . . I would take care of it on my own," she stammered uneasily.

"You couldn't," Angeline countered. "You know as well as I do that such efforts are nearly impossible and you'd end by coming to me."

Elise's gaze dropped to the forest floor. She put her right foot out before her and stood sheepishly drawing doodles in the dirt with the tip of her hobnailed shoe. "Well, after what Luc is doing for you and your father today, I should think you'd be willing to do us a good turn as well."

"Don't delude yourself, dear cousin. It wouldn't be Luc who'd come begging for my help. It would be *you*."

"It would be both of us," Elise maintained, "because he loves me, Angeline. I have a beau who loves me, and that's a great deal more than can be said of you."

Angeline did her best to ignore this second attack. Elise knew as well as she did that it was Angeline's own unwillingess to be courted that kept her out of circulation, not the unwillingness of Grand Pré's young men. The truth was that not a week went by when Angeline didn't hear of one of them inquiring about her, speaking of how intrigued they all were by this lovely, mysterious *sage femme* who had refused her company to so many men already. "If Luc loves you, why haven't you married?" Angeline asked pointedly.

It was Elise who looked wounded now. "Luc . . . Well, we . . . we don't think the time is right yet," she replied. "*Maman* and papa don't want me to marry for a couple of years. That is when they will be willing to give Luc my dowry . . . and we'll really need it in order to get along."

"Looks to me as thought you're *getting along* quite well without it," Angeline retorted with a discerning expression.

To Angeline's surprise, her cousin reached out to her an instant later with an oddly entreating look in her eye. "Just go, dear cousin, before the men change their minds about accompanying you . . . before *I* change my mind about letting Luc go," she added with a strange note of threat in her voice. "Just go, and do what you must, and return to Grand Pré safely."

At this, Angeline let her gaze drop to the ground and, after several seconds, she nodded thoughtfully. "Oh, I see. So, you're worried about my safety in all of this, as well? Not just Luc's?"

"Of course," Elise replied, reaching out again and giving Angeline's left hand an affectionate squeeze. "Of course. Just as you are worried about my fate, should I find myself with child. But just go now," she urged again, "while you still have the twilight of early morning to shroud you from the British. You're always taking care of everyone else, Angeline. Now, it is time you started looking out for yourself," she concluded with a bolstering smile.

This was sound advice, Angeline realized, as she leaned forward and gave her cousin a farewell kiss on the cheek. It was true; she *had* always taken better care of others than she had of herself. Her willingness now to risk her young life for those of her father and his cohorts at Beauséjour only served to underscore this. But what was she to live for, really, if she let her father die? All she would inherit was the same nagging loneliness he'd felt since the death of her mother, and somehow, risking execution or imprisonment by the British seemed a happier fate to Angeline now than continuing to live as a lonely *femme solitaire* in her father's cabin at the west end of Grand Pré. The time had finally come for Angeline to take some risks with her life. She sensed now that the circumstances were right for it—for better or worse.

Chapter 5

Richard Brenton took a commercial schooner from Boston to Annapolis Royal in Nova Scotia. It was, indeed, a bleak two-day journey, the dreariest of his life thus far. Once he reached Annapolis Royal, he donned a British naval captain's uniform before going aboard the ship he was to command. It was as though he was regarding a total stranger as he stood before the full-length looking glass in his quarters at the fort. It had been over half a decade since he'd worn a naval uniform, and he'd never dreamed he would see himself in anything quite as grand as this. His breeches, stockings, and vest were chalk-white, and they were topped off by a dark-blue knee-length coat with white facings, which were trimmed in shimmering gold lace. All in all, the uniform struck him as more befitting an admiral than a captain. He reminded himself, however, that it had been years since he'd had any exposure to the Royal Navy and its dress, so of course he was bound to be a bit baffled by it all.

"*Captain* Brenton," he said to himself, before gathering up his attendant sword and tasseled hat. "Most odd," he concluded seconds later, as he left his quarters and headed for the pier. He doubted that he would ever readjust to naval life after so many years as a landsman.

Though he'd been given ample time to powder his own hair or don a white wig—something that was expected of any officer in His Majesty's navy over the rank of lieutenant commander—he had refused to do either, and he could see the resultant look of surprise in the eyes of his subordinates as he ascended the gangplank of his ship minutes later.

His crew, probably a mix of British-born and Colonial seamen, stood at attention now on the gun deck, as a pudgy middle-aged man in expensive civilian clothing stepped forward to greet him.

"An honor to make your acquaintance, Captain Brenton," the stranger said, reaching out to shake Richard's hand. "I am Horace Chumley, one of Charles Lawrence's aides, and I will be acting as your assistant and guide in the coming weeks. Before you meet your officers, let me be the first to assure you that your good ship and crew are most anxious to get under way."

"So am I, Mr. Chumley," Richard replied guardedly, reciprocating the gentleman's handshake, "so am I." Anxious to get this whole ordeal behind him, Richard thought, but of course he kept himself from saying it. There seemed no advantage, after all, in purposely getting off on the wrong foot with his *assistant* and *guide*. Despite Richard's efforts to appear cordial, however, Chumley looked rather disapproving now, as he spoke again.

"I fear, sir," he said, eyeing Richard's sandy-brown hair and then reaching up and purposefully fingering a few strands of his own white wig, "that, in our mutual haste to embark, we may have rushed you too much. If the captain would like more time to prepare himself, surely we have it to spare," he added, lowering his voice considerably.

"No, thank you, Mr. Chumley," Richard replied firmly, subtly clenching his jaw. "That won't be necessary, because, you see, I'm as prepared as I care to be."

At this, Chumley drew up closer to him, much closer than the deferential boat-hook length that Richard's crew would be required to maintain from their captain, and he again began speaking in a patronizing sort of hush. "With all due respect, sir, I think . . . well, I can't help feeling that the crew would have far more confidence in their captain, if he at least tried to appear a trifle older."

Richard could feel his forced smile fading, and he couldn't help narrowing his eyes to an angry squint. Though he'd never met Charles Lawrence, he already greatly resented the man for exerting such power upon him as to draft him up to this godforsaken land and assign him so officious an "assistant." If he was condemned to spend the next few months here, he was hell-bent on conducting matters in his own way. "My age is my age, Mr. Chumley, and if any of these men care to mutiny over it, I suggest they do so now, before we cast off. It will, doubtless, be a far less distressing endeavor than if undertaken later amid the icy waters of Fundy." With that, Richard shifted his gaze over Chumley's shoulder to his crew, who still stood at attention. "Do any of you care to rebel because my hair isn't white?" he shouted over to them.

At first his question was greeted with uneasy silence, and Richard looked back again at Chumley and saw that his face and neck had reddened all the way down to the shirt ruffles at his throat, due to either embarrassment or anger. Seconds later Richard heard some scattered laughter among his crew.

"There, you see, Mr. Chumley? They're not provoked by it, by my unwillingness to either coat my hair with all manner of ill-smelling white glop or else shave my head each morning to accommodate some poor cadaver's white crop. On the contrary, I believe they find the whole matter quite laughable, and certainly as trifling as it indeed is." Richard considered asking the crew to confirm this conclusion for him, but he decided that there was no point in embarrassing Lawrence's man any further. God only knew how often Chumley's services might be required in the next several weeks.

"If you don't mind, Mr. Chumley," Richard continued in an even voice. "I would rather not be introduced to my officers just yet. I think I'll dismiss the men and proceed to my quarters, if it's all the same to you. I would very much like to get settled in before we sail."

"By . . . by all means, Captain," Chumley replied, still looking taken aback by Richard's informal manner.

"Dismissed," Richard shouted an instant later, giving his crew a hurried salute and turning to head for the ladder which led below deck. He could hear Chumley walking behind him in the seconds which followed, and the sound that was made as he did so indicated that he was dragging Richard's ditty bag along with him.

Richard, still not accustomed to his uniform, found the costume's sword most unwieldly now, where it hung from the waist of his breeches in its black leather scabbard. Its brass hilt clanked annoyingly against the ladder's rungs with each step of his descent. When he got to the berth deck, he turned back to the ladder and reached up to receive his ditty bag from Chumley, as Chumley finished climbing down.

"It's quite a small ship, really, isn't it," Richard

noted as an afterthought, feeling it was best to try to clear the air now with some light conversation, after the showdown on the main deck. "Not much bigger than the schooner I took from Boston."

Chumley's tone was chilly as he replied. "As you might well suppose, Captain, full-scale battle ships don't fare well deep within rocky bays."

"No, no. I guess they wouldn't, would they," Richard replied amenably.

"Your quarters, Captain, are straight back in the rear, of course," Chumley declared, once his feet touched down upon the berth deck as well. In that same instant, he reached out for a lit lantern that hung on a wall peg adjacent to the ladder.

Richard was beginning to feel nauseous as he followed Chumley down a dark corridor, and the below-deck smells of bilge water, pitch, and what must have been game stored in the hold filled his nostrils. "I'd forgotten how much I hated being below deck," he muttered uneasily.

"You'll grow accustomed to it by day's end," Chumley retorted rather scoldingly. "I did on my first day, and I was never even in the navy. Besides," he added, holding up the lantern now to illuminate the wooden door that apparently led into Richard's quarters, "your cabin is the best on board, sir. Even my lodgings pale by comparison," he said grudgingly.

Richard followed Chumley into the moderately sized quarters an instant later and, by the light of the official's lantern, had a look around. There was a long, narrow bunk in the far left corner of the room, with a lantern suspended from a rib beam at its foot. Just to the right of that was a roughly hewn slant-top desk and an accompanying hooped-back chair. On the right-hand side of the cabin was Richard's own traveling trunk, which some second lieutenants had conveyed to the ship from Annapolis Royal only an hour earlier.

"Well, I trust you'll find everything you need here, Captain," Chumley muttered, crossing to the desk and setting his lantern down upon it.

Richard walked over to the bed and set his ditty bag down upon it. "Yes, thank you," he said with a note of finality he hoped would prompt the man to go away and leave him alone for a while.

"Before I take my leave, sir," Chumley went on in a far sterner tone than Richard had yet heard from him. "May I remind you that, no matter how far from England, this is still His Majesty's ship and crew and there are still rules to be followed and examples to be set."

Richard sat down abruptly, resolutely on the bed. "If you are again referring to my refusal to go about with white hair, Mr. Chumley, I'll thank you not to waste your breath."

"It isn't simply the matter of the wig," Chumley snapped, all of his previous deference seeming absent from his voice now. "It's your entire demeanor, Captain Brenton. Governor Lawrence was told that you were considered one of the finest men in officers' training. But after only a few minutes in your presence, I can't help feeling that there has been some mistake. You appear to lack the very discipline that you have been hired to maintain in this crew. Not only do you lack it, but you seem quite contemptuous of it."

"Mr. Chumley," Richard replied with equal sharpness. "I gather from what you have said thus far, that you have never been part of a naval crew before."

Chumley pursed his lips. "That is correct, sir."

"Well, then, you couldn't possibly know that men restricted to the confines of a ship for long periods are soon tempted to turn against harsh and overbearing officers, and the most sensible course for us is to allow the crew a kind of regimented freedom, wherein their daily tasks are completed, but no attempt is made to dampen their spirits. That, I assure you, sir, is the first lesson an officer learns. And he adheres to it, unless he relishes the idea of having his throat slit in the middle of the night. Now, this ship shall sail according to plan, and it shall fulfill its mission. And I will do my damnedest to see to it that not only will the crew go unscathed in the process, but we won't lose so much as a splinter off the bow. But understand, sir, that I cannot and will not be bothered with pointless regulations. Nor will I expect such trifle from my crew. I've been too long ashore for that, I'm afraid. And, if this is not to your liking, Mr. Chumley, I suggest that you and Acting Governor Lawrence send me back to Boston at once."

At this, Chumley swallowed loudly and took a couple of steps backward. Just as Richard had suspected, the official didn't have the clout to discharge him without some kind of permission from his superiors; Richard could see it in his eyes. And given the distance from Annapolis Royal to the governor's citadel at Halifax on the other side of the Nova Scotian peninsula, it was likely to take him days to obtain such sanction. Therefore, he was probably stuck with Richard for at least a week or so longer, and Richard was determined to conduct himself just as he pleased until then.

"Will I be seeing you in the wardroom at the noon meal, sir?" Richard inquired coolly, as he crossed to the cabin door and swung it open more widely to facilitate Chumley's exit.

Chumley clucked and turned abruptly on his heel. "I prefer to take my meals in my cabin. I'm not one of your officers, after all, Captain," he answered bitingly.

Richard offered him another forced smile. "Of course you're not, sir. I think we're all in agreement, after all, that a warship is no place for a civilian."

At this, Chumley turned and cast him a final, parting glare. "It may be no place for a spoiled Bostonian shipping heir either, Captain Brenton . . . but I'm afraid time alone will have to tell on that."

"Indeed it will," Richard agreed, wrapping an arm about the man's shoulders and moving forward briskly to hasten his departure.

It was late afternoon and the ship had nearly reached the mouth of Chignecto Bay when Richard finally went to the wardroom to meet the officers who could be found there. They were playing cards and drinking ale as Richard entered, and upon seeing him, they sprang to their feet and saluted.

"At ease," Richard said with a nonchalant smile, and he crossed to take a chair at the long table where they sat. There were four of them present, a commander and three lieutenant commanders, and they hurriedly reached out to shake Richard's hand and introduce themselves.

One of the lieutenant commanders, apparently still shaken by Richard's sudden entrance, dropped a couple of his playing cards, and they chanced to land face up upon the table.

"When I said 'at ease,' Lieutenant Commander, I meant it," Richard said to him admonishingly. "You can't expect to win at this, after all, mate, if your opponents know what you're holding," he concluded with a teasing smile.

The lieutenant commander gave forth an abashed laugh and quickly gathered up what he'd dropped. "Aye, Captain . . . I know."

Not wishing to cause the young man further embarrassment, Richard turned his attention to the commander. "So, *you're* my assistant and guide," he acknowledged. "I was told by Mr. Chumley that he was," Richard added with a broad smile.

The commander, a redhead who had introduced himself to Richard as Kyle McGraw, shook his head and smiled wryly. "Yes, I fancy he would say that, Captain," he replied in a heavy Northern English accent, "seeing as how he was assigned to us by the acting governor himself. But you had best come to me, if you have any questions about these waters or the people here, because Mr. Chumley seems to know very little about either . . . if you'll pardon me for saying so."

"No pardon needed. I am quite certain you're correct," Richard assured.

McGraw smiled at him, as though relieved by this reply. "That was a wonderful business, Captain," he said with a blush, "that bit about your not wanting to wear a powdered wig earlier."

The other officers laughed quietly and nodded their heads in agreement. "Wonderful, Captain," another of the lieutenant commanders declared, his eyes sparkling with obvious admiration. "I think it really did a lot to break the ice with the men."

"Well, I didn't say it to amuse the crew, gentlemen," Richard explained. "I said it because it is how I feel."

"Yes, sir," the commander replied tractably, looking about now at his companions, obviously to convey a silent warning not to attempt to become too familiar with the captain before they knew more about him. "I think what the men mean, sir, is that they're pleased to have a bona fide captain on board now, rather than continuing to have to take orders from some acting governor's secretary."

Richard fought back a laugh. "You mean to say he's nothing more than a scrivener?"

McGraw nodded, attempting to hide his amusement as well. "Aye, sir. Or so I was told."

Richard shook his head in amazement and reached out to accept a mug of ale that one of the lieutenant commanders had poured for him. "Your daily ration of spirits?" he inquired, taking a sip of the brew.

"There's little need for rationing, sir," his commander explained, "when we're only twenty miles from shore at any given time."

Richard could feel his face growing a bit warm with embarrassment. "Of course. How silly of me not to realize that."

"Ah, 'tis a common mistake up here, Captain," McGraw replied. "We're trained for life on the open sea, after all, not duty offshore of such remote ports. In truth, though," he continued, "this is probably the best assignment I've had since joining the navy. The Acadians harvest a wide variety of wonderful crops, and there's plenty of game, beef, seafood, and poultry . . . anything a man could want. So, we never go without."

85

Richard smiled, feeling quite relieved at hearing that the meals on board weren't likely to be as dreadful as he'd imagined. "Good news, indeed, Mr. McGraw . . . So, the Acadians are an industrious lot, I take it?"

The commander looked rather nonplussed by this question. "Yes and no," he answered finally with an awkward laugh. "They work as much as they need to to survive, but when it comes to drinking and making merry, there are none more fond. The main thing is, Captain, they know these waters and how to survive in this cruel land in a way that our men, newly from Europe, do not. They've learned to build dikes and turn marshland into pasture, to survive the bitter winters off the Atlantic, and navigate these treacherous bays. It is said that, were we British to try to do the same, without the aid of the local Indians, we would lose five men to every Acadian who died trying to settle these shores."

Richard raised a brow at him in bewilderment. "Then let us hire the damned Indians, if they could be of such help to us."

McGraw shook his head. "Begging your pardon, sir, but I can tell you have not been in Acadia long. The Indians want nothing to do with us, and they are not in the least bit interested in our money or our goods. They know that, unlike the French, we are not willing to share the land with them, that we will do as we have in the colonies, if given the opportunity, and drive them westward so that we might take full possession of this region. They are quite loyal to the French, having even interbred with them," he added, rather blushingly, "and they are, therefore, most dangerous, Captain. We English are best advised to avoid them as much as is possible . . . most savage," he declared, again shaking his head with repulsion, as though he had actually borne witness to some of their terrifying massacres.

Richard scowled in confusion. "But I'd heard that the French had converted them to Catholicism."

Again the commander gave forth an uncomfortable laugh. "Aye, sir, all the more reason for them to hate Protestants such as ourselves. And to make matters worse, it is rumored that the French have also told them that we British are responsible for the killing of *Christ,* of all things. So you can imagine what wrath we'll face if we come to blows with Le Loutre and his Indian followers at Beauséjour."

Richard sat back in his chair with a dry swallow and tried to recall the conversation he'd had in Boston with Dolman and his father. Dolman had been quick to point out that the Acadians had had their weapons confiscated by the British, but there'd been no mention that night of the possibility of Richard's having to contend with flaming arrows and scalping parties. What on earth had Dolman gotten him into? "Perhaps I'm again misinformed, Mr. McGraw," he began once more in a markedly quieter voice, "but I thought our assignment was simply to sit in this bay and keep watch to make certain there is no smuggling to Fort Beauséjour."

At this, McGraw turned his chair toward Richard and, looking rather furtive now, began addressing him in an undertone. "Well . . . maybe 'tis only conjecture on my part, sir, but I've been in Acadia for nearly a year now and there is much talk that Governor Lawrence probably won't be satisfied until he has driven the French and Indians out of these lands altogether."

"Why, that's madness," Richard replied in a whisper, bending his head forward now to help assure that only his first mate would hear. "The French have lived here peacefully for over a century. What right have we to expel them?"

McGraw offered a resigned shrug. " 'Tis British land now, I'm afraid, sir. It has been for over forty years. And with the Acadians offering such resistance to taking an oath to His Majesty and so frequently refusing to follow the orders of our governors here, Lawrence may ultimately decide that it is better to drive them out than to continue to tolerate their opposition."

"A most disturbing prospect, Commander," Richard mumbled, having never before found himself in a position where he would have to lead men into battle. His only consolation now was that the other officers had long since resumed their card game and appeared not to be overhearing much of his hushed conversation with McGraw. There was, after all, no point in fostering trepidation in his crew by letting them know how dangerous this conflict with Le Loutre might become.

"Aye, sir. It is disturbing. Especially in light of the fact that the Acadians are such peace-loving people. Not particularly given to warring. In fact, I'm told that they don't even have locks on their doors or bars on their windows. It is a most unique society, Captain, one which conducts its business entirely by bartering. Short of a few iron pots and bolts of our red English cloth, they need and want virtually nothing from us . . . except, of course, that we let them live in peace. They seem to know nothing of the attendant necessities of the Old World, a world based on money. They're quite content, you see, to live without such things as banks, government, and soldiers . . . and it would be a shame to be forced to crush such a utopian society . . . don't you agree?" he asked sheepishly, as though it was dawning on him that he may have just spoken too candidly, perhaps even treasonously to a superior officer. "No disrespect intended, of course, sir, to His Majesty or His Majesty's will," he added hurriedly.

Richard reached out and gave him a consoling pat on the shoulder. There was no way the poor man could know that he was speaking to a captain who not only agreed with him whole-heartedly, but who actually believed that the world would be a much better place if monarchies were abolished altogether. "Of course not," he replied. "I quite understand what you mean, Mr. McGraw." Try as he might to smile, however, in those seconds, to offer his first officer added reassurance, Richard knew that his face was betraying his own misgivings. He was finally realizing that Dolman and his circle of imperialist associates had very likely drafted him into a far bigger mess than they had portrayed this as being.

Chapter 6

According to Commander McGraw, Fundy's wicked tides in the Chignecto region made it nearly impossible for even the most skilled helmsman to navigate all the way inland to Beauséjour. It was clear to Richard that their ship would simply have to continue to hover off Cape Chignecto indefinitely, keeping watch for any suspicious vessels. This was all just fine, as far as Richard was concerned. He would happily have spent his obligatory few months in Acadia drifting about in Fundy's waters, having no more interaction with the locals than was absolutely necessary. In fact, he realized that it might actually prove to be an excellent respite for him, a much-needed break from the many demands of the family business in Boston.

Unfortunately, however, it wasn't long before

Richard saw that things weren't destined to go quite so smoothly for him. He and his crew hadn't even passed four hours at their lookout point when a suspicious craft was sighted just three miles off their starboard bow, and Richard's first dreaded encounter with the locals was imminent.

Richard considered fleeing to his cabin and bolting its door, as one of the watchmen called the tiny boat to his attention and Commander McGraw handed him a spyglass through which to view the vessel more clearly. The watchman's call had been so loud, however, that Mr. Chumley had apparently heard it in whatever part of the ship he'd been dwelling in, and as he came thundering to Richard's side at the helm, Richard saw that a graceful retreat on his part would prove impossible.

"Well, what are you going to do about it, Captain?" Chumley demanded, linking his pudgy hands behind his back and rocking officiously up and down on the balls of his feet.

Richard gave forth a dry laugh. "What should I do about it? Open fire? Why, it appears to be nothing more than a little fishing boat."

"Out at this hour?" Chumley countered skeptically. "It will be dark in just a few minutes. Who fishes in the dark? Huh?"

"Perhaps they're simply heading for shore now," Richard answered with a shrug. "We'll keep an eye on them, and if there's anything out of the ordinary, sir, you'll be the first to be told," he promised, looking the official in the eye with a sincerity he hoped would induce the man to return to whatever hole he'd come darting out of.

To Richard's disappointment, however, Chumley simply snatched the spyglass out of his hand with a critical cluck. Richard, in turn, rolled his eyes at his first mate and issued a weary sigh.

"Why, they're pointed southwest, Captain," Chumley declared, as he stood studying the shoreline of Advocate Bay through the glass. "They're not headed to shore at all."

"Perhaps their port is farther down the coast," Richard suggested hopefully.

Chumley clucked again and thrust the spyglass back at him. "Oh, nonsense! The Acadians know they're not to be out on the waters after dark for any reason. Now, give the orders to sail over there and intercept them."

"May I remind you, sir, that I am the captain of this ship and I, alone, give the orders here?" Richard inquired in a growl.

"You won't be for long, *richling,* if I have aught to say about it," Chumley threatened in return. "You'll find yourself in irons at Halifax if you don't start following the acting governor's orders at once!"

The official was so unflinching that Richard almost found himself believing that Chumley really possessed the influence to condemn him to such a fate.

"Perhaps Mr. Chumley is right, sir," McGraw said to Richard out of the corner of his mouth.

"Our orders *are* to search every vessel we consider suspicious in this area and seize any contraband on board. I don't suppose it would do any harm to have a look, Captain, seeing as how they appear to be headed this way in any case. And it is an Acadian boat, sir, not an Indian birch bark. So I doubt we will meet with any resistance."

Richard was silent for several seconds as he considered his first officer's advice and tried to keep his anger at Chumley in hand. Because McGraw's look was one of such concern, one that said he was far more interested in protecting his captain from Lawrence's retribution than in simply following the acting governor's edicts, Richard could feel himself beginning to acquiesce.

"Oh, very well, Commander," Richard snapped after a moment. "Give chase and board the damned thing, if it will keep everyone happy. I'll be in my cabin, if you have need of me." With that, Richard jabbed the spyglass back into Chumley's grasp and, turning on his heel, stormed away from the helm. He figured it was probably wiser to leave the scene than to risk losing his temper altogether and running Chumley through with a boarding pike.

"And, Commander," Richard shouted back to McGraw as an afterthought an instant later.

"Aye, Captain?"

"Do try not to capsize the poor souls or run us aground in the process."

"Aye, sir," his first mate called back with a

nervous gleam in his eye. "I shall do my very best not to, Captain."

Angeline froze as she saw the British ship in the distance beginning to turn its bow toward the fishing boat she occupied with Luc and Marcel.

"*Mon Dieu!* They're heading this way," she exclaimed. "Let's turn and paddle to shore!"

Her companions sat silently observing the British ship for several seconds.

"We can't, Angeline," Luc said finally. "They're within firing range. We would never make it to shore."

"I can't believe they spotted us," Marcel declared, shaking his head. "We must be little more than a dot to them in this dim light."

"Well, it appears they did, nevertheless," Luc retorted bitterly.

"We could jump overboard and swim to shore," Marcel suggested. "They can't seize us if they don't get their hands on us."

Luc scowled at him. "You must be mad, Lagrange. We'd freeze to death trying to swim that far this time of year. Even if we made it to shore, what would we live on if we leave all our food behind in the boat? No. We're just going to have to stay here and pray for the best," he concluded.

"I have an idea," Angeline announced suddenly.

"Oh, fine," Marcel replied with a huff. "That's all we need, another idea from you. You were the one with the idea to come out here in the first place, and look where that has gotten us!"

"Shut your mouth, Lagrange," Luc ordered, "and let her speak."

"Well, I think we should tie the food hampers to our anchor rope and drop them overboard before the British reach us. That way, they're not as apt to find them, and at least the meats and bottled goods will be salvageable."

The two young men stared blankly at each other. Angeline wasn't sure if their silence meant that they were trying to envision what she was proposing or that they were surprised by her quick thinking.

"*Mon Dieu,* mademoiselle," Luc said finally with a broad smile. "I guess they don't call you a *sage femme* for nothing . . . Yes! Let's do it," he exclaimed, and seconds later Angeline started working to carry out the plan, as her companions positioned themselves so that their bodies would block her actions from the British ship's view.

Richard sat fuming in his cabin as he felt the ship being navigated at his first officer's command. It had been terribly amateurish of him to have stormed away from the helm at such a time. He rather regretted it now. But every time his thoughts returned to the image of Chumley standing so impertinently at his side on deck, attempting to give him orders, he realized that he'd made the wisest decision in choosing to absent himself from the potentially volatile scene.

He turned his desk chair to face the direction of the helm. As he sat staring up at the ceiling, trying to predict each of his commander's moves, he was amazed at the memories of chasing and boarding procedures that came flooding back to him in such detail. The wind was from the southwest this evening, and his good first officer was doing just what he should have been, running, with the wind astern at thirty degrees of either side of the ship, so that the aft sails could steal the wind from those up ahead and propel the vessel along at the highest possible speed. Judging from what Richard had seen through the spyglass, McGraw would be attempting to board the Acadian boat while it was at anchor, against the wind. Fortunately, this was a classic, textbook situation, one that dictated a very specific procedure. The prescription came rushing back to Richard now, out of the murkiness of six years' absence from such naval exercises, and he took a great deal of comfort in realizing that he hadn't forgotten his training entirely.

"No attempt should be made to throw grapplings and tow the enemy into a boarding position," his mind declared by rote. "To do so is to risk casualties by enemy gunfire." According to what Dolman had told Richard and his father back in Boston, however, the Acadians were no longer in possession of arms, so perhaps McGraw would consider this precaution unnecessary.

Richard couldn't help wondering what he

would do in such a situation. *Follow procedure,* he decided in those tense seconds. It was doubtful that the Acadians could have been forced to surrender all of their weapons. Surely they were sharp-witted enough to have hidden some of them for future use, even if only against the attack of wild animals . . . Yes, Richard concluded, he'd follow the prescribed plan were he in McGraw's place now—which, he again sorrily acknowledged, he should have been.

"Approach to the windward," Richard found himself whispering to the ceiling several minutes later, as the ship's race to the suspicious craft finally started to wind down and they were beginning to slow to a stop. "Cease your headway, McGraw, and pass them by a ship's length. Then, drop anchor and let us drift head to wind." Richard began to feel foolish at finding himself speaking so fervently to a ceiling and, gathering up his hat once more, he rose and rushed out of his quarters. McGraw had done beautifully so far, but the most critical part was yet ahead of them, and no matter how much he objected to Lawrence's policies, Richard knew he could no longer afford to sit by and make his first officer take the helm for him.

"Slacken your cable and fall off, Commander," Richard heard himself shout as he reached the main deck seconds later. To his great relief, a couple of his second lieutenants, hearing the urgency in his voice, ran ahead to relay this message to his first officer, and McGraw had the order well under way by the time Richard reached him.

"Aye, Captain," he called back as Richard came up behind him. "We'll let the wind drift us up to her. Glad to have you back, sir," he continued, his voice reflecting marked relief.

Richard reached out and patted McGraw on the shoulder as he drew up beside him. "I should never have left," he confessed sotto voce. "But well done, Commander, nevertheless. I couldn't have done better myself. Now, let's rake her and see what terrible threat she poses," he added sarcastically for Chumley's benefit, glancing over to where he stood at McGraw's other side.

"They say they're not armed, Captain," a deck hand called over to the helm minutes later.

"Draw arms and go down to frisk them, nevertheless," Richard called back to him. "And don't let them come to any harm," he said sternly.

"Aye, sir," the deck hand replied, joining some of his mates as they tossed a rope ladder over the side and hurried to carry out the captain's orders.

"Well, Mr. Chumley. Since you are the one who insisted on this ridiculous encounter, be my guest. Go down and be the first to search them and their boat."

Chumley stuck out his chin with an indignant huff, which seemed half intended to mask the fear that shone in his eyes. "I will not, sir," he growled. "That's a lackey's task!"

"A lackey with more courage than you possess, sir," Richard replied with a knowing smile, and before Chumley could seem to formulate a retort, Richard strode over to the starboard side to have a look at the craft in question.

By the time he reached the rail and stood trying to survey the boat by the glow of a deck lantern, a few of his second lieutenants had already descended to it and had begun frisking its occupants. Richard was getting his first glimpse of the "enemy" he'd been drafted to Acadia to oppose, and he felt a bit of a lump forming in his throat as his own eyes stood witness to the fact that these French settlers appeared to be little more than sheep. Anyone could see at a glance that they were simply the plain, peace-loving people McGraw had described them as being.

It was difficult to make out much in the dim light, but Richard was able to determine that they were wearing an antiquated sort of fishermen's apparel, topped off by knit caps. "Are they armed?" he called down to his men.

"No, Captain," one of his lieutenants shouted up.

"Then, do they have any contraband aboard?"

"Nay to that as well, sir," another of his men replied.

"Well then, come back aboard at once," he ordered impatiently. "And be quick about it, so these good people can return to their village before dark."

"Not likely, sir," that same lieutenant yelled up again.

"What do you mean?" Richard demanded, and he couldn't help noting how comical the lieutenant in question looked as he turned and stared up at Richard by lantern light with a strangely awkward expression.

"Well, beggin' your pardon, sir, I don't speak much French. But, from what we can gather, they hail from the Petitcodiac River region, some forty-eight miles northwest of here. So it would be impossible for them to make their way back yet tonight. I think they drifted off course or something, sir. And the other strange thing, Captain," he added with obvious embarrassment, "is that one of them . . . well, one of them—"

"Out with it, man," Richard interrupted, growing more and more impatient with this absurd exercise. "This wind is freezing. Let's not tarry out here all night!"

"Well, one of them seems not to be a . . . a *man,* sir," he stammered.

"You mean there's a woman on board?" Richard asked in amazement.

"Aye, sir. It's a woman dressed as a man . . . or so it feels through her clothing, sir."

"Well, have you asked her what she's doing out here?"

"Aye, Captain. But it didn't do much good, 'cause none of us speaks enough French to understand her answer."

"Oh, for Christ's sake, bring her up here then," Richard ordered with an exasperated cluck. "I speak French."

"You do, sir?" the lieutenant asked, his voice rising with surprise.

"Yes, I studied it for many years in England. Well, you needn't stand there gaping, lieutenant," Richard scolded, when the man failed to respond after several seconds. "I hardly think French such an unusual second tongue."

"It's just that none of the other officers I've met here speak any, sir."

Richard could feel his nostrils beginning to flare as the man continued to stand and stare up at him. "Lieutenant?"

"Aye, Captain?"

"Do you or the others relish the idea of standing down there until you catch your deaths from this night air?"

The second lieutenant cocked his head at Richard in bewilderment, as though he had no idea where this line of questioning could be leading. "Why, no, sir. I don't think so, Captain."

"Well then, kindly shut your gaping mouth and get yourselves and the 'fisherman' in question up here at once, before I draw a gun on the lot of you. And step lively!" Richard thundered.

No more than two minutes later Richard found himself surrounded by several curious deck hands and a suspicious Mr. Chumley, as a short, slightly built Acadian "fisherman" stood before him, shivering in the cold evening wind.

"Well, go ahead, Captain. Ask her why she's dressed this way," Chumley ordered, keeping his distance from the Acadian as though he half expected her to draw a weapon on him.

"Why don't *you* ask her?" Richard retorted, folding his arms over his chest. "Since you're so quick to dictate what should be asked . . . go ahead," he prompted again when Chumley failed to respond.

"I . . . I can't," the official confessed in a low voice. "You see, I don't speak much of the local tongue either. None of us in the governor's charge do. So, 'tis not so odd," he defended.

Richard scowled. "You mean to tell me, sir, that you and Lawrence and the rest actually presume to 'govern' these people and none of you speak their language?"

"They should speak our language," Chumley grumbled defensively. "This is British territory now, you know!"

"Yes, but . . . nevertheless, I should think at least some of you might trouble to learn to understand what these subjects of His Majesty are saying," Richard contended, not taking his eyes off the Acadian before him as she stood staring steadily downward.

"They are not subjects of His Majesty, Captain Brenton, until they take an oath of allegiance to Him, and so far, they have shown themselves to be most unwilling to do so. Now, let us please get on with this, while there is still enough light out here for a man to see a step or two ahead of himself!"

"Oh, very well," Richard conceded with a weary sigh. "*Que faites-vous ici, mademoiselle, vêtue de ces habits?"*

Though he'd tried to ask the question in the most disarming voice he could muster, the Acadian remained silent in the seconds that followed. She did, however, lift her eyes slightly to look at Richard, and her expression told him that she was quite amazed at finally having encountered an Englishman who spoke French.

"Perhaps she didn't understand you," Chumley suggested.

"Of course she understood. If she speaks French, she understood," Richard said firmly. "It was a very simple question, after all, gentlemen."

"Maybe she's too frightened to answer you, Captain," a second lieutenant volunteered, and as Richard continued to stare into the young lady's captivating dark eyes, he did see a hint of fear in them.

"Ask it again," Chumley ordered. "If she doesn't bloody speak up soon, *I'll* loosen her tongue for her," he blustered, as though starting to lose all patience with the situation.

Seeing the flash of terror in the Acadian's eyes at Chumley's threatening tone, Richard reflexively reached out and drew her to him. "You'll do nothing of the kind! I am the captain here, and I'll do any questioning necessary. She's coming below deck with me," he announced an instant later, as it finally dawned on him that he might have more luck with getting the woman to reply if she were removed from the large and somewhat bawdy group of onlookers.

"Come with me, if you please, mademoiselle," he said to her in French as he ushered her away, toward the ladder which led below deck. "I will not harm you."

Though she appeared hesitant to move at first, she seemed to take comfort in this assurance from him, and it was evident that she was really trying to keep up with his long-legged stride seconds later, as he drew her along.

"Where are you taking her, Captain?" Chumley called after them.

"To my cabin for a moment. We'll be back directly," Richard replied, not bothering to look back at the official. "Do assure her companions of that, won't you?" he added, as he stooped down to hold the berth-deck ladder steady, so the girl could climb down ahead of him.

"This is most irregular, Captain Brenton," Richard heard Chumley bellowing after him, as he began his descent seconds later.

"I said I shall be back up shortly, Mr. Chumley, and I shall be back—with answers," he declared, shutting the hatch after him with an angry slam.

Chapter 7

Richard told the young lady to be seated when they had reached his quarters. Again she seemed hesitant to move, and she stood in the middle of his cabin with her gaze directed downward, as it had been up on the main deck.

"Please, mademoiselle," he said entreatingly, still in her native tongue. "I assure you that I am no happier about any of this than you are. So do please cooperate and answer my questions, so that I can let you and your companions be on your way."

At this, she turned around, backed up a step or two, and sank down resignedly in Richard's desk chair. With her back to him in the instant before she sat down, Richard was able to see that she had what appeared to be two thick black braids of hair tucked up under her knit fisherman's cap. Some wisps from her windblown mane protruded from beneath the hat, and they hung over the nape of her neck in silky tendrils.

She was seated now, as he'd requested, but she still refused to look at him.

"You do speak French, don't you?" he queried, striking an impatient pose in the frame of his cabin's doorway and crossing his arms over his chest. The last thing he'd expected to find himself doing in Acadia, after all, was coaxing some French maiden in mannish apparel to account for herself, and the whole encounter struck him as being exceedingly irksome now.

Her only response was a nod.

"Then, my question on the main deck still stands; what are you doing out here, dressed that way?"

"I was fishing. We weren't anchored, and our boat drifted too far," she replied in a sweet, airy voice that took Richard a bit by surprise. He supposed that, because of her attire, he'd been expecting a tone of voice that was more masculine. "What else does one do in fishing clothes, but fish?" she added after a moment, staring up at him with huge beseeching eyes, like those of a fox he'd once seen caught in a trap. As with that animal's eyes, hers were silently pleading with him now to set her free.

Richard's gaze remained fixed on hers for several seconds as her lilting words echoed in his mind. It had been years since he'd heard French

107

spoken by a native, and he found himself wanting to bask for a moment in its lovely lingering musicality. There was something more, however, that was making him regard her with such fascination. She was obviously of French descent. That much was evident from her flawless pronunciation. Yet she was so unlike any of the French women he'd encountered during his university years abroad. There was something more exotic, more bewitching about her, than anything he'd seen in the Parisian ladies he'd met.

The very sight of her sent an odd sort of chill running through him, as though he were coming down with some strange illness, and he seemed to lose track of what he'd been saying . . . *Indian* blood, he suddenly realized. Mr. McGraw had told him of how the French had interbred with the local Indians, and perhaps that was what he was witnessing now, the rare hybridity of one wildflower having been crossed with another, provoking the breathtaking realization in its beholder that it might, truly, be one of a kind.

Her beauty hadn't affected him on the deck. She hadn't looked up enough to be seen by him or the others, and it had been too dark to make out much about her features, even if she had. Here, however, by the bright light of the lanterns that Richard's steward had kept glowing in his cabin, there was no mistaking the fact that, despite her attire, this was a wholly feminine creature. Her delicate, yet sharply boned face had a celestial kind of glow about it, and her eyes were growing more and more mesmeric by the moment.

"What is your name?" Richard suddenly heard himself asking. It didn't matter a damn what her name was, and he knew it even as he asked it. That wasn't the information he and Chumley and the others were really seeking from her. Richard realized, however, that he was thinking with his emotions, not his mind, and he truly wanted to know what she was called.

"Angeline DuBay," the young woman replied.

"And how old are you, Angeline?" Richard pursued.

"Nineteen," she answered without hesitation, but her eyes seemed filled now with the same question that Richard was silently asking himself. What did her name and age have to do with any of this? He'd been asking about the way she was dressed. He wanted to know what she and the others were doing out on the bay at such an hour. Yet he seemed to have lost his train of thought somehow, and he was so ovbiously enthralled with her that he thought she must have been starting to fear that matters might get out of hand, that he might attempt to take things much further than simply questioning her about her suspicious actions.

"*Capitaine,*" she began again gingerly. "I will be happy to answer your questions. But please do assure me that, once I've done so, you will let me go directly back to my friends."

Richard blinked and shook his head a bit,

trying to get a grip on himself. "Yes. Of course," he promised. "How silly of me to have gotten away from my original question to you. I . . . I simply wanted to know why a woman would dress as you have."

"I was fishing," Angeline said again evenly. "Is this not what fishermen wear?"

"Yes. But it's not what women wear. At least not where I come from."

"And where is that?" Angeline inquired innocently.

"Boston."

She nodded. "Ah, yes, Boston. You're a Puritan," she concluded in a chilly voice, "like so many of the others."

Richard flashed her a bemused smile. He hadn't expected her response to be such a negative one. He had never before thought of his bloodline as being in any way objectionable to any other. "Yes," he said with a soft laugh. "One of those despicable Puritans."

"Not so despicable, *Capitaine,*" she allowed after a moment. "Because, unlike the others, you, at least, have the decency to speak the Acadian language."

Richard found himself feeling quite bolstered by this comment, and he crossed now to his traveling trunk and sank down upon it, smiling as though he'd just been praised by His Majesty Himself.

"Where did you learn to speak French?" she asked, leaning forward in the desk chair with an expression of great interest.

"In England . . . In France, as well, I suppose," he added after a moment. "I am a great admirer of your French writer, Voltaire, and of course, of Jean Jacques Rousseau," he continued, and Angeline couldn't help taking comfort in the enthusiastic glow about his face. "Naturally, one cannot fully comprehend the ideas of those illustrious men without learning to speak and read their native tongue."

Angeline nodded and offered him an encouraging smile, but she knew that that was, sorrily, about all she could offer. While it was clear now that this most unusual British captain wanted to burst into a learned discussion of the books of these French writers, she knew that she could not take part in it — in this golden opportunity to butter the captain up and persuade him to let her and her escorts go unscathed. The truth was she'd never even heard of Voltaire and Rousseau. What was more, she had never been taught to read and write, in French or any other language. "I am happy for you, *Capitaine*," she said softly, her gaze dropping to the floor once more. "I am glad that you like our French writers."

"Well, who wouldn't?" he asked with an amazed laugh. "Who wouldn't applaud them for their daring, new ideas? Why, they have altered my entire perspective, transformed my thoughts and perceptions of just about *everything!* Haven't they yours?" he asked with continued zeal.

"*Mais oui,*" Angeline answered tentatively after

111

a moment, feeling an embarrassed flush finally beginning to come over her. She had never before felt ashamed of the fact that she couldn't read. No one in the Acadian settlements could, except the priests. They, or so they maintained, were the only ones who had need of such skills. It was necessary that they know how to read the Holy Scripture and the liturgy, and they were always more than willing to decipher any which arrived in Acadia from the settlers' native France. There had simply been no call, therefore, for Angeline to learn to read, and she had never regretted not having done so, until now, with this extraordinary colonist who seemed to be saying that reading was so crucial to one's awareness.

"Then you agree with the view, of Voltaire and Rousseau?" she suddenly heard the captain asking.

She simply nodded, continuing to avoid his gaze. She hated herself for lying to him, but all things considered, it did seem in her best interests to do so.

"Splendid," he replied, leaning toward her with a delighted twinkle in his eyes. To Angeline's surprise his smile slowly gave way to a befuddled scowl.

"What is happening?" he demanded. "I brought you down here to find out what you were doing out there, forty-eight miles from your alleged home, dressed as a man, and all I've learned from you so far is your name, age, and reading preferences!"

Angeline offered him an allaying smile. "*Pardonnez-moi, Capitaine* . . . but those are just about the only questions you've asked."

Richard could feel his face growing a bit warm with embarrassment. "Yes, well. Well," he stammered. "What kind of parents would let a girl your age float about, unchaperoned, in a boat for hours with two young men like that?"

"Oh, the young men will not harm me," Angeline explained, finding herself almost amused by his concern over such a matter. "They are my friends. And," she added, feeling somewhat less reserved now, "my parents are dead."

Richard swallowed dryly at this wrenching bit of disclosure. As if it weren't bad enough that she was the most captivating woman he'd ever set eyes upon, to discover that she was an orphan to boot seemed almost overwhelming to him. "Both of them?" he asked in a pained voice.

"Well . . . not my father," Angeline conceded. "But he will soon die, I'm sure. He is among those being starved out by you at Fort Beauséjour."

Richard could feel his heart beginning to sink to his feet. He'd wanted as little contact with the locals as possible during his brief stay in Acadia, and now he realized precisely why. It was because he didn't want to see their faces, to know what suffering he was causing in their lives by simply having agreed to follow the acting governor's orders. It would have been so much easier, all of it, if the Acadians could simply have remained faceless and nameless to him. Nevertheless, here one of them sat, a young woman whose unusual beauty virtually took his breath away, and he knew he would have to endure, probably for the rest of his days, knowing that his actions had helped to leave her an orphan. This wasn't a simple interrogation anymore; it was rapidly becoming a nightmare for him. "Well, for Christ's sake, girl," he snarled with exasperation. "Why don't you go there and tell your father to leave? He and the others are free to leave the fort at any time without fear of retribution."

"*Oui, Capitaine,*" Angeline concurred, "*if* they are willing to surrender the fort to the likes of you. But they are not."

Once again Richard found himself staring at her speechlessly. There were dozens of questions he should have been asking her. They echoed in his mind now. How had a sail-less little boat drifted so far southeast of her alleged home in the course of just a day? Especially with the winds blowing toward the west most of the morning and afternoon? Why had she, a young woman, joined a fishing party, a realm that was traditionally reserved for men? The questions were churning in his mind, but he couldn't seem to voice them. He simply sat looking at her in an odd state of wonderment, a state that he had never before experienced.

"We are, neither of us, happy to be here, *Capitaine,* are we?" she said suddenly, as if reading this truth in his eyes. Her stare was so probing that he knew he should turn away and not allow her to read any further, but in spite of himself, his eyes remained fixed upon hers. What was more, a sort of tunnel vision descended upon him, and it was as though his surroundings and circumstances fell away from him and she was all he could see.

"You are here at someone else's bidding, as I am," she suddenly declared in a monotone that Richard found quite unsettling. For some reason, though he'd never witnessed such a thing, it was a tone that struck him as being akin to that of a soothsayer in a trance. "Your father's bidding, perhaps," she continued, "as I am. And you want so desperately to be somewhere else, don't you?"

He didn't bother to respond. It was quite clear she already knew the answer.

"We've much in common, you and I," she affirmed in a voice so soft that it was almost as hypnotic as her eyes.

Richard cleared his throat after several seconds and, rising, finally managed to tear his gaze from hers. "Do you always do that?" he asked sternly, assuming a rigid posture and locking his hands behind his back. Before she could answer, he began pacing about his quarters with his eyes directed steadily downward.

"What?" she asked with a guilelessness that irked him a bit.

His tone continued to be cool and slightly accusing. "Read people's thoughts like that."

She didn't answer immediately, and he looked

over at her to see a subtle smile tugging at the right corner of her lips. "Then I was right about your father?" she asked hopefully.

"For courtesy's sake, *mademoiselle*," he retorted coldly, "you answer *my* question first."

"In the very asking of it, *Capitaine*," she said with a self-assurance that made Richard bristle, "you've answered mine."

"Just respond to what I asked," he thundered with an intensity that surprised him almost as much as it appeared to surprise her.

She recoiled a bit at his outburst, and her expression grew sober. "No. I am not clairvoyant. There are others with much more of a gift at that than I possess. I am, instead, a healer."

"A healer?" Richard repeated, reaching up to scratch his chin and making no effort to hide his skepticism.

It was she who dropped her gaze now, as though she regretted having made this disclosure, and Richard couldn't imagine what was going through her mind. What was she afraid he would do with such information? Perhaps she thought that he would take her prisoner indefinitely, make her the physician that almost every British ship lacked, yet needed so badly at times. "*Oui,*" she replied finally, in an almost inaudible voice.

"And whom do you heal, pray tell?" he asked pointedly.

"My people . . . whoever needs me."

"And what do you heal?" Richard pursued, not knowing why he cared about such trivia now,

116

when his real questions, the questions Chumley would have demanded that he ask, still went unvoiced and unanswered.

She looked up at him again, the glimmer in her eyes reflecting an odd mix of resentment and pleading. "What do you mean, 'what do I heal'?" she asked in a tone so artless that he knew she had been genuinely confused by the question.

"I mean, do you rid people of the gout or warts or what?"

"I . . . I stop bleeding, *Capitaine*," she answered, her voice faltering, but her eyes focused steadily upon his once more.

"Bleeding?" he echoed back, as though it were the first time he had heard the word.

"Yes . . . you know . . . when one has been shot or injured."

"Ah, yes. Bleeding," he acknowledged. *You'd like to make me bleed, wouldn't you?* an odd little voice within him wanted to say to her. And strangely, it was *he* who seemed capable of reading her thoughts now. *That savage Indian blood in you would like to take a knife to my throat and bleed me like a pig in a slaughterhouse.* Her eyes, which had seemed so captivating to him only minutes before, were frightening to him now. He could see his own demise in their dark pupils. They seemed black as coal, black as the abyss of death itself, and he felt a shiver run through him.

"What are you warning me of?" he suddenly heard himself asking. He didn't fully understand the question, but mercifully, it appeared that she did.

"Of the danger of fighting other men's wars," she said simply. "Of not listening to yourself, *Capitaine*. I fear it could be very bad for you. And what you do now, tonight, with me," she added in an entreating tone, "could make all the difference."

Again he tore his gaze from hers. "I'd expect you to say that," he said cynically. "You would say or do anything to be let out of here, wouldn't you? You hate us British. I can see it in your eyes."

"*Oui,*" she answered candidly. Then, again, her voice assumed a strange, prophesier's sort of earnestness. "But I don't hate you. Anyone can see that you are not like the others. You are, as you say in English . . ." She paused for a second or two, obviously searching for the right word. "A gentleman," she said at last. "Yes, a *gentle* man. Isn't that how you English say it?"

Richard nodded, managing to hide the surprise he felt at hearing her dissect the word in this way.

"There is much 'gentleness' in your eyes, *Capitaine*. And one should always look into the eyes of one's opponent, because they often tell more truth than the lips."

Richard was silent for a moment. Part of him wanted to lash out at her for having seen through him so quickly, for somehow deducing that he lacked the detachment necessary to captain a British warship. Yet, another part of him was so stunned by her uncanny ability to read him that he found himself continuing to say nothing at all.

"Up with you. Come on," he ordered several moments later, crossing to her and reaching out to help her to her feet. "Let's get you back to your friends before they decide to leave without you."

"Then, you're letting us go?" she asked, her tone reflecting an equal mix of relief and surprise.

"Yes," Richard confirmed, taking her arm and leading her out of his cabin. "I'm letting you go. And good riddances to you, *mademoiselle*," he added in a frosty voice. "I wish you and your father and friends all the best. Now, please do be on your way," he continued, moving her down the passageway that led from his quarters to the berth-deck ladder.

He found that he was walking at a ridiculously hurried pace. He simply wanted her and her unnerving regard out of his cabin, out of his sight, and off his ship. He had let her extract far too much from him already. He could only conclude, from what he'd heard and seen of her, that she was some sort of Acadian sorceress, and the sooner he was rid of her and allowed to return to his former, normal state of mind, the better. Not only had she succeeded in reading his thoughts, but he was convinced that she was also responsible for beclouding his mind as he'd tried to question her, and he had no doubt now that such a woman was dangerous.

"Well," Chumley hailed pointedly, as Richard and the girl emerged from below deck several seconds later, "what did she tell you?"

Richard pushed Angeline forward, past Chumley's rotund figure, which hovered in front of them, obviously attempting to block their way. Richard rushed past the official as well an instant later, not stopping to address his question. "Nothing," he called back over his shoulder. "It's just as it appears. She was out fishing with her companions, and their boat drifted off course."

"*Huh!*" Chumley thundered, chasing after them, as they made their way to the starboard side of the boat. "Fishing, with a fortnight's supply of meat and ale tied to their anchor rope? Not likely, Captain!"

Richard turned about and stared at the official. "What?"

"Oh, yes, Captain Brenton," Chumley continued imperiously, strutting up to him. "While you were off having your tête-à-tête with the young lady, one of your second lieutenants chanced to discover how heavily the Acadians' anchor rope was weighted, and when he pulled it up to the surface, lo and behold, there was the contraband I suspected they were carrying."

Richard stood looking at the official in stunned silence for a second or two more. "Then we'll simply have to take it from them," he said finally with an uneasy swallow. "Aren't those the acting governor's orders?"

"Indeed, Captain," Chumley confirmed, and

120

Richard could see an unmistakably sadistic gleam in his eyes as the man drew up even closer. "We are to confiscate everything, including their boat."

"And then what?" Richard asked in amazement. "Make them swim to shore in this dreadful cold? Why, they would freeze to death in these waters!"

Chumley donned a ruthless smirk. "Well, they should have thought of that, shouldn't they have, before they rowed out here with those illegal goods."

Richard looked away from Chumley's brutish expression and called out to his first officer, who had left his place at the helm and was standing at the starboard rail. He was, evidently, supervising the deck hands' interactions with the remaining occupants of the Acadian craft below.

"Lower the longboats, Mister McGraw," Richard ordered. "We'll be escorting the Acadians back to their settlement."

"We shall do nothing of the kind, Captain," Chumley bellowed. "We shall relieve them of their belongings and be on our way!"

As Richard turned back and saw Chumley's nostrils flaring with rage, it occurred to him, however fleetingly, to tell the official about the strange conversation he'd had with the girl below deck, of how she'd been able to read his thoughts, and, apparently, warn him of his future. Surely, even one as devoted to procedure as Chumley would understand the dangers implicit in crossing such a woman, what negative consequences it could bring. On the other hand, Chumley wasn't a seaman, Richard reminded himself. He probably wouldn't know of or believe in the superstitions of true navy men. He wasn't likely to be familiar with the evils that could befall a ship if certain warnings went unheeded. In fact, Richard sorrily concluded, he was very apt to greet talk of such things with ridicule and laughter. Such a landsman could spit into the wind, hand some article to a shipmate through the rungs of a ladder, and turn a hatch cover over, all within the space of an hour, and have no idea what dreadful fates might betide the entire crew because of such reckless actions. Even the most blatant omens were ignored by landlubbers, so Richard held out little hope now that he could persuade Chumley to heed the one he'd just heard from the Acadian's lips.

"I give the orders here, Mr. Chumley," Richard finally replied in a fierce growl. "And I say we shall confiscate only their contraband and escort them and their boat back to the Petitcodiac River region, from whence they claim to have come."

"This is treasonous, Captain," the official countered.

"On the contrary, sir," Richard retorted with equal vehemence, "it is following the acting governor's orders to the letter. His orders were only that we confiscate the offending cargo. Nothing more nor less, as I recall," Richard concluded. With that, he turned away and began heading toward the starboard side of the ship once more to oversee the lowering of the longboats.

"And just how far do you suppose your longboats will get in the dark?" Chumley demanded.

Richard froze in his tracks. He'd been so hellbent on getting the ominous visitor off the ship that he had never even stopped to consider how foolish it was to have his men try to escort the Acadians such a distance in total darkness. "They shall get as far as the nearest shore for tonight, Mr. Chumley. Then they shall accompany the Acadians to the Petitcodiac region at daybreak."

"That's madness, Captain. Making them sleep ashore with known lawbreakers. Why, your men could be overpowered in the middle of the night!"

Richard gave this possibility a few seconds' thought. Maybe Chumley was right. Given the fact that Indian blood seemed evident in the girl, there might be a chance that these Acadians were in cahoots with some of the local natives and Richard would find his longboat party massacred by morning. On the other hand, the threesome claimed to be from the Petitcodiac region, not from Advocate Bay where they were at present, so the likelihood of such collaboration with the Indians was probably not high. In any case, Richard knew that, as the ship's captain, his primary responsibility was to act in the best interests of the majority of his crew, not simply a small portion of it. He therefore concluded once more that getting the menacing Acadian woman

123

off his ship was the wisest course for all concerned.

"I shall see to it that the longboat party is amply armed," he said to Chumley through clenched teeth. "And our frisking has already established that the Acadians are not. What more, Mr. Chumley, it takes at least three men to pilot a longboat and at least two longboats to accompany such a fishing craft to its destination, so my men will outnumber them two to one." Feeling certain now that he had successfully countered each of the official's arguments, Richard again began heading for the starboard rail.

"Any sane man would simply hold the Acadians in the brig overnight," Chumley called after him.

Richard came to an abrupt halt, and he turned back to address the man, his lips pursed with rage. "I don't think you understand, sir. So, please do allow me to make myself more plain. I don't want those people aboard this ship. Not even for one night," he exclaimed with such volume and rage that he could see his crew freezing in their tracks all about him at his outburst. He was quite confident that Chumley would have the good sense not to question him any further. To his amazement, however, Chumley's next words rang out like those of an impudent child.

"Why not?"

At this, Richard lost all composure. He stormed over to the man and seized him by his

124

shirt ruffles. Chumley, in response, issued an astounded gasp and his eyes seemed to grow as large as sand dollars.

Richard could feel the tightness in his lips as he spoke, and he knew that they were nearly colorless with fury. "I have my reasons, dear sir, and that is all you need know!"

Chapter 8

Angeline felt numb with cold and fear as she was escorted back down to the fishing boat by two of the British second lieutenants, just minutes after she and the captain had returned to the main deck. She understood very little English, and she hadn't heard much of the captain's conversation with the plumpish man who had greeted them at the top of the ladder. She had, however, heard enough to know that the man was telling the captain about the contraband she had tied to the anchor rope. The British had obviously discovered their little cache: that much was evident from the expressions Luc and Marcel were wearing when she was reunited with them.

"What will they do with us now?" she whispered to Luc as she stepped back on board the boat.

Luc's tone was equally furtive. "God alone knows," he said out of the side of his mouth. "I'm sorry, but you were so long with them up there that we couldn't keep their deck hands from nosing around. One of them chanced to catch his foot on the anchor rope, and when he felt how weighted it was, one thing just led to another," he explained, throwing up his arms with a frustrated huff. "Even if they did speak enough French to understand me, I couldn't think of a believable cover story for it."

"I doubt whether I'd have been able to either," Angeline replied.

"What on earth went on up there?" Marcel asked, as Angeline sat down beside him on one of the boat's seats. "Why were you gone so long?"

"The captain took me below deck and questioned me."

Luc raised a skeptical brow. "Well, I hope you didn't tell him too much."

"What sort of fool do you take me for?" she snapped. "Of course I didn't. I simply told him again that we were from the Petitcodiac region and that we were out fishing and we drifted off course."

Marcel leaned up even closer to her in his obvious effort to keep their conversation as inaudible to the nearby British deck hands as possible. "Do you think he believed you?"

Angeline shrugged. "I guess so. He said he intended to let us go, in any case."

"Well, he probably won't now," Marcel predicted with a grim shiver. "If I know the British, they'll most likely row us to shore and shoot us, after finding those hampers."

"Yes," Luc agreed with equal trepidation. "That's probably why they're lowering their long-boats. They plan to take us to land and execute us."

"Nonsense," Angeline declared. "They never kill smugglers. You two know that as well as I. Lawrence has decreed that they simply confiscate our cargo and send us on our way. And even if they do take our boat, at least it looks as though they plan to see us safely to shore."

"It's not *our* boat," Marcel corrected. "It's my father's, and if they do confiscate it, I'm a dead man, whether they execute us or not. Papa will have my hide if I return to Grand Pré without it!"

"Oh, but the British captain was a very nice man," Angeline maintained. "If you could have seen his face, you would realize that he is not the sort to take the boat and strand us out here."

Luc rolled his eyes at her. "Honestly, Angeline, you're as naive as Elise sometimes. There are no 'nice' men among the British! You should know that by now."

"But the captain is a good man. I shall show you," Angeline replied in a determined whisper.

With that she rose slowly and called up to the rail of the ship. The captain had been nearby as she'd climbed down to the boat a few minutes earlier, and she was hopeful that he was still within earshot.

"*Capitaine?*" she yelled up in her most disarming voice. "Oh, *Capitaine?*"

"One of the Acadians is asking for you, Captain," McGraw called out as Richard made his way back to the helm.

Richard stopped short and turned about to face his first officer with a blank expression.

"It's the girl, Captain," McGraw explained. "I think she has something more she wants to say."

Though reluctant to have any further dealings with the frightening young woman, Richard walked over to the rail and peered down at her. She didn't seem nearly as threatening from this slightly dwarfing, overhead view, as she had face to face with him minutes earlier.

"*Oui?*" he shouted down to her in as diplomatic a tone as he could muster.

"Pray tell, where are the longboats taking us?"

"To shore for the night. Then back to the Petitcodiac River in the morning. Isn't that where you came from?" he replied in French.

"Ah, *oui, Capitaine,*" she called up to him with a smile in her voice. "*Merci! Merci beaucoup, mon Capitaine,*" she concluded, giving him a grateful wave.

"Amazing," Luc said under his breath as Angeline sat back down across from him in the

129

little boat. "Not only are they taking us safely to shore, but they're bringing us so much closer to Beauséjour and out of the range of the fleet Lawrence is assembling in Fundy. What in the world could you have said to him to make him so willing to do that?" he continued with a suspicious gleam in his eye.

"I don't know," Angeline answered with a slight smirk. "I think he is simply kind. I told you he was. He is truly a 'gentle' man, as they say in English," she added with a gratified chill running through her. She had never had much rapport with men. She had always been rather afraid of them. But this fancy British captain had been different. He had been considerate enough to speak her language and do right by her and her companions. If anything, she'd sensed that it was *he* who had been afraid of *her*. Yet, for the life of her, she couldn't imagine why.

"Begging your pardon, sir," McGraw said in a low voice to Richard.

"Yes, Commander?"

"We've confiscated the contraband, Captain, per the acting governor's orders, and the long-boat pilots now have your instructions to see the Acadians to shore for the night and on to the Petitcodiac region at dawn. But I was wondering, sir, if I . . . I might have a word with you alone," McGraw added in a faltering voice.

Richard raised a questioning brow at him, unsure of why he was making this request so gingerly. "Certainly, Commander."

"Below deck, sir, if you wouldn't mind."

"Of course not," Richard assured, his brow now knit in perplexity. "We'll go down at once, since the men now have my orders. Just tell the next in command to see to all of it, and come down to my quarters straightaway. I'll be waiting for you there," he concluded with a mystified shrug.

McGraw issued an uneasy sigh, as though he wasn't entirely pleased with this arrangement. "Aye, sir," he replied, turning away with a resigned posture and going off to speak to his subordinate at the helm.

Richard's first officer was still wearing that same pained, yet cautious expression when he appeared in the doorway of Richard's cabin a few minutes later.

"Come in, Commander. Sit down," Richard greeted, raising a brimming mug of ale to him. "May I have my steward bring you some of the local brew? I found that I quite required some this evening," he confessed with a weary laugh.

"No, thank you, Captain," McGraw replied, maintaining his tense deportment as he seated himself on Richard's traveling trunk.

Richard couldn't help chuckling a bit as he continued to observe him. "Good God, man, whatever is the matter? You look as though you were about to be shot."

"Well, begging your pardon, Captain, but as your first officer, I do feel obliged to tell you that the orders you issued up there just now were . . . were . . . well, most curious, sir," he choked. "I mean, Captain, that at the risk of having you believe that I am siding with Mr. Chumley, which I am not, I must tell you that we are all a bit mystified as to why you would send a longboat party to shore for the night. I mean, it is, after all, threatening to rain this evening, from the looks of things, and it would just seem to me, Captain, a wiser choice to have brought the Acadians aboard until morning."

At this point, the commander looked so apprehensive, so drained of color, that Richard feared he might keel over where he sat.

"And you were afraid I would lose all composure again and holler at you on deck, as I did Chumley. Is that it, Mr. McGraw?" Richard inquired with a smile.

His first officer gave forth a nervous cough. "Aye, sir, it is," he confessed.

"Well, I won't, Commander, and I'll tell you why," Richard continued, still smiling.

"Why, sir?"

"Because, being a navy man, I'm certain you will understand what harm could come to this good ship and crew if even the smallest omen should go unheeded."

"I think I will take that drink now, Captain, if it isn't too much trouble," McGraw interjected with an awkward expression. It was as though he wasn't entirely sure at this point whether or not the captain had taken leave of his senses.

"Fine," Richard answered, calling out for his steward.

"What omen is it you speak of, sir?" McGraw inquired in the seconds that ensued before his mug of ale was served.

"It was the girl, Commander," Richard explained, more soberly now. "After speaking with her for just a few minutes, I was convinced she was some sort of sorceress. Though when I confronted her on it, she claimed she was nothing more than a healer."

McGraw's beverage arrived, and he took a long, nervous swallow of it, before responding. "A healer. Aye, sir," he confirmed. "The Acadians do have a few of those among them. *Sage femmes,* I believe they are called. But they are not generally thought of as sorceresses, Captain. I mean, as I understand it, they're midwives and angel-makers mainly."

"Angel-makers?" Richard echoed, furrowing his brow.

An odd blush came over his first officer. "Abortionists, sir . . . you know," he added clumsily in the higher-pitched tone of a schoolboy.

Richard leaned back against his desk and propped his chin upon his upraised left hand. "Most interesting, Mr. McGraw."

"Well, yes, sir . . . I guess they are. But they're also rather rare, so I do find it surprising that we would chance to have one on board."

"But that's just the point, isn't it, Commander. I mean, given what I learned about her, I thought it best not to have her on board a moment longer than was necessary."

"I can understand that, Captain."

Richard nodded and smiled. "I felt certain you would."

"Tell me, Captain. I didn't get much of a look at her, because I was at the helm so much of the time. Did she, by chance, appear to have any Indian blood in her?"

"Indeed she did. Enough to make her quite a temptress, in fact," Richard added with a sheepish smirk.

McGraw nodded. "Oh, aye. Then your suspicion that she possessed some sort of magical power is even more founded. That is to say, sir, that most of the *sage femmes* are rumored to be *métisse* . . . partially of Indian blood."

"She could read my thoughts, you see, Mr. McGraw. That was what was so astounding. She knew things about me that no man on this ship could have guessed at."

The commander drew back a bit at this disclosure. "Good heavens, Captain! Are you quite sure?"

"Positively. It was most unsettling, I assure you!"

"Oh, I'm certain it was, sir."

"And she kept muddling my thinking," Richard continued. "I mean, I brought her down here

134

to question her about what she was doing out there with those two fishermen, and I ended by discussing French writers with her, of all things," he concluded with an irritated cluck.

"Couldn't have been much of a discussion, Captain," McGraw said laughingly. "The Acadians don't know how to read for the most part, sir. Their priests do their reading and writing for them. Part of how the Catholic church has maintained such control in Nova Scotia all these years, I imagine."

As before, when McGraw had given Richard his first information on the natives of this region, Richard found himself comforted by his first officer's apparent expertise on the subject. "How pathetic," he said suddenly, again experiencing the same wrenching sensation in his stomach that he'd felt when he'd spoken to the girl.

"Yes, it is, rather," McGraw agreed. "But then I suppose there are many in *our* ranks as well who know little of reading and writing. Tell me, sir," he continued after a moment, looking quite concerned. "You don't believe she cast some sort of spell on you, do you?"

Richard swallowed dryly and tried not to let his great uneasiness show. "I don't think so. That is to say, I'm feeling pretty much myself again now."

"Ah, that's good, sir," his first officer replied with obvious relief. "After all, I can't help feeling that we would find ourselves hard pressed to counteract such a thing, sir, given how little any of us know of those sorts of practices by the locals. They keep such matters quite a guarded secret, Captain. Rumor has it they even have some sort of black-magic Bibles among them. Volumes called the *Petit Albert* and the *Grand Albert,* I believe."

Richard somehow managed to swallow back the sense of panic that began welling up inside of him in response to this.

"Well, it is a good thing, in any case, that she didn't bring her basket on board, sir," McGraw continued.

Richard's mouth felt almost too dry for him to speak. He simply stared at his first officer with a questioning expression.

"Her basket of local herbs and such, sir. She left it with her companions on the fishing boat, and I think it is just as well."

Richard's face continued to reflect his bewilderment.

"They use them for healing, Captain," McGraw explained. "The Acadians often carry them wherever they go. We saw no reason to confiscate them. They're probably quite harmless, really," he added after a moment, as though trying to convince himself of it now. "I mean, it's not too late, sir. We could still take them from her before they leave for the Petitcodiac region, if you wish."

"No, I don't wish," Richard said firmly. "Just leave that woman and her friends alone," he growled, waving his palms out before him defensively. "Let them return to their settlement in peace! We don't need some hex put upon us now. Life is miserable enough with Mr. Chumley aboard!"

McGraw laughed. "I quite agree, sir."

"So then, I trust you understand now, Commander, why I acted as I did up there a few minutes ago," Richard concluded, getting up and beginning to pace anxiously about his cabin.

"Oh, aye, sir. I would have done the same in your place."

Richard looked up from his pacing and tentatively met his first officer's gaze. "You would have?"

McGraw nodded resolutely. "Oh, aye. We know too little of their local magic, sir, to risk treating it lightly. Many ships have been sunk, after all, due to far less ominous encounters."

"Yes. I'm sure they have," Richard answered, still keeping an eye fixed on McGraw's, searching for any indication of insincerity on his part. Fortunately, there appeared to be none. He was obviously taking all of this as seriously as Richard was.

"She tampered with my thoughts," Richard said again after a moment, his voice cracking. "That is what concerns me most, Commander," he confessed. "I've never had anyone do that to me before, let alone some little waif in fishing clothes!"

McGraw reached out to him now, rather reflexively, obviously in an effort to comfort him. Then, apparently seeing the stoic expression that Richard donned in those seconds, he drew back his hand once more.

"I'm sure it was most disturbing for you, Captain. I know it would be for me. But I assure you that you do seem to be of sound mind now. And you acted precisely as you should have, sir, in the interests of your ship and the majority of your crew. Do try to keep in mind, Captain, that those Acadians will be forty-eight miles from here by tomorrow evening. I think you would do well to remind yourself of that from time to time. They can hardly vex us any further from that distance." With that, McGraw rose, as though wishing to be dismissed.

"Yes. Thank you, Commander," Richard replied resignedly. "You may go now, if you wish."

The Englishman gave him a slight salute and headed for the door. "Give yourself some time, sir," he added awkwardly, turning back to face Richard before taking his leave. "It has, after all, been six years, I'm told, since you last served in His Majesty's Navy, and you've been with us for only a day, scarcely time enough to gain back one's sea legs, do you think?"

"No, of course it's not. You're quite right, Commander," Richard agreed in an equally tactful tone. "Scarcely time enough at all."

At that, McGraw offered him another hurried salute and went on his way, leaving Richard alone in the eerie silence of his dimly lit quarters.

Richard, had, by his own admission, met and bedded many women in his day, more than he cared to number, in fact. He had, however, never met any who were even remotely like that Acadian maiden with the provocative brown eyes. The very thought of her made his palms become moist with nervous perspiration.

This was quite a reversal for a man who had become known to many as the "Romeo" of Boston, and Richard doubted whether he would ever fully accept it. He hadn't been the seducer this evening, a little *métisse* peasant girl had. Sorceress or not, she had seduced him into letting her go and into furnishing her and her friends with a six-man escort back to their village. Acknowledging all of this now, Richard knew that he would somehow have to come to terms with the fact that he had finally encountered someone whose charms were far more potent than his own.

Chapter 9

The pilots of the British longboats accompanied Angeline and her companions as far as Rocher Bay before turning around to head back to their ship. This was the most convenient port for them in the Petitcodiac River region, and it was clear to Angeline and her friends that the pilots' only concern was ridding themselves of their charges and getting back to their ship as quickly as possible. They were so lax about the assignment, that they even neglected to confiscate the trio's fishing boat, as was often done in such cases. So, counting themselves fortunate, Angeline and her companions wasted no time in pulling the boat out of the water and beginning their supposed portage to the Petitcodiac settlement. Then, once they were certain, that the British longboats were well out of view, they launched their fishing craft once more, about seven miles northeast of Rocher Bay, and headed for Fort Beauséjour.

It took them half a day of rowing to reach the basin adjacent to the fort, and the journey went surprisingly smoothly. Much to Angeline's dismay, however, when they came within sight of Beauséjour, they could see that its port was crowded with British boats.

"Well, that's it then," Luc declared. He shook his head resignedly as he finished scanning the congested harbor, and sank down in the fishing boat once more. "The starve-out has ended, and Lawrence has won the fort."

"Nothing left to do but head home," Marcel added evenly.

Angeline could feel her eyes widening with amazement at them. "But we can't turn back now, not without my father! I mean, that's why we've come so far, to help him."

Luc scowled at her. "Now look, Angeline, Marcel and I have done all we can for you. We've been intercepted by the British, we've had our provisions taken from us, and we've spent the last twenty-four hours living on nothing but nuts and berries! You really can't expect us to row right into that nest of British soldiers, can you? You can see for yourself that the fort is surrounded by them, on the water and the land. Not even your father would expect us to go in there."

Angeline could feel her posture stiffening defensively. "Maybe not. But he would expect it of me."

Marcel rolled his eyes at her. "*Mademoiselle,* you saw how many British ships were gathering in the bay when the longboats led us to Rocher. If we are able to make it back to Grand Pré now without being apprehended again, it will probably be a miracle!"

"Marcel is right," Luc agreed, "you must come back with us. If your father is still alive, and the British decide not to take the fort's occupants prisoner, he will probably return to Grand Pré very shortly."

Angeline couldn't hide the desperation she felt. "But what if they *do* take him prisoner and he needs someone to help set him free? Or what if he's too weak to travel? What then? I can't turn my back on him, after coming this far. He would never desert me, were I in his place."

Luc reached out and wrapped a consoling arm about her shoulders. "You're just hungry and tired, *mon amie*. We all are. You'll be able to think more clearly once we've returned home and you've had some food and rest."

Angeline gave an angry shrug, causing his arm to fall away from her. "And how much food and rest do you think papa has had in the last few months? He did not only come here to hold the fort for himself, but for all of us, for every Acadian. He is not cowardly and self-serving like you two! He is a hero and he deserves a hero's rescue, and I am going to see that he receives it."

"Well then, you'll see to it on your own," Marcel retorted, crossing his arms over his chest with a resolute huff.

Luc assumed the same pose, but there was still an empathetic glimmer in his eyes. "I'm sorry, Angeline, but I must agree with Marcel on this. Maybe you have no life, no family back in Grand Pré, but both of us do. And we must be reunited with them, just as you must be reunited with your father."

Several seconds of silence ensued, and Angeline stared pensively downward, trying to come to terms with the fact that she was condemned now to go the rest of the way to Beauséjour alone.

"Very well," she said at last, bravely lifting her chin. "Row to shore. I will get out here and go to him on my own."

"But it's madness, Angeline," Luc protested almost pleadingly. "How far do you suppose you will get without food or a gun? Why, the only weapons you have are the surgical blades in your medicine basket. What help can you possibly be to your father without weapons and supplies?"

"More help than I'll be if I simply turn away with you now and go home," she replied without hesitation, reaching down to gather up her pannier of herbs.

Once the two men had rowed the boat to shore and she rose to step out of the craft, she saw a final entreating gleam in the eyes of her cousin's beau.

"Are you certain, then, that this is what you

want to do?" Luc asked with a definite note of finality in his voice.

"I am," she answered, stepping agilely onto the shore.

"We won't be well received, you know, when we return to the village without you. We can ill afford to lose our *sage femme* at a time like this, with the British ships surrounding us this way."

"Then, you'll understand, Luc Léger, when I tell you that I can ill afford to lose *my* father."

"As always, dear girl, there is no arguing with you," he said sadly, reaching down and pulling the last of the nuts and berries, which they'd found along their way, from his pocket. They were wrapped in his clean linen handkerchief, and he extended the bundle to her with tearful eyes.

Angeline reached out to accept it from him. "*Merci.*"

"Go to your father then, *mon amie,* with our blessings," he said in a wavering voice. "And Godspeed to you."

"Call out to us, mademoiselle, if you should change your mind," Marcel added, as they used their oars to push away from shore seconds later. "We'll come back for you, as long as we are able to hear your call."

Angeline's heart was beating like a rabbit's as she turned away and began heading northward a moment later. She was terrified of being on her own, yet she knew that she wouldn't be calling back to have her companions return for her. Luc

144

had been sadly correct when he'd said there was no kin, no life left for her anymore in Grand Pré. Without her father's help, the family farm they had always run would continue to deteriorate, and Angeline would soon be forced to marry, simply to keep herself alive. Given her fear of men, on the whole, that was a dreadful prospect indeed. It seemed strangely more threatening to her now than running the risk of falling back into the hands of the British. In fact, if the captain she'd met the night before was any example, she felt sure she could make the assumption that the British would, at least, be decent enough to either execute her or take her prisoner and keep her fed. That did seem to her a preferable fate to that of slow starvation on her family farm or having to depend upon her cousins for handouts the rest of her days — undoubtedly the only other choices left to her, if her father never returned to Grand Pré.

Weak with fear, her vision blurring a bit with hunger, she could understand why Le Loutre and the others had finally succumbed to starvation and let the fort fall into the acting governor's hands. Hunger was the most ruthless of masters, and she knew that she, too, was beginning to become a victim of it. Her only prayer was that it would not claim her before she was able to find her father.

To Angeline's great surprise, a few minutes later her trek was interrupted by the sound of male voices shouting from the adjacent waterway.

145

She cautiously emerged from the cloaking shadows of the shoreline's woods to again see Luc and Marcel in the fishing boat.

"We've changed our minds," Luc called out to her with a smile in his voice. "We couldn't leave you."

"Well, I'm not going back with you, if that's what you think," Angeline retorted firmly.

"No, no. We know that. It's just that we have decided to stay here and wait for you and your father," he continued. "We'll come to shore and hunt for more berries and fashion some spears to stab fish, while we wait for you."

"But only until morning, mind you," Marcel added admonishingly, and it was again apparent to Angeline that he was the less willing of her two companions on this journey. "If you're not back here by then, we'll be on our way for good. Fundy is becoming too cluttered with British ships for us to wait here any longer than that."

Angeline moved nearer the water and stood staring at them with a sudden surge of gratitude running through her. "I understand. I realize that, and *merci, mes amis!* How can I ever thank you?"

"It is not us you should thank," Luc called out again rather sheepishly. "It's Elise. She would never have spoken to me again if she learned we simply left you here on your own."

"But we're only staying till morning," Marcel said again, this time even more sternly. "So you had better get going, *mademoiselle!*"

"Oui. Of course. Of course," Angeline replied under her breath, still feeling stunned by their sudden change of heart. She gave them a slight curtsy, feeling a sort of renewed strength filling her. The doubts and apprehension she had experienced only minutes before seemed to melt away, and she knew now that she could make it to Beauséjour and rescue her father in the time allotted to her. The very fact that there would now be someone waiting for her to return — friends with fish and berries to quell her gnawing hunger and that of her father, comrades with a seaworthy boat to take them all home — made her feel strangely certain of success.

Angeline reached the woods surrounding Beauséjour a few hours later, and setting her basket of herbs down behind a memorably large evergreen, she began her stealthy approach to the fort. To her surprise, however, she quickly discovered that surreptitious means would not be necessary in rescuing her father. The truth of the matter was that most of Beauséjour's former occupants were already outside the fort's walls, sitting up against the palisade with a cadaverous kind of stillness. The British troops, meanwhile, were so busy moving their armaments and personal belongings into the fort that it was clear none of them were taking notice of her. She, of course, took full advantage of the hubbub, coming up closer to the fort than she would have dared under any other circumstances.

In the minutes that followed, she scanned the long row of faces of the Acadians who'd been expelled from the fort, in search of her father. In the end however, it was not her father's face which identified him to her, but his apparel. She recognized his clothing and the unusual, multi-colored neck scarf that she, herself, had knit for him a few years earlier.

"Papa," she called out to him in a low voice as she drew closer. *"C'est moi . . . Angeline."*

The emaciated man in the brightly colored scarf did nothing but stare up at her blankly. For a moment, she feared that he was not her father at all, but some scavenger who had found him dead and taken his clothing. As she came within inches of him, however, she could see the familiar features more clearly; the dark hair, the patchy black beard, and the large brown eyes. Finally, as she knelt down before him, she saw a definite flicker of recognition register on his gaunt face.

"Oh, papa," she sobbed, reaching out and hugging his skeletal form to her. *"C'est moi, ta fille,* Angeline . . . I have come to take you home," she continued in a tearful whisper. "Elise's beau has a boat waiting for us just a few miles from here."

She pulled away slightly and again got little more than a blank expression from him. He, like the others around him, was obviously too weak to respond. It was then that Angeline began to fear that he wouldn't be able to walk even the short way back to the fishing boat, that he might, in fact, be too near death for even one with her healing prowess to save.

"Papa," she said firmly. "Listen to me. You must get to your feet and walk with me now, out of the sight of the British. We have to get you away from here, before they decide to shoot you or take you prisoner. Do you understand?"

To her horror, his eyes fell shut, and she began to feel panicky, fearful that he would slip into a coma before she could do anything more for him. Then, to her great relief, he nodded his head and weakly wrapped an arm about her, as though he did wish to cooperate and let her help him to his feet.

"Oh, thank God, thank God you're still alive," she gasped, as she summoned every ounce of her strength to bring them both back up to a standing position. "Come along. It's just a few yards to the woods, papa, where I can hide you."

Though her father's once brawny form had been reduced to little more than skin and bones, it seemed to take all of Angeline's might to shoulder his weight as she made her way with him to the cloaking shade of the nearby forest. With a great deal of silent prayer, however, she did manage to move him well out of the British soldiers' sight and prop him behind the wide trunk of the evergreen under which she'd left her basket.

Her mother had taught her that the first thing to do with a patient in such a state was to coax him or her to drink water. She therefore proceeded to do so now, with only marginal success. Though her father appeared to be swallowing very little of it, she stubbornly tilted the mouth of her deerskin water flask to his parched lips several times in the minutes that followed.

"You rest, papa," she ordered finally, seeing what effort it seemed to be taking for him to keep his eyes open for her. "I'll build a stretcher and take you to my friends. They'll have smoked fish waiting for us when we reach them," she assured, pulling his knit cap more tightly down about his ears. She had come to the rescue of a starving animal or two back home in Grand Pré, and she knew how important it try to keep her father warm now. The body's heat seemed to try to escape at every turn when starvation set in, and with that renewed realization, she took off her own jacket and hung it over his shoulders and chest. She wouldn't be needing the garment, she stoically reasoned. The work she had ahead of her of finding wood and assembling a stretcher would keep her amply warmed. She wasn't surprised to note either that the hunger pangs she'd been feeling for the past day or so were subsiding now. As with her awareness of the chilly sea air, her hunger somehow seemed swallowed up by her deep concern about her father's grave state.

No more than half an hour later, Angeline had built a stretcher using the branches and sticks she'd found about the forest floor and a ball of twine she'd had in her basket. She wasn't altogether sure that the device would be strong enough to support her father's weight for the entire trek, but she knew she'd have to give it a try and pray for the best. One thing she was certain of was that the longer she and her father remained near Beauséjour, the greater was the chance that the ruthless acting governor would issue orders that the fallen Acadians be rounded up and shot or taken prisoner, and that was clearly not the fate she wanted for either of them now. She tied her father to the stretcher using what twine she had left. Then she rolled her jacket up into a pillow of sorts and placed it under his head to cushion it from any jarring or bumps that would be encountered as she dragged him along the forest floor on the laborious journey back to Luc and Marcel. She knew that, under any other circumstances, such an undertaking would be agonizing for one as slightly built as she. Yet, step by step, she made her way along, with a merciful kind of numbness taking effect. Her great relief at having found her father alive seemed enough to quell any physical pain she might otherwise have felt.

Angeline reached her companions well before sunset, and together, the three of them began trying to nurse Daniel DuBay back to life. He did his best to choke down the mash of berries and the smoked fish he was fed. To everyone's dismay, however, he quickly became sick on them, and it was clear to Angeline that his body was too weak to tolerate solid foods. She sorrily acknowledged that she would have to use what few cooking utensils the British had left them to start the whole feeding process over again. For a while, her father would have to be given liquid only, and under their present circumstances, this would limit him to water, fish broth, and berry juices.

There was something else that was clear to Angeline as well that evening, and that was that her father would be in no shape to travel, by land or sea, for at least a few more days. She therefore told Luc and Marcel that they were free to leave at this point, that she understood the urgency of their making their way back to Grand Pré now, with the British increasing their fleet in the Bay of Fundy to such a threatening number. Surprisingly, however, her companions didn't seem nearly as anxious to head back into Fundy and on to Grand Pré as they had that morning. They explained to Angeline that, while she had been off at Beauséjour, Marcel had rowed back to Rocher Bay to make a reconnaissance, and he had returned to Luc with the news that the British had started closing in on a few of the ports in that area. From the looks of things, they were beginning some sort of siege of the surrounding Acadian settlements. After giving the matter much consideration, it was clear to both Luc and Marcel that the wisest thing for them to do was to stay put for a while and wait for the British activity to die down, before attempting to row their boat across Fundy once more.

Marcel suggested that they try making their way back to Grand Pré via a landlocked back route. Given the fact, however, that Daniel Du-Bay was in no condition to make such a journey and that his companions would be stuck taking turns dragging him most of the way on the stretcher, it was finally decided that the best idea was for all of them to travel the relatively short distance to the Petitcodiac settlement. There, well away from the range of British encroachment, they were sure to find shelter and a lasting supply of food. They hoped to dwell there until it seemed safe enough for them to travel back to Grand Pré by water.

While none of them knew much about the Acadians who lived near the Petitcodiac River, it was a common practice among such French settlers to be very hospitable to strangers. Considering the seriousness of their plight and Angeline's willingness to ply her exemplary skills as a *sage femme* in exchange for room and board, the foursome was fairly certain that they would find themselves welcomed there.

Chapter 10

By the end of Richard's third week in Acadia, it had become apparent to him that he and his crew were not going to escape the fate of having to take part in Charles Lawrence's newly disclosed plan to expel the Acadians from Nova Scotia and New Brunswick.

After the fall of Fort Beauséjour, Lawrence's men had taken occupancy of the Acadian stronghold and decided to rename it Fort Cumberland. That defeat seemed to mark the beginning of the end for the Acadians, as Lawrence's subsequent orders to his naval forces began to be delivered to one after another of his ships in the Bay of Fundy.

His orders were monstrous, but easily understood. Each of his ships would be assigned to various Acadian settlements. The crews were to travel to said villages and systematically evacuate them. This entailed setting fire to the Acadians' homes and crops and herding the villagers into ships bound for various cities in the colonies, where they would either be sold into slavery or indentured servitude.

Given Richard's aversion to the practice of enslaving human beings, these orders did not sit at all well with him, and he was doing his level best to have his ship fall back in order to get lost amidst the British fleet in the huge bay. In this way, he hoped to avoid the notice of the dispatch-bearers who would eventually deliver such an evacuation assignment to him and his crew. He reasoned that, if he could steer clear of such orders long enough, his tour of duty in Acadia would draw to a close before he was called upon to carry out such atrocious commands.

In the weeks that followed, Richard and his first officer had several secret discussions about the situation in the privacy of Richard's cabin. Neither of them, however, managed to come up with a way to avoid such a loathsome assignment indefinitely. Short of staging a mutiny of some kind or stealing the ship and crew away to freedom on the open sea, there seemed no way around having to carry out such orders when they arrived.

Richard had become increasingly introspective since rumor of the acting governor's ultimate plan had reached his ship. He often spent several hours a day sleeping and brooding in his quarters, and he did little more than make an obligatory appearance at the helm once or twice daily. He did, however, feel compelled to dine with his officers each evening in the wardroom—a practice made infinitely easier by Chumley's habit of eating every meal alone in his cabin. Nevertheless, Richard's supper conversations with his officers were always painfully trivial, and he usually found himself feeling utterly drained upon returning to his cabin at night. He was finding that maintaining a confident and contented facade in the presence of his subordinates was simply getting to be too taxing for him.

After dark his sleep was usually restless. His dreams were often filled with the nightmarish images of the carnage that was sure to ensue should he and his crew be assigned to evacuate a local settlement and find the Acadians unwilling to cooperate with them. To make matters worse, these hideous nightmares were frequently interlaced with memories of the disquieting Acadian girl he'd met.

The irony was that his thoughts of her extraordinary beauty actually bolstered him by day, renewing his will to survive this dreadful tour of duty and get back to his amorous pursuits in Boston. He had come to think of Angeline DuBay, as she had claimed to be called, as somehow being synonymous with the brightly colored clumps of wildflowers that he could see through his spyglass along the Acadian shores. His recollections of her did almost as much to brighten his otherwise dreary days as did such ornaments of nature. At night, however, when all color and sunlight seemed to leave his mind with the snuffing of his cabin's lanterns, all he seemed capable of focusing upon was the memory of the black pupils of her eyes, enshrouding him like night's darkness, and the hair-raising way in which she'd said the word *saignement,* "bleeding." "I stop *bleeding, Capitaine"* she'd said, "you know, when one has been shot or injured."

It had come to be quite a mystifying dichotomy to him. By day, the young woman's words didn't trouble him in the least. In the rationality of broad daylight it only made sense that a people as isolated as the Acadians would have developed such sorcerous healers among them, especially when the craft was supplemented with the curative wisdom of the local Indians. By night, however, there was nothing rational about it. Richard was terrified by what the girl had said and even more so by the unspoken warnings that had shone in her eyes. He would, as a result, often wake before dawn, his body wet with perspiration, and he would call out to his steward for a change of nightclothes and some sane, calming conversation. Fortunately, his steward seemed to possess those most sought-after of traits; a sympathetic ear and a very discreet tongue. Richard was, therefore, fairly certain that no one else among his crew knew just how sleepless his nights had become or how apprehensive he was about what fate lay before all of them in these freezing foreign waters.

Through all of his mental turmoil, however, a few things had become clear to him. The first was that it had been his infatuation with Angeline DuBay that had muddled his thoughts when he'd met her, and not necessarily any sorcery on her part. His pride had blinded him to this fact before, but he was somehow self-effacing enough to admit to it now. The second was that, no matter what magical powers Mademoiselle DuBay possessed, Richard knew that she couldn't be anywhere near as evil a force as Charles Lawrence was proving to be.

At the end of Richard's second month in Acadia, he and his crew finally did receive the evacuation orders they'd been avoiding. One of his second lieutenants conveyed the note to Richard from a dispatch boat that had pulled up alongside their ship. Richard's breath caught in his throat as he read it. The *Petitcodiac* region. He and his crew were to round up all of the Acadians who had settled there and send them on to a lifetime of servitude in the colonies. It was as simple as that; families torn apart, scores of lives destroyed in just a few strokes of Charles Lawrence's pen.

As Chumley looked on with his accustomed sadistic smirk, Richard handed the note to his first officer and retreated once more to the privacy of his cabin. In choosing to steer clear of Lawrence's orders all this time, he had wound up in a worse spot than he would have if he'd simply allowed himself to receive the assignment in the first place. As a result, he and his crew had ended up being appointed to evacuate one of the most remote and allegedly militant settlements in Acadia, the very settlement he had most wanted to avoid.

When Richard's ship reached the mouth of the waterway that led to the Petitcodiac settlement the following morning, he committed what he deemed to be his first truly rash act since assuming the role of a British naval captain. He went to Chumley's cabin at dawn, before most of the day crew were up and dressed, and he informed the official, at gunpoint, that he, Chumley, would be accompanying the longboat party that would be rowing in to evacuate the settlement.

"This is kidnapping!" Chumley exclaimed, his face reflecting both outrage and fear from where he lay beneath his bed's linens.

"Not at all, sir," Richard countered coolly. "You'll simply be following your superior's orders, along with the rest of us."

"But you will have no need of the likes of me

there, Captain! I'm little more than a scrivener, after all. I'm no soldier."

"Then what have you been doing, these many weeks, aboard a warship, sir?"

"Well . . . overseeing matters," the official stammered.

"Then it only stands to reason that you should continue to do so today, Mr. Chumley, at the Petitcodiac settlement. Now get up at once and get yourself dressed for battle," Richard ordered, cocking the pistol that he was aiming steadily at the official's head.

"This is madness, Captain! You would never be fool enough to shoot me, because Lawrence and the rest would know someone on this ship was to blame. The Acadians had all of their guns confiscated months ago, after all."

Richard met his confident glare with equal assurance. "Not all of them were gathered up, surely. Doubtless, some of the Acadians were bright enough to hide a gun or two away where they were certain our men would not find them. In any case, I'm sure a suitable alibi can be conceived in the time it will take to sail all the way to Halifax and deliver your *corpse* to the acting governor."

"You'll never bring this off, Captain," he hissed.

"On the contrary. Considering that I probably won't live long enough to be tried for it, I think I am quite likely to bring it off. Word of Lawrence's evacuations of so many other villages

160

has surely reached the Petitcodiac settlement by now, and I, for one, will not make the mistake of assuming that those settlers intend to let us round them up without a fight. Many of us will very likely die before the day is out, and as the man who must lead the longboat party into the settlement, I fully expect to be one of those casualties. So it matters little to me whether I shoot you now or later."

The official's face suddenly took on an allaying expression. "But there's no need for *you* to lead them into the settlement, Captain. You're the highest-ranking officer here, after all, the man the crew can least afford to lose. Why don't you treat this like any other march into battle and have your first officer lead the men?"

"Because, unlike you and your superior, Mr. Chumley, I won't require my men to do anything that I, myself, would not be willing to do. Now get up, you doughy little coward," he ordered again, "before I pull this trigger and splatter the better portion of your head across that wall!"

Chumley, obviously seeing the determined gleam in Richard's eyes, began trembling like a frightened animal. He climbed out of bed and hurriedly got dressed.

It took over five hours for Richard's longboat party to reach the landing that led to the Petitcodiac settlement, and Richard saw to it that his pistol remained stealthily pressed to Chumley's back during most of the journey. Short of the periodic perspiration that trickled down Chumley's forehead, it was doubtful that Richard's men saw anything that might have led them to suspect that the official was not accompanying them on the mission voluntarily.

Richard had left Mr. McGraw in charge of the ship in his absence, and he had brought over forty men along with him, all armed with sea-service muskets and boarding pikes. Though he'd told them that he hoped for a peaceful evacuation and he doubted that they would need to use their weapons against the Acadians, he didn't really believe this claim himself and he was certain, judging from Chumley's apprehensiveness now, that the official didn't believe it either.

As the longboats neared the end of the waterway, Richard gazed up at the clear, blue sky and drew in the verdant, summer scents that were afloat upon the breeze. This was as good a day to be wounded or killed as any, he supposed, but he did want to take in as much of the world's beauty as possible before he had to do so.

There were several streams of dark smoke trailing up over the treetops far to the east, indicating that the Acadians were cooking their midday meals, and the distant sounds of dogs barking and geese honking seemed to prove that life in the settlement was going along as usual today. Perhaps the Petitcodiac villagers weren't keeping a watch for approaching British vessels, and Richard's men really would catch them by surprise as they marched into the settlement. *One could always hope,* Richard supposed, trying to maintain an optimistic air for the sake of his men. Deep within him he knew, however, that things probably wouldn't go smoothly.

"Bring our boat to shore first," Richard said to his pilot as they came within just a few yards of land. "Mr. Chumley will be leading us into the settlement," he explained, pressing the muzzle of his pistol even more firmly to the official's back.

"Without a musket?" Chumley asked imploringly under his breath. "Not even the acting governor would be so heartless!"

"Here's your damned musket, Chumley," Richard snarled in a whisper, reaching out and taking up one of the shoulder guns from the arms-rack beneath their seats. "But mind you, sir, if you dare turn and point the thing at me, it will be the *last* of your deeds here on earth! I promise you!"

The surrounding woods were ominously quiet as the boat containing Richard and Chumley reached the shore seconds later. Richard, however, was too busy keeping an eye on the official to really notice the telltale absence of chirping from the crickets and other insects that generally inhabited such grassy banks.

"Slowly take up your musket now, Chumley,

and get out of the boat, with your face and hands directed forward," Richard ordered in a threateningly low tone near the official's ear.

Richard, of course, followed him very closely as he carried out this command. Then he gave the rest of his men the signal to march up behind them in formation. To his great relief, there seemed to be no hesitancy on the part of his crew, as its members got out of the boats, one by one, and joined their captain and Chumley on the sandy landing. All clad in full naval dress, they proceeded to move with admirable silence down the wooded footpath that obviously led to the Acadian settlement.

They walked for several yards with Chumley leading, and Richard couldn't help noticing that the tenseness in the official's back and shoulders seemed to lessen with every step they took. He was, apparently, starting to really believe, as Richard was, that all was normal with the settlers today and that they didn't have the slightest idea that a British battalion was approaching. This mutual belief proved to be incorrect seconds later, however, as he and Chumley were suddenly knocked down by an assailant who leapt upon them from out of the arching boughs of the treetops overhead.

It all happened so quickly—the blinding blow to Richard's head, his fall to the ground, the subsequent war cries from the attacking band of Acadians who'd been hiding in the woods, and the deafening blasts from the muskets of Richard's men—that Richard had no time to come to Chumley's rescue before another Acadian pounced upon the official's prone form and began pounding him with what appeared to be a sledgehammer.

"Dear God, they're armed," Richard heard one of his men exclaim from just behind him. "They still have their tools!"

As Richard lay on his back, frantically feeling about for the musket he'd been carrying before he was knocked down, he learned how sorely correct the man behind him was. Not only did the Acadians have some of the tools of their trades among them, but a few bona fide weapons as well. Richard knew he would bear the evidence of this for quite some time to come, as two Acadians set about attacking him—one with an antiquated-looking saber and one with a musket. The saber slashed down between his legs, causing excruciating pain in the inner part of his left thigh, and the musket, turned butt-end against him now, was brought down with shattering force upon his ribs. He reflexively lifted his hands up to shield his face and head as he struggled to raise himself to a sitting position and get up off the ground. His efforts, however, were in vain. An instant later, the musket's butt was directed at his face, and the last thing he saw, before losing consciousness, was the butt plate coming down upon his forehead.

* * *

Angeline's father, now almost full recovered from his period of starvation at Beauséjour, had left strict orders with Angeline that she remain behind at the Petitcodiac settlement while he and the other men of the village went to ambush the approaching British troops. This band of Acadians knew that they were among the last whom the British had come to banish and enslave, and finding themselves both forewarned and forearmed with their farm tools, they weren't about to allow it to happen.

Angeline, having obediently stayed behind with the other women and children of the settlement, waited a full twenty minutes after the last of the British musket fire was heard. Then she gathered up her basket of healing herbs and implements and began her cautious walk to the scene of the battle. There were, fortunately, two other women among the Petitcodiac settlers who possessed some skill as healers as well. They would accompany Angeline now, and she was hopeful that the three of them would arrive at the scene to find that the Acadians had, indeed, won the battle, and that three healers was a sufficient number to handle what wounds needed immediate treatment.

As the trio started down the footpath that led out of the settlement minutes later, Angeline suddenly gave forth a sigh of great relief. She'd spotted her father heading back from the scene of the skirmish with Luc and Marcel on either

166

side of him.

"They've gone, *ma cherie,*" Daniel DuBay called out triumphantly upon seeing his daughter. "The British have retreated!"

Even from a distance of roughly fifty yards, Angeline could see blood smeared on her father's forehead, and she rushed down the footpath to him and gave him a tearful hug.

"But, papa, you're hurt," she declared, pulling away from him slightly and beginning to rummage through her basket for some linen with which to dab his wound.

"It's nothing, *chouchou,*" he assured, waving her off. "It's the others we must worry about now. Many of them shouldn't be moved until they've been tended to. We were just heading back to fetch you."

"Are there many dead?" Angeline asked with a slight grimace.

"A few," her father answered soberly. "But I'm happy to report that the British lost far more men than we did."

"You should see all of them," Marcel exclaimed, his eyes widening. "They're lying all over the footpath and the woods. We must have killed at least two dozen of them! And the rest retreated, like a pack of startled wolves, and they quickly rowed away in their longboats."

"Oh, yes," Luc chimed in proudly, fighting like the other men to catch his breath. "You should have seen us! We took them completely by surprise. There are so many of them lying back there that I fear we'll be stuck digging a pit grave for them before the day is out."

"Good tidings, indeed," one of the other healer women proclaimed, raising her fist victoriously to the heavens.

"We'll have plenty of time for celebrating later," Daniel DuBay admonished. "Let's just get back to our wounded men and start the work of treating them."

This advice seemed to sober the group once more. Angeline, accordingly, asked Luc and Marcel to head back to the settlement and return to the scene of the battle with a few buckets of boiled water so that she and the other women were sure to have enough to clean the wounds of all those who had fallen. They seemed more than willing to comply with this request, and they continued heading east to the village, as Daniel DuBay turned about and accompanied the women to the site of the skirmish.

"This may be difficult for you, ladies," DuBay cautioned as they made their way briskly down the path. "I mean in all of your healing, I doubt that any of you have seen the likes of this. So for you own sakes, brace yourselves."

Angeline gave forth a confident laugh. "Good heavens, papa. I've been treating people since I could walk, it seems. There'll be nothing up ahead that can shock me."

To Angeline's dismay, however, she discovered how wrong she could be, once they reached the surprisingly large dispersion of dead and wounded several minutes later. There were men lying in all directions, suffering every manner of mutilation. It was so appalling that all Angeline could do, as she stood surveying the scene for the first few seconds, was to keep repeating the words *"mon Dieu"* under her breath.

But she felt relieved as well at seeing that she and the other two healers would not be alone in their efforts. Several of the Acadian men, who'd apparently fought in the battle without incurring serious wounds, were coming to the aid of their fallen neighbors. Angeline saw them kneeling down here and there, wrapping wounds with strips of torn clothing and gathering up the limp Acadian bodies to convey them back to the village.

"Over here, *ma cherie*," Angeline heard her father calling, as he stood beside a particularly bloody form much farther down the path. "It's Henri Parell, daughter. I think you can still save him, if you come at once."

Continuing to feel repulsed and unnerved, Angeline made her way gingerly toward her father, stepping over several British bodies en route. She was nearly to Monsieur Parell's side when she looked down to see a face along the footpath that made her come to an abrupt halt. It was that of a British soldier in naval captain's attire . . . that of the captain who'd let her go a few months before, on the night she and her "fishing" companions had been abducted near

169

Advocate Bay. His features were a bit obscured by a streak of blood that had descended from a wound in his forehead, but Angeline was certain that this was the same man. She hesitated a second or two more and saw that his chest was still rising and falling with his breathing, however faintly.

"*Angeline,*" her father called out again, this time rather sharply. "You didn't come out here to treat the British! Come along with you now, girl, while there is still a chance that Monsieur Parell can be saved!"

Angeline found herself biting down upon her lower lip as she left the captain's fallen form and continued on her way to Mister Parell. She wasn't sure why, but there was a terrible lump forming in her throat, and the only thing she could seem to think about, as she knelt at Henri Parell's side a moment later, was getting back to the captain—the enemy officer who had shown her such mercy months before.

"Try to keep your mind on what you're doing, child," she heard her father scold minutes later, as she continued striving to get Monsieur Parell's bleeding to stop.

"I am, papa," she snapped up at him, her hands trembling with her torn emotions. "Just you go and see to some of the others, will you? You're making me nervous, standing over me like that."

At this, her father issued an offended cluck. Then, apparently deciding to take his daughter's advice, he mercifully walked away. Angeline, in turn, gave forth a sigh of relief. She tried again to clear her mind of all concern about the captain, and she began an even more determined effort to stanch Monsieur Parell's bleeding enough so that she could begin stitching up his life-threatening pike wounds. Fortunately, the pain, or perhaps, his bleeding, had left him unconscious, and she was able to work on him without the wrenching distraction of agonized groans. It was, after all, difficult enough for her to hear such sounds from those lying all about him.

Less than twenty minutes later, Angeline had Monsieur Parell's wounds amply sutured, and he was ready to be carried back to the settlement. He had obviously lost a lot of blood, but Angeline was certain that, with the right care and plenty of rest in the coming weeks, he would recover fully.

Despite this triumph and her subsequent success with the men she treated after Parell, however, she knew that half of her mind was still fixed upon the captain, and she couldn't help feeling a shameful blush come over her at her realization of this. He was the enemy, she kept reminding herself. The *enemy*. Her thoughts and her efforts should have belonged exclusively to her own people. Yet, she couldn't seem to ignore the urge to rush to the captain's side and see whether there was any hope of saving him as well. He had shown her mercy, after all, she

171

rationalized. When so many other ship's officers would have stranded her and her friends at Advocate Bay, *he* had arranged to have them escorted all the way to their alleged home. Finally acknowledging that it had been the captain's orders and not simply laxness on the part of his longboat pilots that had allowed her and her companions to keep their fishing boat, she knew that she had to do something for him now. Even if it had to wait until after nightfall, when the rest of the villagers had all returned to the settlement, she knew that she would have to make her way back to the captain and see what she could do to save him.

She sorely realized that none of her fellow Acadians, not even Luc or Marcel, were likely to approve of such actions on her part. But that didn't really matter to her now. What mattered was what her heart was telling her to do, and she only hoped that the time required for her to treat the wounds of her own people wouldn't cost the good captain his life.

Chapter 11

The Acadians, having had dozens of wounded to attend to and several graves to dig for those of their people who had been killed, were grateful that this could be accomplished in daylight. Angeline, however, had counted the hours till dark with great anxiousness. She was doing whatever she could find to do in order to have some excuse to stay at the battle site until everyone else had left.

"Come along with you, girl," her father called out to her as he and some of the others who had been digging graves finally started back toward the village. They had cast their shovels up over their shoulders like muskets as they walked.

"I'll be along in a few minutes," she called

back in as pleasant a voice as she could muster. It had been a long, exhausting day, and in spite of their victory, the awareness that the British would probably be back fairly soon had them all a bit on edge. "I've a few more things to do."

Her father shrugged and raised his palms upward in a questioning fashion. "What's left? All of ours are either back at the village now or buried, *ma cherie.* And we'll return and dig a pit grave for the British in the morning. Let their bodies serve as a warning to the others until then," he added bitterly. "Now come along, child. It's not safe out here for you. The British could be back at any time."

"I'll be along in a minute, papa. Really I will," Angeline assured again. "I simply want to stay and say a prayer for those who died here today. We've no priest to do it, after all," she added entreatingly.

"Very well," her father replied, giving another mystified shrug. "But see that you're back to the settlement in a few minutes, or I'll return to fetch you!" With that, he turned and continued walking eastward along the footpath with the other men.

Once they were out of sight, Angeline wasted no time in rushing to the captain's side and kneeling down to find out if she could hear a heartbeat in his chest. To her great relief, there was one, albeit faint.

She would have to move him, she decided,

174

hide him where the grave-diggers weren't apt to find him in the morning. She looked about in the last rays of sunlight for one of the stretchers that her people had been using all day to convey the wounded back to the settlement and the dead to their graves. Unfortunately, there were none in sight. She would have to return to the village and sneak back with one for him tonight, she concluded, when everyone else was asleep. It would be frightening, she realized, finding herself here in the woods in the darkness with so many dead bodies all about her. There would be many angry spirits afloat by midnight, but it was a risk she would have to take. She knew she owed the captain more than a slow death in a pit grave.

He groaned once or twice, as if in a delirious sleep, as she tried to examine him. She saw no point, however, in rousing him. She would have to clean and suture his wounds soon, and there was no sense in subjecting him to any further pain, if it could be avoided. She would simply leave him here for the time being. She would return to the settlement, tell her papa she was retiring early, and sneak back out to the captain at her first opportunity. She'd bring a stretcher and all the necessary supplies along with her.

From the looks of things, she doubted that there was any danger of the captain bleeding to death in her absence. His only serious external wound was one in his groin area, a long slash that appeared to have been made with some sort of sword, and the blood in the crotch of his breeches felt dry now, as though the wound had already begun scabbing over. He would need some stitches there, nevertheless, she concluded, because it was such a long wound and there was some danger of it starting to bleed again if he attempted to move. Other than that, however, she saw and felt nothing to cause her great concern.

"Where . . . where am I?" Angeline suddenly heard the captain stammer as she rose to head back to the village a moment later.

His speech was somewhat garbled, but Angeline understood enough English to make out the question. She kneeled down once more and gently brushed the blood-hardened strands of sandy hair from his forehead.

"At the Petitcodiac, *mon capitaine,*" she said in a soothing whisper near his ear. "And you are going to be fine. Put your faith in me."

He gave forth another pained groan, and his eyes flickered open slightly. He squinted up at her as though fighting to see her clearly.

"*C'est moi, Capitaine* . . . Angeline DuBay . . . the girl you let go that night so many weeks ago. And now it's my turn to do you a favor," she explained in French, having already exhausted her English vocabulary. She doubted, however, that in such a state he'd be able to understand her in any language. But, though she knew she had to get back to the village soon or risk having her father return for her, she couldn't help feeling that the captain deserved some sort of explanation and reassurance now.

"Ange . . . Angel," he repeated groggily, his eyes closing once more.

"*Mais oui, Capitaine,*" she replied in a soft, understanding voice. "*Angeline.* Surely, you can't have forgotten me so soon. I didn't forget you in this short time . . . and I won't forget you now," she promised, giving his right upper arm a reassuring squeeze. "I'll be back very shortly to tend to you."

Angeline wasn't sure if he heard her words now, as he seemed to sink back into unconsciousness. She only knew that, as long as he was out, he couldn't feel the pain that, doubtless, filled his body. Until she could return to him with time enough to give him some of the anesthetizing solutions she had on hand, she would simply have to let sleep be his nurse. With that sorry realization, she gathered up her medicine basket and hurried home.

Richard knew that he had been slipping in and out of consciousness for hours, and considering the pain that swept through him every time he made the slightest move, he far preferred his blackouts to being awake. He was being drawn into another dream now, a dream about an angel. He'd heard himself say the word *angel* for some reason and an angel was precisely what had seemed to come to him. She wore the typical seraphic gown, which he'd seen in many of the Renaissance paintings in Europe. The only difference was that her sleeves were unusually long and trailing.

Once she was just a foot or two from him, he could see that her gown was made of a whisper-light gauze of the kind sometimes used to bandage wounds. Her sleeves were like gossamer caught upon dewy blades of grass on a summer morning. As the heavenly creature drew nearer yet, he could see that the garment was meant to stream over him and stanch his bleeding, as the sheerest of gauze would.

Saignement . . . bleeding . . . Angel . . . *Angel* . . . *Angel* . . . *ine.* He was filled with both wonder and terror as he looked up at the creature, where she hovered above him now. Her flowing webs hung over him, shrouded him, and she looked, at once, like an angel and a spider in that strange, aerial position. Nevertheless, he knew that *whatever* she was, he desperately needed her.

As Angeline sat at the dinner table with her father half an hour later, she could tell that he was surprised to see how quickly she was eating.

"I haven't eaten since morning . . . like everyone else," she explained with an uneasy blush. "I'm absolutely famished."

After several seconds he lowered his questioning brow, as though satisfied with her explanation, and went on eating.

"Maybe we can still sail back to Grand Pré this summer, Papa . . . before the fall gales set in," she said hopefully.

Her father rolled his eyes at her wearily. "You know as well as I, Daughter, that the British have probably evacuated Grand Pré by now. Word has it that we are among the last of the French still in Acadia."

Angeline met his gaze somewhat tearfully. "Oh, it can't be true. I could hardly get through another day if I believed such talk."

Her father gave forth a cynical chuckle. "We scarcely got through this one with the British marching upon us. You're just a hopeless optimist," he said, shaking his head critically.

"I must be," she countered, her great conviction evident in her voice. "We all must be these days if we are to survive."

When several minutes ensued with nothing but silence between them, Angeline found herself finally giving into her urge to tell her father whom she'd seen among the fallen British soldiers. "It's the oddest thing, papa," she began cautiously, faintly hopeful that his response wouldn't be the one she was anticipating, "but I thought I saw a familiar face among those that the British left behind this afternoon."

He again raised an eyebrow at her as he finished off his bowl of potato soup. "Who would you know among the British, *chouchou?* We haven't been anywhere near them since we left Beauséjour."

"Well, Papa . . . I meant to tell you about this, but you were in such a poor state when I found you that I forgot to mention the British ship that intercepted Luc and Marcel and me before we reached Beauséjour. I mean, we told you about how the British had stopped us and confiscated the food we were trying to smuggle to you, but I forgot to tell you about the ship's captain."

"What about him? The filthy swine," he added in a grumble.

Angeline could feel her heart starting to beat more rapidly now with her mounting hopefulness that he would, at least, try to keep an open mind about the situation. "Well, he spoke French, Papa—"

"Ah, hell," DuBay interrupted. "That's no great feat. There are a few men among them who deign to speak our tongue."

"When they have to, yes," Angeline conceded. "But this man talked to me at length in French. He was even concerned about my being out upon the water after dark unchaperoned."

Her father reached out and gave her hand a rather patronizing pat. "It's just the strain of the day, Daughter. It's the first time most of us have seen so many dead and wounded men. It's making you speak nonsense."

"No, it's not," Angeline insisted, the great emotion she'd been hiding evident in her voice now. "I'm trying to tell you, don't you see? I'm trying to tell you how he let us go . . . how he had some of his men escort us all the way to Rocher Bay, and how he didn't take our boat when so many other officers would have."

Angeline saw her father's hand tighten angrily about the spoon he had been holding, and she felt herself drawing back a bit in her chair.

"I don't care, child," he thundered. "I don't care if the man rescued you from a boiling caldron! If he is the same man, then all you need know is that he came here to *kill* us today or round us up for slavery, and that's all there is to it!"

Angeline backed her chair away from the table at this outburst. It was clear to her from the furious flush that had spread over her father's face that she couldn't risk saying another word on the subject.

"He's probably dead by now, anyway," Daniel DuBay added in a quiet voice after two or three minutes of strained silence.

Angeline rose from the table and started gathering up their dirty dishes. "Probably," she agreed, choking back her urge to cry.

"In any case, he'll be buried with the others tomorrow morning, and then there'll be no need to give him another thought. You'll have enough to do, trying to get this village packed up with the rest of us," he concluded admonishingly.

She turned from the dish-washing basin, which her hands were submerged in now, and stared at him with wide, questioning eyes. "We really are leaving the Petitcodiac?"

Her father nodded. *"Oui,* though it hasn't yet been unanimously decided when and where we should go. It's clear, in any case, that we can't stay here much longer. After what happened today, we would be fools to believe that the British won't be back, and with twice as many men and weapons as they had this time."

"But, where . . . where could we go?" Angeline stammered. "Back to Grand Pré?" she asked, knowing even as she said it that the question would only serve to anger her father.

"No," he snapped. "Don't you understand? Grand Pré isn't safe anymore. It's too close to Halifax. Even if Lawrence hasn't had it burnt to the ground yet, it won't be long in coming. We'll simply have to head farther west. Maybe south as well. I'm just glad your dear mother didn't live to see such horrible days," he added sadly.

Angeline turned away from him and continued washing the dishes. She bit her lip and went on trying to fight her aching urge to weep. She thought she had broken her emotional ties with Grand Pré when she'd left for Fort Beauséjour months earlier, but she realized now that she hadn't. If the rumors among their neighbors were true, it was very likely that the home and life she'd known in her native village had already been completely reduced to ashes and that her cousin Elise and her other loved ones had been shipped off to serve as slaves in the colonies. Angeline had been too busy trying to

182

help her father carve out a life for them in this struggling little village to give much thought to such things before tonight. It was all finally beginning to sink in now, however, and she had everything she could do to keep from falling apart.

The captain probably knows whether or not Grand Pré has fallen, a voice within her suddenly prompted. She could ask him tonight and, at least, be relatively certain that his knowledge of such evacuations would be more accurate than any reports she'd heard in this remote settlement. Realizing this, she sped up her dishwashing and drying. Right or wrong, she couldn't deny the fact that she was very anxious to get back to him.

"I'm going to bed now," she declared a few minutes later when her work was done. "I'm too tired to stay awake any longer."

Her father, engrossed in dividing up some of the gunpowder he had taken from the priming horns of the fallen British troops that afternoon, offered her a wave. "Sleep well, my dear. Tomorrow will probably be another long, hard day."

Chapter 12

Two hours passed before Angeline was convinced that her father had retired and was fast asleep in his bed in their cabin's loft. She hadn't heard a sound from him in over thirty minutes, and she knew the time had finally come to begin gathering up the necessary implements for her trip back to the captain. With a musket and stretcher under her left arm, a birch-bark pack of supplies strapped to her back, and a dimly lit lantern in her right hand, she crept out of the cabin's back door and made her way surreptitiously through the outskirts of the village. When she was certain she was out of the line of sight of any of the settlers who might have been tending to evening chores, she headed for the woods that lined the footpath and continued her hurried walk due west.

In spite of all her father had said at supper, her heart began to sink with sympathy for the Bostonian once more, as she again beheld him where he lay at the battle site. She set her gear down, dropped to her knees beside him, and quickly withdrew a clean rag from her backpack. She wetted the rag with some water from one of the flasks in her pack and began wiping the dried blood off his face, following its wide path up to the gash in his forehead from which it had emanated. "*Capitaine,*" she said softly, trying to prop him up to a sitting position, once she had cleaned him up, "I've returned."

He let out a pained gasp as she attempted to lift his torso, and she instantly realized that something had escaped her notice earlier. He had obviously suffered some internal injury which made sitting up excruciating for him. "My ribs," he exclaimed in English, his eyes falling open now. "Dear Lord, it feels as if my ribs have all been broken!"

Angeline, able to make out a few words of what he'd said, drew a quick repentant breath in through her teeth and instantly lowered him back down to a supine position. "Oh, I'm sorry. I'm so sorry. I should have known. I should have examined you more thoroughly before I tried lifting you."

By her lantern's light, she could see that he

185

was squinting at her now, as though having great difficulty focusing his vision and making out her features.

"My God," he exclaimed after a moment, "you're that sorceress from the fishing boat!" To Angeline's utter amazement he began struggling to sit up again, as though he wanted desperately to get to his feet and run away from her.

Angeline reached out and tried to hold him down. "Shhh! *Capitaine,*" she whispered scoldingly, "you must not raise your voice like that! I've come back here to help, not harm you. Don't you understand?"

Too weak to continue fighting her, he let his torso sink back down upon the ground in acquiescence. His eyes, however, continued to be locked upon her steadily, as though she were some sort of venomous serpent that he feared provoking.

"Sweet Jesus, where am I?" he asked under his breath. "This must be another one of my nightmares."

"Not at all," Angeline replied with a soft smile. "I assure you that this is all quite real. Here," she continued, pulling a wineskin out of the pack of supplies she'd been carrying. She uncapped it and turned back to him. Reaching back behind his neck, she slowly brought his head forward and tipped the flask to his lips.

"What is it?" he asked uneasily, obviously

186

unwilling to drink until he knew. Richard noted as she brought the wineskin up to his mouth that she did so with her left hand. She was left-handed, he concluded; it was a well-known fact that all those who possessed truly magical powers had that particular characteristic in common. He froze, too filled with misgivings to do anything but stare up at her apprehensively.

"Come on now, my friend, and drink," she urged. "It's just some strong ale to help you rest. You can't expect me to stitch you up with nothing to kill the pain, can you?"

"I don't think I want any," he said gingerly, finding himself able to address her in French once more.

Angeline gave forth a light laugh. "But of course you do, *mon capitaine*. I insist that you drink some."

After several seconds, he took a reluctant sip or two. Seeing that he was refusing to drink any more, Angeline lowered his head to the ground again.

"There, you see," she encouraged. "Not such awful-tasting stuff now, was it? And the more you drink of it, of course, the less pain you will feel. So you must tell me when you want more."

Richard was sorrily discovering that he was too weak and disoriented to do anything but issue another groan. The intense pain in his head, chest, and groin was almost overwhelming. Yet, the pain was all that assured him he was awake, and considering who appeared to be nursing him now, he wasn't sure he wanted to risk losing consciousness again. On the other hand, taking into account the gravity of his situation, he also wasn't sure that he dared do anything that might offend her and drive her away from him. He needed her help, a voice within him warned. It wasn't what he wanted to hear right now, but he sadly acknowledged that it was true.

"So this was what you meant in my cabin that night, when you warned me to let you go?" he asked with a wry smirk as she slipped some sort of pillow under his head.

She returned his ironic smile. "*Oui*. I suppose it was. Not even I know what such warnings mean sometimes, *Capitaine*. I simply relate them, if they come to me."

Her patient seemed to be relaxing a bit, she noted, running her hand over the slowing pulse at his temple. His voice, however, still sounded tremulous as he spoke.

"And where do you suppose such warnings come from?"

"From God, of course," she replied without hesitation. "Where else would they come from?"

Richard studied the innocent expression on her face, doing his level best to keep telling himself that there was nothing to fear from her.

She probably wouldn't have bothered coming to him in the darkness like this if she did not mean well.

He drew in a pained breath as she attempted to remove his breeches. He had already felt her take off his buckle-topped shoes and knee-length stockings. His breeches, however, feeling stuck to the wound in his groin, were not being nearly as cooperative for her.

"I'm going to have to cut these off of you," Angeline declared after a moment. Realizing now how adherent the breeches had become blood-soaked, she knew there was no alternative. "I'm very sorry, *mon capitaine,* but you might start bleeding again if I continue trying to tear the cloth from the wound. I'll simply have to cut them," she concluded, reaching into her backpack and withdrawing a pair of scissors.

"That's all right, Miss DuBay. I quite understand," he replied with an anguished smile. "I've never been fond of lying about in wet breeches, in any case." With that, he shut his eyes and turned his face to the side, wondering what further degradation he could be subjected to before the day was through. He had already lost a battle to a pack of virtually unarmed peasants. What survivors there had been in his battalion had obviously turned tail and run for the longboats, leaving him there to die. And now, some adolescent was busy cutting him out of his soaked breeches! He could feel the night's chill upon his suddenly bared lower body as she carefully cut each inseam, from the pants cuffs just below the knees to his crotch, and part of him couldn't help wishing that she had simply allowed him to pass away there. That seemed, by far, the most respectable of his alternatives.

"Where are the rest of my men?" he inquired as he felt her unfastening the bottom buttons on his vest and slowly cutting his breeches open, from the waistband downward.

"Brace yourself, *Capitaine,*" she warned, as she began easing the blood-hardened fabric of his pants away from his wound once more.

Richard, deciding this was probably pretty good advice, reached down and gripped the now-vacant mouth of his black leather scabbard, as the pain of her tearing ran through him. The Acadians had taken his sword, he realized, as he continued to keep his left hand locked upon the hollow sheath. They had taken his sword and, quite probably, his musket and pistol as well.

"Where are the rest of my men?" he asked again, clenching his teeth.

"The ones who did not retreat are all dead," she answered in an expressionless voice.

"Are you certain?"

"I haven't examined any of them," she admitted. "But, yes, I am certain."

"How can you be?" he pursued, turning his face to her once more and again opening his eyes.

She looked up and met his gaze coldly. "I am certain because you are the only one any of us are of a mind to save. The rest shall be buried tomorrow morning in a pit grave. I am very sorry, my friend," she added, and in spite of the indifference in her voice, he did detect a glimmer of sympathy in her eyes.

"How many men did I lose?" he inquired with a remorseful swallow.

"Two dozen maybe. I haven't really had time to count them, *Capitaine*. And, as I said, the rest retreated."

"What kind of warfare was that anyway?" he asked. "I have never heard of men fighting like that in my life. Pouncing on us from out of treetops and woods as we marched!"

Angeline couldn't help laughing a bit under her breath. "It's the kind of warfare the Indians taught us, *Capitaine*. It's the way men fight when the other side's men and guns far outnumber their own. And you needn't bother complaining about the dreadful wounds you and your men suffered. As far as I'm concerned, the day you British took our guns away was the day you *chose* to be hacked to pieces by my people," she added frostily.

"I see," Richard replied, deciding it was best to change the subject now if he could. She was right, of course. It was *his* people who were to blame for the bloodshed that had taken place that afternoon, and he was wrong to have tried to construe it any other way.

"Though I shudder to ask," he began again in a wavering voice, "what . . . what has happened to me?"

As he strained to sit up and have a look at the wound, Angeline pressed his torso back down to the ground.

"Someone slashed you with a scythe or saber, it appears. You're fortunate that you didn't bleed to death. It has actually begun to scab over slightly," she declared, shaking her head a bit with wonder. "I suggest, *Capitaine,* that you drink more of my ale. I see no danger for you if it thins your blood now, and you're going to need it to help dull the pain when I start suturing."

"Oh, very well," Richard replied with a weary sigh. "But I hardly think stitches will be necessary."

"They will be, if you care to try to walk or move about at all in the next few days. As it is, if you take one step or even attempt to lift a leg, you could tear the wound wide open again." With that, Angeline brought the flask of ale up to his lips once more. Again she gently tilted his head forward to help him drink, and to her great relief, he did so quite heartily.

"Isn't that work better suited to a man?" Richard asked, as she lowered his head to the pillow a moment later and began dabbing the delicate region of his groin with a cleansing, wet rag.

"*Oui*. But it will have to be done by me, because all of the men here want you dead, I'm afraid."

"Well, at least you're frank, mademoiselle," he said with a grimace. The wound began to burn terribly as she sprinkled it with some of her ale. "I admire that in a lady."

"*Merci*," she answered, feeling a slight blush warming her cheeks. She was realizing, for the first time, that he might have found her as attractive as she found him. "I trust you will be frank with me, as well, *Capitaine*, when I ask you questions."

"*Mais oui*," he assured, his voice still a bit shaky with the pain. "Tell me," he began again guardedly, "just how do you intend to keep the other villagers from finding out about me? I mean, if they're coming back here to bury my men in the morning, won't they bury me as well?"

"No. Because I am going to hide you in the woods. Far into the woods, on the other side of the settlement, so that none of my people will have reason to walk by and chance to see you."

"But, as you have already established, Miss

193

DuBay, I can scarcely sit up, so how am I going to walk that far?" he asked with a sorry laugh.

"You won't have to. I've brought a stretcher for you. I can probably pull you most of the way. I'm very strong, *Capitaine*," she added with a note of pride in her voice.

"Oh, I don't doubt that you are, my dear," he confirmed. "But why would you want to bother? Why are you troubling yourself over me this way?"

"Because I owe you a favor. I thought that was clear to you. You let me and my friends go, without taking our boat, and, in exchange, I will nurse you back to health." With that, she took from her dress pocket what appeared to Richard to be a black cross on a rosary with black beads, and closing her downturned right palm around the crucifix, she held it just over his wound. Then she squeezed her eyes shut and began to utter some sort of incantation in a tongue that was totally foreign to him.

"Good heavens! What are you doing?" he asked in a horrified whisper.

Her eyes fell open and she glared down at him. "Helping to assure that no evil spirits will enter you through this wound."

"Well, stop it at once," he ordered. "I'm neither a Catholic nor an Indian, and I can't imagine that that hocus-pocus will do me a bit of good."

"Very well, *Capitaine*," she replied, withdrawing the crucifix from him with a bewildered shrug. "I shall stop, if it disturbs you. But just remember, if this wound should fester, I did offer to purify it."

"Your wet rag and ale have offered purification enough, my dear," he replied. "Now, please do get on with your suturing or whatever it is you plan to do to me."

"Very well," she said again, reaching back and taking a painkilling salve from her pack.

"What is that, now?" Richard inquired warily, as she started applying it about the periphery of his wound.

Angeline's fingers froze. "It's a painkiller, *Capitaine*. A balm of clove oil and ginger, which my grandmother taught me to concoct. It really is quite effective," she assured. "It will deaden you for my suturing. You'll be glad of it, when the time comes."

Richard, seeing the sincerity that shone in her eyes, gave her a resigned wave of consent. "Oh, very well. I don't suppose it can do any harm."

Angeline continued applying it. "On the contrary. Most of my patients tell me it does them a great deal of good." As her fingers glided over this delicate part of him, Angeline began to experience an odd feeling of arousal. She thought she had treated enough men in her time to be somewhat at ease with touching such an intimate part of a male. However, given her conflicting feelings for this particular patient, she couldn't seem to fight her abashment. Now that she'd wiped most of the blood away, his privates were very well exposed to her by the lantern light. She was doing her best, nonetheless, not to look at them and simply to concentrate on tending to his wound. In spite of this effort, though, she couldn't deny the fact that her breath had long since caught in her throat and she was almost numb with the odd melting sensation that even her mere glimpses of such forbidden terrain were causing in her now.

Richard, feeling the pleasant, almost tickling sensation her fingers were producing as she applied the salve, couldn't help issuing a soft laugh and trying to pull away from her a bit. It was a laugh that confused Angeline somewhat, because she wasn't sure if it was provoked by ticklishness on his part or embarrassment.

Richard finally flashed her a grateful smile. "It must do a great deal of good, mademoiselle," he confirmed. "It's the first time I've felt anything but pain in hours."

He tried to lie still and compose himself. Nevertheless, his faith in her was still only marginal. He reasoned that there was probably not a man on earth who wasn't a bit skittish about entrusting such a personal part of his anatomy to the care of a virtual stranger—and a female one at that.

"Just relax, *Capitaine*," Angeline said to him in a tone which he realized was meant to sound reassuring, but actually did little to mask her own uneasiness with the situation. "I'll be finished here in no time. We'll let this balm have a minute or two to do its work, and you'll scarcely feel a thing after that."

"Most unique," he remarked, feeling the tension in his torso beginning to ease up as she finished applying the salve. "It stings a bit at first, and then it leaves you feeling cold and numb. It's a bit like ice, isn't it?"

"*Oui*. Very much like ice, but better, because one doesn't need to trouble with keeping it frozen."

A terribly awkward silence fell between them, and Richard, feeling he couldn't bear the discomfiture of it any longer, began to speak again. If she had been any other woman, a pub maid in Boston or even the pristine daughter of some wealthy colonist, he would have felt much more at ease. She was so foreign to him, however, so frightening and exotic, that he just couldn't seem to bring himself to feel comfortable with her touching him in such a private and vulnerable place. "Pardon me for asking, Miss DuBay, but you are quite young, as I recall. I wonder, are you . . . are you accustomed to treating men with such wounds?"

"Would you prefer I let you die out here instead?" she asked in a voice which told him she was still striving to sound as detached as possible.

"No. Of course not. It's just that—"

"A wound is a wound, *Capitaine,*" she interrupted coolly. "It matters little to me where it's found. They are all just as capable of festering and killing one, if not properly treated."

"Of course," he replied, finally deciding it was best to adopt the same detached air she was feigning. Even though the pain in his groin was starting to subside a bit now, his ribs still felt as though they had been crushed in a vise, and he knew she'd been right to warn him once more of the gravity of his condition.

"Don't misunderstand me, mademoiselle," he began again seconds later, his speech starting to sound somewhat slurred to Angeline, as the ale he had drunk began to take effect. "It's not that I'm not exceedingly grateful for your assistance. It's simply that I can't help feeling that I am the enemy . . . don't you think? I mean, my men and I marched in here this morning with orders to round you people up like cattle."

Angeline knotted the suturing thread that she'd poured out of a second container of ale. "With *whose* orders, *Capitaine?* Not yours, surely."

"Well, no," he conceded. "They were Charles Lawrence's orders, of course. I suppose everyone in Acadia knows who is behind this expulsion by now."

"Indeed, we do," Angeline confirmed with a bitter edge to her voice. "And since *you* are not to blame for this, I am not wrong for coming to your aid."

"But the other men here . . . those of my men who might still be alive, as I am . . . they're not to blame for the orders either, Miss DuBay."

She shrugged. "No. But they are also not the ones who gave the orders to let me and my friends keep our boat. You are feeling guilty, aren't you?" she suddenly acknowledged, looking up at his face with the same unnervingly knowing expression she had worn when she'd spoken to him in his cabin so many weeks before. "You are feeling guilty because a captain is always taught to die with his men, and I am not allowing you to do that, am I?"

"No," he answered with an apprehensive flush coming over him, as she bent down once more to begin stitching his wound. "It doesn't appear that you are."

Angeline looked up again and saw how his eyes were locked, with obvious trepidation, upon her suturing needle. "Please put more faith in me, *Capitaine,*" she said with a heartening expression in her eyes. "My needle is very sharp and I am very fast. And, if you'll kindly lie still, I assure you that you won't feel much

199

at all."

"Quite," he replied with a dry swallow, trying to reciprocate her confident air. Nevertheless, he knew that she saw his fingers reach down to grip his shirt's cuff ruffles in those seconds, as he braced himself for the pain to come.

To Richard's relief, however, he discovered that her assurances were well-founded, as she began to stitch a moment later. It was the oddest sensation, really. He could feel her needle entering and leaving his skin and the thread drawing the edges of his wound together like lacings in a corset. Yet, mercifully, none of what he was feeling could be described as pain. Apparently, the swelling of his wound, combined with the effects of the ale and her extraordinary balm, were numbing him quite adequately.

"Can you talk while you stitch?" he asked entreatingly.

She gave forth a soft laugh, but kept her eyes directed intently on her precarious task. "I guess so. Why?"

"I would like for us to go on talking. It would help to take my mind off myself."

"Very well. What shall we talk about?"

"About you . . . yes. I think that's best," he added with a slight gasp, as she ran into a bit of resistance in what felt like the center of his gaping slash wound.

"What about me?" she asked in a monotone,

quite engrossed in her work.

"Where did you learn such skills? They're really quite remarkable, you know," he praised. "I've never seen or *felt* the like of them in Boston."

"I learned them from my mother, who, in turn, learned them from hers. My great-grandmother was an Abenaki Indian, you see, *Capitaine*. A very gifted *sage femme*."

"Ah, yes. Well, she must have been," Richard replied, continuing to feel tremendously grateful that she still hadn't caused him much discomfort.

"And your good father, did you ever meet up with him? Or, Heaven forbid, did he suffer the misfortune of dying at Beauséjour?"

Angeline emitted a dry laugh. "Oh, no, *Capitaine*. On the contrary. It was some of your men who suffered the misfortune of dying at *his* hand this afternoon."

"So, he's alive and well with you here then?"

"*Oui*. Alive enough to finish us both, if he should catch me tending to you."

"So, you snuck out to me?"

"*Oui*. I saw you among the fallen this afternoon, and I snuck back after supper. Papa would forswear me, I'm afraid, if he knew what I was doing."

"Yet, you came," Richard noted, his admiration and gratitude more than evident in his voice.

"*Oui.* I came. I felt I owed you at least this much for the kindness you showed me and my friends, *Capitaine.*"

Richard felt a twinge of conscience at recalling that it was fear and not kindness at all that had motivated him to act as he had the night he'd met her. "It's Richard. Richard Brenton," he said after a moment.

"What?" she asked, stopping her work just long enough to look up and meet his eyes once more.

"My first name is Richard. *'Capitaine'* is a bit formal now, don't you think . . . all things considered?"

She saw his face flush slightly before she looked down to resume her stitching, and she knew he was thinking precisely what she was; that it was not simply a sense of indebtedness that had brought her to him, but some sort of attraction between them. She found, however, that she was still too afraid of such interactions with a man to continue contemplating it. "We're strangers, though," she said finally. "And enemies. Let us not forget that."

"But I have a rule, you see, Miss DuBay. I always let those who have saved my life, enemies or not, call me by my Christian name. I would hate to see you end that fine tradition."

She couldn't help smiling a bit at this obviously tongue-in-cheek remark. "Oh, *oui?* And how many have saved your life so far?"

202

Richard pretended to give the question some serious thought. "You're the only one, I think . . . that is, if I don't count my sister Amelia."

Angeline found herself fighting a laugh now. "And what did your sister do to save your life, pray tell?"

"She didn't tell my father that she caught me in the hayloft with one of her girlfriends when I was seventeen."

A smile continued to tug at the corner of Angeline's lips. "You're becoming drunk, *Capitaine*. I will have to feed you some supper after I've bandaged your chest."

"It's true though," Richard maintained. "I think he would have killed me, had he learned of it."

"How old was the girl?"

"Fifteen, I believe."

"Then, he *should* have killed you! My papa would have, had he caught you with me at that age."

"Your papa would *now*," Richard retorted with a dry laugh. "Even without such provocation."

Angeline shrugged. "Ah, you were just a boy then. You would never provide such *provocation* today, would you?" she asked, surprised at the uncharacteristic sportiveness she heard in her voice.

"I'm hardly in any state to, mademoiselle," Richard conceded. "But yes, given the right circumstances, my dear, I believe I would."

Angeline, in response, felt a provocative tingle run through her, and her fingers froze, hovering just above his wound. She realized that, under that gentlemanly veneer of his, another kind of man lurked. She could see it in his eyes, the worldliness, the roguish twinkle that told her he had bedded more than his share of women in his time and he wouldn't mind at all if she were the next on his list. But instead of feeling the swooning sensation that had come over her earlier, she wanted to run away from him and hide in her father's cabin, bolt the door behind her and dash to the safety of her warm bed.

She was *touching* him. She was drawing in the heated, manly scent of him, as she worked so closely upon his flesh, and she was starting to feel so overwhelmed by the experience that she found herself torn between flustered tears and the possibility of fainting from fear.

"I . . . um . . . I am finished here now," she declared after a moment as she gathered her wits about her and gently cut her suturing thread. She tied its ends into a knot at the base of his wound, being exceedingly careful all the while not to brush up against the prohibited region just an inch to the left of her hands.

"You were right," Richard said with a sigh of relief and a clearly approving smile. "I didn't feel any pain. You really are quite gifted at this."

Angeline put her suturing implements away and began rummaging through the contents of her pack for one of the blankets she'd brought along. *"Merci, Capitaine . . . Richard,"* she corrected herself, lending the name more musicality with her French pronunciation. "I told you I was a healer on your ship, and I did not lie. I'll . . . um . . . I'll try to smuggle a pair of papa's breeches out for you in the morning," she added, still feeling embarrassed by his nakedness as she hurriedly spread the blanket out over the lower half of his torso and legs.

"Yes, please," Richard encouraged with an awkward laugh. "It won't do to have me lying about like this, I'm afraid."

Angeline cleared her throat with a dutiful air. "We must try to have you sit up now," she declared. She reached out, slipped her hands under his coat, and gently ran her palms over his rib cage in an effort to assess what damage had been done. "I have to try to get you onto this stretcher I brought. Then I can pull you up to one of these tree trunks and prop you up against it, while I wrap your chest. I fear that some of your ribs may have been broken, as you suggested earlier. At least, that's how it feels when I run my hands over them."

"Oh, yes. They're definitely broken," he confirmed with a groan. "I remember a musket butt being hammered down upon them before I blacked out this afternoon."

"Do you need more to drink, before I move you?" Angeline asked tentatively. She was afraid that any additional swigs of the strong brew might cause him to speak too candidly with her again, as he had a few minutes earlier. But considering how difficult moving him was going to be if he was in great pain all the while, she decided that offering him more was the lesser of two evils.

He simply nodded in response.

"I wonder," he asked a few seconds later as she lifted his head and brought the flask up to his lips once more, "could you trouble to find my musket, when we're finished with all of this? I dropped it when I fell this afternoon, and I would feel a great deal better about spending the night out here in this state if I had a weapon at my side."

Angeline smiled down at him sardonically. "Now, you can't honestly think, my friend, that our men would leave your weapons out here, can you? Not after you British confiscated all of ours so many months ago," she added pointedly.

"No, I suppose not," Richard conceded. "It's just that . . ." His words broke off with a sudden wave of pain as she began trying to help him slide onto the stretcher she had pulled to his side.

Angeline had draped his left arm up around her shoulders in preparation for the move. As his left hand tightened about her upper arm and he clung to her with what strength he could summon, she couldn't help feeling an odd sort of affection for him, like what a mother might feel for a small boy. "Have no fear, my friend," she said in a hushed, consoling voice, finally centering him upon the blanketed stretcher. "You'll have a musket with you tonight. I'll stay and keep watch over you till just before dawn. You're in no condition to look out for yourself at present."

She felt very relieved that she had managed to help move him without hurting him much. To her horror, however, she did something then that she would never have expected from herself. Having his face so near to hers and the warming feel of his arm wrapped about her, she was somehow compelled to bend down and plant a soft kiss upon his left temple. She gasped and bit her lower lip, then froze just above him and squeezed her eyes shut regretfully, wondering what on earth could have possessed her to do such a thing.

"Miss DuBay?" she heard him inquire seconds later. "Are you all right?"

Angeline gradually let her eyes fall open, and she gazed down at him with an expression that must have betrayed both her remorse and her great chagrin. *"Oui Capitaine,"* she answered in a faint, wavering voice, finding herself beginning to feel rather sick inside.

"That was very sweet of you," he whispered, reaching up and catching one of her hands in his as she started drawing away from him. "Thank you."

"Yes . . . well . . . I don't, I don't know what came over me," she declared, knowing that her cheeks must have been as red as a lobster's shell. "I'm not in the habit of kissing strange men, you understand. Any men at all, for that matter," she added defensively. "It's just that it's been a very long and trying day, and I'm *tired*."

Though Richard didn't know a great deal about the Acadians, he had spent enough time in France during his university years to know that the French were, on the whole, much more demonstrative than those of British descent. It stood to reason that her kiss really was as innocent as it seemed.

"I quite understand," he said, continuing to smile up at Angeline with a nonchalance that she found almost annoying. It was as though being kissed by young female acquaintances was a common occurrence for him.

"No harm done, my dear. I promise you," he concluded.

Angeline was so torn with emotion, she was tempted to jump to her feet and dash home. She couldn't help wondering if it was possible for one to simply drop dead of humiliation, and all she could seem to bring herself to do was stare numbly down at the ground.

To her surprise, she felt him give her hand a gentle tug, and she fell into a kneeling position beside him once more.

"It shall be our little secret, Angeline. I shan't tell a soul," he vowed in a murmur that, to her further chagrin, she realized was somewhat patronizing in tone. But she noted that he'd called her by her first name as he spoke, and that meant something too. Evidently, his intention had not been simply to tease her about her obvious innocence, but also to seize the opportunity to break down more of the social barriers between them.

"Well, you must understand," she continued, the words flowing out of her in an embarrassed gush. "I felt so sorry for you, having to lie out here for so many hours in such pain, so far from your home in Boston—"

"Shhh," he urged, stroking her hand with an expertness that took her breath away. "You needn't say another word, my dear. I quite understand, and I assure you that that single kiss shall do more to heal me in the next few days than all of your other generous efforts combined."

Mon Dieu, what a charmer, Angeline thought, feeling as though she might simply melt into the ground. She was clearly no match for one as experienced and mature as he, and she silently scolded herself for even toying with the thought that she might have been.

"Well," she began again, easing her hand out of his grasp and reaching up to smooth the sides of her flat linen bonnet about her face. He was staring at her with his winning dark eyes. She could feel them upon her, but she was determined not to look at them and risk revealing further what a novice she was at this business of interacting with men. "There's still much to be done for you, *Capitaine*," she continued in a prudent tone. "I have to wrap your chest and feed you some supper. You must be famished by now."

"I am. Yes," Richard confirmed, watching with satisfaction as her fingers nervously fiddled with the ends of her long black braids and she reached down to flatten the heavy skirt of her gray jumper dress with the palms of her hands. She was quite a prize, really, he thought with a whisper of a smile—once one got past that awful "sorceress" business.

"I didn't recognize you at first. I mean, dressed like a lady and such now," he remarked.

Angeline gave forth an awkward laugh. "Ah, *oui*. That's right. I was dressed as a fisherman that night on your ship, so I suppose you wouldn't have." Once she'd reached the Petitcodiac settlement, one of the Acadian maidens had given her some of the traditional women's clothing to wear, and she had worn it day in and day out ever since, only exchanging it for a nightshift in the evenings, so she'd have the chance to launder the outfit. It was quite simple really. It consisted of nothing more than a flaxen jumper dress with a scoop-necked bodice, which was worn over a long-sleeved white, linen chemise. In addition, Angeline always donned a matching linen bonnet. And, though the captain didn't say as much, she felt certain now that this attire must have seemed rather drab and unsophisticated to one as obviously worldly as he.

"You're quite lovely, you know, in a frock," he suddenly declared, and Angeline couldn't help letting her surprise at the compliment show.

"You should make a practice of wearing them," he added teasingly after a moment.

"*Merci, Capitaine,*" Angeline replied, somewhat indignantly. "I assure you that I do."

She decided at this point that her words to him were doing precious little to alleviate her continued embarrassment over what she had done minutes before, and since conversing with him now only seemed to keep leading to gibes from him, she felt it was best for her to remain silent as she worked from that point on.

She dragged the stretcher up to a nearby tree, and though the thought of having to

211

touch him again was making her palms moist, she reached under his arms and slowly, arduously, propped him up to a sitting position. To the captain's credit, he did offer her as much assistance as he could seem to muster in his incapacitated state.

"How does that feel?" she asked, grimacing a bit herself as she saw the pained expression on her face.

"Only slightly better than excruciating, I'm afraid," he confessed.

She extended her wineskin of ale to him once more. "Here. Drink. I'll work quickly. Once your chest is wrapped, I know you'll feel better."

He groaned and took a swig from the flask. Then he gave forth a languid laugh. "It's unlikely, my dear, that I could feel any worse."

At this point, Angeline was forced to begin the unnerving task of disrobing the upper half of him, a task only made easier by the fact that she had already endured working on his lower half. The first thing she removed was the priming horn that hung from a leather strap across his chest. She was somewhat surprised that he still had it on. Most of them had been confiscated by her father and the others earlier, but this one had, somehow, been passed over. Then, with the captain's fumbling assistance, she managed to pull his arms free of his coat, and she folded it up and laid it on the ground to the right of him. Finally, she began unfastening the brass buttons on his white vest, moving on to unbutton the ruffled white shirt under it. Not wanting to fully expose the muscular, moderately haired chest beneath, she simply left his arms in the shirt's sleeves now and let the garment continue to hang about him, as she began methodically winding her wide roll of bandaging about his rib cage. It took a great deal of strength and dexterity to wrap him as firmly as she knew was required, but fortunately, he made the whole process easier for her by leaning forward and back as needed.

"Feeling any better?" she inquired, once she'd finished the task and secured the bandage at its base with a tight knot.

"Except for being unable to breathe, my dear, this is the best I've felt since before the battle."

"Really? Is it too tight?" Angeline asked with great concern.

To her surprise, his lips spread open to a broad grin. "No. I'm only teasing. You've done quite a commendable job, in truth. I just thought we could do with a little levity now," he continued, raising the wineskin giddily over his head.

Angeline reached up and snatched it from his hand with a glower. "Enough of that! You're apt to hurt yourself, flailing your arms about that way. I'll get you some soup," she concluded, turning to withdraw a flask of it from

213

her pack.

"What kind of soup?" he asked anxiously.

"Turkey broth and vegetable for you, I'm afraid. I would have brought you some of the potato and ham my father and I had for supper, but this is the best kind for one who has lost so much blood."

"I'm sure that anything you offer will be delicious, my dear. If you are half as good at cookery as you are at concocting balms, I'll be eating like a king."

Angeline felt herself blush a bit at the praise, as she eased up closer to him with a spoon, her flask of soup, and an earthenware bowl a moment later. "Can you lift both arms enough to feed yourself, *Capitaine,* or shall I do it?"

"Better let me try," he replied as she poured the steaming soup into the bowl. "You've troubled yourself enough over me as it is."

Angeline helped him to hold the bowl steady in his left hand, as he dipped the spoon into it seconds later with his right.

"It's downward that my arms don't seem able to reach," he explained between mouthfuls. "I seem quite capable of reaching up without much pain, though. And I was correct, my dear, you are an excellent cook," he confirmed.

Angeline shook her head humbly. "Oh, it's just all that ship food you've been eating. How fresh can anything be on a ship?"

"Quite, dear. But I think it's marvelous,

214

nonetheless. Our chief cook at home couldn't have done better."

"Your wife does not cook for you?" Angeline asked, biting her lip repentantly an instant later at the realization that it had never even occurred to her until now that he might be a married man.

Richard laughed. "No. She doesn't, and that's primarily because I don't have one."

Angeline was almost certain that she managed to conceal her great sense of relief in those seconds. "So, then, you have a cook?" she pursued, handing him the end of a loaf of bread she'd brought along as well. "To dip," she interjected.

He gladly accepted it from her. "Oh, how wonderful. *Merci*. You French bake the most delectable bread, as I recall from my time in Paris. But, to get back to your question. Yes, I have a cook, or, more specifically, my parents do."

"You live with your parents, then?"

"Well, yes. It's quite a large estate, you see, my dear. Plenty of room for the lot of us. I've never seen much advantage in living elsewhere."

"Oh, so your papa is wealthy?"

Richard froze for a second, surprised to hear her use such a term. Thus far, he had gotten the impression that the Acadians were too far removed from the rest of the world to have much of an awareness of wealth and poverty.

215

Considering, however, that this young woman's ancestors had come from France, it was possible that talk of such economic states had been passed down through the generations.

"Yes. I suppose you could say he is. But it's my wealth as well, you see. I'm his partner in the family business."

Angeline flashed him a warm smile. "Oh, how nice for you. Then you have plenty of reason to recover quickly and return home. Plenty to look forward to."

"Indeed. I do look forward to getting back to it. Indeed I do, *ma cherie*. And, because of your kind care, I once again have some hope of it."

This comment triggered Angeline to wonder once more whether or not the same could still be true for her. "*Capitaine . . . Richard,*" she corrected herself again with a slight blush. "Can you tell me if the village of Grand Pré is still standing?"

"Grand Pré," Richard repeated thoughtfully. "I am rather a newcomer to Acadia. But I seem to recall that that village is just south of Cape Sharp. Is that correct?"

"*Oui.*"

"Then, I doubt very much that it is still standing. I believe the villages in that area were among the first that Lawrence had destroyed."

At this, Angeline let her gaze drop abruptly to the ground. She didn't want him to see the

216

great sadness in her eyes.

"Was this Grand Pré important to you for some reason?" he inquired softly after a moment.

"*Oui*. It was my home," Angeline confessed.

"But I thought you told me that *this* village was your home."

She shook her head, still not willing to look up at him. "My friends and I lied to you, I'm afraid. We told you we came from the Petitcodiac settlement in the hopes that you would bring us here. It's so much closer to Beauséjour, you see."

Richard was silent for several seconds, finding himself a bit surprised by this deceitfulness on the part of Angeline and her friends. After what he'd heard from his first officer, he had expected the Acadians to be quite artless. "How clever of you," he said at last. "I would have done the same in your place, I suppose."

"So, then, you're not cross about it?" Angeline asked, lifting her face just enough to see him from beneath her long dark lashes.

"Not in the least. As you pointed out earlier, this is Charles Lawrence's campaign, not mine."

"Then, why are you here?"

"But you've already answered that, my dear, haven't you. That night in my cabin, *you* told me it was at my father's bidding, and you were quite right. A most disturbing business that, reading other's thoughts," he added with a disapproving scowl.

Angeline emitted an allaying laugh. "Well, I don't do it very often. It just sort of happened that evening. You have very telling eyes, after all, *Capitaine.*"

Even though Richard knew it wasn't a subject he cared to delve into, he couldn't help feeling intrigued by this observation. "I do?"

"*Mais oui.* In fact, at this very moment, they are telling me you want more soup."

"Right again," he confirmed, handing her his now-empty bowl. "I really must guard my thoughts with you, mustn't I, my dear. There is no telling what other appetites you'll detect," he concluded with a roguish smirk.

Angeline hoped he didn't see how her hands trembled in response to this as she quickly refilled his bowl and gave it back to him. "So, tell me. Why would your father send you here?"

"The merchant business he and I operate made it necessary, I'm afraid. If I had not agreed to come, I would have been faced with losing some of our most important patrons. And I was also likely to be charged with treason for not acting in accordance with His Majesty's wishes."

"Ah, *oui,* His Majesty," Angeline said with a disgusted cluck. "You British have been chasing my people about for nearly fifty years now, demanding our pledge of allegiance to him."

218

"Perhaps you should have given it," Richard replied charily. "You might have saved a lot of poor souls like me the trouble of having to sail up here to round you up and expel you. To say nothing of the trouble you would have saved yourselves."

"We don't like sovereigns, *Capitaine*. We would have stayed in France if we had wanted a king!"

To her surprise, he simply laughed at this sacrilegious remark. "Oh, there's no need to tell me that, I suppose. I've been reading about such sentiments in the books of many of your great writers for years."

"And do you agree with them?"

"Yes. I do," he admitted, though somewhat guardedly.

She cocked her head at him. "So, you needed books to tell you how you feel?"

Richard gave forth an amazed laugh. "Well, yes. It seems I did, doesn't it. Though I've never thought of it in quite that way, my dear. But, having been raised under a king's rule, it simply never occurred to me that men could live any other way. So I suppose I did need you French to come along and make me mindful of such possibilities."

"And now you believe there should be no king of England?"

Richard felt his face flush due to his continued uneasiness with the subject. "Well now, I didn't say that exactly. A man could find himself hanged with great dispatch because of such talk. I guess I simply feel that this world would be much improved if kings did more to keep men like Charles Lawrence from enslaving good people like yours."

"And yet, you're here," she noted again critically, "enslaving us for Monsieur Lawrence."

"Yes. I do appear to be, don't I?" he conceded. "Although I have suspected, for some weeks now, that it is possible that this is all just some sort of long horrible dream."

"I'll have you know that *I*, for one, am quite *real, Capitaine*," Angeline retorted indignantly.

He set his spoon down in his bowl and reached out to her amenably. "Oh, I know. I know you are, my dear," he replied, caressing her hand once more. "I could feel how warm your hands were, how warm your soft breath, when you stitched me up earlier," he added, letting his eyes look entreatingly into hers. "I simply find that I need some way to justify my part in this whole dreadful affair."

As before, Angeline found that he was obviously too versed in the realm of relations between men and women for her gaze to be any match for his in those seconds. She tore her eyes away and stared down at the ground again. "I'm staying with you tonight, *Capitaine*, because of the wolves," she stated coolly. "They are very attracted by the scent of human blood, of course, and I'm sorry to report that a lot of it was spilt here today. I just don't want you to get the impression that I am in the habit of spending nights with strange men, because I am not." With that, she withdrew her hand from his and quickly turned to dig a flask of water out of her pack of supplies. Without an instant of hesitation, she uncapped it, tipped it to her lips, and took a few long swallows from it.

"Oh, I am quite clear on that, *mon amie*," Richard assured. "Have no fear. What is it you are drinking so heartily there?" he suddenly inquired, his brow furrowed with curiosity.

"Oh, it's only water. Do you want some?" She extended the flask to him. "You probably should, you know. It is much better for you than ale," she coaxed.

"No, thank you. Maybe later," he said politely. "You finish it off, if you'd like. It appears that you're quite thirsty."

Angeline shook her head. "Not at all. It's just that I have to make certain I wake before dawn, and this is the best striking clock I know of out-of-doors."

Richard felt his face flush a bit as her meaning became clear to him. "How clever of you," he said simply, feeling a bit taken aback by her candor. Given her vocation, however, he realized it probably shouldn't have surprised him. "Well, Angeline, it is good of you to want to keep me company out here tonight," he began again, deciding it was best to move on to a different subject. "But let me remind you that you have yourself to worry about as well in all of this."

She cocked her head at him once more, wondering if this was some sort of coy way of leading up to the subject of lovemaking again. "What do you mean?" she asked cautiously.

"Well, only that my men will be returning very soon. You can't expect a small band of farmers and fishermen, armed with nothing but hatchets and hoes, to keep His Majesty's troops away forever, now can you? Why, I, for one, left a first officer on that ship who I know won't sleep a wink until he has personally come here in search of me."

"Then, let him come, *Capitaine*," she said, squaring her shoulders with a stubborn air. "I'm staying with you. You're in no condition to be left alone tonight. Besides, you would come to my defense with them again, wouldn't you?" she inquired gingerly. "Surely, you wouldn't let them harm me."

"Of course not," he pledged, giving her hand a gentle squeeze. "I would do everything in my power to save you, my dear. Just as you are doing for me now."

"And what about that horrible fat man on your ship? The one who was trying to give you orders on deck. He frightened me terribly," she confessed. "Will he be with them when they return?"

Richard suddenly donned an odd sort of knowing expression. "I believe that, if you take up your lantern and walk just a few paces up the footpath, you'll see for yourself that you have nothing whatever to fear from him now."

"You mean, he was with you today?"

Richard nodded.

"But he didn't look like a soldier to me."

"He became one just this morning," Richard explained with an ironic smirk. "He was one of Charles Lawrence's assistants, so I only thought it right that he join us in coming here. Of course, it took some persuasion on my part."

"What sort of persuasion?" Angeline asked, reciprocating his now-vengeful smile.

"A pistol to his back."

Angeline gave forth a dry laugh. "Ah, *oui*. That would persuade most anyone, I suppose."

"Go and check, my dear," he urged, wanting confirmation himself that the official was, indeed, dead.

"Oh, all right," Angeline agreed in a faltering voice, feeling afraid of the prospect of looking into the face of a dead man with the night's darkness all about them. Nevertheless, she managed to rise slowly and take hold of the lantern. Then she began moving cautiously up the path.

Richard heard her let out a frightened gasp an instant later. "What is it? Is he dead?"

"Oh, *oui, Capitaine,*" she answered, as if repulsed by what she was seeing. "Someone crushed his skull, it appears."

"And high time it was, too," Richard retorted. "I've been tempted to do so myself for weeks now. But at least this way the bastard died in the service of his country. The acting governor should be pleased to hear that."

Angeline, unaccustomed to making light of the dead and considering it a most unwise thing to do, especially after dark, simply bit her lower lip and hurried back to the captain's side.

"So, my people killed at least one of the *right* men today, apparently," she said, continuing to shudder with repulsion.

"Indeed they did, *ma cherie.* So, you see, the day wasn't a total loss. Are you cold?" he asked finally, seeing her shiver where she stood beside him.

"*Oui,*" Angeline replied, realizing that it was the night's chill, as well as fear, that was making her continue to tremble now. "It gets cool out here after dark, so close to the water."

"Come lie beside me, then," Richard invited, holding the right side of his blanket open to her. It was already clear to him that she was ill at ease with amorous interactions, so he did his best to look and sound as innocent as possible now. To his dismay, however, she appeared quite flustered by the invitation.

"Oh, no, *Capitaine*. That won't be necessary. I believe I remembered to bring a cape along for warmth." With that, Angeline walked over to her pack of supplies once more and began searching through its contents for the garment. "*Sacrébleu,*" she snarled after a moment. "I forgot it, and it's too long a walk back to get it now. I'm afraid I might wake papa trying to sneak in at this hour."

"Have you any more blankets?" Richard asked, hoping to allay her obvious frustration with the situation.

She shook her head. "No. Two was all I could fit in my pack, what with all of the other things I knew we would need."

"Then wear my coat. It's lying here somewhere, isn't it? I distinctly remember you taking it off of me to wrap my chest."

"That's right," she confirmed, searching about for it now by the light of her lantern. She did finally spot it lying just a foot or two from his right side, and she hurriedly slipped into it.

"Rather large for you, my dear," Richard noted, chuckling now at how the bulky garment dwarfed her delicate frame. "Not a regulation fit at all," he continued, shaking his head with a teasing sternness.

Angeline glared at him, and it was clear to Richard that she was not in the least bit amused by the comment. "I'm not worried about what your people would say at seeing me in it, but what mine would."

Richard, though soberer now, continued to fight a smile. "Yes. It would look rather traitorous, wouldn't it, you lying here in the darkness in a British naval captain's coat. Perhaps you had better give it back to me, and crawl in under this blanket, as I first proposed."

Angeline, feeling surrounded and overwhelmed by the scent of him, the manly citrus smell of barber's cologne that seemed to have permeated the collar of his coat, stepped forward and hurriedly surrendered the garment to him.

"Don't be silly girl," he chided as she continued to stand, shivering, in front of him in the seconds that followed. "Come lie beside me for the night, before you catch your death! We'll keep each other warm."

To Angeline's chagrin, she found that she couldn't move. She just continued to stand, staring nervously down at him.

"You've never been with a man have you, *ma cherie?*" he acknowledged with a strangely sympathetic expression.

She simply shook her head, seeing no point in trying to pretend she was more sophisticated than she was.

"But those two young men in the boat with you. You spent the night with them at Advocate Bay when my men saw you to shore.

There's no question of that."

"That was different," she answered defensively.

A knowing smile tugged at the corner of Richard's mouth, but his tone remained innocent. "Why?"

"Because. Because they were my friends."

"I'm your friend now, as well, aren't I? One hardly goes to all the trouble you have, Angeline, for an enemy. Oh, don't be ridiculous, my dear. What possible harm could I do you in such a state? As it is, I'm afraid you'll have to come over here and help me back down to a lying position, so I can get some sleep," he added with a sorry laugh.

Angeline, always willing to respond to the requests of a patient, wasted no time in going to his side now. Once she reached him, she knelt down, threw his right arm up over her shoulders, and carefully helped him back down to a supine state. To her relief, he made far fewer sounds of discomfort than he had when she'd propped him up, and she had to conclude that her bandaging had really done him some good.

"What? No kiss this time?" he asked, again catching her hand in his and smiling up at her waggishly, as she began to pull away.

She scowled at him. "Just how old are you, anyway, *Capitaine?*" she asked suspiciously.

"Thirty. Old enough to be your big brother,

my dear. And that is how I swear to you we shall treat this, just as if you were one of my little sisters climbing into bed with me, frightened of a thunderstorm. Oh, Angeline, can't you see how silly you're being about all of this? You must realize by now that I am as helpless as a babe in this condition."

Angeline, faced now with the choice of either running home—with all the possible encounters with ghosts and wolves along the way—or settling to the ground in a shivering heap for the night, finally decided that taking the captain up on his invitation was definitely the most preferable course. "All right," she agreed at last. "I'll share the blanket with you, then. But one false move, *Capitaine*," she continued in a hiss, "and, as God is my Witness, I'll take up the musket I brought along and finish you!"

Richard drew his head back with a stunned expression. "Good heavens, girl. Such a viper's warning! What makes you think I would *want* to have my way with you, after such a nasty show?"

Angeline swallowed dryly, feeling rather wounded by this retort. "Just see to it you stay on that stretcher," she cautioned again finally, rising once more and gathering up what she thought she would need for the night; her lantern, the primed musket, and her pack of supplies. With all three items in hand, she walked over to his right side. Then she set it all down within reach and crawled reluctantly in beside him under the blanket. She was careful to keep her back to him all the while. She would let the lantern burn as long as possible, she decided. Its flame would probably help ward off any wolves.

"Here," he said after a moment, and she could tell he was still fighting his show of amusement.

All she saw through her peripheral vision in that instant was him reaching over her for some reason. "*Capitaine,*" she snarled, turning back to him now with a threatening glare. To her further embarrassment, she realized that he was simply trying to hand her his coat.

"Here. To roll up and use as a pillow," he explained. "You'll sleep better with something under your head."

She accepted the garment from him with a blush. "Oh, *oui. Merci,*" she replied, folding it up and slipping it under her head as he'd suggested.

"I suppose you slept with some *French* girls while you were in France," she said with a critical air after a moment.

Richard, mystified as to why she would make such a comment, simply stared up at the stars with his mouth gaping. "Slept with or *bedded?* Which are you asking?" he finally inquired.

Angeline clucked at him with feigned disgust. "*Bedded,* then. What's the difference?"

229

"Oh, there's a great deal of difference, my dear. I assure you. With one, you are asleep, and with the other, you're very much awake."

An aroused tingle ran through Angeline, and she fell silent again.

"But you didn't answer my question," she said at last.

"All right, then. I bedded many of them when I was there. And they were all quite willing, I might add. Is that what you wanted to hear?"

"I simply wanted to hear the truth."

"And so you have, my dear. Would I dare lie to you, knowing how capable you are of reading my thoughts?" he asked with a gibing edge to his voice.

"Well, I've told you, *Capitaine,* I don't do it all the time. It simply happens to me once in a while. I just couldn't help being curious as to whether or not I will be the first girl you have slept with, *without* bedding."

Richard rolled his eyes wearily. It had been a very traumatic day for him, and the ale he had drunk was starting to make him feel drowsy. "Frankly, I fail to see why such a thing would matter to you."

"Well, it does," she countered, though she wasn't quite sure either why it did. For some reason, she just wanted his assurance now that she had a chance of standing out in his memory against all of the fancy women he had

230

obviously met during his many travels.

"All right then. Yes, my dear, short of the occasional frightened little sister, yes, you are the first."

"Ah, then, you're sure to remember me, aren't you?" she replied in a cynical tone.

"Quite," he confirmed. "In fact, I can say, without hesitation, that you are one of the most memorable women I've ever met, Angeline."

She felt her breath catch in her throat at hearing him call her a woman. She knew she was an adult now, at nineteen, but she simply had never thought of herself as a woman. "Is that good or bad?" she pursued.

"Good," he answered in a winning whisper. "Now, *bonne nuit,* my dear. Under the circumstances, I think it's best that we both try to get as much sleep as possible, before we're roused by one side or the other."

"That has a frightening sound to it, doesn't it?" she asked soberly after a moment. "One side or the other?"

"Yes. I'm afraid it does. Perhaps God will lend you more of that prophetic power, so you can predict what will become of us in all of this."

Angeline rolled over onto her back in those seconds and joined him in staring up at the stars. "I'm sorry, *mon ami,* but I'm not receiving anything so far. I'll be sure to let you know, though, if I do."

"Yes. Please do," Richard urged, feeling most anxious now to find himself healed and headed back to Boston. He had somehow resigned himself that morning to dying in Acadia, but now, with this young lady's kind intervention, his hopes of getting home alive had been revived. "I have a feeling we'll be needing all the divine guidance we can get," he concluded.

Chapter 13

As Angeline had hoped, she was roused by
nature's call well before sunup the following
morning, and she felt fairly sure that she would
have time enough to hide the captain in the
woods and get back to the cabin before her
father awoke.

The candle in her lantern had long since
burned out, so she fumbled about in the morning twilight in search of one of the extra tapers
she had brought along in her pack. Once she
found it and her flint and striking steel, she lit
it and carefully anchored it in her lantern's
holder.

She gingerly shined the lantern toward the
captain and saw that he was now sleeping quite
soundly. It had been a wakeful night for him,

unfortunately. Angeline had heard him issue many soft groans throughout the past several hours, apparently because his painful attempts to get comfortable on the stretcher, and due to his discomfort, she hadn't gotten much sleep either. Given their dangerous circumstances, however, she doubted whether getting any real rest had even been a possibility.

She quietly rose and crept off into the adjacent underbrush to relieve herself. When she returned to the captain she saw that he hadn't stirred at all. Continuing to be careful not to wake him, she began gathering up her belongings. There was no point in rousing him any sooner than was necessary, she reasoned. His body needed all the sleep it could get in order to mend itself.

Once everything was returned to her birchbark pack, she slipped her head and shoulders through its huge strap and centered it securely on her back. Taking up her lantern once more, she knelt down and whispered to her companion. *"Capitaine."*

He didn't respond.

"Richard?" she hailed again.

The captain's eyes drifted open, and he looked up at her blankly.

"It is nearly dawn, time for me to hide you and get back to papa, before he's up. Go on sleeping, if you can. I just didn't want to frighten you by moving you without warning."

Richard couldn't help flinching as her face

came into focus. Where was he? Why was the sorceress he had met on his ship leaning over him now? And why did his body ache as though he had been beaten nearly to death by someone? The answers to these questions quickly fell into place for him as he recalled all that had happened the day before.

"Are you all right?" Angeline inquired with a smile as he continued to stare expressionlessly up at her.

"Yes . . . I think . . . think so," he answered in broken French.

"*Bon.* Can you hold onto the stretcher as I drag you? Or should I go ahead and tie you to it?"

"I can hold on, I guess," he said tentatively. He really wasn't certain whether or not he actually had the strength for such a thing, but he didn't want to trouble the girl any more than he already had.

"*Bon.*" Angeline said again with a hurried nod. Then she tucked the blanket in snugly all about him and rose once more.

Richard looked on helplessly in the minutes that followed, as she placed the lantern's rope handle about her right wrist and bent down to steer the head of the stretcher away from the tree she had butted it against the night before. Then she turned around, got a backward grip on the front of the stretcher, and began dragging him deeply into the woods to the north.

He, of course, weighed a great deal more

than she did, and she had to pause frequently along the way in order to rest and catch her breath. Richard, in turn, did his best, in his still-sleepy state, to keep some conversation going between them. He had never before seen a female take on such an arduous task, and he figured that the least he could do was to try to make it all a little easier for her by distracting her from it with some engaging chat.

"Well, you see?" he began hearteningly. "You spent the entire night with me, and I never once attempted to violate you, now did I?"

He heard her give forth a dry, weary laugh. "No, Richard. You didn't."

"It wasn't because you're not desirable, mind," he quickly added. "I wouldn't want you to get that impression at all, my dear. It was simply that I have far too much respect for you to chance offending you in such a manner."

"It might also have had to do with the fact that you can scarcely roll over on your own at present, my friend, let alone ravish anyone," Angeline gibed, stopping now and setting the stretcher down with an exhausted sigh.

"Yes. I must confess, it might have had something to do with that as well," he said with a laugh. "You're really quite remarkable, you know, Angeline," he continued much more soberly after a moment. "I know of no woman in Boston who would go to such trouble for me. But then, I know of very few *men* who would either," he added with a wry smile.

Angeline sank down in a tired heap beside the stretcher and set the lantern to the right of her. "The people of Boston don't like you, *Capitaine?*" she inquired, fighting to catch her breath.

"Oh, it's not that exactly. Some of the women, in fact, seem to like me far more than they ought. It's just that they're not given to engaging in such heavy tasks, you see. They are rarely dressed suitably for them."

"They dress differently than we do, then?" Angeline asked, knowing from having seen the apparel of the British officials in Acadia that they probably did, but anxious to hear whatever details the captain could give.

"Indeed they do. I'm afraid your style of dress ended with my grandparents' time," he explained gingerly. "Our Puritan forefathers had the good sense, as you do, to wear clothing they could move about in. But now that everything's become so civilized in Boston, we dress as they do in the Old World. You should see our women in their ridiculous billowing gowns, trimmed all over with bows and lace. Why, a lady's so bound by them that she can barely climb out of a carriage without chancing to have a whale bone pop out of her corset and puncture a lung!"

"Oh, surely you jest," Angeline replied with a disbelieving laugh.

"I wish I did. But it's the God's truth. Quite pathetic, really," he added, shaking his head with disgust.

"But why would a woman wear such a dangerous garment?"

"Well, you see, it's a much more complicated society than this. People become slaves to their own fashions. They worry far more about what their neighbors think than you good people do."

"It sounds like rather an unhappy place, this Boston. Are you sure you want to return to it?"

Richard gave the question some thought. It simply wasn't something he had ever had occasion to ask himself. "Well, for all of its social restraints, Angeline, life is far easier in Boston than it is here. I mean, there is more time for leisure activities, for one thing."

"What sort of activities?"

"Fox hunts, horse racing, things of that sort."

Angeline gave forth a critical cluck. "That doesn't sound like much fun to me."

"I suppose it wouldn't," Richard agreed. "You would probably prefer more ladylike pastimes. We have those as well."

"And what would those be?"

"Oh, there are many of them. Chess, cards, lawn bowling, fan talk."

Angeline cocked her head at him. "What is this last one? 'Fan talk'?"

"That's when a young lady talks to a man with her fan . . . you know, at gatherings where she doesn't feel they should be seen speaking together."

Angeline leaned forward, clearly intrigued. "How does one talk with a fan?"

"I'll have to show you when we have more time for it, my dear. It's really quite amusing, actually."

"*Oui*. It sounds that way."

Richard couldn't help noticing that her inquisitive expression suddenly became one of disapproval.

"I think," she said after a moment, "that the only reason why your people have time for such silliness is because they go about enslaving people like us!"

Richard was silent for several seconds, finding himself sorrily unable to argue the point with her. "Well, my family owns no slaves," he said at last. "And even though we are shippers and merchants, we do not buy or sell them either."

"But most of the other colonists do, don't they?" she countered.

There was a kind of resigned sadness apparent in his voice now. "Yes. I'm afraid they do."

"So, why don't you?" she pursued in an even voice.

"Because my father and I don't believe in it. We couldn't be more adamantly against it."

"But that is not adamantly enough, it seems," she retorted, "if you would lead men here to the Petitcodiac in order to enslave *us*."

Richard could feel himself growing a bit

239

impatient with her reminders of how wrong he had been in agreeing to come to Acadia at Charles Lawrence's request. "Look, Angeline," he began again in a slightly irritable tone, "you must understand that, when I was drafted into His Majesty's service months ago, I had no idea that the acting governor had anything more in mind than simply taking occupancy of Fort Beauséjour. This is, after all, British land. It has been for half a century. So you must have expected that, sooner or later, our British governors would object to you French maintaining your own military fortresses. And by the time I realized that Lawrence had plans to drive your people out of here altogether, it was too late. Short of deserting, I had no choice but to stay on with my ship and see this whole horrible business through."

To Richard's surprise, her voice was not reproachful, but almost entreating as she spoke again. "But all of that is behind you now. Don't you see? By the time your men come back here, my people will probably have buried your dead, and your first officer and the rest will simply assume that you were buried with them."

Richard again fell silent. It simply had not occurred to him, until she pointed it out, that the tragedy of the previous day would afford him such a golden opportunity to "legitimately" relinquish his duties as captain. He would have to devote some serious thought to the matter.

Considering that he was destined to spend the next several days lying around in an Acadian forest, waiting for his body to mend, he knew he would probably have all the time he would need for such pondering.

"Thank you for calling that to my attention, my dear," he said finally. "I'm afraid my thinking has been much too cloudy since the battle to be of any use in arriving at such conclusions."

"So you would consider it?" Angeline asked hopefully. "You would consider simply staying here and not going back to your ship?"

Richard strove to keep his face, as well as his voice, completely unreadable now. "I might," he answered simply. "But if I know the British Navy, and after all the time I have spent in it through the years, believe me, I do," he added with a sorry laugh, "they will probably demand that your people dig up my dead crew members so they can positively identify them all."

"How gruesome," Angeline said with a gasp. "Would they really?"

"They very well might, and if they do, they had better find someone in a captain's uniform among the corpses, or they'll believe I simply fled from the battle."

Angeline's eyes grew wide, as a solution to this obstacle dawned on her. "So, you give me your shirt and vest and coat, *mon ami,* and I'll go back and re-dress one of your dead men in them."

Richard scowled at her, his mind still seeming too foggy to keep up with her now. "Then, what will *I* wear? I'll have no part in wearing a dead man's clothes," he said firmly.

"I'll bring you some of the clothing my papa borrowed from the villagers when we came here," she declared without hesitation.

Richard was seized with almost agonizing indecision.

"Well, it is up to you, *Capitaine,*" Angeline said finally. "If you wish to go on doing Charles Lawrence's evil bidding for him, you can simply rejoin your crew when they come again. Considering the shape you are in, they probably wouldn't expect you to raise a musket against us a second time."

"But they will eventually," Richard replied with a knowing expression. "My injuries will probably heal within only a week or two, and I *would* be expected to resume my part in this monstrous campaign at that point."

"Well, you must decide, Richard, which it will be. We haven't got much time before the sun comes up and my people come back to bury your men."

"Oh, very well," he agreed reluctantly after a moment, reaching down and beginning to un-button his vest. "But just you see to it, Missy, that you get back to me soon with those clothes of your father's. I won't have you stranding me out here, naked as a babe!"

Angeline smiled, relieved that he didn't plan

242

to return to Lawrence's ranks. "Have no fear, my friend. I'll be back to you with some clean clothes yet this morning, if at all possible. But we must hurry now! Time is running out for me. There's a small swell near here, behind which I can hide you for the time being."

Richard suddenly donned a worried expression. "But aren't we still too close to the scene of the battle?"

Angeline shook her head. "With having to go back and put your uniform on someone else, this is as far as I'll be able to take you for now. And believe me, you'll be safe enough behind the swell. Though I haven't been here long, I know this settlement very well, and I assure you that no one strays this far from the footpath. The only reason why *I* know of the swell is that I'm so often out gathering herbs in the forest and fields. Trust me," she concluded, rising and taking up her lantern. Then she proceeded to lift the top end of the stretcher once more and resume her strenuous walk toward the north.

Richard couldn't help continuing to feel concerned as she pulled him along. He had scarcely even entertained the thought of doing anything as treacherous as deserting. Yet in agreeing to let this woman take his clothes, that was clearly what he was doing. He only hoped that the pain of his injuries and any lingering effects of the strong ale she had given him the night before weren't clouding his judgment too drastically now.

"You will have to choose a man who was wounded beyond recognition. I do hope you realize that, my dear," he cautioned.

She laughed softly at his lack of confidence in her. "Have no fear, *Capitaine*. There were many of those, I'm certain. And I'll be sure to slash your uniform as needed, to make it all look believable. What is more," she continued, winded again with the heavy task of pulling him, "once you are in Acadian clothing, you can simply pretend to be a passerby, a refugee from some other settlement in this region, should any of the villagers happen upon you. Your French is certainly good enough to be convincing, provided you do what you can to conceal that English accent of yours."

"I'll have you know that my French professor claimed that mine was one of the best Parisian accents he had ever heard from a student, mademoiselle," Richard replied with a sort of teasing indignation.

"Well, I'll have you know that Acadians are not Parisians, *mon capitaine*," Angeline retorted in an equally teasing tone. "So, try, if you will, to speak as I do."

"I thought you said that none of your people would find me here," Richard challenged, as they finally arrived at the partially eroded swell she'd mentioned. He noticed that there was a large evergreen growing out of the top of the swell, as Angeline rounded it and centered the stretcher behind its sheer, root-riddled face.

"They *won't*," Angeline maintained breathlessly, setting the stretcher down and then her lantern and her backpack. "Just trust me, my friend. They *won't*. Now, there are some apples and bread and venison charqui in the pack, in case you get hungry before I return. And I will also leave you the musket and the lantern," she concluded, kneeling down beside him and helping him out of his garments.

"I hope you can leave a chamber pot, as well," he said blushfully.

"Oh, dear heavens," she replied with equal embarrassment. "I forgot all about your having to relieve yourself. I'm so sorry, dragging you all this way in such an uncomfortable state! I'll get it for you now," she declared, again beginning to rummage through her pack.

"Just leave it next to me, please," he requested with an uneasy wave as she turned back to him with the vessel seconds later.

"Are you sure you can manage it on your own?"

"Quite," Richard assured, still feeling a self-conscious flush warming his cheeks. "Just help me to a sitting position before you go, my dear, and leave everything within reach, and I should manage quite nicely until you can return."

Angeline, feeling more comfortable with him this morning than she had the night before, did not hesitate to take hold of his now-naked torso and prop him up, so he could lean back against the face of the swell. To her surprise in that instant, it was *he* who pressed a soft kiss to *her* temple, and she responded by pulling away from him with an astounded expression.

"Merely to even the score," he explained with a smirk. "And to thank you for being such an angel, *Angel*ine."

She knew he could see the continued surprise in her eyes. For some reason, in the course of her nineteen years, she had never heard anyone make this play on her name before.

"So, we're one for one now," he continued. "I spared you, and you saved me. And we're one for one when it comes to kisses, as well."

"Yes, well," she stammered, stepping away from him with an uneasy laugh. "I suppose it is best to keep things equitable between us."

"Indeed."

"I will leave some of my willow powder with you," she declared, her fingers trembling because of the flustered state his kiss had induced. She turned back to her pack and withdrew the tiny pouch of powder. "It's for pain," she explained, handing it to him. "Use it sparingly, because it can upset your stomach. But do take it, if you need it. It will help you rest. You simply mix a couple of pinches of it in some ale or water. Here," she continued, reaching into her pack once more and taking out the earthenware bowl he had used the night before. "I'll rinse this out, and you can mix it in here. And I'll leave you the flasks of water and ale, as well. Then you simply swallow it down, and, in less than half an hour, you should be feeling better."

Richard accepted the bowl from her and set it down beside him with a grateful smile. "Go now, Angeline," he said, looking earnestly into her eyes. "As it is, you will barely have time to take my clothes off to the battle site and get back to your father before the cocks crow."

"I know, I know," she said hurriedly, rising and rushing about to gather up some of the evergreen branches that were strewn upon the forest floor around them.

Richard scowled at her. "What are you doing?"

"Collecting some branches with which you can hide yourself should anyone happen by. I mean, as I said, I know of no one among these villagers who would have cause to wander this far off the footpath. But should it happen, you can simply cover yourself with these, and you're sure to go unnoticed."

"Another trick you learned from the Indians, right?" he asked with a knowing laugh.

Angeline nodded. "And a good one too, *Capitaine*. Rest assured," she added, as she set the branches down beside him.

"Very well. I'll cover myself, if need be. Now just *go*, Angeline," he admonished again, handing her his shirt and vest, "or there won't be enough branches to hide either of us in these

247

woods!"

She nodded mindfully. Then she bent down and dug his dark blue coat out of her pack. "I shall return, my friend, perhaps even before the midday meal," she pledged in a wavering voice, as she backed away from him once more.

He flashed her a confident smile. "Of course you shall. You're one of the most amazing women I have ever met, after all," he declared before she turned away, and the sincere gleam in his eyes as he said it told her that he really believed this to be true.

Knowing she couldn't afford to stay a moment longer, she turned and hurried off in the direction of the battle site, with his clothes bundled up in her arms. She wished there had been more time for her to savor his soft warm kiss, more time for her to make him comfortable in this new location. But there would be more time later, she tried to assure herself as she ran now. If she managed to re-dress a suitable corpse and get back to her father's cabin before daybreak there was no reason why she and the captain couldn't spend a good deal more time together.

She remembered that Luc and Marcel hadn't been close enough to the captain, on the night their boat had been intercepted, to recognize his face now. With that potential stumbling block eliminated, Angeline reasoned that she was very apt to be able to convince the Petitcodiac settlers that Richard was just who she had suggested he pretend to be earlier; a refugee who had escaped a British invasion of some other village in that region. Once he was clad in Acadian dress, such a claim would probably seem quite plausible to her fellow villagers. For the time being, however, Angeline thought it safest to simply have him remain her little secret.

Chapter 14

Angeline's good luck held out, and she managed to dress one of the more defaced of Richard's men in what remained of his captain's uniform and make it back to her father's cabin before he got up. Nevertheless, once Monsieur DuBay awoke and came down from the loft, he did look a bit suspicious at finding his daughter already dressed and preparing breakfast. Angeline wasn't usually an early riser, so of course he was curious as to what had roused her at such an hour today. She, in turn, simply told him that she had suffered a very sleepless night and had decided it was best to get up and make herself useful, rather than continuing to toss and turn. This wasn't really a lie, after all, she rationalized. It was true that her night had been quite sleepless, though for reasons her father would probably have never been able to guess.

"We are burying the dead British troops this morning," her father announced for the second time once he finished eating breakfast. "I just want you to bear that in mind, so you don't have to go on worrying about that captain you thought you knew among them. Whoever he was, he'll be dead as a shotten herring when we're through with him! You needn't give his fate another thought."

"*Oui*, Papa," Angeline replied, clearing the breakfast dishes from the table. "I think now that perhaps I was mistaken about him anyway. I mean the man's face was so badly wounded that I guess there was really no way of telling if he was the same captain," she conceded.

He crossed to her and patted her on the shoulder, before climbing back up to the loft to get dressed. "*Bon, chouchou*," he praised. "I knew you would take a wiser view of it all, once you had had some rest."

"I probably will not be here when you get back from the digging, Papa," she called up the loft's ladder a few minutes later.

"Why not? Where will you be?" her father inquired loudly from up above, and Angeline noted that his voice was filled with more concern now than it ordinarily would have been with such a question.

"I'll be out in the woods, replenishing my

medicine basket. I used up almost all of my herbs and such yesterday, I'm afraid. And with the threat of the British returning, it seems best that I try to replace what is gone as soon as possible."

"Very well," her father called down to her reluctantly. "But just you be back by supper-time, and if you hear any signals from our lookout men while you're out there, you return here at once!"

"*Oui,* Papa," she answered, giving forth a relieved sigh. For the next several hours, any-way, he was simply going to be too busy to keep track of her comings and goings, and she found tremendous comfort in this realization. To her dismay, however, things got a bit stickier as he was leaving to join the other grave-diggers several minutes later.

"Where is that third British musket I brought back here from the battle last night, Angeline? Have you seen it?" he queried.

Angeline turned about slowly from her dish-washing to face him, but all she could bring herself to do was offer him a slight shrug and turn back blushfully to her basin of hot water.

"But you must have seen it," he maintained. "It was propped up right here, beside the door, with these others."

"Are you sure you brought home three, Papa, and not just two?" she asked, her cheeks feel-ing almost ablaze now with the uneasy flush that had come over her. She hated what this

252

situation with the captain was making both of them do. Richard had, in effect, become a deserter, which had to be unimaginably degrading for an officer of his rank, and she, at the very least, had become a liar, finding herself having to deceive even her father now.

"Well, I *thought* there were three," Monsieur DuBay replied in a vague tone after a moment. "But perhaps I was wrong."

"Perhaps," Angeline said under her breath.

"Ah, well," he began again resignedly, crossing to give his daughter a parting kiss on the crown of her head before leaving. "I shall see you at supper, *chouchou,* if not before. *Adieu.*"

"Adieu," she replied in a tremulous voice. To her great relief, she heard the cabin door close behind him seconds later.

Her hands were tremulous as well, in the minutes that followed her father's exit, and she knew it wasn't simply worry over Richard's situation that was causing it. Besides being frightened of what might happen to Richard and her, should either side catch on to what they had done, she realized now that she was also afraid of Richard himself. She felt as if he were some huge wild animal she had captured, an uncontrollable male wolf, who was sure to overpower her if she continued trying to tend to him.

Though she had been fighting it, the vivid memories of his naked body the night before, the images of the forbidden area she had had to work so near, kept returning to her mind, and she felt torn with emotions. On the one hand, she liked Richard. She still believed, as she had on the night she had first met him, that he was a nice man at heart. Having led such a sheltered, backwater life thus far, she couldn't help finding his comments about life in Boston utterly fascinating. On the other hand, he was a *male,* she kept reminding herself, a gender she had always felt it wisest to keep at a respectable distance, and she was deeply afraid of what might happen between them if she spent too much time with him in the days to come.

She was fairly safe with him for now, she reasoned. He really was too incapacitated to try to force himself upon her, if he were even inclined to do such a thing. Yet he had, indirectly, warned her just the night before that he was indeed so inclined, and she knew she would be a fool not to take that warning seriously.

What scared her most, she realized at last, was not so much his feelings for her—whatever they were at this point—but *her* feelings for him. She was terrified of that irrational part of her that had compelled her to press a kiss to his temple the night before. She couldn't remember ever having acted so impetuously, and she just wasn't sure now whether or not she could trust herself to behave properly with him in the long run. She *liked* what she had seen under his uniform, the sinewy thighs, arms, and chest, and she hated herself now for liking them, for wanting to dally with the man until he was finally goaded into taking her into his arms, as he obviously had so many of those frilly European and colonial women.

She silently scolded herself as she continued to stand before the dishwashing basin, staring into space. She knew she didn't have such time to waste, so she began rushing around, gathering the additional food and supplies the captain would be needing. Then she climbed up to the loft and helped herself to some of her father's clothes. She tried to choose the garments she felt he was least likely to miss, those items she rarely saw him wear. Then she hurried back down the ladder and began bundling everything up in a blanket. She had chosen to leave her birch-bark backpack with the captain, and she realized that it was just as well that she was forced to use a blanket now. Considering how chilly the nights were near the waterway, Richard was sure to need it for extra warmth.

Finally, she tore a piece of paper from a crops ledger, which her father was keeping, and she tucked it in with the other things she was taking to Richard. She would fold it into a fan, she decided, so her newly found friend could show her how to "talk" with it. Considering how grave matters between the villagers and the British were apt to become in the next few days, she figured that she and Richard would probably need whatever diversions they could think of to keep their spirits up.

Then, on a last-minute whim, she went into her sleeping room and withdrew a tiny bottle of perfume from a wall shelf that her father had put up for her. It was a meadowy fragrance she had distilled from wildflowers, some ground cinnamon and cloves, and the scent-extending fixative, castor. She dabbed a bit of it on her neck and wrists and hurried back into the fire-room to finish her packing. She somehow felt that by moving quickly enough now, she wouldn't have to acknowledge the fact that she was going to lengths for the captain that she had never gone to for any other man. But he was accustomed to fancy women, she kept telling herself, women who, no doubt, had the leisure and the means to literally bathe themselves in the sweet oils of flowers that Angeline had probably never even heard of, and if a few drops of her own homespun perfume could help to make her more acceptable to the wealthy Bostonian now, she saw no real harm or vanity in applying it.

When she had everything adequately bundled up, she left the cabin via its back door. She wanted to do all she could to avoid her neighbors' notice, as she snuck off into the woods to the north and made her way westward back to her patient.

"It's just me . . . Angeline," she called out softly to Richard several minutes later. She was now just a few feet from the swell, behind which she had left him a couple of hours earlier.

He looked very relieved as she finally came around to the back side of the mound. "Oh, I was so glad to hear it was only you," he muttered, setting the musket down. "I didn't have enough time to cover myself with these branches, and I really wasn't up to shooting anyone this morning. Did you put my uniform on someone else?" he asked with a concerned expression as she set her bundle of supplies down beside the stretcher.

She nodded. "He was a lieutenant, I think, though I don't know much about your ranks. Anyway, his hair was about the same color as yours, and his face was pretty well destroyed," she added with a nauseated swallow.

Richard looked rather queasy, too, in those seconds. "You know . . . I wouldn't have thought that a woman with your calling would find herself sickened by such a thing," he commented after a moment.

"Oh, but I am, *mon ami,*" she confessed. "I'm a good healer, but, nevertheless, a squeamish one on the whole," she added with a sheepish laugh.

Richard laughed softly as well. "And what about your father? Did you get back to the cabin before he awoke?"

"*Oui.* I think so. At least he didn't seem to hear me come in, and it was several minutes after I arrived when he finally came down from his bed in the loft."

"So you don't think he suspects anything?"

"Not so far. But he did notice that one of the muskets he collected after the battle yesterday was missing."

"What did you tell him?"

"Nothing. I only shrugged and suggested that perhaps he had counted incorrectly and had collected only two."

"Good girl," Richard praised.

At this, Angeline let her gaze drop to the ground. "I don't think so. I hated having to lie to him. I never have before."

"We all hate what we must do sometimes, Angeline. I hate passing myself off to my crew as a dead man, as well. But it is what is in one's heart that matters most at times such as these."

She knelt down and unfastened the tied ends of the blanketed bundle she'd been carrying. Then she quickly withdrew the clothing she had brought along for him and handed it to him. "And what is in your heart now, Richard Brenton?" she asked, looking him squarely in the eye. "Are you really a man who objects to what Charles Lawrence is doing? Or did you go along with my suggestion that you pass yourself off as dead for convenience's sake alone?"

She could see the pain and weariness in his eyes as he began slipping into the shirt and sack jacket she had brought him.

"Read my mind, Angeline. What do you see?" he asked in an even voice.

She studied him for a moment. "I see someone who is just as unhappy about this situation as I am," she answered sadly.

Richard nodded. "Indeed . . . But it's not all for the worse, is it?" he continued with a soft smile. "It has brought you and me together, hasn't it? And I must tell you, *ma cherie,* you've been, by far, the nicest part of my stay in Acadia."

Angeline again let her gaze drop abruptly to the ground.

"Why do you do that whenever I pay you a compliment, my dear?"

"What?" she asked, feeling a terrible lump forming in her throat.

"Look away from me? Stare downward?"

"Because it embarrasses me, I suppose," she replied in a barely audible voice.

"Do compliments always have that effect upon you?"

She shook her head. "Not always."

"But when *I* give them they do?"

"*Oui.*"

"Why?"

She shrugged uneasily, knowing her face was much too flushed now to risk lifting it enough for him to see it again. She was kneeling right next to the stretcher, however, and he was able to lean forward a bit and reach out to raise her chin gently with his right hand.

"Good heavens, it *is* me, isn't it?" he acknowledged. "You're afraid of me for some reason, aren't you?"

"Teach . . . teach me to talk with a fan, *Capitaine*," she suddenly suggested with a wavering smile, still trying to avoid his gaze. "I would like it very much if you would."

Richard leaned back once more, but Angeline was sorry to see that he still wore a quizzical expression. "Very well," he agreed after a moment. "But what can we use as a fan?"

"I brought some paper along," Angeline declared brightly, reaching over to pull it out of her bundle. Then she folded some fanlike pleats into it.

"I thought you said you disapproved of such silliness," Richard said with a teasing smile as she handed the makeshift fan to him seconds later.

"It could be amusing though," she conceded.

Richard laughed. "All right, Miss DuBay, your lessons in being a lady of Boston shall hereby commence."

"But where did you learn this fan talk?"

"From my younger sisters."

"And where did they learn it?"

"In finishing schools in Europe, I guess. It is said to have originated with the señoritas in Spain."

Angeline could feel her eyes widening now with interest. "Oh, Spain is very far away, isn't it?"

"I should say it is, my dear. Not much closer than your native France."

"And they speak English in Spain?"

Richard furrowed his brow in confusion. "Well, of course not, Angeline. They speak *Spanish* in Spain. Surely someone must have taught you that by now." He couldn't help noticing that she looked a bit wounded, and he tried to sound less critical as he spoke again. "Why would you ask such a thing?"

"Because, if the Spanish were able to teach you English this fan talk, I figured they must speak English too."

Richard chuckled. "How charming you can be, my dear. But, no. Don't you see?" he continued, reaching out to her now and taking one of her hands in his. "Fan talk is the language of love, and every man and woman can understand that tongue, no matter what language he or she speaks."

"I don't think *I* understand it," Angeline admitted, her voice breaking off with her continued embarrassment.

He gave her hand an affectionate squeeze. "But of course you do, *ma cherie*. Surely you're old enough to have such feelings. Let us just say, for instance, that you saw a man you fancied at some festivity. What would you want to say to him?"

Angeline thought about the question for several seconds. *"Bonjour,"* she answered finally with a crooked smile and a shrug.

Richard gave forth an amazed laugh. "That's all? Just *bonjour?*"

Angeline continued to wear an awkward expression. "Well . . . yes. It's all I can think of right now."

"Very well. But I know of no fan signal for something as simple as *bonjour,* my dear. We would have to choose something else, I'm afraid."

"Such as?"

"Such as, 'I am desirous of your acquaintance,' Or 'Come and talk to me.' "

"*Oui.* 'I am desirous of your acquaintance,' " Angeline repeated enthusiastically. "That is what I would want to say."

Richard eased his hand out of hers and showed her how this would be done. "Then, you simply hold the fan in your left hand like this, *ma cherie,* and you make certain it is covering your face."

She cocked her head at him. "But, if it's covering my face, how will the man know whether or not he wished to make my acquaintance?"

Richard issued another amazed laugh. "He would have seen you before you raised the fan, of course. You only cover your face for a few seconds. That's all it will take for him to get the message, unless of course he's totally dull. In which case, I would strongly suggest that you try some other lad!"

Angeline laughed as well. "And then, what

else should I say?"

"Well, that's up to you, isn't it?" he asked rhetorically. "You ladies are the ones who must make most of the choices under such circumstances. Why, women's fans have become rather like men's swords in Boston, and there are dozens of possibilities." Richard suddenly began demonstrating some of them. "You can say, 'You have won my love,' by placing the fan near your heart, like this. Or, if you close the fan and rest it over your right eye, like this, it means, 'When may I be allowed to see you?' And, if he should leave that answer up to you, you could respond by opening the fan to reveal the number of sticks that equals the hour you have in mind for such a rendezvous. So, three sticks for three o'clock and so on, you see. You *do* have stick fans here in Acadia, don't you?" he asked suddenly. "You know, the ones from the Orient with blades of carved ivory strung together with silk ribbons and such?"

Angeline nodded.

"Ah, fine. Then, you know how they open and shut."

"*Oui.*"

"Do you want to know how to say '*oui*' with a fan?" Richard inquired with an affable smile.

Again Angeline nodded.

"You simply let the fan rest on your right cheek, like this. And, to say 'no,' you do this," he explained, letting the fan rest on his left cheek. "And, if you and the young man you're

263

signaling to have a secret you don't want divulged, you would cover your left ear with the open fan, like this, to say, 'Do not betray our secret.' "

"Show me more, *s'il vous plaît,*" Angeline urged with an eager expression. "I've a very good memory."

"I suppose you would," he replied, smiling at the simple delight that shone in her eyes, "what with having to recite those incantations of yours," he added pointedly. His tone, however, was far more tolerant now than it had been before on this subject.

He pressed the half-opened fan to his lips. "This is how you give a young man your permission to kiss you. And this," he continued, hiding his eyes behind the fully opened fan, "is how you say 'I love you.' "

"Have you ever had a woman say that to you?" she asked shyly.

"One or two maybe. I really can't recall, to tell you the truth."

Her look now was one of critical disbelief. "Well, I surely would recall such a thing, if it were said to me."

"Oh, but you don't understand, my dear. Sometimes a woman doesn't really mean that she loves a particular gentleman, when she gives him that signal. Sometimes she simply wants to be made love to by him."

"And what do you do, when that is what a woman wants?"

"I usually oblige her," he confessed with a smirk. "That is, if she's pretty and unmarried."

"But that's committing the sin of fornication," Angeline retorted sternly. "Don't you worry about what will become of your soul?"

Richard laughed under his breath. "To be frank, my dear, my soul is usually the *last* part of me that I'm worried about at such times."

"You're wicked, you Bostonians," Angeline declared with a cluck. "Devils all!"

Richard was taken aback for a moment at the irony of hearing this declaration from her lips. Just the day before, he had thought that the same was true of *her*. He had honestly believed her to be a sorceress. He was realizing now, however, just how wrongful such assumptions could be. "Not all of us are so promiscuous," he defended at last. "Please don't judge my people solely by what I do, Angeline." With that, he suddenly made a show of clasping both of his hands under the open fan.

"And what does that mean? Dare I ask?" she inquired with an expression that reflected her continued disapproval.

"You may dare," he assured with a soft smile. "It means 'Forgive me.' "

"You're asking me to forgive you?" she queried when he continued to hold the fan in this way for several seconds more.

"Yes. I guess I am," he answered, sobering a bit now.

"For what?"

"Well, for the sin of fornication, I suppose. Clearly it offends you."

"But such sins are not mine to forgive, Richard. They are God's, of course."

"You are quite a believer in God, aren't you?" he noted.

"*Mais oui.* I have seen His healing power many times."

Richard gave her a thoughtful nod.

"It was He who helped me to treat you last night, in fact."

"He did?"

"But of course He did. He stopped your bleeding. He kept you alive until I could come and stitch you up."

Richard found his thoughts wandering back to the angel about whom he had dreamt the evening before. "Yes, well," he stammered. "Perhaps you're right, my dear. Perhaps I'm sinning in even teaching such an emissary of the Lord so decadent a thing as fan talk."

Angeline studied him for several seconds, unsure now whether or not he was being sarcastic. To her surprise, he appeared to be quite sincere. "But I asked to be taught," she said after a moment. "Surely God won't blame you, if I, myself, requested it."

"Maybe not," Richard agreed, directing his gaze downward with a repentant air that was only partially feigned.

"What would you say to me, Richard, if we were at such a social gathering and men talked

266

with fans?"

He looked up at her once more, and she was again surprised to note how seriously he was taking the conversation. "I would want to say *'merci,'* but there is no signal for that, I'm afraid."

"So, pick one that's on the same order," she encouraged.

He gave the question several seconds' thought, and then he placed the fan behind his head.

Angeline, assuming he was simply teasing her now with some nonsensical signal he'd made up, couldn't help laughing and waving him off. "And what is *that* supposed to mean?"

To her amazement, he was completely straight-faced as he answered her. "It means 'Do not forget me.'"

"You're afraid that I'll forget you? You mean, that I'll just return to the village and strand you out here in that condition?"

"Oh, I suppose I'm afraid of that, as well. But, mainly, it just means what I said. *'Don't forget me,'* Angeline."

"You mean ever?" she pursued, her brow furrowed now with perplexity.

"Yes. I guess that's what I mean," he replied, again taking hold of one of her hands. "I've grown quite fond of you, you know, in this short time."

Angeline, unable to bear looking into his entrancing dark eyes in those seconds, again dropped her gaze.

"There. You see?" he asked admonishingly. "There you go again. Looking away from me. What are you so afraid of, *ma cherie?* Has some man wronged you in some way?"

"No, it's not that," Angeline stammered. "It's just that I've seen what a man can do to a woman, and I don't want it to happen to me."

"Want what to happen to you?"

"I don't want to die that way," she confessed, feeling near tears now for some reason. "Oh, *sacrébleu,*" she snarled. "I always get like this when I haven't had enough sleep."

He gave her hand a consoling squeeze. "Like what?"

She reached up to blot her eyes with the band cuff of her bishop-sleeved chemise. "Teary-eyed."

"Come sit up here by me," he coaxed, patting the ground beside him, "so I can put an arm around you."

She hesitantly obliged him, and he slipped his right arm around her shoulders and drew her up against him with such practiced agility that her breath caught in her throat. He was very experienced at consoling women; that much was clear. But maybe this experience had simply come from having younger sisters to counsel, Angeline rationalized.

"Now, tell me," he began again in a whisper near her ear, "what you meant a moment ago when you said you didn't want to die that way."

"The way . . . the way my mother died," Angeline choked, atingle now with the pleasant sensation of having him speak so closely to her ear. It was quite a painful contradiction for her in those seconds, having to talk about something as harrowing as her mother's death with a man who caused such indescribable arousal in her.

"And how did she die?"

"Trying to give birth to my little brother."

Richard drew a breath in through his teeth, making a clearly sympathetic sound. "But I thought you said some man killed her?"

"Well, he did, don't you see? It was my father who made her that way."

"What way?" Richard pursued gingerly, already pretty sure he knew what she meant.

"That way—with child."

"But not every woman dies in childbirth, Angeline. You must know that."

"I know. But many do," she maintained. "And, believe me, it's a horrible, torturous way to die! I saw it for myself. And I was helpless, powerless to stop the bleeding," she added with a sob. She was so upset now that she hardly knew what was happening, as he reached up, pressed her head down to his chest, and sat gently stroking her hair.

"Shhh. Shut your eyes," he murmured. "You're just tired, as I am, and you're frightened by what has happened. You'll feel better

269

if you sleep awhile."

"But it's true, isn't it?" she continued, striving to sound as rational as possible. "Men are the ones who make women that way."

"Well, of course. But it doesn't necessarily mean you'll die if it happens to you. Why, my mother had four of us, and my sister, Margaret, and I were twins. And, through all of that, she never even came *close* to dying."

"But my mother did die, and that means I'm likely to as well, because mothers and daughters are usually alike in that way."

"Well . . . Angeline," Richard began again awkwardly. "I must confess to not knowing much about midwifery. But I do know that, just because a woman lies with a man doesn't mean she will end up with child. I mean, I've been with many women and none of them, to the best of my knowledge, have found themselves in such a state because of me."

"Oh, you mean like last night?" she asked, again reaching up to wipe her eyes.

He issued a soft laugh "Well, no. Not like last night exactly, because all we did was sleep together."

"But some people say that is all it takes."

"Well, that may be what they say, *mon amie,* but that's not what they mean. As I told you last night, there is a great deal of difference between 'sleeping' with a man and being 'bedded' by one. You, my dear, only slept with me," he declared, continuing to stroke her hair.

"So you have nothing whatsoever to worry yourself about now."

"Yes. But someday there will have to be more, if I marry."

"Why don't you worry about that when the times comes? I see no point in being so concerned about it now, when we are faced with so many other problems."

"But I don't want to be afraid of men anymore, you see. Now that I'm getting to know you, I want to be able to trust you."

"Well, of course you can trust me. I've trusted you, haven't I? I've trusted you not to strand me here in this state."

"*Oui*. You must, I guess."

"Of course, I must. I have no other choice. And, I guess, in some ways you must trust me as well . . . dear heavens, Angeline," he began again in a fervent whisper, "you're the sweetest, dearest, loveliest creature the good Lord could have sent to nurse me back to strength, and I wouldn't harm you for the world." He noticed now that he didn't feel as he usually did when he praised a woman. This was different. Not only was it quite heartfelt, but it was very important to him that she realized it was heartfelt. He concluded the claim by bending down and pressing a lingering kiss just beneath her ear.

Angeline, in turn, felt her entire body freeze.

"Come back to Boston with me," he began again in an urgent whisper. "I can't bear the thought of you being killed by my people or sent into a life of indentured servitude."

Angeline knew she had to find the self-possession to look him in the eye in those seconds. Theirs was no longer the coy conversation of prospective lovers, but of adversaries in a deathly serious struggle. "No, Richard," she replied after a moment. "It is you who must come with my people, wherever we are going, now. Don't you see? When you chose to pass yourself off to Charles Lawrence and the others as dead, you gave the *coup de grâce* to going back to Boston. And your people might just hang you for it, if they ever get their hands on you again."

Richard, having drunk all of the ale that remained in her flask that morning in the hopes of quelling his continuing pain, knew that his thinking was probably still clouded now. However, he just couldn't bring himself to believe that he wouldn't ever be able to return home.

"Nonsense," he countered, beginning to feel angry about the situation. "It wasn't me who deserted back there, it was those of my men who turned tail and ran back to the longboats! *They* deserted me and all of the other men whom they left here for dead! Once I'm re-united with the British forces here, I'll simply tell them the truth; that my men deserted me and the others who fell and that my only chance for survival, once I found that I had been stranded, was to accept your kind aid and dress myself as an Acadian so I wouldn't be killed by the other settlers."

Angeline gave this explanation several seconds' thought. "All right," she said finally. "But who will look after you, once I've gone? My people are preparing, even now, to evacuate this settlement."

"And where will you go? This is British land for as far as the eye can see in almost every direction. And the colonies will offer no refuge, because they are British-owned as well."

Angeline grimaced with uncertainty. "I don't know. I only know we can't stay here and continue to risk being enslaved."

"But enslavement is not the worst of it, my dear," Richard warned. "Rumor among the crews in the fleet has it that nearly half of all the Acadians we've tried to expel have been *killed* for resisting our troops. I just don't think you understand the gravity of this situation, Angeline. Even if your people left here right now, Lawrence would have troops at your heels in no time. My men retreated yesterday afternoon and it could not have taken them more than five hours to get back to my ship. That means that even if they have informed Lawrence of their defeat and are stuck awaiting more orders from him, they will probably be back here within twenty-four hours or less, and they'll return with more men and more muskets than you can even imagine!"

"Well, what must be, must be," Angeline replied with a resolute air. "We must flee, Richard. You can't expect us to simply stay here and willingly be taken!"

Richard couldn't continue to hide the great concern he was feeling. "But you don't know what those troops will do, once they catch up with you. They have orders to separate family members, children from parents, husbands from wives, and ship you all off to very different destinations, where you will live out your days in slavery. The odds are that you and your father and friends won't end up together, even if you do flee together now. And, in case any of you manage to get away from our soldiers and are, somehow, left behind, they will see to it you have nothing to eat by burning this settlement to the ground and turning your livestock loose."

Angeline was silent for several seconds. He was right; she hadn't realized how catastrophic Charles Lawrence's campaign had become. She couldn't have known, nor could her fellow villagers, that there was a fifty-fifty chance that any loved ones they had left behind in other Acadian settlements were dead now at the hands of the British.

"But what threat did we pose?" she asked tearfully. "What could Lawrence have feared so much from us that he would go to such monstrous lengths to drive us out of here?"

Richard hugged her tightly to him and again

sat stroking her hair. "I don't know. I doubt whether even those above him know or *care*. But I do know that it is happening and I don't want you to become another of its victims. That is why you must agree to stay behind with me when your people flee, and you must say you'll come to Boston with me when I'm sent home."

"In what capacity?" she asked. Tears were streaming down her face now as she stared up at him. "As your 'indentured servant'?" she spat, wanting to lash out at him for the atrocities those in his ranks were committing.

Richard was stung by her comment, but seeing the great anguish in her eyes, he offered her a gentle smile. "No, Angeline, it is *I* who should be *your* servant, after all you've done for me."

"But I'm terrified of you," she confessed in a whisper. "You asked earlier if I'm afraid of you. Well, I'm not. I'm *terrified*."

"No you're not, *ma cherie*," he replied, lowering his head now so his lips hovered just over her ear. "Any woman who comes to a man smelling as heavenly as you do isn't really afraid. You must have realized, when you put it on, that that woodsy perfume of yours would speak more clearly to me than any fan ever could," he continued, pressing his lips to her neck, then opening her drawstring collar and baring her flesh as he kissed it. He knew, even as he did so, that he was running the risk of having her become more frightened and flee, but he realized that he had drunk too much ale today and been too long away from the young women of Boston to stop himself now. He wanted so desperately to lay claim to her, to make her stay with him—not only for his sake, but for hers.

"I know ways to make love to you that you've never even imagined," he declared, and to Angeline's amazement she felt the tickling wetness of his tongue entering her ear and stroking its sensitive interior with astounding adeptness. "Ways that will bring you to untold heights of pleasure, yet still leave you chaste and quite without child. I swear it," he vowed in a fevered whisper.

Angeline found that she could do nothing more in response but shudder and sigh beneath his skillful caresses.

"Because," he continued, still in a reverent murmur as he went on hugging her to him, "what you don't know, my angel, is that I've thought about you almost constantly since the night we first met. The exotic image of you never left my thoughts or my dreams. And now, having you so close to me, having the wildflower scent of you filling my senses," he added, letting his left hand slip into the gauzy bodice of her chemise and then into the warming cleavage of her breasts, "my body aches to make love to yours."

Angeline felt paralyzed in those seconds. She

knew she should pull herself away from him and hurry home to the imagined safety of her father's cabin, but something was keeping her in his embrace, a hidden desire that seemed too strong to fight.

"I was afraid of you, too, my love, when you came to me last night," Richard confessed, amidst the ardent stream of kisses he was pressing to the side of her face and neck. "I was afraid that you were a sorceress of some kind, some strange, Acadian witch who had cast a spell upon me. But now I realize that it is simply your beauty, your kind, healing ways that have bewitched me, and I want so desperately to bring that same heavenly magic to you, Angeline, to take care of you and renew your life, as you have mine. My . . . my body can't make love to yours in this state," he stammered.

With her eyes pressed shut now, Angeline could really hear the heartfelt emotion in his voice. And even though she felt one of his hands inching up her skirts, an action that would have brought the encounter to an abrupt halt were he any other man, it seemed she was powerless to do anything but continue to recline there in his arms.

"Let me take care of you now, Angeline. Let me minister to you with the same tenderness and kindness you've shown me. Say that you will," he urged, tightening his grasp upon her and feeling quite unwilling to let her go. He didn't honestly know why he was speaking so ardently, why he was running the risk of saying words to her that he would never have dreamt of saying to another. But he was sure that it was a great deal more than gratitude that he felt toward her now. "I know how to get that aching, that longing in you to stop for a while. Just as you quelled my suffering, my aching last night, I know how to quell yours, to fill you, to *satisfy* you, my angel, if you'll let me."

His right hand was well under her kirtle now, easing up the inside of her right thigh with a breathtaking lightness, and still Angeline felt no will to stop him. She realized, in fact, that she wouldn't have stopped him for the world. After all, her misgivings and embarrassment were safely buried now, buried, with her face, in the warm musculature of his chest.

"Ah, it's open," he murmured, letting his fingertips explore the forbidden place between her legs with whisper-soft agility. "Open as a chapel door on a fragrant summer Sunday. And I have come to pray, Angeline. To pray that you will Heaven find in my touch. Have no fear, as these harmless pilgrims enter such a hallowed place as this," he directed, closing his eyes as he let first his forefinger, then his longer, more penetrating middle one slip carefully, expertly into her and begin to stroke the creamy warmth within. "What higher praise can I offer you, my angel, than to lovingly caress every blessed inch of you and feel for myself that you are not a sorceress, but simply a woman, an innocent, saintly woman who will, so kindly, allow some part of me to find refuge within you."

Angeline couldn't help gasping a bit as his fingers moved more deeply into her.

"Shhh," he whispered in her ear. "That is all the discomfort you will feel for today, my love, all a sweet angel such as yourself should ever have to feel. Just lie back and let these gentle messengers of my passion fondle you, make love to you."

It was, accordingly, with pleasure, not pain, that Angeline gasped once more.

"Let them be the blades of the fan with which I speak to you, my beloved," he continued, his adroit manipulations quickening now. "And let them say so much more than the stilted language of the fan could ever say about how I pray that it is that swollen, aching part of me beneath you now that will first lay claim to you. How envious it is of these fortunate pilgrims who have been allowed inside you, inside this sacred part of you. And only the two of us shall ever know, Angeline," he pledged. "With my hand hidden under your skirts, no one would know, even if they came upon us now, what sweet communion we are both partaking of."

His fingers were moving so incessantly inside her by this point and with such masterful attentions to the most sensitive part of her, that

Angeline felt her thighs reflexively drawing together, closing around his large, strong hand and causing his fingers to be thrust even farther into her. And then, as he had promised, it did feel as though Heaven itself was descending upon her, and her heart began to beat thunderously as she let out an ecstatic cry. Fortunately, it was muffled by his linen shirt, as she continued to press her face to his chest and she felt her body opening and closing about his long stout fingers in an uncontrollable series of spasms. Then he bent down and helped to silence her subsequent sighs by again pressing his lips to hers in a heated kiss.

"Heaven help me, I think I'm falling in love with you, Angeline DuBay," he declared in those impassioned seconds, as though in spite of himself. "I've never spoken those words to anyone before, and now I realize I must have been saving them for *you*."

Chapter 15

A few hours later Angeline woke on Richard's lap. His act of love had left her feeling so drained, so satisfied that she'd slipped into a much-needed nap, and she had come to rest upon him with a peaceful, sated feeling she had never before known. As her eyes began to open, however, her thoughts brought her back to the intimate interaction she and Richard had shared, and she wished with all her heart that she could simply slip back into sleep again and not have to endure the embarrassment of talking to him.

He was still holding her. She could feel his chest rising and falling against her cheek as she lay with her face turned toward the line of buttons on his shirt. He was obviously awake, because she heard him softly humming some tune that was completely foreign to her.

How long had it been? she wondered. How much time had passed since she had fallen asleep in his arms? Not wanting to let him know she was awake, she simply peered farther downward at the ground and tried to determine what distance the sun had traveled since she'd dozed off. It was no use, she realized. She just couldn't see a wide enough range of ground without lifting her head, and that was sure to tell him that she'd awakened.

"Angeline?" she suddenly heard him say in a soft voice.

Her breath caught in her throat. She had no idea how he could have surmised that she was no longer asleep. She was certain that she hadn't stirred even an inch in the past several seconds, and she'd been very careful to keep her breathing even.

She lay tensely listening to his heartbeat as she felt him slide himself into a more upright position against the face of the swell.

"Are you awake, love?" he asked in a whisper.

Again she didn't answer. After several seconds of his quizzical silence, she found herself shaking her head where it still rested against him.

At this she heard him issue a soft laugh. "You must be, you know, if you can answer me. Come on, my dear. Time to get up. I'm afraid that your patient is frightfully hungry, and I can't reach anything with you resting on me."

This appeal made her feel a bit guilty, and she finally lifted her head from his warming torso with a resigned sigh.

"Now what was that about?" he inquired with a smile, as she rose and began smoothing down the skirt of her dress.

She didn't look at him. After what had happened between them, she found that she simply *couldn't*. She only shrugged in response to the question and bent down to begin rummaging through the supplies she had brought, in search of something for him to eat. She had thought that, once she had her first amorous encounter with a man, she would be more comfortable with the opposite sex, but she was finding, instead, that she'd never before felt so bashful with a male as she did now.

"I hope you slept well," he continued softly, and there was a knowing, almost sportive kind of smile in his voice as he said it that made her feel even more ill at ease. She knew that he was intimating that what he'd done to her was part of the reason she'd slept so deeply.

She only nodded in reply.

"How . . . how long did I sleep?" she asked timidly after a moment.

Again she heard a slight smile in his voice, and she was amazed to note how calm his tone continued to be, how unruffled given the magnitude of what had passed between them. What a seasoned lover he was, she thought again, and she felt an odd mix of admiration and contempt for him.

"I don't know," he answered evenly. "I fell asleep, too, I'm afraid. And I don't have my

283

pocket watch with me. But no longer than a couple of hours, I'm sure. I'm not quite famished enough for it to be noon just yet."

At this point, she walked back over to him with a half a loaf of bread and some venison charqui, and keeping her eyes directed down at the ground all the while, she handed these to him. He accepted them from her an instant later, and she was surprised to see him set them down on the edge of the blanket on his other side. Then, to her dismay, she felt him reach up once more and, with one firm tug, pull her back down to where he sat.

"Now, tell me, *ma cherie,* what the matter is with you," he said, again in a hushed voice.

Angeline froze in the kneeling position she had fallen into and shook her head. "Nothing . . . nothing is the matter," she replied, almost choking on her words.

"But of course there is." He reached out and lifted her chin so that she was forced to meet his eyes. "You haven't so much as looked at me since you awoke. Did I offend you in some way?"

Again she shook her head and directed her gaze downward as best she could with her chin still cradled in his hand.

"Well, what is it then? Please tell me."

She shrugged uneasily. "I'm just embarrassed, I guess," she confessed in a whisper. To her surprise, she felt very close to tears in that instant.

He must have heard this tearfulness in her

tone, because his voice softened considerably, as though he were addressing a little child. "Embarrassed by what?"

"I . . . I don't know," she stammered. "It's just that I'm not accustomed to . . . to what happened between us. Not like you are," she added with a critical edge to her voice. "It's difficult for me to just go on as before."

She heard him fighting a laugh as he replied. "Come here," he said, reaching out and pulling her to him. "Just come here," he continued, hugging her now and giving her back a series of comforting pats. "*Pauvre petite*. You're having to grow up very fast with us British and colonists tromping through here these days, aren't you? It's nothing to feel embarrassed about, Angeline. It's what lovers do, after all. It's all just part of . . . of *it*," he concluded awkwardly. "I'm sure you'll acquire a taste for such things as time goes on."

"That's just it," she replied, heaving a sob now. "I think I already have. And it frightens me terribly!"

Richard found that he couldn't fight back a laugh as he sat rocking her slightly in his arms. "Oh, Angeline. I do wish you would stop troubling yourself with all of this business about sinning and having babies. There's nothing shameful in allowing yourself to enjoy a man's touch. God knows that shame would be the *last* thing I'd feel at having you touch me in that way. And it was really quite innocent, I assure you. No harm will come to you because of it.

You have my word on that."

"Just hold me," she heard herself whisper, and she squeezed her eyes shut as he continued to embrace her as tightly as he could seem to in his wounded state. "What's to become of us?" she asked almost pleadingly, realizing that what she felt more than anything else now was apprehension, the nagging awareness that no matter how she clung to him, one side or the other in this struggle was bound to come along and tear them apart. "This is such a dreadful time for us to have been brought together."

He offered her a consoling "shush" and shook his head. "Maybe not. Maybe all we're suffering through now will somehow assure that we will stay together. You of all people must know, my angel, that the ways of the Lord are often mysterious. I'll tell you what," he began again more hearteningly after a moment. "Let us try to take our minds off of all that's happened. What do you say?"

"Well. All right. But how?" she asked, drawing away from him and reaching up to blot her tears with the cuff of her chemise. Then she turned around and settled into a sitting position at his side.

"I'll have a bit to eat, while you tell me all about life with your people. Then I'll tell you about life in Boston. That way, no matter which side claims us first, we'll both be prepared for what lies ahead."

Angeline gave the idea several seconds' thought. "*Oui*. I suppose that that is the practical thing to do now. But where should I begin? What could you possibly want to know about my people?"

Richard shrugged as he helped himself to the bread and charqui. "Everything. How you came to befriend the Indians here. How you survive the winters. Anything you think I must know if I'm to pass myself off to your people as being one of you."

Angeline again thought about this for a few seconds, then she launched into some detailed answers to these questions. Richard, in his turn, did the same regarding life in Boston, and before they knew it, the sun was beginning to set, and it was clearly time that Angeline get back to her father's cabin.

They parted rather tearfully, with Angeline promising to sneak back to him at her earliest opportunity. Then she hurried home, being careful all the while to escape the notice of any lookouts her people had posted in the treetops. She couldn't help thinking, as she rushed along, how suddenly this bond of hers had been formed with Richard, how few hours they'd really had together thus far. But then, she reminded herself, they had actually had many weeks in which to consider one another. Though she hadn't admitted it to Richard, or to herself for that matter, she really had thought of him several times since she'd met him a few months before, and she always found herself smiling a bit as she did so. She remembered him so fondly as the only kindhearted Englishman she'd had occasion to meet. He, too, had thought of her often in those many intervening weeks. He'd come right out and said so that very morning, as his hands had caressed the most intimate parts of her. She recalled it all now with a chaste flush, and she couldn't help feeling weak in the knees as she continued to make her way back to the settlement.

The truth was that they were anything but strangers now, anything but enemies. They had known one another in spirit from the moment they'd met months before, and even then, this mysterious bond of love had begun forming between them. She recalled her words to him on the night they met. "We've much in common, you and I." And she realized now how right she'd been about that. It wasn't just their circumstances they had in common. It was far more. They were, in fact, kindred spirits, and even when she wasn't at his side, part of her felt as if she were.

Daniel DuBay was very late in getting to bed that night. He and Angeline spent hours packing their belongings for the evacuation of the village and lending their hands in helping the more burdened of their neighbors to do likewise, and it was nearly three in the morning before Angeline had the chance to return to Richard's hiding place. She wasn't sure, as she hurried back to him, what decision she would make with the coming of dawn. Her father had informed her

288

that the villagers planned to leave the settlement at sunup, and either she and Richard would have to join them or be left behind. She hoped that Richard would finally agree to flee with her people; but even if he did, she knew that there would be a chance that her father or some of their neighbors would be suspicious of him and refuse to bring him along. On the other hand, given what she might suffer at the hands of Lawrence's troops, the risks seemed equally high if she decided to stay behind with Richard.

Again, she called out softly to him as she neared the swell, and she found him very much awake.

"I'm sorry it took so long for me to come back. I had to help papa and the others pack. They plan to leave at dawn."

"I was afraid of that," Richard said sadly, gesturing for her to come and lie beside him. "In fact, I haven't slept a wink since you left, for fear you wouldn't come back."

She sank down at his side and slipped in beneath the blanket with him. "Of course I came back. *Of course,*" she whispered, pressing a kiss to his cheek. "I wouldn't have slept a wink either, if I'd tried to force myself to stay at the cabin tonight," she confessed. "And no matter how in vain, Richard, I know I must try to persuade you to come with us at dawn. Please say that you will."

"But I'm in no shape to travel, Angeline. You know that. Who among your people would volunteer to tow me along on such a journey?"

"*I* would," she said in a wavering voice. "And perhaps Papa or Luc or Marcel would agree to help me."

"And if they don't?"

Angeline shook her head sadly after several seconds, and Richard found himself unable to do anything more than drink in her lovely, haunting features in the blue glow of the moon.

"We must try, though, *mon ami*," she continued after a moment. "We must, at least, try to persuade them to help. I simply won't leave you behind," she declared, looking him squarely in the eye.

He hugged her more tightly to him and bent over to give her a lingering kiss. "Just sleep now, love. Let's try to get at least a few hours' rest before morning. Maybe you're right. Maybe we'll have to leave with your people and run the risk of being hunted down by Lawrence's troops. Perhaps, with all that has happened to me these past couple of days, I'm just not thinking clearly enough to make the best decision now."

"Then you will come with us?" Angeline asked hopefully.

"Probably," he answered with an air of resignation. "But just sleep now," he urged again. "And we'll see what the morning brings."

Before shutting her eyes, Angeline reached down and laced her fingers into those of Richard's right hand, then closed her grasp around them. No matter what fate lay before them, she wouldn't allow herself to be separated from him.

It was the tenseness in Richard's body that woke Angeline the next morning. And then, at seeing that the sun had already risen, she sat up suddenly and emitted a horrified gasp. At this, Richard clapped a hand to her mouth and shushed her sternly, and she looked over to see that he was sitting bolt upright, clutching the musket as though ready to aim and fire. His hand fell away from her lips, but she could tell from his perturbed expression that he wanted her to remain silent. He was obviously straining to hear something in the distance.

"What is it?" she asked in a whisper.

He glared at her like a stern parent. "Shhh! Someone's coming. I can hear footsteps," he explained in a voice so low she could barely make out his words.

"But what time is it? My people should surely have left by now. Why didn't you wake me at dawn?"

"Angeline," he hissed, "I wasn't awake at dawn either, so how could I wake you? And it doesn't matter now," he continued in a heated whisper. "I can tell from the sounds I've been hearing from the direction of the settlement that your people are still here."

"What?"

"And mine are here, too," he added, pressing a silencing finger to her lips. "So please do stay quiet and let me keep an ear out, lest we find ourselves in the very middle of this mess!"

"I'll take the musket," Angeline suddenly volunteered in an urgent whisper. "Let me take it and go see who it is."

"No," he growled. "You stay right where you are! I won't have you shot over this!"

They both sat in total silence for the next several seconds, and even over her thunderous heartbeat, Angeline could finally hear the noise to which he was referring. It was the unmistakable sound of footsteps, not one set, but many, and she could even feel the forest floor beginning to vibrate as the parties in question continued to approach from the direction of the village. To her further dismay, she heard words from them, *English* words, and despite Richard's efforts to stop her, she instantly bent over to her birch-bark pack and withdrew her scissors from it. From that point on, she knew there was nothing more either of them could do but stay as quiet as possible and pray that whoever was coming would not bother looking on the other side of their concealing swell.

This prayer was not answered, however, and Angeline found herself frozen with fear as a British second lieutenant came around to the back side of the swell, and seeing Richard with his musket aimed, shot at him.

Angeline looked over at Richard in that instant and saw that the shot had hit him in his left shoulder. She flung down her scissors, took the musket from Richard's hands and cast it aside as well. Then she threw her body over his, in an effort to dissuade the lieutenant from shooting again. She could hear that her cries of protest were being drowned out by the shouts of some obviously higher-ranking officer as he rounded the swell. He was, apparently, telling the lieutenant to hold his fire. She could make out that much of it, and, what was more, she distinctly heard the officer say Richard's name, and she felt certain that these troops now realized what a grave mistake had just been made.

"I'm all right," Angeline heard Richard whisper to her in French, as he reached over her and cupped his wounded shoulder with his right hand. She looked into his eyes and saw a pained, but somewhat reassuring, gleam in them. Then they were looking at someone else, looking beyond her at the officer who apparently stood just behind her now.

"McGraw," Richard said evenly.

"*Captain?*" the officer replied with an incredulous rise to his voice. "We thought you were dead! The men who returned to the ship said you and the others were dead. We've just come from the pit grave the Acadians dug for all of you."

"Well, not for me, Commander, obviously, or I wouldn't be sitting here bleeding because of your second lieutenant's musket fire, now, would I?" he retorted testily.

By this time dozens of the other troops, which McGraw had apparently brought with him, had rounded the swell as well. They stood watching the scene dumbfoundedly as the second lieutenant who had shot Richard stood before their captain now with the crimson glow of chagrin on his face.

"Sweet Jesus, I'm sorry, Captain Brenton," the second lieutenant blurted in his own defense. "All I saw was your Acadian clothing and your musket pointed at me, and after what we were told went on here day before yesterday, I figured it was either you or me!"

"Understandable, lad," Richard said grudgingly after several seconds, his voice starting to waver with pain. "Just, please do try to refrain from shooting me again!"

"Begging your pardon, sir, but just what is going on here?" McGraw asked. "Why are you dressed that way? And why did the troops you brought here claim you were dead?"

"They fled, Mr. McGraw. Isn't that much clear to you by now? We were ambushed by the Acadians, and those who didn't fall obviously fled to the longboats and deserted us. I suppose, in such a case, I would have reported my senior officer dead, too!"

"Well, for what it's worth to you now, Captain, I'm happy to report that the settlers here haven't given us that sort of trouble today. We snuck in on the village from the east this time, and caught them quite by surprise, and the evacuation has gone fairly smoothly."

Richard could hear Angeline draw an anguished breath in through her teeth as she apparently deciphered the commander's words, and he hugged her more tightly to him. "It's finished, then?" he asked McGraw gingerly.

"Very nearly. Some of the men are bringing

out the last of them now. And we were just combing the area for any escapees when we came upon you two. Shall we escort the young lady to the longboats that are headed for the expulsion schooner, sir?" he inquired guardedly.

Richard felt Angeline clutch him even more tightly, as she obviously continued to make out McGraw's words. His tone was very firm as he answered. "No. She stays with me! If it weren't for her, Commander, I would be dead and buried with the others. She hid me here, treated my wounds, gave me food and drink, as well as these clothes, so that none of the other settlers would shoot me as the enemy. And she comes with me now, wherever I go. Is that understood?"

Again his first officer nodded, but his expression was much more tentative at this point. "Sir, it's not that I doubt your claim that she helped you. Obviously someone must have, or you wouldn't have survived. But if you don't mind my asking, Captain. Why would she do such a thing? I mean, you're clearly the enemy."

"Because the young lady and I were acquaintances, Commander. We met one night, when our ship intercepted her fishing boat."

McGraw furrowed his brow. "You mean, she's that sorceress you spoke to?"

Richard flashed him a wry smile. "No 'sorceress' would cross her people to save me from the grave. On the contrary, she has proven herself an angel of mercy. Wouldn't you agree?"

"Well, of course, Captain. There's no question

that her actions were extraordinary, given the circumstances. But she can't . . ." The commander's words broke off as he saw the threatening expression on Richard's face. It was obvious that he was about to remind Richard of the many reasons why the young lady could not stay with him once they returned to the ship, and it was also obvious that Richard didn't care to hear them.

McGraw's tone was suddenly obliging as he spoke again, and Richard could see that his eyes had focused upon the blood that he felt trickling over his fingers from his shoulder wound. The commander would try to keep the peace for the time being, Richard surmised. For fear of making his Captain's condition any worse than it already was, he would avoid mentioning the fact that Richard and the girl would, ultimately, have to part company.

"Let's get you to the longboats, Captain," he said softly. "One of the other ships in the bay was good enough to lend us their physician last night for the wounded who returned from here, and it really looks as though you could use his services now."

"Very well," Richard agreed, after letting several seconds of reluctant silence fall between them. "But the girl is not to be taken from my sight for any reason! Is that understood, Commander?"

McGraw simply nodded again and gestured for a couple of the second lieutenants who stood behind him to take up Richard's stretcher.

As they did so, Angeline had to be pried free of their captain, where she still lay over him. Her right hand was nearly as wet with blood as Richard's now, due to her efforts to help him stanch his bleeding.

"It's all right," Richard assured her again in French, as his men lowered him to a supine position once more for the walk to the long-boats. "They won't try to separate us. They'll take you with me, back to my ship."

"But Papa," she replied with a sob, and the grievous look on her face in those seconds pained Richard more than his latest wound. "He'll be worried sick about me. I don't know how your men could have made him leave here without me, Richard. I can only believe that they must have killed him!"

Richard reached out and took her left hand in his right as his men lifted the stretcher, and the firmness of his grasp upon her told Angeline that he was hell-bent on keeping her at his side.

"See to it her things are brought along," Richard called back to his first officer as they left the swell. "Have any of the Acadians been killed or wounded during the evacuation this morning, Lieutenant?" he continued to one of his stretcher-bearers.

"No, Captain. I don't think so, sir," the second lieutenant replied.

"There. You see?" Richard said hearteningly to Angeline in French as they progressed. "This man has just told me that he doesn't think that any of your people have been killed or even wounded, my dearest. So you needn't go on worrying about that. I'm sure your father is fine and headed for the schooner to the colonies now, as are the rest. As soon as we reach my ship, I'll see to it word of your whereabouts is sent to him."

To Richard's relief, Angeline did look as though she believed this claim, or at least that she desperately wished to believe it.

"Your shoulder," she said, shaking her head and looking over at his wound with deep concern. "They shouldn't be moving you." With that, she reached across him with her free hand, pulled his blanket up a bit and pressed its absorbent wool to his torn flesh with a practiced firmness, all the while managing to keep pace with his stretcher-bearers.

When they arrived at the landing, Angeline saw several of the British longboats, loaded with her fellow villagers, hundreds of yards ahead of her on the waterway, and she couldn't help tearing up a bit and reaching up to wipe her eyes with one of her cuffs. When she looked down once more, she saw that Richard was being carefully loaded onto one of the longboats. Another of his men reached out to help her into the same craft a moment later.

It dawned on her in those seconds how odd it was to have an enemy soldier smiling so amenably at her now, helping her to be seated beside Richard with such a gentlemanly air, when only a little while before, those same hands had been raised against her people, herding them at gunpoint into those horribly overcrowded vessels in the distance. Such were the privileges that came with befriending a British captain, she told herself. But rather than feeling honored by such deferential treatment, she felt shamed by it. She felt utterly traitorous to Acadia.

The only thing that kept her from dwelling on her sense of disgrace and her apprehension in those moments was her concern about Richard's condition, and once the commander arrived at the landing and handed her her birch-bark pack, she immediately began trying to stop his bleeding.

"You must try to relax now," she told him in a whisper. Her efforts to treat him were made more difficult in those seconds by the lurching and swaying of the boat as it was pushed away from the shore. "Shut your eyes, *mon ami,* and concentrate with me upon slowing the beating of your heart," she continued once the boat was finally under way and its movement became less erratic.

Richard gazed up at her with a slightly glazed look in his eyes, and she could tell that he was dangerously close to losing consciousness once more. " *'Mon amour,'* not *'mon ami,'* " he corrected with a faint, sweet smile that made her eyes well up with tears all over again. "We're lovers now, Angeline. What happened yesterday between us," he added in a voice so low she knew it was meant only for her to hear, "made us lovers. And I'm not about to let you go again. I may have, that first night on my ship.

299

But I'm taking you 'prisoner' this time," he vowed, in a tone that told her that the comment wasn't meant entirely in jest.

It was evening by the time they reached Richard's ship, and in spite of Angeline's efforts to treat him, Richard was clearly in a serious state. She had, somehow, succeeded in stopping his bleeding and suturing his wound on the rocking boat, but unfortunately, a fever had come over him during the last couple of hours of the journey. Angeline believed that it was probably a result of some sort of infection, which had started in the wound he had received the day before. But whatever its cause, she was having no luck now with getting it to break.

The man whom Richard had kept referring to as McGraw at the swell had chosen to ride back to the ship in the same longboat that Richard and Angeline occupied, and though he obviously couldn't speak French or understand what Angeline was saying to him, she could tell that he was very concerned about the captain's condition as well. She could even see in his eyes that he was sympathetic to *her* plight. To her surprise, however, he refused to let her board with the captain, once their longboat was brought up alongside the ship.

Angeline began to panic as Richard and his stretcher were hoisted to the main deck seconds later. As if it weren't bad enough that the only friend she had among them, the only one of them who spoke her language, was being taken from her now, it was also clear that Richard was

300

too delirious with fever to have any say at this point as to what was, ultimately, to become of her. She screamed his name several times as the stretcher was raised and taken out of her view, but she doubted whether it did much good.

Once McGraw climbed the rope ladder to the main deck, she was left alone with the pilot of the longboat, and his only response to her continued protests was a glower. Finally, he gestured for her to be seated once more, and the look on his face warned that he would take physical action against her if she didn't silence herself immediately. Her only possible weapon, the scissors she'd had in her birch-bark pack, had been tossed aside when Richard had been shot and, consequently, they'd been left behind at the swell. So, she knew that her sole option at this point was simply to cooperate with the captain's crew and pray that his commander would call down for her soon.

Richard had been jolted back to consciousness seconds earlier, as Angeline's outcries filled the evening air. She'd been calling his name for some reason, and he suddenly realized that he was up on the main deck of his ship and she was no longer with him.

"McGraw?" he heard himself mutter. "Where is she? Why isn't she here?" He had just entered another chills phase of his fever, and he could feel his teeth starting to chatter as one of his men lifted him from the stretcher and proceeded to carry him below deck.

"I'll explain, Captain," Richard heard his first

officer reply from somewhere overhead, and he wasn't sure, with his vision somewhat blurred and so limited in the below-deck darkness, whether or not the man following them down the ladder now was, indeed, McGraw. "She'll be just fine, I promise you, sir," the voice from above continued.

Richard could feel himself slipping back into semiconsciousness in those seconds, and it wasn't until he was laid upon the bed in his cabin and someone began removing his clothing that he again heard what he thought was McGraw's voice.

The light from the lantern, which hung from a beam overhead, stung Richard's eyes as he opened them once more. And, yes, it did appear to be McGraw who was standing at his bedside now, along with the gentleman who was disrobing him.

"This is Doctor Davis, Captain, from our neighbor ship, the *H.M.S. Valiant*. He's a fine physician, sir, and he shall have you well again in no time."

Richard groaned as the doctor began examining the wound in his shoulder. "Where . . . where is Angeline?" he stammered, and it seemed as though each word required herculean effort to voice.

"She can't stay on this ship, Capitan. I'm sorry, but you know the rules as well as I. She is to be sent to the colonies, and this ship is not bound for them."

"Then let me go with her," Richard said

weakly, feeling the way he had when he was sick as a child; out of control of his emotions and frightfully close to tears.

"You can't, sir. While I have no doubt that you, too, will be headed for the colonies in a few days, we must work through the usual channels, I'm afraid. Unfortunately, Captain, because of an inquiry made as to Mr. Chumley's whereabouts, you've already been reported as dead to Lawrence's staff, and, obviously, we must put that right and get you properly discharged. To say nothing of the fact that you're simply in no condition to make the voyage home yet. But don't worry, sir, please," he added, bending down even farther now in order to look Richard in the eye. "I'll see to it that the young lady is reunited with any family she may have and sent to your home in Boston. Just give me her name and those of her kin, if you can, and then your address, and I will give the information to the captain of the schooner straightaway."

"DuBay," Richard replied, his voice cracking. "I don't . . . don't remember her telling me her father's first name. But his last name is DuBay . . . as is hers. Angeline DuBay."

"Let me get a quill and paper, Captain, and write it all down," McGraw replied, and Richard was relieved to note how compliant his tone was as he said it.

"In the desk," Richard directed, making a feeble attempt to lift his arm and point at the pertinent drawer. He found the physician clucking at him in that instant for moving, as he tended to the powder burns about Richard's shoulder wound.

McGraw's face came into focus again for Richard seconds later, and Richard dictated the address of his family's estate to him. Though he was disappointed by it, he truly understood his first officer's unwillingness to let Angeline on the ship. Unless she was being taken prisoner and held in the brig, all sorts of violations of navy regulations would occur. Even if they tried to keep her a secret from the rest of the crew, word was bound to leak out, sooner or later, that the captain and his first officer had gone against Charles Lawrence's expulsion orders by harboring an Acadian maiden aboard their ship. The penalties for such an act were simply too severe to risk, and Richard had to admit to himself that he knew this as well as McGraw did.

"Just, please see to it that she and her father are reunited and kept together," Richard said, taking hold of the commander's hand as he spoke. He felt himself on the verge of blacking out again, as the physician began poking about his obviously infected groin wound. He knew, however, that he had to stay conscious long enough to finish his request. "And promise me, *swear* to me she will be delivered to my family's address, along with a letter of explanation to my father."

"And what should be said in the letter, Captain? That they are to be treated as your guests?"

"Precisely, Commander. Treated as my guests,

until my return."

"I swear to you, sir, that it shall be done," McGraw replied.

Richard, in turn, feeling unable to endure the pain of the physician's probing any longer, finally shut his eyes and let unconsciousness engulf him once more.

Chapter 16

Boston, Massachusetts

Margaret Brenton was beside herself with joy when her parents received the dispatch from Charles Lawrence's staff in Acadia stating that her twin brother, Richard, had been killed in battle. She knew, however, that she couldn't afford to let her elation show. Just as before, her efforts to win control of the family estate and business had to remain covert. Nevertheless, the dispatch did finally confirm for her that there was a force of justice in the universe, that the good Lord had, at last, seen fit to grant her what would have been her birthright had she been born a male. This tacit reassurance did much to lift her spirits as she witnessed her grief-stricken family mourn the loss of her brother. She seized this opportunity to take advantage of their defenselessness and move even further ahead with the takeover plans she had been entertaining for years.

The dispatch had gone on to say that His Majesty's Navy was unsure, at this point, whether or not Richard's body would be recovered and returned to the family for burial. Mr. and Mrs. Brenton had, in turn decided it was best to postpone funeral services for their son until that matter was settled.

On the evening of the third day after the dispatch arrived at the Brenton estate, Margaret and her husband, Nathaniel, went to her parents with an emotional appeal. They asked that Mr. and Mrs. Brenton consider accepting Nathaniel as their new son, if only in the adoptive sense. Nathaniel said that he was more than willing to have his surname changed to "Brenton," so that the family appellation could be passed along to his children and grandchildren. In this way, Margaret told her parents, she hoped that she and her husband could help to quell their profound grief at the loss of her twin. Mr. and Mrs. Brenton seemed too disconsolate to respond to this appeal, so Margaret resolved to try again later, when life at the estate started to get back to normal.

Five days after the first dispatch was sent from Lawrence's staff, a second one arrived at the Brenton estate. This one was, apparently, from the ship on which Richard had served, and it was signed by one Commander Kyle McGraw, Richard's first officer. It stated simply that Charles Lawrence's staff had been misinformed as to the events that took place at the Petitcodiac River settlement some days earlier and that Captain Richard Brenton, though seriously wounded in battle, was still very much alive. It went on to explain that Richard would be honorably discharged and sent home within a fortnight. In conclusion, it stated that Captain Brenton's homecoming would be preceded by the arrival of two Acadians by the last name of DuBay, whom Richard had requested be received by his family as his guests at the estate, until he could return and arrange other accommodations for them.

Richard's parents were, of course, so overjoyed at the news that their only son was still alive that they gave little thought to the portion of the message that spoke of the houseguests who were to precede his arrival. Consequently, it wasn't until Richard showed up at the estate two weeks later and found that Angeline and her father weren't there that this matter was finally addressed.

Richard's mind was racing as the family coachman drove him home from the pier on the morning of his return to Boston. His wounds still ached periodically, but he honestly believed that most of the pain of his ordeal in Acadia was behind him now.

The inquiry into Chumley's death at the Petitcodiac settlement had been mercifully brief, and in the end, Lawrence and his staff seemed satisfied with Richard's claim that Chumley had fought and died there voluntarily. And while it was true that Lawrence's staff had mistakenly sent a dispatch to the Brenton estate saying that Richard had died in that same battle, Richard's family had obviously received the subsequent dispatch from McGraw, explaining that he was still alive. The very fact that the family coachman had been there at the pier awaiting him minutes before was absolute proof of it. It seemed to Richard that his life was on the upswing once more, and he could return to the amenities of Boston knowing that they would be even sweeter now with his dear Angeline at his side to share them with him.

Seeing her again was, of course, what he looked forward to most. But he shouldn't expect her to come dashing down the walk of the estate to greet him, he warned himself. Given Angeline's obvious ancestry, an ancestry that Richard's mother was sure to find dubious, Mrs. Brenton would probably forbid the girl to make such a public show of her delight at seeing her son arrive. Rather, Angeline would probably be asked to await him well within the entrance hall. Having deduced this, he wasn't in the least surprised to see only his mother and two of his sisters come and peer out of the estate's front doorway when the coachman finally pulled up to the gate and came around to help him out of the carriage.

Richard could see the pity and surprise in the eyes of his family as he began making his way up the cobblestone path. They hadn't been expecting to see him walking with a cane, he concluded, smiling and waving at them now. His mother threw social restraint to the wind and rushed down the estate's front steps to greet him in her dressing gown and dust cap.

She was, clearly, near tears as she spoke. "Richard! My dearest darling. We would have come down to the pier to meet you ourselves, but we weren't told *which* morning you would be arriving. The poor coachman, bless his heart, has been waiting for you down there every morning for a week! What on earth did those savages do to you?" she continued, not allowing him the chance to get a word in edgewise, and nearly causing him to lose his footing as she threw her arms about him with a great gush of emotion.

Over his mother's shoulder, Richard saw his two younger sisters hurrying down the front steps to greet him as well. They, too, were wearing tearful expressions.

"They weren't savages, Mother," Richard replied in a low, almost scolding voice, leaning back a bit and kissing her on the cheek. "They were white men, Frenchmen, simply fighting, as we would in their places, to save their homes and their land. Charles Lawrence is the only savage in Acadia, I assure you!"

His mother drew back slightly at his suddenly caustic tone, as though a bit surprised to hear her once-easygoing son speak in such a way. She looked up into his face and offered him an amenable smile. "I meant only that, as your mother, I can't help being concerned about what they must have done to you to make you walk with a cane like this. It *is* only temporary, isn't it?" she asked gingerly, tears glistening in her blue eyes. He could tell she was afraid that it was some sort of amputation that had disabled him.

"Quite," he answered with a soft smile, patting her back consolingly, as his sisters finally reached him and stretched out their arms to embrace him as well. "My limp is simply due to a slash wound in a location that modesty prohibits me from specifying in the presence of my sweet, innocent siblings here," he explained, smirking, as he hugged each of the girls.

At this, his mother pulled him aside and addressed him in an even more worried whisper. "Good heavens, Son. You'll still . . . still *function,* won't you? I mean you haven't lost—"

"I know what you mean, Mother," he interrupted, meeting her eyes reassuringly. "And, no, I don't believe we need worry about that."

His sisters looked a bit blushful as he turned back to face them once more. But their subsequent barrage of questions about life in Acadia and the experience of captaining one of His Majesty's ships seemed to quickly supersede any embarrassment they might have been feeling.

"Did they have muskets, the Acadians?" Amelia asked with a kind of childishly morbid twinkle in her eyes. "Or is it true they fight with bows and arrows, like the Indians?"

"They had muskets once, Pudding," Richard answered, wrapping an arm about her shoulders and letting her help him up the walk. "Pudding" was a rather derogatory nickname that she had acquired in her pudgy childhood. Though she was as tall and willowy now as any of Boston's most coveted maidens, she still permitted Richard to call her this because she realized it was meant affectionately. "But Charles Lawrence had their weapons taken from them months ago, so they were forced to fight with farm tools and such," Richard concluded.

311

"Oh, how absolutely dreadful," his youngest sister, Louisa, chimed in, insisting upon doing her part to help her wounded brother up to the estate by taking hold of his other arm as they progressed. "You will tell us every little detail at dinner, won't you?" she asked entreatingly.

"That's not the sort of thing a young lady asks to have discussed at a meal or at any other time, Louisa Marie," Mrs. Brenton scolded, from where she walked just behind the threesome. "I'm sure your brother would rather be allowed to forget it all."

"It's quite all right, Mother," Richard replied. "Acadia is a most interesting place, and I'll be more than happy to tell the girls about it in the coming days." He suddenly stopped walking and turned back to her with an anxious expression. "Angeline is just inside, isn't she?"

Mrs. Brenton furrowed her brow as though she didn't have the slightest idea who he was referring to.

"Angeline DuBay," Richard clarified. "You know, one of the Acadians my first officer mentioned in his dispatch."

"Oh, yes . . . the 'houseguests,' " his mother replied after a moment.

"Yes, Mother," Richard confirmed, his anxiousness evident in his voice. "Where are they?"

She shrugged. "I haven't the slightest, my dear. You see, they never arrived."

Richard felt his heart beginning to sink as he stood staring at her blank expression. Over her shoulder, he could see his father up ahead of them, standing in the doorway of the estate with the stolid

312

air of a true patriarch. Even at seeing his allegedly dead son returning home alive at last, William Brenton clearly refused to let his feelings show. Nevertheless, Richard knew that he should continue walking and properly greet him, before getting any further into the conversation with his mother. He just couldn't seem to bring himself to do so, however. He cared too deeply about Angeline, about what had become of her, to take another step until he had obtained more information.

"You mean, there's been no trace of them? No bill for their passage? No message as to where they might be at present?"

His mother looked quite at a loss, though it was clear that she could see how concerned her son was over the matter.

"Who were these people, Richard?" she asked finally. "Were they friends of yours? I thought you went up there to oppose the Acadians."

"I did. But you see, one of them, a young woman with great healing powers, was good enough to save my life after I was wounded at the Petitcodiac settlement. And with Lawrence sending them all off to serve as slaves in the colonies, I felt it only right that I make some effort to save her and her father from such a fate."

"Well, of course, of course," his mother agreed, pulling a lacy handkerchief from the cuff of her elbow-length sleeve and blotting her forehead and neck with it, as though already uncomfortably warm in the sun of that September morning. "And we shall look into it, Son. I promise you," she said hurriedly. "Now just go and give your father a proper greeting, before he grows annoyed with us."

Richard, knowing that this was very sound advice, forced himself to continue walking, and with the somewhat overzealous help of his sisters, he managed to climb the three steps up to the estate door and give his father a hug. As he did so, he could see how tear-filled his father's eyes were, how stoically fixed his jaw in an obvious effort to choke back his emotion, and it was finally clear to Richard how devastating the mistaken report of his death must have been to the entire family.

"Still standing," his father croaked, coughing as they continued to embrace, apparently in order to mask his weepiness.

"Still standing, father," Richard replied with a bolstering steadiness to his voice, as his father's hugging arms tightened about his still-mending shoulder and ribs. "As only a true Brenton can."

His father must have heard him as he drew in a pained breath an instant later, because his hold upon him suddenly loosened. "What's hurting here?" he asked, easing away and looking his son in the eye with a worried expression.

Richard gave forth an uneasy laugh. "Only some broken ribs and a wounded shoulder."

"Dear God," Richard heard Amelia exclaim from where she still hovered to the left of him. "Dear God, Louisa, did you hear that? He was wounded in the shoulder and chest as well!"

Louisa responded with an anguished sigh.

"Well, good heavens, girls," William Brenton bellowed. "Don't just stand here, chittering like a pair of squirrels! Help your brother inside. Get him into

314

a chair and off his feet at once!"

The sisters did so, dutifully, and several seconds later, Richard found himself seated in the most plush of their parlor wing-chairs — the one usually reserved for his father. To his further surprise his shod and travel-soiled feet were planted comfortably out before him on the chair's matching footstool.

"Bring us some tea, Mrs. Brenton," Richard heard his father call back to his mother as he strode into the parlor a moment later and sat down across the hearth rug from his son. Richard noted that his air was markedly more accommodating now, almost compassionate, in fact. In those same seconds, the Brenton girls each dragged a chair up close to where Richard was seated, apparently so that they wouldn't miss a word of what he had to relate about his adventures in Acadia.

"Can we have a party for Richard, Father? A welcome home party?" Amelia asked eagerly. "I mean, with half of Boston believing he was dead for so many days, they'll come in hordes to see him now!"

Her father scowled at her, as though certain that she should understand why Richard might find such a remark rather offensive. "Your brother is not a carnival animal to be put on display for our neighbors," he snapped. "He's a hero, for heaven's sake, a man to whom we should pay homage for his willingness to fight to protect all of us!"

Amelia looked amply shamed. "I'm sorry," she choked. "I only meant that there are so many of our friends who want to see him again and to wish him a speedy recovery."

Richard nodded and smiled softly at her. "I know what you meant, Pudding. And yes, I think I would quite like a party. That is, when I'm up to dancing again."

This response, as Richard had hoped, seemed to do much to alleviate his sister's chagrin.

"Business went well in your absence," William Brenton declared, leaning back rather proudly in his chair.

"I'm sure it did, Father," Richard replied. "And you will have to tell me all the details in the days to come, so that I'm adequately versed to return to it. But to be frank," he continued, "there is a matter that concerns me far more at present."

"And what is that?" his father inquired, looking as though he hadn't the faintest idea what his son was leading up to.

"It's the DuBays, Father, the Acadians who were to be sent here before my return. Mother says you've seen no sign of them."

"None," William Brenton confirmed as his wife entered the parlor a moment later and placed the silver tea set upon the Queen Anne tea table that was situated between the men. Her daughters, in turn, rallied round to help her with the pouring and serving. "What were they to you, anyway, son?" his father asked.

"Friends," Richard answered simply. "The best of friends, it seems, because as it turned out, one of them, a female healer of sorts, actually saved my life after I was wounded at the Petitcodiac settlement."

"Saved your life? Why? I mean, didn't they consider you one of the enemy?"

"Indeed, Father, much more so than our friend Mr. Dolman would have had either of us know," he added pointedly. "But odd things happen in battle, I'm afraid. It seems I left with more than enemies in Acadia."

"And you sent this DuBay woman here to Boston for some reason?"

"Yes. And her father, as well, in order to save them from being enslaved in one of the other colonies, you see."

"Enslaved? Dolman said nothing of enslavement."

"There was much Dolman failed to mention. I've also learned that Charles Lawrence didn't even obtain the consent of the Secretary of State before expelling the Acadians! But that's yet another subject for us to discuss. For now, I simply *must* learn what has become of the DuBays!"

"I told Richard we would gladly help him with it, William," Mrs. Brenton explained as she handed her husband a cup of the steaming tea with a half a slice of marmalade-slathered toast resting next to it on its china saucer.

Richard eyed it hungrily. It really had been far too long since he'd known the luxuries of home. His serving was handed to him only a few seconds later, and he found his words impeded by his mouthful of the sweet toast as he began trying to speak again. "I'll check with the navy, of course. Perhaps there has been some confusion as to our address somewhere along the way. But in the meantime, if you would just be good enough to ask around with your friends in commercial shipping, it would be very

317

much appreciated."

"So it was a commercial ship that was to bring them here?" his father asked.

Richard nodded. "I believe so. And with the Du-Bays unable to speak anything but French, I can't help worrying that they've ended up in altogether the wrong place."

"Understandable," his father replied, noisily supping his tea. "But, Son, one can't help wondering what it is you plan to do with these DuBays if they should arrive. I mean, surely you don't intend to try to keep them as houseguests indefinitely."

"Well, no, Father," Richard stammered, having given that end of things very little thought thus far. "It's just that they're clever people, you see. Very inventive and skilled, on the whole. And what with the need for craftsmen here in the colonies, I felt certain that Monsieur DuBay could be quite gainfully employed in that area."

"Yes," his father agreed. "But what about the young woman?"

Richard was silent for several seconds, unsure of what to say. *What about the young woman,* he heard a voice within himself ask. *I want to marry her, Father,* he thought. *My mind has been filled with nothing but her for weeks, months. The image of her, the poignant memory of the perfume she wore has haunted me so relentlessly that my body aches more now with desire for her than it does from my wounds. And I don't care what you and Mother think of her. I don't care that she is a Catholic and a* métisse *at that. I want* her, *desperately, obsessively, and I won't rest until I find her!*

318

"I want to . . . to look after her, Father," Richard answered finally. "I mean, I owe her that much, after all she did for me up there. That is to say, had it not been for her, I simply would have perished, and you would be holding a funeral for me now, rather than our sitting here together, having a nice cup of tea."

Despite Richard's efforts to hide his feelings for Angeline, he could tell from his father's expression that they showed.

"Very well," William Brenton replied, letting out a long, thoughtful sigh, as he set his tea cup down on his saucer once more. "We must do our best to find her then, I suppose. The Brenton family has never defaulted on its debts, be they monetary or otherwise, and we will do our very best to pay this one, as well."

At this, Richard breathed a soft sigh of relief. He settled back in his chair to finish his tea, confident now that his father would help him in every possible way with the task of finding the DuBays. Just as he was finally starting to feel more at ease, however, his youngest sister, Louisa, blurted a question that upset him all over again.

"Did you kiss her?" she asked zealously.

Richard, in turn, found himself choking on his mouthful of tea. "Who?" he inquired with a scowl, knowing perfectly well to whom she referred.

"Why, this DuBay girl, of course. The one who nursed you back to life," Louisa clarified.

"*Louisa,*" Mrs. Brenton hissed. "What kind of question is that for a proper young lady to ask? I'm sure he did nothing of the sort, did you, Richard?

319

Knowing what an unwholesome lot they are up there, tainted with the blood of Indians and French pirates as they are. Of course he didn't kiss her!"

Richard felt no obligation to answer the question. It seemed his mother had done a sufficient job of it for him.

"Was she pretty?" Louisa pursued, seeming surprisingly unintimidated by her mother's tongue-lashing.

Richard looked at her from beneath hooded eyes, sure that his annoyance with her line of questioning was more than apparent. "Yes. Since you've asked, dear sister, I must be truthful and tell you that she was very pretty."

"And she was the one who tended to that wound that makes you walk with a cane?" Amelia chimed in with a coquettish giggle.

"*Amelia,*" their mother hissed again. "I shall have the pair of you thrashed before the morning is through!"

Richard could feel his cheeks flushing a bit. "That's none of your business, Amelia Brenton!"

"Well at least tell us how old she was. What harm can there be in our knowing that?" Louisa coaxed.

"Your age, maybe," Richard answered with a shrug, doing his damnedest to appear blasé about the matter.

Louisa gave forth what seemed almost an involuntary squeal. "Oooh, how provocative," she said, leaning over to elbow her sister. "Can you imagine, Amelia, nursing some enemy soldier and disrobing him and such? *Oooh,*" she squealed again, and it was such a comical sound she made that Richard

320

suddenly found himself chuckling at her adolescent musing.

William Brenton, on the other hand, seemed quite appalled by these remarks. "What kind of young women are you raising here, Mother?" he snarled at his wife. "Why, have they lost all sense of decency?"

"Off to your rooms now, girls," Mrs. Brenton commanded in turn, clapping her hands twice to shoo them.

This order, of course, caused a duet of groans, as her daughters rose and dragged themselves out of the room—doubtless to go on listening from some secret location in the adjacent entrance hall, Richard concluded.

"They're just glad to have their brother home again," Mrs. Brenton said to her husband in an assuasive voice once the girls were gone. "Apparently it has made them silly with glee."

The patriarch continued to scowl. "Well, we had best get them married off, Mother, before we find ourselves with *more* children to raise!"

Richard could tell from the slight blush that colored his mother's cheeks that his father's meaning was quite clear to her.

"It certainly is quieter, isn't it, with the two of them gone," Richard observed after a moment, wanting to put an end to the clumsy silence among them.

"Blessedly so," his father replied, rolling his eyes.

"And where, dare I ask, is my charming twin this morning?" Richard inquired. "I must say that she and Nathaniel are certainly—*tellingly*—absent from all of this."

"They are down at the shipping office," Mr. Brenton answered uneasily. "I mean, with you gone all this time, they've had to help a bit, here and there, with the business."

"Doubtless," Richard replied with a cynical cluck.

"Well, you must understand," his father continued apologetically, "with you having been first reported to us as dead, it was, in a measure, assumed that Margaret and Nathaniel would—"

"Please, Father. There's no need to go on," Richard interrupted, raising a halting palm to him. "I know precisely what was assumed, and I don't think I can bear to go on contemplating it. I'm sure dear Margaret sobbed her heart out when she heard I didn't die after all."

His mother gasped. "Oh, on the contrary, Richard! She and Nathaniel seemed just as happy to hear it as the rest of us."

Richard rolled his eyes toward the ceiling and sat shaking his head with a weary sigh. "Really, Mother, you needn't waste your breath."

"But it's true, isn't it, William? You should have seen, Richard, how devastated they were to hear of your death when that first dispatch came. Tell him, William," Mrs. Brenton urged again.

"Yes. Quite devastated," his father said in an odd monotone.

Richard was silent for several seconds, trying to figure out what his father's deadpan response meant. His mother had lied or, at the very least, exaggerated quite a bit in order to spare his feelings and keep the peace, he concluded finally. "Well, it's from one battle to the *next* then, I guess," he declared with a resigned expression as he rose to head up to his bedchamber. As always, he was angered by his parents' failure to put a stop to Margaret and her husband's conniving, and it was abundantly clear that nothing had changed on that score. If anything, matters were probably far worse than they'd been before he'd left for Acadia.

"Oh, leaving us so soon?" his mother asked in a slightly hurt tone.

"I'm afraid so. I want to make certain that the footman got all of my luggage at the pier, and I'm quite exhausted from the voyage. These wounds have really left me flagging, as I'm sure you can imagine."

His parents both rose as he made his way out of the room.

"See you at dinner, then," his mother called after him.

"Yes," Richard replied, exiting.

"He's not at all himself, is he?" Richard overheard his mother say to his father in a low voice an instant later. "Perhaps 'tis some sort of wound shock."

"No. 'Tis more than that," Mr. Brenton returned in an equally quiet tone. "I fear he has come back to us wounded in body *and* soul. Did you see how distracted he was all through tea? It is as if he left some part of himself up in that godforsaken place."

"It was his talk of that Acadian girl that shook me," his mother declared, lowering her voice even more. "You don't suppose he's gone and gotten himself entangled with her, do you?"

"Oh, why would he?" Mr. Brenton retorted in an

almost arrogant tone. "He knows he can take his pick of all the young ladies in Boston."

"Yes . . . well, whatever the cause, his manner troubles me," his mother maintained, sounding even more concerned, "it troubles me greatly."

Chapter 17

Over two weeks had passed since Richard had returned to Boston, and still he'd found no answers as to the DuBays' whereabouts. Charles Lawrence's staff had responded to his inquiry with a note stating that Mlle. DuBay had, indeed, been placed aboard a commercial schooner bound for Boston and that that schooner had begun its voyage to the colonies early on the morning following Richard's return to his ship, after he'd been found at the Petitcodiac settlement. Commander McGraw, too, answered Richard's inquiry by stating that one of the senior crewmen serving on the schooner upon which Angeline DuBay had been placed was definitely given the Brenton family address, along with the strictest orders that the young lady be delivered there promptly upon the vessel's arrival at Boston Harbor. In light of all of this, Richard could only conclude that the foul-up had probably occurred once the schooner reached Boston.

It seemed he had mulled over all of the possibilities hundreds of times. Nevertheless, he lay on his bed, holed up in his suite on yet another sunny September morning, pondering it all again like a lovelorn schoolboy. His only hope, it seemed, was that his father might have some luck in contacting the captain of the commercial schooner upon which Angeline was said to have been transported. So far, William Brenton hadn't been able to find the man, and he and Richard could only conclude that said captain had already returned to Acadia to convey another shipload of New Brunswickers or Nova Scotians to their lives of servitude in the colonies. But this schooner captain couldn't remain thusly occupied forever, Richard told himself hearteningly. Acadia, after all, was rumored to have been pretty well emptied of all of its inhabitants by the time Richard had left there a couple of weeks earlier.

There was, of course, the possibility that Angeline had been hurt or killed somewhere en route. Richard had to admit to himself that she had seemed to be the fiery sort. There was no denying that, and judging from the reports Richard had heard of all of the deaths that had occurred among the Acadian people at British hands during the expulsion, it would probably not have taken much provocation for some crewman on the schooner to have gotten angry and dispatched her. Then, too, in the overcrowded conditions, which surely must have existed on such expulsion vessels, one was very apt to contract some death-dealing disease and simply perish.

These possibilities, however, were just too grim for Richard to go on even contemplating, and he found himself blocking them out of his head now. Perhaps his combat experience in Acadia *had* left him as morose and soul-sick as his parents kept accusing him of being. But for whatever reason, Richard found that he simply couldn't bear to think of Angeline dying, because it would, in the end, prove a death sentence for him as well. During the last several days, he had reached the conclusion that a life without her wouldn't be worth living. He had, finally — after over a decade of philandering, sampling the nectar of scores of beautiful young ladies in both the Old World and the New — found a woman who really cared about him, who, in fact, risked her very life for him, and he knew that returning to his previous ways would never take the place of what he'd found, at last, with Angeline.

Just as it seemed he was about to sink back into a pit of despair, however, there was a loud knock on his chamber door. His subsequent inquiry as to who it was revealed that his dear old friend Peter Tyler had come to pay him a call. Richard had known Peter since they were both toddlers, and fortunately, the similar circumstances of their adulthoods had helped to keep them close through the years.

Peter, like Richard, now played a key role in running his family's business, a thriving bindery, and, also like Richard, Peter had chosen to remain unmarried thus far and to take part regularly in the "merry chase" of Boston's most eligible young women. Most importantly, however, Peter was one of the few men

Richard had come to trust and confide in through the years, and Richard realized that Peter's visit was probably the most heartening thing that had happened to him since he'd come home.

"Don't bother getting up, you lazy swillbelly," Peter snarled teasingly as he let himself into Richard's suite a moment later and closed the door behind him. "I wouldn't want to trouble that gamy leg of yours."

Richard couldn't help laughing as his friend strode across to the windowseat of his bedchamber and settled down upon it with a completely irreverent air.

"It might interest you to know, Mr. Tyler, that neither of my legs is gamy. And is that any way to address a war hero?" Richard countered with almost equal cheekiness.

"Hero? Rubbish," he replied, laughing under his breath. "That wasn't a war up there, that was Charles Lawrence laying the flattering unction to his soul! And with *our* tax money, no doubt."

"Well, I'm glad someone was forewarned of that fact. It did seem to have escaped my father's notice, to say nothing of some of our most prominent patrons."

"So that's why your mother tells me you've been sealed up in this room for a fortnight? Because you're cross with your father and your patrons?"

"They sent you up here to worm things out of me, didn't they?" Richard acknowledged in a bitter tone, rolling onto his right side so that he was no longer facing his friend.

"Dear God, you have become a whiny little milksop, haven't you," Peter noted with a bit of surprise in his voice. "I wouldn't have believed it if I hadn't come over here and had a look for myself. No, Richard, my dear old compeer, fellow rider in the autumn hunt for young lovelies. I'm a friend, remember? Not to be confused with your kin, who are simply stuck with you these days. I came here entirely of my own accord, and I warn you that is how I'll choose to leave."

Richard found himself chuckling a little as he rolled back over to again face the ever-candid Mr. Tyler. "So what is it you wish to discuss?"

"Pompous bugger!" Peter blared. "I need no topic with which to call upon you! My loyalty and unflagging friendship through the years more than qualify me to simply lounge here in your windowseat and gawk at you, if I wish, and I *do* wish."

"So my parents didn't send you up here?"

Peter stuck his right hand out before him and made a seesawing motion with it, while turning down the corners of his mouth. "They might have had a little something to do with it, I suppose. But in the main, I simply came to visit you. You were, after all, originally reported as dead, chap, so one does rather more relish the idea of tipping a couple off with you, than winding up a pallbearer at your funeral, you see. Strange as it may seem, it was your parents who discouraged me from paying you a call any sooner. You were made out to have been a bit of an invalid when you returned. You know how mothers and little sisters so love the drama of a wounded soldier coming home. Dear heavens, half of the petticoats in Boston are spending their days now just itching to catch even a glimpse of the valiant Captain Brenton! I would have gone off to expel Acadians myself had I known the residual benefits of it! So you see, the best I can hope for now is to simply be allowed to be at your side when you put in your first public appearance during this promising season."

Richard groaned. "Impossible. Sorry, mate. But I'm afraid I don't care if I ever attend another gala or dance. In fact, after what I weathered in Acadia, I don't think I could bear the frivolity of such gatherings anymore."

Peter sat up a bit, having spent the last several minutes lying back in the windowseat, with the masterful air of a lion. "Oh, so now we're getting to the heart of it, are we?"

"What's that supposed to mean?" Richard asked defensively.

"Well, only that something's clearly afoul with you, my good man. Your family says you haven't done or said a thing since you returned that's in any way characteristic of the nonchalant Romeo we all used to know and love."

"Not *all*," Richard corrected in a resentful tone. "Margaret has never loved me. Nor do I expect she ever will. In fact, I'm sure she's utterly grief-stricken that I have indeed returned home . . . outside the confines of a pine box!"

Peter raised a quizzical brow. "Her nastiness never bothered you before, Richard. Why should it suddenly bother you now?"

"Because I've already done all of the fighting I care to," he replied wearily, propping himself up against his carved cherry-wood headboard. "You don't know what it's like. You couldn't know," he continued, looking his friend squarely in the eye, "what it's like to have your life really threatened, to be slashed by swords and bludgeoned by musket butts, and lie about waiting to die, with your subordinates groaning and dying all around you. A man's simply never the same after such experiences."

Peter swallowed loudly and his gaze dropped to the windowseat cushion. "I suppose not," he returned in a wavering voice after a moment.

"And you see, the worst of it was that I didn't *want* to be fighting the Acadians. I didn't want to be entrusted with the monstrous task of herding them all like cattle off to lives of slavery! What man, in his right mind, would?"

Peter shrugged. "Ne'er a one, I suppose. You really have changed, you know," he continued, looking up at Richard again. "I didn't believe it when your mother told me you were a changed man, but I certainly do now."

"I'm sorry," Richard said testily, "if my new bearing doesn't suit you. You're free to leave at any time, you know."

"Yes. But I don't care to just yet," Peter countered, more of his previous jocularity returning to his voice. "I would rather stay long enough to wangle you into attending a gala dinner with me Saturday next."

"Whose gala dinner?" Richard asked pointedly, knowing what a good one Peter was for attempting to match him up with any young lady who had taken a fancy to him.

"Burnard Canfield's," he answered simply. "I'm sure you don't know him. He lives on the other end of town. He's remarkably wealthy, a leading patron of the bindery for years, and I could hardly say no to

331

his invitation. But I don't want to have to go alone, you see, mate. I'd far prefer the company of an old and trusted friend such as yourself. So please say you'll come. I'll only make you stay through dinner, and then, if you wish to leave, we'll do so forthwith. You have my word."

"Why don't you simply ask one of your many lady friends to join you? I'm sure there are several who would be more than happy to accompany you to a function of that sort."

"Because you require such a social diversion far more than any of them do at present. And I've come to see to it you get one," Peter answered in a blatantly parental tone.

Richard rolled his eyes wearily. "Oh, do go away and leave me alone now, Petey," he replied, hoping that the use of his friend's childhood diminutive might irritate him enough to cause him to do so. "You are thirty years old, for God's sake! Can't you tell by now when a fellow just wishes to be left alone?"

"Why?" he fired back. "So you can go on mourning the deaths of a pack of crewmen who had no more say in being drafted to duty in Acadia than you did? Honestly, Richard, you should have asked the navy to give you a sound flogging before you were discharged! Would have saved you having to do all this self-flagellation now, don't you think?"

"Oh, it wasn't just the casualties," Richard admitted after several seconds. "I realize there wasn't much I could have done to prevent them."

"Then, what is the matter? Is it that Acadian girl and her father who have you so upset?"

332

Richard scowled at him. "Who told you about them?"

Richard shrugged. "Word travels, chap. I'm only a few doors down, after all."

"Well, they . . . they should have been here weeks ago," Richard stammered.

"They might yet turn up," his friend reminded him with a heartening smile. "In any case, it's hardly the kind of thing one goes into weeks of seclusion over, now, is it?"

"It is when one . . ." Richard's words broke off as he suddenly realized he was about to confess his love for Angeline.

"When one *what?*" Peter pursued with an oddly knowing expression. "When one *loves* one of the parties in question?"

"God damn it! Who told you that?" Richard asked again, now in a furious growl.

"Your face told me that. Blame your face and your eyes and your lovesick demeanor, Richard old boy, for they are your greatest betrayers."

Richard fell silent, and he found he could no longer meet his old friend's gaze. "This goes no further," he warned finally, his voice ominously low.

"I'll not say a word about it," Peter assured. "She must be quite grand, though, to have snared a reveler such as yourself," he added, obviously very curious now as to the particulars.

"I've never seen anyone like her," Richard confessed sotto voce, worried, for some reason, that a passerby might chance to hear him through his closed bedchamber door.

Peter was leaning toward him in the windowseat as

though quite intrigued. "Do tell! I presume she's French, then?"

"French and Indian and glorious, Peter! Words are inadequate to describe her long black hair and huge twinkling dark eyes, her grace and wisdom. I'm quite shamelessly smitten with her, to tell you the truth," he concluded, feeling his face flushing a bit.

"Yes. You do appear to be."

"She saved me, you see," he continued now, taking unexpected pleasure in finally being able to tell someone about her. "When I was wounded by the Acadians, she came to me, I swear to you, like an angel of the Lord, and treated my wounds."

"But I thought you said she was an Acadian."

"Well, she was . . . is," Richard corrected himself. "But she had met me prior to the battle, and I had done her a good turn. So I guess she felt she owed me one."

Peter nodded thoughtfully. "Lucky thing."

"Lucky thing indeed," Richard agreed, feeling a soft smile forming on his face. "But now it seems I've lost her, and I don't think I can bear it."

"Now, now, mate. Let's not lose all perspective on this thing. If you had her sent to Boston, as I'm told you did, she must be here somewhere. I'm sure she'll come to hand. In the meantime, what better way to take your mind off of her than by feasting your eyes on some of the young lovelies at Canfield's dinner?"

" 'I'm sure she'll come to hand,' " Richard mocked. "You speak of her as if she were a lost kitten! Haven't you ever been in love?"

"Frankly, I'm appalled that you would ask such a thing! Of course I've never been in love. I'm far too wise a fellow for that! And I'm sure that, once you've had a bit more time to think about it, you'll come to your senses and realize you are, too. After all, it's probably not love you feel for that girl. Rather 'tis gratitude or some such thing," he concluded, waving him off. "I suppose it was only natural to grow attached to her given the circumstances," he conceded. "But you're back in Boston now, old boy, and it's time you began conducting yourself accordingly. Your father needs you at the shipping office. *I* need you in the social sphere. And we simply can't continue to let you lie about in this suite and rot!"

"Oh, very well," Richard began haltingly, realizing now that his friend didn't intend to go away and leave him in peace unless he accepted his invitation to Canfield's. "If I agree to go with you to this bloody gala, Peter, will you promise not to pester me again about attending any more of these ridiculous gatherings?"

Peter gave this question some thought. "Well, for the duration of this season, at least," he agreed at last. "I'll leave you alone till spring, if it will make you happy," he added grudgingly.

"Good enough. We're in agreement, then."

"But in that case, you must promise me you'll stay through to the dancing at Canfield's," his friend specified.

"Very well," Richard assented again, getting up from the bed and hobbling to the door in the hopes of finally inducing his old friend to leave.

Fortunately, Peter followed his lead and rose as well. "Yes. Thank you, old chap, but I'm quite capable of finding my way out on my own," he said with a biting smile as he crossed the room to take his leave. "Just you see to it that you don't start taking root in this bedchamber floor. All right?" he asked in parting, the accustomed sportiveness returning to his voice.

"All right," Richard called out to him as his friend made his way down the second-story hallway to the staircase. Just as Peter had said, there was no reason to show him all the way out. He had practically grown up in the Brenton estate and knew it nearly as well as his own.

Richard smiled slightly now, as he shut his door once more and returned to his bed. As galling as his conversation with his old friend had been, he could already feel that it had jarred him a little, cheered and jolted him out of some of his moroseness, and he realized that this had, in fact, been sorely needed.

This newly found spurt of optimism, ended however, when the steward of the estate came to Richard a few minutes later with another response to his continued inquiries as to whether or not anyone on the servant staff had seen Angeline and her father arrive on the grounds at any time.

The steward explained that one of the stablemen, a man employed only part time at the Brenton estate, had, indeed, seen a young woman who met Mlle. DuBay's description, near the carriage entrance some sixteen days earlier. It seemed that said stableman hadn't had occasion to work for the Brentons since that time and had, only today, heard of Richard's inquiries.

In any case, the stableman reported that a young woman with long black braids, wearing what he described as "rather old-fashioned clothing," had, in fact, been seen speaking to Madame Margaret near the carriage entrance on that day, and that, save for that one brief sighting of her, no one working in that area of the grounds had seen the girl since.

Richard, his nostrils flaring, barely took the time to thank the steward before gathering up his walking cane and storming off to find his twin. Fortunately for his still-painful slash wound, he found her within just a few minutes, and despite vehement protests from Margaret's handmaid, he barged in upon his sister and found her at her French writing table, working on what appeared to be some ledgers.

She turned to him instantly with a dour expression. "And what, pray tell, do you want?" she asked pointedly. "Isn't my slaving away night and day at all this paper work, while you, the blessed heir, loll about, 'on the mend,' enough to ask?"

"I want to know what you did with her," Richard growled.

Margaret appeared genuinely puzzled. "With whom?"

"Angeline DuBay. The Acadian girl who was sent down here a few days before my return."

Margaret turned her back on him once more and continued making her entries. "I have no idea what's become of her," she replied coldly. "And I really don't care to. So do go away now and let me finish this."

He strode over to her and snatched the quill from her hand in mid-stroke, leaving a blotchy streak of ink across the page's columns. She issued a horrified gasp in response.

"I'm not one of your little brats to be sent off to the

green when you're too busy working to talk," Richard thundered. "I said I want to know what you did with her, and I want to know now!" He used his free hand to jerk her chair about so that she was forced to face him once more. As he did so, he noticed that she had become almost ghostly white with either shock or fear, and having never raged at her this way before, he couldn't be sure which it was.

"Did with whom?" she asked again, her voice rising anxiously.

"Angeline! And don't try to deny it! One of our stablemen saw you speaking to her a few days before I came home."

Margaret's eyes suddenly narrowed into an analytical squint. "Have you quite lost your mind, Richard? I swear to you I'm going to go to Father at once and tell him you ought to be shut away somewhere! Whatever has come over you?"

To Richard's own amazement, he responded to this by taking hold of her fichu collar and pulling her face up toward his. He had never handled a woman in this way, but then, he reminded himself, Margaret was different. She didn't *want* to be a woman, and somehow, at the height of his fury now, that seemed to justify his actions. He spoke to her again from behind clenched teeth. "Don't deny it! You were seen speaking to her. Long black braids, the stableman said, and old-fashioned clothing."

He grew even angrier as she met this claim with nothing more than a blank stare.

"Oh . . . oh, yes," she stammered finally as his grip upon her collar tightened. "I think I do remember speaking to a girl who met that description one morning, before you came back."

"So, where is she now?" he demanded.

"Back at Pudley's dairy farm, I imagine. At least, that's where she said she came from."

Richard furrowed his brow. "You mean, she spoke to you in English?"

"Well, of course. How else was she going to sell me milk and butter?"

"Are you saying she was a milkmaid?"

Margaret shrugged, as well as she could in her somewhat suspended state, and she continued to offer him an allaying expression. "That's what she claimed to be, in any case."

Richard searched her eyes for several seconds hoping to catch the telltale glimmer of a lie in them. He saw none, however, so he finally released her, causing her to fall back down into her chair with a resounding plop.

The suspicious tone still hadn't left his voice, however, as he spoke again. "And what were *you* doing answering an inquiry about this estate's dairy needs? I would think Mother or the chief cook would have been better equipped to talk to the girl."

Margaret hesitated before answering him, but her voice didn't waver for an instant as she finally did so. "Mother was ill that day, as I recall, and I was told that the cook was off at the marketplace. So that left me, you see."

"Who was this milkmaid?" Richard persisted, still watching her intently. "I shall ask for her at Pudley's! What was her name?"

Margaret was starting to look indignant again. "I don't remember her name," she snapped. "I don't go

339

about asking milkmaids their names! And it was weeks ago, Richard. Really," she exclaimed, reaching up and straightening her collar. "I'm afraid I am going to have to tell Father that you have lost your mind!"

"You do that," Richard spat as he stomped out of her suite seconds later, furious that yet another avenue of investigation had seemingly led him nowhere. "You go ahead and do that, straightaway!"

Margaret could feel her lips curving up into a subtle smile when she was sure her brother had gone. She had handled his inquisition brilliantly, by her own assessment, and naturally she was rather proud of herself. The DuBay girl was safely off on the other side of town, living the life of servitude which she probably deserved, and Margaret had thought that she'd arranged it all without leaving a trace. She hadn't realized that some stableman had chanced to see her talking to the Acadian. She'd been so engrossed that morning in trying to determine, from the girl's facial expressions, what the nature of her brother's relationship with her had been, that she'd probably been oblivious to any passersby. But fortunately she had come up with an apt alibi to cover that, as well.

As incredible as it seemed, Richard *loved* this "Angeline". That much was clear. If it hadn't been apparent in the reverent, receptive twinkle in the eyes of the Acadian, it certainly was now, in Richard's passionate anger and lovesick conduct. And what better way for Margaret to keep her primary competitor for the estate sidetracked, but to force him to go off on a wild-goose chase for the girl? It seemed to

Margaret small retaliation, in fact, for what had happened to her and Nathaniel. It felt as though they had had the estate and the business in the palms of their hands the night they had received that first dispatch saying Richard was dead. For days they'd been allowed to muse, to dream, to plan for their future as the mistress and master of it all, and then, that second bloody dispatch had arrived, explaining the erroneous assumption made by Charles Lawrence's staff, and Margaret's parents had actually expected her and her husband to look happy about it!

Yes. In light of what she and Nathaniel had suffered in the last few weeks, selling Richard's latest bedmate into servitude seemed small retaliation indeed. And what had made it all the sweeter for Margaret these past several days was watching her brother's mounting anguish over it, seeing him wilt like a plant in parched soil and seal himself up in his suite, when it was so clear that their father needed his help with the business. Surely, if enough of that went on, their father would, at last, come to realize that Richard was no longer capable of serving as his partner and that such position should finally be given to Margaret and Nathaniel, since they had proven themselves so helpful in Richard's absence.

To Margaret's further satisfaction, she again acknowledged that the situation wasn't apt to get better for her twin in the near future. She had it on the best authority that Richard had never met the man to whom she'd sold the Acadian, a Mr. Burnard Canfield. And since Canfield lived a good ways off and claimed to have few dealings with the local shippers and merchants, Richard wasn't likely to run into him—let alone to have occasion to make inquiries about the members of his servant staff.

Chapter 18

Life had become a kind of nightmare for Angeline since she had arrived in Boston. It was a nightmare from which she kept praying she'd soon
awaken, but she never seemed to do so. When she'd
first arrived and was taken to what she believed was
Richard's address, her heart was still filled with
hope that she would be reunited with him and that,
even apart from her father and the life she'd always
known back in Acadia, she could survive with Richard at her side. She had prayed that, in time, she
could resign herself to the fact that Luc, Marcel,
and her father had not been on the commercial
schooner that she had been forced onto. What had
made things worse, as she'd left her homeland, was
that none of her neighbors from the Petitcodiac
settlement seemed to have had a clue as to what had
become of the three men, and Angeline had to con-

clude that they had either been slain by Richard's subordinates or that they had somehow managed to escape the troops. Perhaps in time, she told herself, Richard would be good enough to look into the matter and ask Lawrence's staff to try to locate her father and have him sent to Boston to be reunited with her.

Such hopes, however, had grown dimmer and dimmer for her since she had been sold to Canfield by the severe-looking woman she had met at the first address to which she'd been taken. Though Angeline had never seen coins before, having come from a society that did not use money for exchanges, such currency had been described to her by those of her people whose ancestors had recounted the details of life in the coastal towns of France from whence they had come. If such descriptions were indeed accurate, coins had been given to the woman who had brought her to Master Canfield's estate to work as a kitchen servant. Angeline had, in short, been *sold* to Canfield. That much was made clear to her from the moment of her arrival at the estate, in spite of her limited ability to understand English. The fact that she had been *paid for* was apparent every day, as well as during the nights, which she spent in the crowded servants' quarters in the backstairs portion of the mansion. Though no one had laid a hand upon her since she had come, she had seen a few of her fellow servants caned, apparently for disobedience, and she knew that she had no other choice but to do as she was told — insofar as she was able to understand such English instructions.

The man who was apparently head of Canfield's

servant staff had given Angeline an ill-fitting uniform to wear upon her arrival, and she had worn it every day since. She only removed it in late evening in order to exchange it for the threadbare nightshift they had also furnished for her. The uniform included a head-hugging kind of bonnet. It was similar to the one she had worn in Acadia, except that it was edged with a wide strip of ruffles and there was a dark ribbon encircling the area between its ruche and its gathers. In spite of these differences, however, Angeline did take some comfort in wearing it, because it reminded her of home. Her uniform, on the other hand, was quite a different matter. It was unlike any frock she had seen before, with its shawl collar and tightly fitted waist, and she scarcely recognized herself in it whenever she chanced to pass a looking glass in the mansion.

The only blessing in her plight, she'd come to realize, was that she'd been assigned to do kitchen work, rather than some of the more taxing tasks about the estate, and this allowed her to eat a little better than most of the rest of the staff and to enjoy the warmth of the ovens and stoves as the autumn days began to grow more chilly. She had always found cooking rather enjoyable, and her talent for concocting things as a *sage femme,* coupled with her knowledge of herbs, seemed to make it a natural match for her. But no matter how enjoyable the work was at times, the realization that she had become a slave never left her mind for an instant. She often lay in her bed at night with tears streaming down her face, wondering if she would ever meet up with Richard and her father again, or if she was destined, instead, to live out her days in servitude, in the backstairs quarters of this Bostonian estate.

Had her English been better and had she ever been taught to read and write, she might have stood a chance of finding Richard. God knew she had said his name to almost everyone she had encountered at Canfield's — to the point that her overhearing supervisor had begun raising a disapproving eyebrow at her. Yet no one seemed at all familiar with the name "Brenton," and she was finally beginning to give up the hope of ever being able to locate him.

Perhaps, as time passed, her English would become fluent enough for her to be able to explain to someone in authority what had happened in Acadia, so that she could make it understood that it had been Richard Brenton's intention that she be sent to his home, not Canfield's. But for now she would have to stay where she'd been put. Here, at least, she was certain to be fed a couple of times a day and she was sure of having a warm bed at night, and that seemed far preferable to being beaten or killed for attempting to run away and scrape along on her own in this thoroughly foreign land.

Richard had been right, she thought from time to time with a sad smile; life in Boston was more luxurious, more sophisticated than life in Acadia had been. Angeline, whose only sampling of commercially made goods had been the occasional iron pot that had been shipped to Acadia from England, or a bolt of the red cloth that the British used in replicating their flag, had, of course, been dazzled upon her arrival at Canfield's. Such things as cut-glass chandeliers, gold-trimmed cornice boards and moldings, and interior walls painted in such ethereal hues as sky blue and cherry-blossom pink, had simply been beyond imagining for her. Many of Canfield's furnishings were quite breathtaking as well, and Angeline had been told that some of them were actually patterned after the furniture of the distant peoples of Asia, a part of the earth she had never had reason to even think about until now.

In spite of all of this, however, life was anything but luxurious for the servants and the slaves at the estate. Far from it, in fact. The backstairs quarters were sparsely furnished with rickety ladder-back chairs and beds with unbearably hard mattresses, and except for when the kitchen staff was serving the Canfield family's meals, Angeline caught little more than glimpses of the elegant estate that existed beyond the servants' domain. Life in Boston was as she had told Richard she believed it was, luxurious only for the wealthy, due to the employment of slaves and indentured servants such as herself. Having been right with this prediction, however, felt like anything but a victory for her now, because she was a victim of it all, and she truly did not know if she would ever be rescued from it.

Just as she was beginning to believe that the tide would never turn for her, God did seem to bless her with what struck her as a miracle of sorts. She was out at the barn fetching some buckets of milk one morning about a week after her arrival in Boston, and glancing over the split-rail fence at the next-door estate, she chanced to see a young woman in servant apparel rushing toward the neighboring great house. Something about the servant compelled Angeline to walk up to the fence and study her more carefully, and she saw in those seconds that the young lady looked exactly like her cousin, Elise. Because of this, Angeline arranged to be out at the barn or the nearby well, fetching water, at roughly the same time on the next couple of mornings, and finally spotting the young woman again, she darted surreptitiously to the fence and called out to her. The girl in question seemed not to hear her at first, but when Angeline addressed her a second time in French, the young lady froze in her tracks and turned to face her with a stunned expression.

"Elise, c'est moi, ta cousine, Angeline," she'd exclaimed.

At this, the dark-haired girl set down the load of firewood she'd been carrying and came running to the fence as quickly as Angeline had. Once the young lady was just feet from Angeline, she could see that she was, indeed, Elise, and an instant later, the two of them embraced. Then they stood conversing hurriedly in French, as they finally drew apart. Though Elise looked a little too amazed to speak at the outset, Angeline managed to learn from her that she, too, had been separated from the rest of her family when the British had come to evacuate Grand Pré.

"And what about Luc?" Elise asked with obvious apprehension in her eyes.

Angeline bit her lip and shook her head. "I don't know, dear cousin. I only wish I did! He and Marcel and Papa were not seen by any of the villagers where we were staying the day the British came to expel us. They never boarded the schooner we were herded

348

onto," she added, near tears.

Angeline's immediate supervisor—a short-tempered chief cook who was given to rapping her subordinates' knuckles with whatever kitchen utensil came quickly to hand in her moments of anger—called from one of the cook-house windows for Angeline in those same seconds. Angeline knew she had to conclude her conversation with her cousin with all haste.

"There is yet hope for us, though, and perhaps for Luc and Papa, as well," she continued, taking hold of her cousin's hand and giving it a reassuring squeeze. "I know a Bostonian who was serving as the captain of one of the British ships up in Acadia, and he is the one who had me sent here. But something went wrong, and I ended up at this house instead of at his estate, so I know he's searching for me now. And when he finds me, I'll have him set you free, too. I swear it."

Elise scowled as though she half believed her cousin had lost her mind. "You mean, he's your *friend?* The captain of a British ship?"

Angeline's supervisor called out to her again, this time much more sternly.

"I must go now," she blurted, wishing that the two of them could continue enjoying the luxury of conversing in their native tongue indefinitely. "But take hope and courage in this. He *shall* come for me, Elise, and for you, as well."

Angeline saw the dumbfounded look on her cousin's face as she turned away and hurried back to the cookhouse. She realized how outlandish her claim must have seemed to Elise, how presumptuous she

349

had been to promise such a thing to another, when in fact she had no guarantee that Richard was even going to rescue her. There was, after all, one possibility that she hadn't wanted to consider thus far, and that was that Richard had died. He had been in a pretty serious state when Angeline had seen him last, and she had to admit to herself that it was possible that the fever that had come over him the day his men had found him at the Petitcodiac had ultimately claimed his life. That might have been the reason why she had been taken to one address in Boston, then, almost immediately, whisked off to another. Perhaps Richard had died before he could make any arrangements for her with his family. Or maybe, knowing that their son had been wounded by Acadians, his family had decided that they wanted no part of the Acadian maiden he had sent to them posthumously. It was true that the look on the face of the woman who had sold her to Canfield was anything but genial. Recalling it, Angeline realized it was a look that could almost have been described as vengeful. She had seemed to take pleasure in Angeline's obvious confusion and trepidation all the while! Shivering with fear at the memory, Angeline put the possibility of Richard's death out of her mind, knowing that continuing to believe he was still alive was all that would sustain her in the days to come.

Richard's mood could only be described as foul as he and Peter Tyler approached the Canfield estate in Peter's coach on Saturday evening of the following week. There were still no clues regarding what had become of Angeline and her father, and Richard's hopes were beginning to fade. He had gone to Pudley's dairy farm and inquired about the girl whom Margaret had claimed to have conversed with, but according to the owner, no one meeting Angeline's description was employed there. Once again Richard had reached an impasse. And his only other hope, the captain of the commercial schooner upon which Angeline was said to have been placed, had indeed returned to Boston, but had been of no help either. The captain stated that, while a "Daniel DuBay" was listed among the names of his passengers on the date in question, Angeline DuBay was not, and that if she boarded the schooner much later than the rest of her fellow villagers, no notation was likely to have been made of her boarding. What was more, the schooner had made a few stops en route to Boston and no record had been kept of which of the passengers had been dropped off in which of the colonies. So there was no real hope of tracing Angeline's course once she'd been shipped out of Acadia.

Given all of this, Richard was, once again, finding himself sinking into the depths of despair. As the coachman drove them up to the front gate of the Canfield estate now, Richard realized what a fool he had been to agree to accompany Peter to this ridiculous affair. He could barely force a glimmer of a smile onto his face these days, let alone spend an entire evening wearing one.

"I loathe you for coercing me into coming to this thing," Richard said to Peter under his breath a moment later, as he thrust his walking cane out before him and descended the coach's passenger step. "You do realize that, don't you, old chap?"

"Now, now," Peter retorted, following closely behind him. "Just listen to those lovely strains of Bach in there and think of the marvelous feast that awaits, and you'll stop being so churlish."

In spite of these allaying words, Richard found himself glowering at his friend as they proceeded, side by side, up the cobblestone path that led to the estate.

Once they reached the front door, they were met by a satin-clad butler who led them through the entrance hall and on to the parlor to be officially greeted by Mr. and Mrs. Canfield. Canfield, by Richard's assessment, was best described as fat and jolly, a man whose obviously bountiful way of life was mirrored by his bountiful physique. His spouse, on the other hand, appeared to be the petite shrewish type, the sort of woman who, even as she greeted her guests, had one eye scanning the room beyond to make certain her servants were working as quickly and efficiently as possible.

Richard learned in the minutes that followed that Peter was right; the young ladies of Boston had, indeed, been awaiting Captain Brenton's first public appearance since his return from Acadia. Though Richard had never met Canfield before, he saw many faces he did recognize in the crowd of guests, and he could hear the young women tittering and exchanging whispers all around him. But rather than feeling flattered by this surreptitious attention, he felt annoyed by it. It was as though he had just entered a bog swarming with buzzing gnats, and all he wanted to do was run away from them—as far away as his battered body could carry him.

Fortunately, he and Peter had arrived rather late, so Richard wasn't forced to stand about making small talk for too awfully long before they were ushered in to dinner. Despite Richard's fairly affluent upbringing, he couldn't help feeling a bit taken aback as he entered Canfield's magnificent dining room moments later. It was the size of a ballroom and every bit as ornate, with its gold-trimmed woodwork and the celestial murals on its walls. To Richard's further surprise, the table at which they were all seated was long enough to comfortably accommodate not only the dozens of guests who were present, but probably ten or twelve more. The food, too, looked unusually elegant, where it rested on the platters and dishes held by the many scullery maids who stood about the table.

After the wine was poured, a toast was offered to the host and hostess by a young gentleman, whom, Peter explained, worked at Canfield's place of business. The meal commenced as the servants each stepped up to the table and began passing their respective dishes from guest to guest.

Richard did his best to avoid making eye contact with any of the young ladies who had been tittering over him earlier, and to keep his face and his utterances directed toward Peter. He really was in no humor to be drawn into a conversation with some gabby little hopeful who wouldn't take "no" for an answer this evening. He doubted, given how slow his body had been to mend, that he could even agree to dance with any of them, let alone bed one. Peter, of course, was fighting him all the while. He was busy chatting with everyone who looked their way. And he introduced Richard, to those who claimed not to know him, in such a trumpeting voice that even the servants, who were still busy in the adjacent scullery, must have overheard him. Indeed, an instant later, it was made clear to Richard that the servants did hear, as one of the maids, several feet away near the head of the table, turned her bonneted head and met Richard's eyes with an astounded expression.

Richard's look became one of amazement as well in those seconds as his eyes locked upon hers. It was as though time stood still for a moment, and all he could seem to bring himself to do was tug at the sleeve of Peter's coat and issue some exclamations under his breath.

"Dear God, that's *her,* old man," he heard himself whisper.

Peter, who was just coming out of a bout of uproarious laughter at some amusing story the gentleman on his right had told, turned to Richard with a blank expression. "Whom?"

Somehow Richard had the presence of mind not to point at the maid as he answered. "Over there. The servant girl with the platter of fowl. The one who's looking right at me. That's Angeline DuBay!"

"You mean the Acadian girl you sent down here?" Peter asked out of the corner of his mouth with what seemed almost equal amazement.

"Yes. The very one!"

"Are you certain? She's quite a ways away, after all. And I don't see those long black braids you

354

spoke of."

"But she has her hair up. Don't you see? She has it coiled up under that bonnet. And look how she's staring at me. It's as if she'd seen a ghost!"

"But what would she be doing here, of all places?"

"I don't know," Richard concluded, pushing his chair away from the table. "But I damn well intend to go over there and find out!"

Peter reached out in that instant and, placing a heavy hand on Richard's left shoulder, clamped him down in his chair. "No! That will only knock up the price, don't you see? If she isn't a paid servant and Canfield owns her, he'll probably charge you a king's ransom for her if he sees how much you want her. He might even refuse to sell her to you. He's a very tough negotiator . . . Just stay seated, and I'll look into it for you after dinner."

"But what if she's working here willingly? What if she *is* one of his paid servants?" Richard asked anxiously, feeling barely able to contain himself.

"Don't be a fool! Just look at the way she's staring at you. Does she look like someone who came here to avoid having to go to you?"

Richard's gaze didn't leave Angeline's. Indeed, it did appear that her amazed expression was giving way to a look of relief and elation. But Peter was right, he acknowledged, easing his chair back up to the table; they had to go with the tide for now. They could not betray their secret . . . *Do not betray our secret*. The fan-talk message came rushing back to Richard. *Of course*. He had taught her fan talk!

His eyes left hers for the first time now and feverishly scanned the table before him for some object with which to convey this message to her. A split second later, his hand plucked the stiffly pleated serviette from his lap, and he hurriedly flattened it out and pressed it over his left ear, turning his head a bit so she was sure to see it.

To his great relief, she nodded. Then she offered him an almost shy smile and strode off toward the scullery, apparently to replenish her nearly emptied platter.

Richard's heart was racing so fast by this point that he thought surely it would beat a path right up to his mouth. "I signalled to her," he whispered to Peter. "Did you see?"

"I saw her smile and nod at you, if that's what you mean, old chap," he answered with a laugh. "I guess she must be the right lass."

"I taught her fan talk when we were up in Acadia. And I just told her not to betray our secret."

"How clever of you," Peter praised, reaching out and patting him on the back. "Let's just hope you can keep your mouth shut, until I get the opportunity to corner our host."

Richard realized that some of the young ladies at the table must have noticed his signal to Angeline. They were buzzing louder than ever now and leaning back and forth in their chairs in an effort to determine whom he had signalled.

"Dear God, Peter, I can't believe it! I just can't believe that was her," Richard declared as they went on dining. "I'm simply too beside myself to take another bite!"

Peter elbowed him. "But do try, will you? I fear

Canfield will be quite offended if you don't, and I didn't bring you here to offend him, you know."

"I know, I know," Richard conceded with an almost schoolboyish giddiness. "I'll do my best, old chap. Truly I will. It's just that I'm so stunned."

"I quite understand," his friend assured, still keeping his voice cautiously low. "I'm rather surprised myself."

"Did you see how lovely she is? Did you see those magnificent dark eyes? Almost like a fawn's, aren't they?" Richard asked, with a dreamy airiness to his voice.

"Yes. She is quite lovely. I can see why you took a fancy to her up there."

"But isn't it miraculous that you should drag me to this dinner and she should turn up here, on Canfield's kitchen staff?"

Peter shrugged after a moment. "Well, you knew she had been sent to Boston. Everyone, from those on Lawrence's staff to your first mate, confirmed it for you. And once she got here, she had to feed herself somehow. I guess she was just as likely to end up working here as anywhere else, if she wasn't sent to your estate the way she should have been."

"You don't suppose she came here to avoid going to my address, do you?" Richard asked, suddenly feeling shot through with doubts.

Peter turned and scowled at him. "Dear God! I haven't seen you this unnerved by a petticoat since we were boys! Whatever has come over you?"

"I'm in love, I guess," Richard replied, keeping his eyes trained on the scullery door now, in the hopes that Angeline would soon reappear. "And I just

357

can't bear to think of her giving me the slip."

"You've become quite hopeless, you know," Peter scolded. "Of course she didn't give you the slip! Why would she smile and nod at you like that, if she wished to be rid of you?"

"I don't know. It's just important to me, you see. More important than it's ever been with any other woman . . . what she thinks, what she feels—"

"Oh, do stop going on about her, will you?" Peter interrupted with a groan. "I promise to free her from Canfield for you, but you must realize how sickening I find it to hear you gushing this way. And one of us, after all, has to remain well enough to finish this meal!"

At this Richard gave forth what must have seemed an unduly loud laugh, and he reached out and gave his old friend a jovial slap on the back. "Ah, Peter . . . you'll never change, will you?"

"Hopefully not, if it means being reduced to a quivering clump of jelly like yourself! Now," he began again dutifully, "just concentrate upon how pleasant it will be to get her home and into your bed, and surely your appetite will return."

"On the contrary! You don't understand at all, do you," Richard retorted, shaking his head. "Such a prospect scares me so much that I'll start to tremble if I even entertain it!"

Peter furrowed his brow in confusion. "But I thought that was what you wanted. I thought that was what all this pining was about, for God's sake!"

"Well, it is. But I can't actually think about going to bed with her or I shall come undone, you see."

"No," Peter answered coldly. "I don't see. What is

more, I don't want to see! And, if I ever find myself in the pathetic sort of state you're in now, I want you to swear to me that you'll simply take me out behind the stables and shoot me! Now, just please face your plate and make some effort to eat, or I shall leave you alone here to haggle with old Canfield on your own!"

Richard continued to wear a smile, as he compliantly allowed several minutes of silence to ensue between them. He realized that it had been so long since he had known true elation that he hardly recognized the feel of it.

"Thank you, Peter," he said at last in a soft voice, his eyes still locked upon the scullery door for any sign of Angeline.

"For what?" his friend asked with a continued gruffness to his voice that Richard sensed was largely feigned.

"For insisting I come here tonight."

"You're quite welcome. But to tell you the truth, I suspect that you are going to be the only Brenton who will be thankful to me for it in the end," he added gingerly.

Richard was still too elated now to sound defensive. "Why is that?"

"Don't you know, old chap? Given her ancestry and religion, can't you guess?"

"None of that matters to me, though, Peter. Don't you understand?"

"I understand that in Acadia there were probably no social constraints about such things. But you're back in Boston now, mate, and I wish you would finally realize it."

Richard looked down at the table now to see that his hands were tightening about his serviette with knuckle-whitening anger. "Please don't spoil this for me," he snarled. "I'm well aware that I'm apt to have difficulties with getting the family to accept her, and I'll cross those bridges when I come to them. But the next few days, at least, shall belong to Angeline and me alone. I fully intend to take up where we left off in Acadia and to lay claim to her, with or without my parents' approval."

Peter shrugged resignedly and continued to dine. "Well . . . suit yourself, old chap. You usually do."

Richard could feel his breath catch in his throat as he saw Angeline emerge from the adjoining scullery a moment later, with a refilled platter of fowl. Try as he might not to stare at her in those seconds, not to "betray their secret" to Canfield and the others, he couldn't help observing her. He realized that he was frozen with emotion, experiencing the poignant, tearful feeling one has at seeing a magnificent wild animal taken into captivity.

Angeline, on the other hand, was definitely complying with his request. She did not look at him, but kept her eyes and her attention directed steadily upon the task of passing her platter from guest to guest.

After a couple of minutes passed, Richard began to find that it was just too excruciating to go on watching her in the role of servant — or, perhaps, of slave. Unlike the pack of gluttonous snobs who surrounded him at the table now, he had seen Angeline in her native habitat. He had seen her ply her marvelous craft as a healer, and the very thought of her having been reduced to a life of such menial tasks as clearing tables of dirtied dishes and refilling empty goblets was enough to tear him apart. His feelings were so akin to those he'd had at seeing a majestic lion caged in a carnival in Europe during his university days that he had all he could do to keep from leaping to his feet and whisking her to freedom.

But acknowledging again how prudent his friend's advice had been, Richard forced his eyes downward to his place setting in those seconds and waited, his heart pounding with anticipation for Angeline and her serving platter to finally reach him. And when at last they did, he stared up into her bonnet-framed face, hoping she would not see the sadness in his eyes, the humiliation he felt at what his people had done to her, but rather, his hope for their future together.

"*Je reviendrai pour toi bientôt,*" he whispered, in a voice so low he was certain no one else could possibly overhear. *I shall come back for you soon.*

In return, she offered him a whisper of a smile, stared down at him as he helped himself to some of the fowl she held out before him, and then moved on to serve the gentleman on his left. It was as simple as that. She'd been his for a second or two, and then she was on to the next guest. Richard, in turn, could feel an aching lump forming in his throat as he continued to fight his almost over-whelming urge to reach out, grab her, and make off with her. This did, on some not completely rational level, seem a preferable alternative to waiting to work through the usual channels, running the risk that Canfield might refuse to set her free.

Miraculously, however, Richard did manage to keep his emotions in check throughout the rest of the meal. As he and Peter finally cornered Canfield in the ballroom half an hour later to discuss the matter, Richard could feel all of his pent-up anxiousness surging up into his chest and throat again.

To Richard's great relief, though, Canfield did not appear in the least bit put off by Peter's inquiries about Angeline, and he responded to them with amazing frankness. "Yes. I did buy the girl, as a matter of fact," he answered evenly. "I'm certainly not ashamed to admit that I own slaves. Many of my neighbors do, as well. What else is one to do, with Charles Lawrence shipping so many Acadians here each week?" he asked with a shrug. "We can't very well let them wander about the streets of Boston, begging for their meals! It does seem the only fair way," he concluded, taking some long swallows of his after-dinner serving of brandy.

"Oh, you needn't justify such purchases to me, Master Canfield," Peter assured with an ingratiating smile. "I quite agree that the Acadians should be made, indeed, allowed to fill some useful niche in our society, rather than starve to death. I simply wondered if you might agree to sell that particular lass to me, or more specifically, to my friend here."

Canfield furrowed his brow as though quite unprepared for such a request. "Well . . . I don't know," he stammered. "I only just purchased her myself. Wouldn't you rather buy a maid who can speak some English? I mean, they can only speak French for the first several months, that Acadian lot, and that sometimes makes matters quite difficult for their superiors, as I'm sure you can imagine. Wouldn't you rather buy a girl who's had a bit more breaking in?"

Though Richard realized that Canfield was only trying to be helpful by steering them toward a more considered transaction, he couldn't help bristling a bit now at how similar the conversation was to what one might hear regarding the purchase of a horse or cow.

"Her language is no obstacle, you see, Mr. Canfield, because Mr. Brenton here speaks fluent French," Peter explained.

Canfield's eyes lit up a bit at this. "Oh, you do?" he inquired brightly, focusing his attention entirely upon Richard now. "How very convenient for you. I could do with a part-time translator here at the estate. I don't suppose I could interest you in such a position, Mr. Brenton . . . I mean, as part of my terms for selling the girl," he added with a shrewd twinkle in his eye.

Richard clenched his teeth. *How dare he!* Having already learned from Peter, when they were first introduced, that Richard was a full partner, indeed, the heir to one of the most prosperous merchant and shipping businesses in the colonies, how dare Canfield proposition him with such a demeaning position! But Richard felt Peter elbow him sharply, albeit surreptitiously, and he once again found the will to restrain himself.

"I will gladly act as your translator, Mr. Canfield, and without salary, if you will agree to sell the girl in question to me for whatever amount you paid for her."

Canfield donned a broad smile and reached out to shake Richard's hand. "Agreed, Mr. Brenton, agreed. Though I must, in all good conscience, inform you that such Acadians are getting to be very modestly priced, being shipped down to the colonies in such numbers these days. I'm sure a better deal could be had by you at any pier in the harbor."

"I appreciate your candor, sir," Richard assured. "But I'm quite firm on wanting the lass we have discussed. I do wish to inquire, however, whether or not you bought her at the harbor yourself."

Canfield scratched his chin and narrowed his eyes as though trying to recall the circumstances of Angeline's acquisition. "No," he answered finally. "If memory serves, I believe I purchased her from a family on the other end of town."

"And would you, by chance, remember that family's name?" Richard pursued, fighting to hide his eagerness to hear Canfield's response.

"The name was Prentiss, I believe," he said tentatively. "It was a woman who sold her to me. A dark-haired, rather plain-looking matron. She introduced herself to me as Mrs. Nathaniel Prentiss. Yes, that was the name," he confirmed.

Richard heard Peter emit an involuntary gasp at this, and it was Richard who did the elbowing now. Though he had begun to suspect Margaret earlier, during Canfield's dinner, finally receiving confirmation that she had, indeed, committed such a monstrous act, caused a chill to run through him. He just hadn't realized, until that moment, how much his twin despised him, to what lengths she would go to spite him, and this realization made him shudder.

"I'm not in the habit of conducting business with women, mind," Richard heard Canfield continue. In his now stunned state, his host's voice sounded strangely distant, however.

"I did request that she produce some master of the estate or an epistle from one, in order to validate her authority to sell the girl. But the truth was," Canfield added in an embarrassed tone, "that the price she set for the Acadian was so ridiculously low, I would have been a fool to refuse it. Why, I doubt it was even commensurate with what she must have paid for the girl's passage from Acadia. And naturally, at first, I thought there was some sort of snarl to the deal. I thought that, perhaps, the girl was with child or the bearer of some contagious disease. But I can assure you, Mr. Brenton, that my cooks have reported no such maladies on her part. She is said to be quite strong and a very good worker."

Richard felt Peter elbow him again, this time more adamantly, obviously in an effort to stir him from his stupefied state. "Oh, Mr. Brenton has no doubts about that, do you, Richard?" he declared.

Richard reflexively reached down and rubbed the portion of his rib cage that Peter had so forcefully poked. "No. None," he blurted. "I'm certain I will be quite pleased with her, sir. Quite pleased."

As they left the gala a short time later Peter, clearly astounded by what he'd heard, finally got the chance to speak to Richard alone again.

"Dear God, old chap, this makes your sister guilty of kidnapping, doesn't it?" he asked under his breath, as they made their way down Canfield's front walk.

"Something of the sort," Richard concurred in a growl. "I don't know the legalities of it yet, but I certainly intend to learn of them!"

"Why do you suppose she would do such a dreadful thing?"

"To keep me occupied, I guess. She somehow discerned how strong my feelings were for Angeline, and she figured the next best thing to having me dead or off in battle somewhere was to send me on a wild-goose chase after her."

Peter nodded after several seconds. "Yes. That stands to reason. She's a shrewd one, that Margaret. Always has been. So, now what?"

"I see to it that she's properly punished for it," Richard answered resolutely.

"But how? Have her thrown in gaol?" Peter asked in a skeptical tone. "The mother of five? It wouldn't reflect well upon the family, I fear, old chap. Besides, if Margaret paid the bill for Angeline's passage, perhaps she *was* within her rights to sell her and recover those costs."

"So then what she did was not illegal, just immoral?" Richard asked, his voice growing louder now as he started to slip in his struggle to keep his anger contained. "And that makes it tolerable? Is that what you're saying?"

"Of course not," Peter quickly assured him, looking fearful now of provoking his friend any further. "Of course it doesn't. I'm simply not sure, Richard, as to what grounds you will have for bringing any punishment to bear upon her. That's all I meant by it. And, given Angeline's lineage; French, Indian, *and Catholic,*" he continued, raising a dubious brow, "well . . . all I can say is, you certainly shall have heavy weather ahead with your parents! I mean, I'm sure it will make that irksome negotiation you just had with Canfield seem like mere sport by comparison!"

At this, Richard came to an abrupt halt and stood staring down at the cobblestone walk, lost in thought.

Peter stopped as well, and turned back to him. "What is it? What's the matter?"

"Nothing. It's just that I think I may already have conceived a plan for showing Margaret the error of her ways."

"Well, what is it?"

"I . . . I can't put it into words just yet, but when you mentioned Canfield a second ago it reminded me of something he had said, about how he was suspicious of his deal with Margaret because she had charged him such a low price for Angeline." As Richard looked up again in those seconds, he saw that Peter's coachman was pulling the vehicle up to the gate for them, and they both began walking again, now at a more hurried pace.

"*And?*" Peter prompted, obviously growing frustrated at not being told precisely what Richard had in mind.

"*And,*" Richard returned as they both climbed into the coach seconds later and the driver began to pull away from the estate, "what I'm wondering now, Peter, is this: Do you think if I explained to Canfield that Margaret sold Angeline to him under false pretenses, he might agree to take part with me in a little scheme that would punish Margaret for what she did and, perhaps, clip her wings for good and all?"

Peter turned down the corners of his mouth as though giving the question some serious thought. "Yes. I suppose he would, provided you make it very clear to him that he, too, was duped by Margaret's actions."

"Oh, don't worry," Richard said with a confident smile. "He'll be more than clear on that point!"

Peter leaned forward from where he sat opposite Richard in the coach. "So what is the scheme, then? Do tell!"

"Oh, I'm sorry, mate, but I can't. I still have much of the superstitious sailor in me, after all, and I fear I might jinx it if I speak of it too soon. But I will tell you this. If Canfield *is* willing to cooperate, my father will have Margaret and her husband booted out of the family business so fast it will make your head swim! And in that case, it won't matter who I take for a wife. When compared with their treacherous and quite calamitous daughter, Margaret, any woman will seem to my parents a better choice as future mistress of the estate!"

Chapter 19

Late on the morning following Canfield's gala, Angeline was called away from her tasks in the cook house and summoned to the great house by Canfield's steward. He led her to her room in the backstairs servant quarters and handed her the Acadian clothing she had been wearing on the morning of her arrival at Canfield's. Then he explained to her, very slowly and painstakingly in English, that she was to change back into them and meet him upstairs in the entrance hall. With that, he turned on his heel and left her.

Angeline fumbled nervously with her buttons as she got herself out of her maid's uniform and back into her own clothing minutes later. *Richard had returned for her,* she kept telling herself, her heart soaring at the prospect of being reunited with him. But the truth was she couldn't be certain that was why the steward had made these requests of her. She had already learned that the steward wasn't, on the whole, a particularly patient man, and she had known better than to request that he say more about what was to happen to her. The language barrier seemed just too insurmountable with him. Therefore, she was quite terrified as she finished changing. She felt almost as helpless and frightened as she had on the morning she had arrived in Boston on the schooner from Acadia. But it was the terror of waiting that was the worst in such circumstances, she told herself. So, considering it pointless, indeed torturous, to tarry a moment longer, she forced herself to march back upstairs and, with her legs trembling, on to the entrance hall.

Once she reached it, the steward silently ushered her out of the estate's front door and down Canfield's long walkway to an elegant coach. As they approached the vehicle, Angeline looked up at its windows, and because she was unable to see anyone within, she turned back to the steward with a puzzled expression and tried asking him, in very broken English, where she was to be taken.

He simply clucked at her as though exasperated. Then he strode forward and pulled the coach door open for her. Angeline, in response, hesitantly stepped up inside of it, and to her great relief, she saw that Richard was indeed seated within. He instantly reached out to her, took her hand, and pulled her into his open arms.

Time seemed to freeze for Angeline in those seconds. She only knew that her face was becoming wet with her tears of joy as the steward shut the coach door behind her and she settled into Richard's embrace. She felt almost as she had when she'd been reunited with her father at Beauséjour, like a little child finally finding her long-lost guardian. The only difference was that she felt Richard kissing her now, bowing his head and kissing the side of her neck in a way that a father never would. It was passion he was feeling, that much was clear, and yet, all she could seem to do in response was bury her face in his ruffled cravat and weep soundlessly.

"*Pauvre petite,*" she heard him whisper as he hugged her more tightly to him. "What has Margaret done to you, my poor angel?" he continued, still in French.

She pulled away from him slightly and looked questioningly up into his face.

"My twin sister, Margaret," Richard explained. "She's the one who sold you to Canfield, I'm afraid."

Angeline gaped at him in amazement. Then she swallowed dryly, recalling the spiteful expression on the face of the woman who had sold her to Canfield. She would never have guessed that that gruff-looking matron was her beloved Richard's twin. "Why would she do such a thing?"

He shook his head and fixed his jaw with what looked to Angeline to be intense anger. Then he reached into one of his coat pockets and withdrew a neatly folded, monogrammed handkerchief. "To spite me. It really had nothing to do with you," he assured. "And you have my word that she shall be punished in full measure for it."

"So that is how you knew where to find me?"

Again Richard shook his head, this time with a bitter air, and he began blotting her tear-streaked face with his kerchief. "I only wish it had been that easy, *mon amour*. But the truth is that I came to Canfield's purely by chance. My old friend, Peter Tyler, brought me here to the gala dinner as his guest. And when I saw you . . ." His voice broke off with his obviously deep emotion. "When I saw you, I knew that my prayers had finally been answered, that all those weeks of trying to locate you had finally been brought to a merciful end. But let's not speak of that sadness any further for now. Today . . . *tonight*," he added in a provocative murmur, "will be ours alone. The world has kept us apart long enough," he concluded, pulling her up under his arm and bending down to kiss the crown of her head.

She certainly wouldn't offer any disagreement on that point, she thought with a sigh.

"I thought you might have died," she explained, her voice cracking as she again gave in to her urge to weep. "I mean, you were so feverish the night they took you away from me."

He ran his hand assuasively up and down her left upper arm, as he continued to hug her to his side. "God, no," he exclaimed in a low voice. "Die without having the chance to see you again? *Never, ma cherie!*"

Again she looked up into his face, and once more, the urge to cry about all that had happened overpowered her.

"There, there," he whispered, softly shushing her. "It's all over now. I'll take care of you from this day

372

forward, my love. You'll never want for anything again. I promise you."

"But Papa," she croaked. "I don't know what became of him, Richard! They say he never boarded the schooner for Boston."

Richard looked down into her eyes as though to offer her further consolation, and for the first time she saw it, the bodily desire in him, the great restraint that was causing his features to look almost painfully tight to her now. As if realizing that she perceived all of this, he swallowed uneasily and began speaking to her again.

"We'll find him, Angeline," he said evenly. "I promise you that I'll use every means in my power to find him for you."

"*Merci,*" was all she could seem to choke out in response. She simply hadn't expected to have to deal with it this soon, his physical attraction to her and hers to him, the obviously carnal urges that had scared her so that last day in Acadia. And it was finally clear to her that he couldn't be kept in check much longer, that he was a very experienced man in the realm of love, and he was certainly able-bodied enough now to act on such desires.

"Richard," she began again seconds later in a wavering voice. She was doing her best to keep her eyes directed downward, in order to avoid his penetrating gaze.

"*Oui?*" he asked in a whisper.

"Did you *buy* me from Canfield?"

"Oh, that's so gauche, *mon amour*. Must we discuss the details of it? The important thing is that you're here, in my arms again. Isn't that all that really matters?"

"*Oui.* I suppose so."

"The other important point is that you are truly free henceforth, free of Canfield and any other man who would presume to own you . . . including me. I tossed and turned for hours last night, asking myself what I could possibly be to you now. And I had to conclude, in all good conscience, Angeline, that I am neither your owner, nor your fiancé, for the former would mean that I believe in the buying and selling of human beings and the latter simply can't be true until you, and, if you wish, your father, have consented to such a proposal. I've read through the books by your French philosophers again, *mon amour.* I brought one of them for you, by Jean Jacques Rousseau," he continued, delving into his deep coat pocket and withdrawing a beautifully bound volume for her.

Though she accepted it from him and pressed it gratefully to her chest, her face became quite flushed with what appeared to Richard to be embarrassment.

"*Merci,*" she replied. "But I must tell you that I can't . . . can't read it."

"But it's written in French."

"Not even in French," she confessed. "I can't read at all. I was never taught to."

"So, then, I'll teach you," he declared, reaching down and giving her right hand a reassuring squeeze. "Now that I've found you, we should have plenty of time for it, and you're certainly clever enough to learn. Would you like that?" he asked after several seconds.

She bit her lip, smiled slightly, and then nodded.

"Good. Then it will be done. But that was an easy choice, my love. The next, I fear, will not be nearly so," he cautioned.

She looked up at him, clearly puzzled.

"You see, with the freedom I spoke of, *ma petite,* also comes difficult choices. And above all else, Rousseau here will tell you that we each have the inalienable right to choose by whom we will be ruled. By a king? By God? By a spouse? By the greed implicit in choosing to be the heir of a grand estate? I've made my choice already, Angeline. I've chosen you over my rights as an heir. I will marry you, even if doing so means being disowned by my parents.

"But now, my dear, it is you who must decide where this coach will go from here. To church to be wed to me by our local vicar? Or to a suite in a nearby inn, where you may decide, more at your leisure, whether or not you wish to marry me and, thereby, also run the risk of someday having to become the mistress of my family's estate."

Angeline bit her lip, having never even considered the responsibilities that might come with being re-united with him. "You . . . you mean that you would marry me now, this morning, if I wished it?" she stammered incredulously.

The corners of his mouth turned up into a smile at the childlike wonder in her eyes. "Yes. Of course."

"But we knew one another for such a short time up in Acadia. How can you be so certain that I am the woman you want to marry?"

375

"Because I've seen how empty life is without you, *mon amour,*" he answered, hugging her more tightly to him. "And I don't ever want to know that emptiness again." He expected some sort of response from her, some reciprocation of this sentiment as he stared at her now. But short of looking touched by his words, her expression was fairly blank, and Richard's pride compelled him to speak much more coolly as he addressed her again. "I must tell you that, should you chose to refuse my proposal of marriage, Angeline, you have my word that I will help you to find suitable employment here in Boston."

Angeline couldn't hide the hurt and surprise she felt in that instant at hearing how stoic, how forthright he was in informing her of this. It was rather like watching a small boy set a wild animal free, one he had clearly viewed and loved as a pet for quite some time. She was like that to him, she realized uneasily. She was someone whose freedom would torture him.

"In whatever sphere of work you wish," she heard him go on to say, now in a resolute, though pained voice. "I even know of a physician who will gladly engage you as his assistant, so that you can go on doing what you do best, acting as a *sage femme.*"

At this, Angeline reached up and pressed a finger to his lips. "Please don't speak of that choice anymore, my love," she beseeched him. "It hurts me too much to hear in your voice how much it hurts you."

Richard, in turn, offered her a subtle, resigned smile. "I'm not much good at this business of setting you free, am I?" he acknowledged.

She shook her head and smiled a bit as well.

"But I do mean all of it," he maintained after a moment. "I don't want you cleaving to me out of material need or want, or even out of fear of your new life here in Boston. I want you only out of love. And the other point I must make clear now," he added, "is that I will not take you today, or at any other time, home to my family, unless we are already wed. For reasons I will explain to you later, I will bring you to the Brenton estate only as my wife and nothing less. Only as a Brenton."

"But, Richard," she replied in a guarded voice, "this is all so absurd, don't you see? I cannot even speak your language. How can you possibly hope to make me the mistress of your family's estate?"

"I'll teach you the language. We've plenty of time for that now, love. I'll see to it. I'll teach you *many* things," he added in an enticing whisper, again bending down to kiss her neck.

A timorous chill ran through her. "But . . . but my father," she stammered.

Richard looked at her sympathetically. "If you would rather wait to see if we can find your father and receive his blessings upon our marriage, we certainly can do so."

After a moment, she nodded. "I guess I would," she said gingerly. "It just doesn't seem right without him knowing."

Richard felt tremendously relieved to learn that the need for her father's consent was all that was keeping her from accepting his proposal. He knew that she heard the smile in his voice as he spoke again. "I quite understand. We shall wait, then, for

377

as long as is necessary." With that having been decided, he leaned to his right and called out the coach window to the driver. "To the inn, please."

Angeline could feel her expression sinking into sadness again as the coach finally got under way. "But we may have quite a wait ahead of us, Richard. Papa may not even be alive," she said tearfully. "Wherever he is now, I can only pray that Lawrence's men haven't killed him."

Again Richard reached down and gave one of her hands a heartening squeeze. "We'll find him," he vowed. "My father and I have many powerful friends in the colonies, and whether he's dead or alive, love, we shall locate your father for you."

"But that's not all I have to ask of you," she began again in a tone that was both troubled and apologetic.

He offered her a shrug and a smile. "Ask whatever you will. You saved my life, after all, *mon amour*. And, no matter what you ask of me, I can never hope to repay you for that."

"All right, then," she replied hesitantly. "But, mind you I ask this favor not for my sake, but for someone else's."

There was a teasing sort of impatience in his voice now. "Well, what is it?"

"It's my cousin. My first cousin, Elise Presnell. She's my mother's sister's daughter and Luc Léger's fiancée. You remember Luc, don't you? He was one of the young men who was with me the night your ship intercepted our fishing boat. Anyway, Elise is being held as a slave by Canfield's neighbor," she explained, feeling her eyes brimming with tears.

378

"She and her mother were two of the finest midwives and angel makers in all of Acadia, and now she's been reduced to milking cows and toting firewood for some English *master!* It tears my heart out just to think of it!" she concluded, breaking into a sob.

He hugged her and shushed her once more, knowing precisely how she felt. He had experienced the same feelings the night before, when he'd seen her helping to serve Canfield's dinner, and he knew that it was partly for herself that Angeline cried now. "Of course. Of course," he assured her. "I'll do everything possible to have her set free, my angel. But enough of everyone else. It's you I'm concerned about. Are you well? How did Canfield and his staff treat you?"

Angeline shrugged. "As well as could be expected, I suppose. I wasn't beaten or harmed in any way."

"Lucky for them," Richard replied in an ominous growl.

Angeline furrowed her brow with surprise. "You mean, you would actually avenge me, if they had hurt me?"

"Of course. That goes without saying, doesn't it?"

"But Canfield bought me fair and square, Richard. I was his to do with as he or his staff pleased."

"Only because of treachery on my sister's part. I would still hold him accountable if a hair on your head had been harmed," he declared from behind clenched teeth, "just as my sister will be held accountable now for selling you to him."

Hearing the same, frightening anger in his voice that she'd heard when he'd spoken of his twin earlier, Angeline thought it best to try to change the subject. For the first time since she'd boarded the coach, she noticed the walking cane that was propped up against the seat just to the right of him. It looked like the same cane she'd seen him using when he'd been mixing with Canfield's guests the night before. "I watched you," she said shyly. "I mean, I saw you mingling with the others at Canfield's last night, and you are walking very well now."

A smile tugged at the corner of his mouth. "*Merci*. I couldn't have done it without you, you know," he added, again bending down to kiss the crown of her head. "And perhaps you'll see later that walking is not *all* I am able to do again," he concluded with a schoolboyish blush that really surprised Angeline.

She didn't think a man of his obvious experience would have reason to show embarrassment over such a subject. But perhaps it was her reticence that was making him act this way, she reasoned. Maybe it was his fear of being rejected by her that made him seem so vulnerable now. Whatever it was, it did much to soften her heart, to make her understand what courage it took for him or any other man to risk being rejected in such an intimate realm. "Perhaps," she replied in a barely audible voice, letting her head come to rest upon his chest.

She couldn't help thinking now about her reasons for not agreeing to go directly to the church at this point and marry him. She was somewhat ashamed to admit to herself that wanting her father's consent and blessings upon their union was far from the only reason why she had refused the proposal. It wasn't that she didn't love Richard. In fact, she knew that her love for him and her hope that they would one day be reunited had been about all that had kept her alive the past few weeks at Canfield's. The truth was that it was her fear of being bedded by him, her fear of dying as her mother had, in childbirth, that had held her back, that made her freeze up now at his references to the possibility of intimacy between them.

"You've made a request or two of me, love," Richard began again in a low voice after several moments of silence. "I wonder, then, if I might make one of you."

She raised her head and looked at him questioningly, and she knew, even as she did so, that he could see the apprehension in her eyes, the deep fear that what he was about to ask was something she could not bring herself to grant — something of a sexual nature. "What is it?" she asked timidly.

"I'm only wondering if it's possible for you and me to go back to the way things were between us up in Acadia weeks ago. With your head resting on me just now, it reminded me of how you lay asleep upon me that day when my men found us." He reached out and brushed the stray strands of black hair away from her forehead, his eyes filled with what looked to Angeline to be a mix of desire and melancholy. "I was in such pain then. I thought that the physical agony of those hours would make me want to forget them. Instead I find now that I want to *remember,*

381

to remember how alone we were up there, how separate from my people and yours. It was like a world of our own in that forest."

She laid her head back down upon his chest. "It can be that way for us again, I imagine," she said tentatively. "But this is your country now, Richard, so I guess *you'll* have to find the hiding places for us."

He gave forth a sad laugh. "*Oui*. Well I suppose that Downing's Inn isn't a bad place to start. It will be far more comfortable than the woods. Though, sadly, not as beautiful."

To his surprise, this last comment only served to make her start crying again.

"Dear heavens. Have I said something wrong?" he asked, his tone fraught with concern.

She shook her head and reached up to dab her wet eyes with the kerchief he had given her. "No. It's not your fault. It's just that I miss Acadia so much, *mon cher*. And I can't help wondering if I'll ever see it again."

He reached down, eased her up to a sitting position once more and hugged her to him. "But of course you will. It's not as though my people intend to set fire to all of it. The land, the forests will always be there. I'll take you to visit it whenever you wish."

He drew back a bit at seeing how red and tear-filled her eyes were as she looked into his. "But you don't understand. It won't be the same without my people there, without our villages."

He found himself, for what may have been the first time in his life, truly at a loss for words with a woman. "My God, I don't seem able to say anything of comfort to you this morning, do I?" he acknowledged sadly.

Again she dabbed her eyes. "Oh, it's not you, *mon amour*," she assured. "You are as charming and debonair as ever. It's me. Don't you see? I'm the one who's holding you back, holding us back, now."

"But why?"

"Because I'm afraid."

"Afraid of what?"

"Afraid of losing all hold on my past. Afraid of letting things go too far between us."

He looked genuinely perplexed. "What things, love?"

"Our relationship."

"But I've asked you to *marry* me, for heaven's sake. Isn't that evidence enough of my good intent?"

"*Mais oui.* But it doesn't take all of my fear away, don't you see?"

He still looked mystified. "No. I guess I don't."

"I don't want to be made a wife and mother. I don't want to run the risk of dying as my mother did."

To Angeline's surprise, rather than continuing to look confused now, he simply threw his head back and emitted a soft laugh. "Oh . . . is that all? Is that all that has you so upset? Ah, Angeline, you're such an innocent. Don't you understand? You don't need to worry yourself with having babies just yet. There are ways to prevent that, and I'll happily teach them to you," he volunteered in a winning whisper near her ear.

383

"But you want a mistress for your family's estate, and what does a mistress do, but produce heirs?"

"That can wait," he said again firmly. "Please, my dear, don't concern yourself so needlessly about such things, when we've so many other matters to attend to now, like finding your father and freeing Elise. You're simply going to have to put your trust in me," he concluded, reaching down and lovingly lacing the fingers of his right hand through hers. "I swear to you I won't let you come to any harm, of that sort or any other."

Angeline again blotted her eyes as she sat studying his in those seconds, confirming for herself that it was sincerity that shone in them. "All right," she said softly.

"And you have my word that, if at any time you wish to say no to me, you are free to do so," he continued. "You are free now, Angeline," he declared once more. "And you must believe that I didn't set you free simply to enslave you again myself, in my bed or anywhere else. Do you understand?"

She offered him a grateful smile and a nod.

Chapter 20

Once they arrived at the inn, Richard had his coachman escort Angeline in to the reception counter and sign her in as a guest there. Then Richard snuck up to her room, via the backstairs. As he later explained to her, this was a precaution he took not to protect his own reputation — because, as he laughingly admitted, he had long ago done irreparable damage to that with his philandering — but rather, to protect hers. This surreptitious entry was probably an unnecessary cautionary measure on Richard's part, however, because he had long been a friend of the inn's owner, a Mr. Henry Downing, and Richard was fairly sure that he could count on Downing and his staff to be close-mouthed about his comings and goings. Though Downing's, like most inns of the day, didn't have latches on its suite doors, it was, in fact, part of the Downing family's huge estate and was always, therefore, almost as accommodative as one's own home. It offered chambermaids, who came promptly in answer to the rings of servant bells. There were also such uncommon extras as washbasins, towels, and soap in every suite. In addition, Downing generously employed a fine chief cook in his kitchen, and delicious meals could be delivered to one's room by a maid, provided one requested them at the appropriate times of day.

"These lodgings are so big," Angeline noted, as Richard entered her suite minutes later.

"It's a suite, my dear. With a sitting room and such for you. Haven't you ever seen one?"

"At Canfield's, *oui*," she said sheepishly. "I wasn't supposed to wander upstairs, but I did once," she confessed. "And his family sleeps in rooms such as these."

"Well, of course they do," Richard confirmed with a smile. "This is just the same, you see. A suite. And this one is all yours."

"But it's so big," she maintained. "I mean, I haven't anything to fill it with, Richard. I haven't anything even to hang in its wardrobe."

"Is it a big wardrobe?" he asked with a waggish smile from where he stood leaning upon his walking cane beside the door.

She shrugged. "I haven't looked inside it."

"Perhaps you should," he encouraged. "Maybe it's not nearly so large as it looks."

Though she thought the suggestion rather silly, Angeline crossed to the wardrobe and opened it. She reeled back a bit at what she saw within. *"Mon Dieu!* Someone has left her clothing here."

He laughed. "No. *I* left them here. They're for you. The innkeeper agreed to let my coachman drop them off earlier this morning, in case you chose to come here."

"They're for me?" she asked in amazement.

"Oui. For you. I will have the couturier come by and tailor them to fit you tomorrow, if you'd like."

Angeline found that she could do nothing more than stand and gape at the colorful collection of gowns. They were made of the most breathtaking, shimmering fabrics and hues she had ever set eyes upon, and she couldn't resist the urge to pull one of them out and hold it up to herself.

Richard leaned back casually against the door and watched her with great pleasure.

"But . . . but where is the collar?" she asked, staring down at the scoop-necked bodice she now held to her chest.

Richard tried not to laugh at her. "There is no collar. Don't you see? It's low-cut."

Angeline bit her lip, recalling all of the plunging necklines she'd seen on Canfield's female guests the night before. This, apparently, was the fashion of the day in the colonies. "You mean, my chest should just . . . just protrude . . . like Mistress Canfield's?"

Richard bit the inside of his cheek till it bled to keep from bursting out in laughter at her. "That's right."

"But she's a *madame,* Richard. A married woman."

He shrugged and smiled. "You could have been, as well, my dear, this very morning, but you refused me."

"Oh . . . you know what I mean," she retorted, clucking and waving him off. "I mean that this is hardly what any self-respecting mademoiselle ought to wear."

"They do, though. You saw it for yourself last night. Canfield's dining room was filled with sweet little mademoiselles in such gowns. Besides," he added with a knowing smile, "I think you would look splendid in it."

"Really?" she asked, interrupting her perusal of the garment to look up and meet his eyes once more.

"Really," he confirmed. "I'll even wager that that saffron shade is just your color, what with your dark eyes and hair."

She gave forth an awkward laugh. "I wouldn't know. We only wore black, gray, and white in Acadia. Well, there was the occasional bit of red, too, I guess. Cloth we got from England."

"So put it on," he urged. "There's a dressing screen over there," he continued, pointing to the far corner of the room near the window. "Try it on and see for yourself how you look in yellow."

Angeline could feel her face flushing even more now. "Oh, I couldn't," she said, moving to hang it back up in the wardrobe and feeling tremendously grateful now that those of Boston's servant class

388

weren't expected to dress in such risqué garments. "They are all very beautiful," she assured him. "And I don't want to hurt your feelings. But, I just *couldn't*."

"Why not?" he pursued, walking over to one of the room's wing chairs and leaning up against the back of it. "It's just you and me here. No one will disturb us."

"Yes . . . but, I've never worn such a thing in my life! Papa would never approve."

"But your papa's not here, my dear. And I promise not to tell a soul that you tried it on."

She still looked hesitant, and he finally crossed to where she stood. Then he set his walking cane down, stepped behind her, took the gown from her hands, and held it up to her torso. "Now, let's see," he said in an amorous whisper. "With it up like this, starting just at your shoulders, the neckline only comes down to here," he declared, pressing a finger to a point just above her cleavage. "Now what harm could there be in my seeing that much of you, my angel? Heaven knows, in Acadia, I felt a great deal more than that. Now, didn't I?" he asked in a titillating murmur near her ear. "Or was that just some delirious, joyous dream of a man caught in the grips of a fever?"

She raised her right shoulder to her ear at the feel of these warm, breathy utterances. "No," she said weakly. "It was real."

"*Bon,*" he replied, still in a murmur that had grown quite urgent by this point. "Then, go try it on, *mon amour*. I shall not take another breath until you do."

She laughed at this ridiculous appeal and hurried off to oblige him. A couple of minutes later, feeling as though she might faint dead-away with embarrassment, she forced herself out from behind the dressing screen, with her eyes directed shyly downward.

"Oh, yes! Let me see. Let me see it," he encouraged. "Turn round a time or two, and let me see how it lays on you."

She pivoted rather awkwardly and then started moving back behind the screen. To her surprise, however, he rushed over to her and caught her by the arm. "Oh, don't take it off just yet. You haven't even had a look at yourself in the glass."

"You walked just now," she noted with amazement. "You walked to me without your cane!"

He smiled and looked down the length of his body, as though somewhat surprised by the feat himself. "So I did. You see now how gifted you are?" he asked, pulling her closer to him and wrapping his arms about her. "You healed me *twice!*"

She eased away from him slightly, shaking her head. "No. It wasn't because of me. You did it on your own."

He pulled her up close to him once more and began pressing a hot trail of kisses to her neck. "No. Not on my own. Because of you. I wanted to come over here and hug you so desperately that I forgot all about the pain of walking." Then, as though aware that he was beginning to lose all restraint, he reluctantly withdrew his arms from her and stood trying to regain his composure.

"Go and have a look for yourself in the glass," he said, steering her toward the framed, full-length mirror that stood just a few feet away.

Feeling somewhat relieved to be out of his heated embrace, Angeline stepped away from him and went to stand before the glass. A second or two later, she heard him come up behind her once more.

"Ah, but you must look," he insisted as she continued to keep her gaze locked downward upon the garment's ruffled hem. In that same instant, she felt him reach out from behind her and gently lift her chin, so that her face was reflected squarely in the mirror.

"But it looks silly on me with these long braids and my bonnet."

He reached up and gently untied her cap, then removed it. Then he took the tiny strips of black ribbon from off the ends of each of her long braids and, running his fingers through the braids from top to bottom, he carelessly unplaited them, leaving her hip-length mane to flow down over the sides of the gown's bodice in tangly waves. "I'll have one of my little sisters come up here and style your hair as Boston's women do," he declared, reaching over and setting her cap and ribbons down on the adjacent dresser. "Then you'll be the loveliest lady to grace this town in years. Why, I'll be the envy of every man in Boston, with you on my arm."

"Do you really think so?" she asked in a wavering voice.

"*Mais oui*. I know it. But there is one more thing we must add, I think."

"What?" she inquired, finally beginning to study herself in the mirror.

"A necklace," he replied. "A bit of finery to cascade from around your neck, like this," he explained, letting the index finger on each of his hands trace two titillative paths from either side of her throat, down, down to the ruffled edge of the garment's low-cut neckline. "Pearls I think . . . yes," he continued in an irresistible whisper. "Yes, pearls, framing a large canary diamond to favor the gown's color. What do you say?"

Before Angeline could answer, however, he had turned her around to face him, and he bent down to press a hard, passion-filled kiss to her lips. "Come on . . . *kiss* me, Angeline," he coaxed when she remained frozen in his embrace. "I know you know how to kiss. It was *you* who first kissed me that night not so long ago near the Petitcodiac."

There was something so indisputable, so compelling about this entreaty that Angeline did find herself starting to kiss him back. She was beginning to grow quite weak in the knees, and she couldn't help emitting a muffled groan as his lips and tongue moved ravenously over hers.

It was as though he knew that she was too overwhelmed to remain standing in those seconds, because he swept her up into his arms and carried her to the elegantly carved colonial bed that was situated just beyond in the adjoining room.

"No more skittishness now, Angeline, please,"

he implored in a silky voice, as he laid her down upon the quilt-covered mattress a second later. "It's torturing both of us, this trying to stay apart, and it's so senseless. We're aching for each other. So, please, don't say no to this now, I beg of you."

"I . . . I won't," she stammered at hearing the yearning, the urgency in his voice. Then she looked on in horror as he knelt beside her on the bed an instant later, lifted his vest, and hurriedly unbuttoned the drop-front closing of his breeches.

"Please don't be frightened," he continued quite breathlessly. "You know what lies beneath this cloth. You *touched*, you sutured this flesh on that first night at the Petitcodiac. So don't be afraid of it now. I'll wear a sheath, I swear it," he added, digging into his coat pocket and withdrawing a tiny casing of sheer-looking material. Then, to Angeline's further dismay, he reached inside the half-opened drop-front of his breeches and hurriedly deposited the device somewhere within. At this point, she simply turned her face away, her head resting on one of the bed's ample pillows, and shut her eyes, bracing herself for what was to come.

The next thing she knew, the skirts of her gown were being pushed up around her, until they surrounded her head and shoulders like a sea of bubbly bathwater. Then he was lying over her, breathing heavily, his ruffled cravat hanging softly down upon the bared region just above her cleavage, as she felt him causing the most extraordinary sensations far below. His fingers were opening her once more, as they had in Acadia, but now it was something else he was easing into her, something far larger and much more coarse than his fingers.

"It's all right, my angel," she heard him say in an impassioned whisper an instant later. "You're ready for me. I could feel just now that you are ready. It should only hurt for a second or two, and then you'll join me in ecstasy, *mon amour*."

At this Angeline reached out and dug her fingertips into the hefty layers of clothing about his upper arms, and she went on doing her best not to fight him. Her body, too, seemed to be longing for this union, though she did not yet fully understand the nature of it. And then seconds later she could feel the forbidden part of him, the long, swollen part that she had tried so hard to avoid when she was wiping the blood from his wounds, inside of her, along with the rough, dry sheath he'd apparently put on it . . . to protect her from finding herself with child, she concluded in those feverish seconds. As she breathed a slight sigh of relief at realizing this, she could feel him sliding even more deeply into her, and she began to panic a bit as she wondered just how far he intended to go.

"*Richard!*" she heard herself gasp.

"Shhh," he replied, holding her steady upon the mattress as he began to move rhythmically in and out of her. "Not another word," he directed. His eyes were closed now, and his face took on an almost reverent expression, from where it hovered over hers. "Just let our *bodies* speak to one another, *mon amour.*"

Suddenly she felt the pain he had mentioned, a sharp, stabbing pain deep within her, and her fingertips dug farther into his arms. But this discomfort seemed to pass just as quickly as it came, and a moment later she found herself swept up in the caressing rhythm of his movement. She understood, almost instinctively now, that he wanted her body to envelop him, to bathe this part of him in the desirous fluid within her, as each beat of his cravat against her bared chest paralleled his penetrating movement below. He was right; it was a sensation that could only be described as ecstatic, a union so gratifying to the depths of her that she found herself crying out now, not with pain, but with pleasure.

"That's it. You see?" he whispered, again bending down to her ear. "It's not so terrible. Now, is it?"

"No," she replied, but it sounded to her in those seconds like more of an enraptured groan than a reply.

"That's right," he declared. "*Grip* me, Angeline. My body longs for you, as it did that night when I lay bleeding on your soil. Minister to me again, my bright angel!" But before Angeline could take in these words, his thrusts within her became so forceful and frequent that she was swept up into his feverish climax with him, and she had everything she could do to keep from crying out too loudly.

Then suddenly he lay still over her, and she

could feel his heart pounding in his chest even more frenetically than her own was. He had caused the same heavenly climax in her here as he had with his fingers weeks before in Acadia. But somehow, she knew that this act had been far more significant, because its exquisite culmination had apparently seized him as well.

"Is . . . is that all you wish to do to me?" she asked several seconds later as he continued to rest upon her.

She could see his torso shaking a bit with laughter. Then he raised his head and stared down at her with an adoring smile. "*Oui*. That's all, my dear . . . you're dismissed now," he added teasingly.

She turned her lips down into an offended pout. "No. I just meant that I wasn't sure what else there was to this."

"Oh, there's a lot more to it," he replied, propping himself up on his arms now, as though sensing that he should take some of his weight off of her. "But unfortunately I found myself so overwhelmed by my lust for you, my dear, that I didn't take the time for any of the lovely preliminaries, of which, I assure you, there are many," he continued, bending down to press a loving kiss to her forehead. "I thought it best to simply quell your fear of this business once and for all and cut right to the heart of it. I hope you'll find it within you to forgive me. I promise to make up for it tenfold in the future."

"Oh, I forgive you," she replied with a blushful smile. "I'm relieved, in fact, to have it over."

It was he who looked rather offended now. "Really? Have I lost my touch as much as that?"

"Oh, I didn't mean I was glad to have it over because I did not enjoy it, for I enjoyed it very much! I just meant that I am glad to finally know how it feels, so I can stop being afraid of it."

He looked amply allayed by this explanation. "Ah . . . good. Just as I'd hoped."

"How much longer will you stay inside of me now?"

An odd expression appeared on his face, as though he didn't quite understand her French. "Oh," he said after a moment, glancing down at where they were still joined. "Well, we needn't uncouple at all, if you don't care to. I'm so mad about you that I'm sure to be aroused again in just a few minutes, and we can partake of it a second time, if you wish."

Her eyes widened in amazement. "You mean, people can just keep doing this? Hour after hour?"

"It depends on the man, I'm afraid, *ma petite.* Sometimes he can, and sometimes he can't. And sometimes the lady wishes to have a bit of a rest. Which is what I think is wisest in your case, my dear," he whispered, easing resignedly out of her now. "With this being your first time and all, I wouldn't want to have you overdo. I want you to remember it fondly."

Angeline couldn't help feeling a bit disappointed as he pushed down her skirts a moment later and then glided upward to simply lay beside her.

"What was the sheath for?" she asked, her discomfiture with the subject apparent in her almost inaudible voice.

"To help make certain that you won't be giving birth to any Brentons until you feel you're ready for it."

"That's what I thought."

"Have you never seen one?" he asked, propping himself up on his left elbow and gazing down into her face.

She shook her head.

"Ah, you're a good girl, Angeline," he praised, reaching out with his free hand and brushing the stray wisps of her now disheveled hair from her face. "I can't imagine you would have had reason to see one before now."

"Do they work every time?"

He looked somewhat hesitant to answer. "Not every time," he admitted finally. "But much of the time, love. As I think I told you up in Acadia, I've never caused a woman to be with child, as far as I know, and I've bedded a shamefully immoderate number of them in my day."

Angeline, though troubled by this news, tried to take comfort in this report of his past performance. "Then was I as pleasant for you as all of them?" she asked, finding herself half afraid to hear his answer.

He stared down into her big dark eyes and smiled. "Oh, God, yes. I've never been in love before, you see, and being in love makes it far, far better."

398

He looked so sincere as he said this that Angeline breathed a sigh of relief, and for the first time that morning, she truly began to relax. "So you'll still have me then, Richard? You'll still marry me?"

"Of course. It was *you* who refused me earlier. Remember?"

She bit her lip and nodded, realizing now that his reminders of this were, in part, meant to let her know how hurt he was that she hadn't immediately agreed to his proposal. "I won't always, though," she assured him, reaching up and taking his right hand in hers. "We'll find Papa, and I'm sure he'll give us his blessing."

"Yes. Well. Let's hope so," he said uneasily. "Well, enough of this taking fliers for us," he began again more brightly after a moment. "It's time I cleaned up, like a civilized chap, and ordered us a hot bath and a little dinner. Don't you think?"

She smiled. "I suppose. What are 'fliers'?" she asked as he rose from the bed a moment later and leaned over to empty the pitcher of water, which rested on the adjacent night table, into its accompanying washbasin.

He didn't turn back to face her as he answered, and she wasn't sure if this was because he was embarrassed by the question or because he was busy disposing of the sheath he had worn and doing the attendant cleaning up. "Well, it's not a particularly genteel expression, Angeline, so perhaps it's not the sort of English I ought to be teaching you."

"Have I done it, this 'taking fliers'?"

He gave forth an awkward laugh. *"Oui.* I'm afraid so," he answered, wringing out the washcloth that he'd found beside the pitcher. "But just once, my dear. In this case, it's singular, not plural, you see. 'Taking *a* flier.' "

"Did I do it just now? With you?"

He turned back to her finally with a bit of a blushful expression, and she was relieved to see that he had rebuttoned the closing on his breeches. *"Oui.* Just now. With me," he confirmed, handing her the wrung-out cloth. "There, to clean yourself," he said softly, and he looked as though he was growing even more embarrassed with the conversation now.

She wasn't sure she understood what he meant by "cleaning" herself, but she was still too busy trying to learn what a "flier" was, to concern herself with this second question just yet. "That is what you English call lovemaking? 'Taking a flier'?"

He scowled slightly. "No, Angeline. It's just . . . just some slang, don't you see?"

"Slang for what?"

"Slang for making love with one's clothes on. You know . . . when a man and a woman get a bit overheated, as I did with you . . . It's really quite indelicate, I must admit. I'm sure your papa would have me flogged for teaching you to say such things."

She offered him a demure smile. "Oh, it's not the saying, but the doing that would anger him."

"Yes, well. I do intend to make it all more

400

respectable, you know, by placing an engagement ring on your finger at my earliest possible opportunity. In the meantime, I suggest you clean yourself, so I can ring down for a maid and the aforementioned bathwater. And I promise you that I shall avert my eyes, like a gentleman, and busy myself with getting a fire started on the hearth over there, so this autumn chill doesn't overtake us while we bathe." With that, he crossed to the far side of the room and began the task.

Angeline, in turn, finally deduced that he intended that she use the damp cloth to clean the intimate part of her he'd left feeling curiously wet and sticky. She rose from the bed and went to stand behind the dressing screen in the front room once more. As she removed the gown and began to clean herself, she couldn't help letting out a horrified scream. An instant later, she heard Richard calling to her in a terribly worried tone, and she realized that he was now standing just in front of the dressing partition. She reached up and plucked the gown, from where she had hung it, just over the top of the screen, and she clamped it to herself to cover her nakedness.

"What is it, *mon amour?*" she heard him ask again, this time with even more concern in his voice.

"I'm *bleeding,*" she answered in a terrified whisper. "I'm bleeding and I shouldn't be. This is not the time for it . . . Oh, *mon Dieu,* God is punishing me for what we did! What if I can't get it to stop?!"

Hearing her burst into hysterical sobs now, Richard shoved the screen aside and again scooped her up into his arms. "It's all right," he said softly, as he carried her and the gown, which she still clutched to herself, back to the bed. "I should have explained. I'm sorry, *ma petite*. It's perfectly normal to bleed a little after your first time with a man."

"But are you sure it will stop?" she asked, still looking quite worried as he laid her down once more upon the bed.

He sat down beside her and helped her to smooth the billowy skirts of the gown out over the lower half of her. "Shhh. Yes. Of course it will stop. It's not at all like what killed your mother. It happens to every maiden the first time with a man."

She seemed to take some comfort in these words as she lay staring up at him with teary eyes.

"That's it. Just try to calm yourself," he directed, reaching out and stroking her hair. "I'll go and get the washcloth for you, so you can see for yourself when the bleeding has stopped."

"No," she exclaimed, reaching up and grabbing his left hand. "Don't leave me. Please. Just stay here and hold me for a while."

"Very well," he agreed, noting, as he lay down beside her, how pale her face had become with her obvious panic. He hadn't seen anyone so frightened and inconsolable since his sister, Amelia, had accidentally trodden upon and been stung by a jellyfish, while wading near the harbor when they were children. And it was finally clear to him now how traumatic the death of Mrs. DuBay had been for Angeline. Given her work as a *sage femme,* it stood to reason that she had probably seen more than one person bleed to death in her young life, and it was quite apparent to Richard now that she was terrified of dying in that way herself.

Richard wrapped his arms about her and lay gently rocking and shushing her.

"When will it stop?" she asked in a wavering voice after a moment or two had passed.

"It has probably stopped already, love. It's said to be only enough blood to fill a thimble or two."

"Will it happen every time we make love?"

"Shhh. No. Just this first time, as I've told you. But just rest now. I'll have some hot bathwater brought up for us and a nice midday meal, and then I'll be back to you before nightfall."

"Where are you going?" she asked with great concern.

"I'm just going home for a few hours to take care of a bit of business that can't wait. And then I'll be back directly to stay the night with you, if you wish."

"Oh, *oui.* I *do* wish."

"And you have my word that I won't attempt to seduce you again until you're feeling better."

She seemed to take comfort in this promise. "You'll just hold me, right?"

He smiled and leaned over to kiss her softly on the cheek. "I'll just hold you, *sage femme,*" he assured. "And I won't let anyone know that you're afraid of the very thing you're said to be

403

best at remedying."

"It does seem rather odd, doesn't it?" she agreed after a moment.

"Oh, not really, I guess. It simply means you're human and not a sorceress, as some of my people would think, if they knew of your healing powers." He would have to warn her soon, he thought. She would have to be told that women with her kind of healing ability were still executed by hanging sometimes in Boston, by those who feared that they were witches. She'd have to be informed that, after the punishment Richard was likely to see meted out to his twin this evening, Margaret might choose to retaliate by telling the local authorities that she believed that Angeline was actually a sorceress. But Angeline was clearly too upset at this point to be told of such things. So Richard chose to remain silent and simply go on cradling her in his arms.

After several minutes he saw that she had, mercifully, relaxed enough to drift off to sleep, and he rose quietly from the bed and resumed his efforts to build a fire.

He woke her half an hour later and taught her how to ask the inn's chambermaid for the necessary bathwater, as well as how to order some dinner, once the servant came to the suite's door. Then, again for the sake of Angeline's reputation, he hid in the sitting room while Angeline stepped out into the corridor and rang the servant bell. A couple of minutes later, the maid arrived at the suite door and Angeline made her requests. The servant did look a bit suspicious at the quantity of food that Angeline ordered, but once Angeline handed her the mound of coins that Richard had supplied as a gratuity, the maid's quizzical manner gave way to one of complete compliance.

After Angeline overcame more of her shyness, Richard managed to persuade her to bathe with him beside the warming fire. Then they shared a midday meal of roasted turkey and potatoes, followed by berry tarts.

At five o'clock Richard left the inn, again using the backstairs, but not before he'd given Angeline his solemn vow that he would return within just a few hours.

Chapter 21

There was a lump in Richard's throat as he entered the dining room of his family's estate half an hour later. His father was in the habit of making any important announcements to the family at the supper table, and provided that Canfield had followed through on his end of the bargain that he'd made with Richard early that morning, Richard knew that William Brenton was about to deliver a veritable cannonball of bad tidings to Margaret and her husband.

"You're late," William Brenton declared as Richard rushed to take his place at the long table where the rest of the family was already assembled. Fortunately, Margaret and Nathaniel usually chose to have their offspring fed separately in the nursery at suppertime. So Richard knew that Margaret's children, at least, would be spared the scene that, judging from his father's stern expression, was about to ensue.

"Sorry," Richard apologized, hurriedly sitting down and placing his serviette on his lap. "I was detained by something pressing, I'm afraid."

"Humbug," Richard heard Margaret grumble to Nathaniel.

Richard didn't look at her. As twins, they'd always possessed an uncanny ability to read the other's thoughts. He, therefore, thought it best to avoid her gaze altogether for quite some time to come.

Mr. Brenton, though looking annoyed by his daughter's side comment, proceeded to fold his hands before him on the table. Then he bowed his head and began to lead the family in a prayer of thanks.

Richard's eyes were locked upon him when he finished saying grace and raised his head once more. He was searching his father's face for any further indication that Canfield's message had, indeed, been delivered to the Brenton estate that day. It wasn't until all of the food had been passed around the table and everyone was beginning to dine, however, that the final confirmation of this came.

"I'm afraid I have some rather bad news this evening," William Brenton began in an unnervingly low voice.

Everyone, except Richard, turned and stared at him with wide-eyed uneasiness.

"It seems that a Mr. Burnard Canfield from the

other side of town is suing us."

A dreadful silence followed, and even Richard found that his breath had caught in his throat as he stealthily shifted his gaze to Margaret and Nathaniel. Margaret seemed to freeze in that instant, her food-laden fork stuck en route to her gaping mouth. She set the dining utensil down and turned to flash her husband a horrified look.

"Suing us?" Nathaniel echoed after several seconds, in a tellingly high-pitched voice. "Whatever for?"

"Well, I shouldn't say he's suing *us*," Mr. Brenton amended, clearing his throat emphatically. "I should say he's suing you."

"Me?"

"Yes. Or, more specifically, Margaret."

"Margaret?" Nathaniel echoed once more.

"Yes."

"But whatever for?"

Richard was riveted to the conversation, watching as these utterances were passed from one party and back again across the length of the table. He hadn't thought that he was going to enjoy the scene quite as much as he found he was now, and for the second time that day, he bit down upon the inside of his cheek to keep from showing his amusement.

"For selling him a diseased slave girl from Acadia," William Brenton replied in a tone that said he was finding this cat-and-mouse game with his son-in-law and daughter quite intolerable.

"She was *not* diseased," Margaret blurted. She

instantly bit her lip and fell silent as she realized she had just confessed to at least half of the allegations.

Because his father had mentioned the fact that said slave girl was Acadian, Richard thought it best now to jump into the discussion with as much shock and indignation as he could muster. "An *Acadian* slave girl?" he questioned with a gasp. "Surely you can't mean Angeline, Father, can you?"

His father tore his eyes away from Margaret just long enough to flash Richard a somewhat sympathetic look. "I'm afraid that's precisely who I mean. It seems your sister here saw fit to greet your friend by selling her to a fellow Bostonian as a scullery maid, of all things! Isn't that right, Margaret?" he thundered, turning his full attention back to his eldest daughter.

Margaret, apparently realizing that there was no point in denying it now, simply issued a loud cluck. "Well, I had no idea she was the girl Richard had sent here."

"But according to Mister Canfield, you paid her passage from Acadia when one of the crewmen from the schooner brought her here from the harbor."

"Well, yes . . . but . . . but . . . I didn't realize she was Richard's friend," she stammered.

"How could you not have realized that?" Richard chimed in, joining his father in glowering at her now. "Everyone, from our steward to our lowliest stableboy, was told to keep watch for her arrival."

"Well, I just . . . just didn't," she maintained, leaning back in her chair and crossing her arms over her chest like a disgruntled child.

"For God's sake, where is she, Father?" Richard demanded, doing his best to look and sound convincingly anxious. "Does this Canfield fellow still have her?"

"Apparently. But, dead or alive, it's clear that you can't bring her here now. According to Mr. Canfield, she has infected most of his kitchen staff with smallpox."

"Dear Heavens!" Mrs. Brenton exclaimed, reaching up and pressing her serviette to her mouth.

"Well then, you see?" Margaret began again in her own defense. "I did us all a service, Father. I'd rather have it be Canfield's staff sick than all of us. Wouldn't you?"

"When you see the sum his lawyer is attempting to exact from this family for his losses, my dear daughter, I think you'll feel, as I do, that we would have been better off trying to hold our own with the smallpox!"

"Oh, dear Heavens!" Mrs. Brenton exclaimed again as she leapt from her chair, crossed to where Richard was seated, and clapped a palm to his forehead. "You don't suppose you could have caught that ghastly stuff from her up there, do you?" she inquired, her face paling with fear.

Richard waved her off. "No, Mother. Now, do go and finish your supper, please. I'm fine."

"Oh, yes. He must be all right," Louisa confirmed. "It's been weeks since he was with her last. He would surely have been showing signs of it by now, wouldn't he?"

"Yes, of course," Richard agreed, finally succeeding in getting his mother to return to her place at the table. "I'm just fine. It's Angeline who concerns me."

"Well, Son, the dear girl could be dead and buried by now, for all we know," his father noted gingerly. "Canfield was very vague on that point, and we'll have to make inquiries about it later. For now, let us just settle this matter of the five hundred pounds in goods and Massachusetts bills of credit that he's asking of us in order to defray his staff's curative expenses and the cost of the time lost from their jobs at his estate."

"Five hundred pounds?" Nathaniel repeated in amazement. "Why, that's absurd! That's a fortune!"

"Yes. Well, tell that to Canfield's lawyer," William Brenton replied coldly. "Because I'll have no part of this pretty predicament! It's your wife who did the unlawful selling of that girl, Nathaniel, not mine."

Nathaniel looked as though he had just been sentenced to death. "But Margaret and I don't have that kind of money, sir, and you know it as well as I."

"Then you had better find a way to raise it, hadn't you? Because to come to your aid now would mean that I condone what Margaret did,

411

and you've known from the day you two began working with me in the business, that I am opposed to the buying and selling of human beings. Though it pains me to add to your burdens in an hour as dark as this, I must also inform the pair of you now that your services will no longer be needed with the family business. Richard and I will have to manage it alone henceforward."

"But, Father—" Margaret croaked, looking as close to tears as Richard had seen her in at least a decade.

"No more 'but father's' from you, young lady," Mr. Brenton interrupted, pointing a castigating finger at her. "What you did was not only underhanded, but monstrous, and it has taught me that you simply can't be trusted in the realm of business. For the sake of your children, I'll let the two of you stay on at the estate for a time, until Nathaniel here has found employment elsewhere. But after that, I want all of you out of here. To the best of my knowledge there has never been a Brenton who has stooped to such treachery as this, and I certainly don't want this incident setting a precedent in this household." Looking too perturbed now to continue eating, William Brenton rose and left the room. Even Richard couldn't help feeling a twinge of conscience in those seconds at seeing how distressed the patriarch appeared to be, as he turned away to take his leave.

An awful silence followed his exit, and it was Richard who finally felt compelled to break it. "She wasn't *yours* to sell, Margaret," he said in a growl, rising from the table now himself. "Look at me," he demanded when she failed to acknowledge his words. "God damn it, look at me!"

He could see her flinch slightly at the great volume of this last exclamation. Then, after several seconds, she turned her gaze reluctantly toward him.

"I asked you about this just a few days ago," Richard continued, "when the steward came to me and explained that you had been seen talking to Angeline near the carriage entrance a few weeks back. I asked you about it, and you lied to me. You said she was only a milkmaid."

To his amazement, she offered him nothing more than a snide smirk and a shrug.

He, in turn, clenched his teeth and stormed out of the dining room, as his father had, knowing that to remain another moment was to risk losing all control and tearing his twin limb from limb.

A few minutes later Richard entered his father's study and found William Brenton seated at his desk, brooding. This was the patriarch's usual course, whenever one of his staff or family members disappointed him.

"May I have a word with you?" Richard inquired, waiting until his father responded to be seated.

William Brenton simply gestured for him to sit down in one of the hooped-back chairs before his desk. Then the patriarch resumed his efforts to light his pipe with a smoking punk, which had been resting before him in a cut-glass dish. "You needn't say anything, Richard," he began in a weary tone. "I know why you're here."

Richard couldn't hide his surprise at this claim as he sat down. "You do?"

"Well, of course. You've come to ask that I consent to your bringing that Acadian girl over here to reside, provided she hasn't already passed on."

Richard opened his mouth to respond, to explain to his father that that definitely wasn't what he sought now. Unfortunately, however, the patriarch got up from his desk, raised a silencing palm to him, and launched into one of his sermons for which he was so well known. Richard thought it best, given the mood his father was in, to simply sit back in his chair and hear him out.

William Brenton began pacing pensively about behind his desk as he spoke. "I realize that this news about your Acadian friend being sick, and perhaps even . . . God rest her soul, departed, is very difficult for you. It's apparent to all of us that you grew quite fond of her up there in New Brunswick. And I want you to know that, suit or no, I am more than willing to pay for her curative costs and do all I can to help her recover, if that is still possible."

"But, Father—" Richard interjected. Again however, his effort to speak was met by a silencing palm.

"*But* I cannot allow her to be brought to this house if she is not well. Furthermore, I must ask that you refrain from seeing her until such time as

414

a doctor says she's no longer contagious. After what just happened in the dining room, Son, I'm going to need you more than ever before with the business. We simply can't afford to risk having you become infected as well."

At this point, Richard leaned forward in his chair, staring down at the hooked rug before him in exasperation. "But, Father—" he tried again, this time rather halfheartedly.

"Let me finish," William Brenton interrupted loudly. "Because the most important point I have to make here is that I've stood by you all these many weeks since you returned home from Acadia. I've kept your position as my business partner open and waiting for you, in the hopes that you would recover from this lovesick stupor you've been in and lay your shoulder to the wheel. I've been very lenient, Richard, because I know that I am, in large part, to blame for the state you've fallen into. I, after all, am the one who insisted you go up and serve Charles Lawrence in the first place."

Richard couldn't help nodding his agreement with this admission.

"But, clearly, the time has come for you to put all of that behind you and resume your duties at the office," Mr. Brenton continued. "I've stood by you, and now it's time you stand by me."

"Quite," Richard blurted, in the hopes that this sudden interjection might give his father pause.

"You agree?" William Brenton inquired with a surprised expression.

Richard smiled slightly. "Well, of course I agree. That's why I came in here to speak to you, you see. Because I want your mind free enough of worry over Mr. Canfield's letter to be dedicated fully to our business matters."

His father scowled. "I'm not following you, I'm afraid."

At this point, Richard got up from his chair and hurried back to the study door. Then he shut it and began to speak again in a hushed voice. "Well, you see, Father, there's something I have to explain to you. But first, I must have your word that what I'm about to tell you will, in no way, change the terms you laid down for Margaret and Nathaniel just now."

Mr. Brenton looked quite perplexed by this. "Why would it?"

Richard returned to his chair and slid it up closer to the desk before beginning to speak again. "Because it . . . it just would," he stammered. "I'm sorry, Father, but I can tell you nothing more, until I have your word on this."

William Brenton sat down at his desk again and nodded his head with obvious impatience. Then he issued his reply, along with a stream of tobacco smoke. "Yes, yes. You have it. Now what about Canfield's letter?"

"He's not really suing you. I mean, as things stand now, Margaret and Nathaniel," Richard amended. "He's not suing anyone."

"But I have the letter right here." His father furrowed his brow and opened his desk drawer, apparently in search of the papers that Canfield had had delivered to him.

"No. It was all a hoax, you see," Richard continued.

The furrow in his father's forehead deepened. "What?"

"I knew I had to come to you at once and explain, because I realized it wasn't right to have you and Mother continue to be upset over something that I merely trumped up in order to punish Margaret."

"You mean you had something to do with all of this?"

"Indeed. It was my idea, in fact. Canfield simply agreed to strike in with me, because he didn't like being deceived by Margaret either."

The senior Brenton continued to look confounded. "So, Margaret didn't sell him the girl?"

"Oh, yes. She most certainly did. It's just that Canfield didn't realize she had done so without your permission. He assumed, when he bought Angeline, that Margaret owned her and had the right to sell her, which, we all know, was simply not the case. So when I discovered what had become of Angeline, I discussed the matter with Canfield, and he agreed to send you that letter stating that he was suing you for damages due to Angeline's illness. But Angeline *isn't* ill, you see. She's just fine. So the whole thing was simply a scheme I arranged to even the score a bit with Margaret."

William Brenton leaned back in his chair, and

Richard noted that his face had grown quite pale. "Dear God, you're as designing as she," he said finally, under his breath.

"Hardly, Father. I, after all, only arranged for Margaret to be punished for what she did. It's not as though I sold *her* fiancé to a slave owner!"

"Fiancé? Surely you don't mean to tell me, Richard, that you're *betrothed* to this Acadian girl!"

"Not yet," he conceded, "because, you see, she hasn't accepted my proposal. But she assures me that she shall, just as soon as we're able to locate her father and obtain his consent. Then, I pray she'll have me," he added with a boyish waver to his voice.

"Have you?" his father repeated in obvious amazement, rising abruptly from his desk once more. "Has the whole world taken leave of its senses this evening? *Have you?"* he said again with equal astoundment. "She's a savage, for God's sake! One of those beastly French *Catholics!"*

Richard flashed him an incisive look. "Not nearly as savage and beastly as your eldest daughter, it appears, because I know Angeline, Father, and it would never even occur to her to sell one human being to another. The Acadians don't believe in slavery any more than you and I do. And how can you think of her as a savage, when she saved my very life? Don't you realize, after all I've told you, that I'd be dead and buried in Acadia now, if not for her?"

At this, William Brenton withdrew the pipe from his mouth and began to finger it uneasily. "So then, give her some position here at the estate. Or establish a millinery shop, or some such thing for her to manage. There are many ways to show your gratitude to her, Son. You needn't go so far as to marry her!"

"But I want to marry her, don't you see? I love her, Father. I've known it for weeks."

His father simply rolled his eyes, as though too taken aback by all of this to even try to think of a suitable response now. "You mean to tell me that, for the past twelve years, your mother and I have endured your endless philandering with every eligible maiden in Boston, *only* to have you come to me now and announce that you're marrying some sort of Acadian witch doctor?"

Richard tried not to laugh at this ridiculous term for her. "Angeline is not a witch doctor; she's a *sage femme,* a healer, just as our doctors are healers. And she's quite good at it too, I might add."

"Well in that case, tell her to refuse your proposal and heal your broken heart, so you can give it to one of your own kind!"

Richard felt himself sobering as he rose again from his chair. "You don't seem to understand," he said firmly. "I didn't come here to ask your permission to marry Angeline, for I have every intention of doing so, with or without your consent. I came here to save you from worrying about a lawsuit that doesn't exist and was simply trumped up in order to provoke you to do what you should have done long ago, and that's get my conniving twin and her blood-sucking husband out of your coffers for good. After all, Father, you named *me* as your heir apparent and partner in your business over a decade ago. The matter should have been settled then. Instead, I've been forced to spend the last ten years of my life vying with your daughter and that despicable man she married for what is rightfully mine. And try as I have to persuade you to put an end to it, you've done little or nothing. So, sadly, I came to realize that it would require something as extreme as a trumped-up lawsuit to compel you to finally stop their shenanigans, and I was absolutely right. What is more," Richard continued, feeling as though he was just getting started now, "my dear Angeline was grievously wronged, and I knew that I was the only one in this household who would care enough about that sin against her to see to it that Margaret was punished for it. I'm sorry that it took deception on my part, and on Canfield's, to bring this to pass, but obviously that was what was required. And now, if you'll excuse me," he declared, turning on his heel and striding toward the door, "I've got to get back to Angeline."

"Wait," Mr. Brenton called after him. "Wait just one moment."

Richard stopped walking and turned slowly back to him.

"So what are you saying? Am I to understand that you no longer wish to be involved with the family business?"

Richard shook his head. "Not at all. I simply assumed that, since you don't approve of my choice in spouses, you'd dismiss me now, just as you did Margaret."

"But I . . . I need you," the patriarch stammered, with as much vulnerability reflected in his voice as Richard had ever heard from him.

Richard smiled. "And so you shall have me . . . provided my wife will be welcomed here as well."

Again William Brenton fell silent, as though too appalled by the thought of it to speak. Finally he shook his head. "It's just impossible. Don't you see?"

It was Richard who shook his head now. "No, Father, I'm sorry, but I don't. For over a decade, you've trusted my judgment in business. Why, then, can't you trust it now in the realm of matrimony?"

"But Richard, you must consider the next generation, the heirs you will sire for this estate. Above all else, they must be *Brentons,* don't you understand? They must speak English, not French."

"But I've already begun teaching Angeline some English, Father, and she's doing very well. She's a most clever young woman, I assure you."

"I'm sure she is, Son. But what of her religion? We Brentons are Puritans, not Catholics."

Richard shrugged. "Perhaps she'll agree to convert. I shall ask her."

A strained silence ensued, and Richard could

see his father's pain, the indecision on his face in those seconds. "Ah . . . it's no use, Richard. You'll never persuade our friends and neighbors to accept her."

"I'm not asking them to accept her," Richard retorted. "I'm asking you and Mother to, and even if you can't, I intend to make her my bride . . . if she'll have me." With that, he turned again to leave.

"You're doing this to spite me, aren't you?" he heard his father ask in a knowing tone. "You're doing it to punish me for . . ." William's voice broke off, as he obviously searched for what he thought was the most probable reason, "for sending you off to Acadia. Isn't that right?"

Richard didn't bother turning back to face him now, as he answered. "On the contrary, Father. It's the one thing I thank you most for. Because if you hadn't, I would never have met Angeline. But what you must understand now is that I won't fight any more of your battles, not with the Acadians and not with Margaret and Nathaniel."

"So that's why you're doing this? Because of the trouble I've permitted Margaret and Nathaniel to cause you?"

At this Richard turned back to him with a gentle smile. "Don't you understand? It has nothing whatever to do with them or with you. I'm doing it for the best possible reason, because I *love* Angeline. It's as simple as that." With that, Richard resumed his walk to the door and finally made his exit. To his dismay, however, his father did nothing more to stop him.

It was over, he realized. He had done what he could to allay his father's reservations about Angeline, and he had failed. And now the time had finally come to put his money where his mouth was. He had to back the brave words that he had spoken that morning to Angeline in the coach, and part with his claim to the Brenton estate. He would have to use all that his father had taught him in the past decade and find his own way now in the world of commerce. Such was the price of freedom, he told himself as he made his way down the long corridor that led to the entrance hall. Such was the price of finally breaking the ties that had bound him for so long.

Angeline would understand this relinquishment, he told himself. She, after all, hadn't known whether she was saving a rich man or a pauper the night she'd happened upon him at the Petitcodiac. And considering how she felt about bearing his heirs, she'd probably be relieved to hear that marrying him no longer brought with it the possibility that she'd have to serve as mistress of a grand colonial estate. With that heartening thought, Richard left the manse and headed around to the carriage entrance to summon a coach to take him back to the inn.

He was truly free, he kept telling himself. Free, just as all those philosophers he admired had always encouraged him to be, and though he might, ultimately, find himself penniless in exchange, he did feel a shiver of pride run through him as he continued to walk.

Just when he thought he might succeed in talking himself into being comfortable with his new circumstances, he heard his father's voice again. The patriarch was clearly pursuing him, and though Richard was tempted to stop once more, he forced himself to keep walking.

"Richard!" William Brenton exclaimed, his voice cracking in an odd emotional way, the likes of which Richard had never heard from him.

An instant later Richard felt his father catch his arm from behind, and he realized he had to stop walking now or risk dragging the patriarch behind him on the cobblestone walk that led to the coach house. He therefore brought himself to an abrupt halt.

"Richard," his father began again, obviously winded by his hurried pursuit, "your mother and I thought we lost you once up in Acadia, and we don't want to lose you again. I would rather have you here with us, serving at my side, married to whomever you please, than to have you separated from us again for any reason."

Richard noticed that his father's eyes were tear-filled in those seconds. It was a sight that he couldn't remember having seen in his thirty-odd years of life, and he found that it almost took his breath away.

"Bring her here," William Brenton continued. "Tonight, if you wish. And we will all do our very best to make her feel welcomed as the future mistress of this estate." With that, he reached out and hugged his son, and Richard, stunned by the concession, reciprocated this rare show of affection.

"Yes, Father. I *will* bring her here," he agreed, finding himself a bit teary-eyed as well as he ended their embrace. "But only as my wife," he added, "and that decision, I'm afraid, is up to Angeline now. Do wish me good luck with persuading her to say yes," he concluded with a nervous smile. Then he gave his father a parting pat on the back and hurried off to board one of their coaches.

"Good luck!" his father called after him in a tone that Richard recognized as being quite sincere.

Chapter 22

Three weeks passed, and under Richard's tender tutelage, Angeline's command of the English language improved greatly. She had learned dozens of short, but nonetheless essential phrases from him, as well as how to conjugate scores of verbs, and to her relief, she was finding that English was not so very different from French, that the two languages possessed many similar words. What was more, she was beginning to be able to read, in both French and English, and during the hours when Richard left her alone at the inn to go and work at his family's shipping business, she would sit in her suite and slowly decipher the words in the books he had given her. She alternated these spells of reading with sight-seeing strolls about the streets of Boston and buying sprees at the millinery and wig shops, which Richard encouraged her to patronize. And, while she enjoyed her days of newly found luxury and leisure, particularly after having spent so much time laboring with Canfield's kitchen staff, she far preferred her nights, because that was when Richard always returned to the inn. They would then share a delectable supper, as well as sharing the suite's bed after dark.

Richard was always most insistent that she speak to him in English as she recounted the things she'd done during the day, and he would do the same, until an odd sort of *Franglais,* their own unique blend of French and English, began to develop between them.

Richard, too, was obviously thriving in their relationship. He no longer needed his walking cane, and his limp was almost nonexistent now. The prolonged pain he'd experienced because of his injuries was gone as well, and he adamantly attributed all of this to Angeline's healing abilities, to her therapeutic touch as both his *sage femme* and his lover.

But despite their wonderful rapport and Richard's endless generosity to Angeline with both his time and his money, she couldn't help growing more and more lonely when he was away at his place of business. She began to feel as though her life was in a kind of limbo as she waited for Richard to finally succeed in freeing Elise from Canfield's mulish neighbor, as well as for some word on what might have become of her father.

She knew that Richard was aware of her loneliness, and one afternoon, she answered a knock at her suite door to find a tall slender young lady beaming at her in the corridor. The girl appeared to be roughly Angeline's age, and her honey-colored hair was swept up into a soft bun at the back of her head. She was so beautifully dressed that Angeline knew instantly that she must have been from a well-to-do family. What was more, the look she wore as she studied Angeline was so knowing, so incisive, that Angeline couldn't help feeling that the girl somehow already knew quite a bit about her.

"Hello," the stranger greeted, extending her right hand to Angeline. "I'm Pudding, Richard's sister. May I come in?"

Angeline was hesitant to let her enter at first, but she found the girl's expression so disarming that she finally did so.

"Richard sent me," she explained as she strode into the front room of the suite and had a look around. "He sent me to coif your hair. I'm quite good with it, if I do say so myself, and it looks as though you've a wonderful mane with which to work."

"You really are one of Richard's sisters?" Angeline asked, seeing only a slight resemblance to him in the girl's dark eyes.

"Yes," she answered with a smile.

"And you are called *Pudding?*" Angeline queried, her voice betraying the surprise she was trying to hide. "Forgive my English," she began again, "but is that . . . is that not a dessert?"

The girl laughed. "Indeed it is. It's a nickname, you see. It's what Richard always calls me, so I assumed you would know me by it. My real name is Amelia."

"Ah, yes," Angeline declared, smiling now as well. "Amelia. He speaks of you quite often. He is most fond of you. Do sit down, if you wish."

She gave forth a great sigh of relief. "Oh, yes. I *do* wish," she declared, plopping the large vanity bag that she'd brought along on the floor next to her. Then she turned and sank down into one of the front room's wing chairs. "The coachman let me out a full two blocks from here, because he was having trouble with one of the horses, and he thought it safer for me to go the rest of the way on foot. Consequently, my feet are killing me," she concluded, reaching down and slipping off her shoes now.

"I'm sorry," Angeline replied, taking a seat across from her in the matching wing chair, "but what, pray tell, does this 'consequently' mean? It is not a word I have learned yet."

Amelia laughed softly and reached down to withdraw a fan from the bag she'd been carrying. She opened it with an abrupt snap and sat breezing herself carelessly with it. "Oh, no need to apologize. It's my fault, I fear. I should know better than to use such big words with you. *Consequently* means *therefore, and so . . .* that sort of thing."

Angeline nodded. "Ah, *oui*." She leaned back in her chair now and felt herself beginning to relax a bit. She liked "Pudding," she decided in that instant. She liked her warm smile and almost heedless manner. It was clear that she had a knack for putting others at ease, a trait she had in common with her charming brother.

"You're quite lovely, you know," Amelia suddenly declared. "I can certainly see why my brother took a fancy to you up in Acadia."

Angeline could feel her face flushing at this unexpected compliment. "Why . . . thank you," she stammered.

"You're most welcome. My sister, Margaret . . . that's that horrible lady who sold you to Canfield," Amelia clarified. "Well, she said I shouldn't come up here to see you, because you might scalp me. But I told her that was poppycock, that Richard said you were even more civilized than *we* in some ways, and of course he was right. You're really just a dear little thing," she said with a wide smile of approval. "I knew you would be. Richard has very good taste in women."

Angeline knew that she should feel somewhat offended by all of this, but instead she found herself fighting back a laugh now at how offhandedly Amelia had delivered it. "Yes, well

. . . thank you," she replied again. "And I'm proud to report that I haven't scalped anyone since coming to Boston."

Amelia threw her head back and laughed heartily at this, then shut her fan and pointed it at Angeline. "Excellent," she declared. "A sense of humor. You'll need one, if you decide to marry Richard. The family can be difficult at times. Not me, of course," she quickly added. "I'm an absolute lamb. But, well, the rest of them can be peevish, now and then. I'll teach you how to manage them, though. You'll need to know, if you're going to be mistress of the estate one day. And you needn't worry another moment about whether or not you're up to the task, because believe me, if you managed your family's farm in Grand Pré on your own, as Richard said you did, managing the Brenton estate will be child's play! All you have to do is learn to give orders, and I'm sure you saw how that was done often enough at Canfield's. And don't worry yourself about that nasty Margaret either. She and her husband and children are moving out soon, to a parcel of land Father acquired for them on the edge of town. Phew," she exclaimed, running the back of her right hand across her forehead. "What a relief that will be! Only having to see them and their brood of unruly children at Sunday dinner henceforth. Oh," she concluded, beaming at Angeline once more and clapping her hands together triumphantly. "What fun we shall have together, you and I! And you must promise to tell me all about Acadia and how you healed Richard and such. What a treasure you are! I haven't been this excited since I was sent off to finishing school in London!"

"*Oui,*" Angeline answered, feeling herself blushing again at this stream of praise. "I shall tell you all about it, if you wish."

The two girls went on conversing for hours, as Amelia withdrew her hair-styling implements from her bag and converted Angeline's hip-length mane into the latest look of the day. By the time Amelia left and Richard returned from work at five, Angeline's mind was positively buzzing with all of the new things she'd learned about Bostonian life.

"Ah, good for Pudding," Richard declared, giving Angeline his accustomed evening greeting of a kiss and a lingering hug. "I knew you would like her. Everyone does. She shall prove a good ally for you, Angeline, should you choose to marry me. And she'll cheer you, when you're feeling down. She always does me. She's a godsend, that one. Did you try out lots of the English you've learned on her?" he asked with the officious sort of tone one would expect from a tutor.

Angeline sheepishly dropped her gaze to the Oriental rug beneath their feet as he continued to hold her in their loose embrace. "Well, not much really," she confessed. "I didn't get the opportunity to, because she talked so steadily."

At this, Richard gave forth an impetuous laugh. "Yes. That was definitely Pudding who paid you a call. She's quite the prattle-box."

"But she taught me a lot," Angeline added in Amelia's defense. "She taught me more fan talk. And she told me much about the ways of your people."

To her surprise, Richard suddenly grew quite serious, as she looked up and met his gaze once more. "And did you like what you heard?" he asked, his dark eyes quite penetrating now, as though he were about to propose to her again.

Angeline swallowed dryly, sensing a painful sort of urgency in him. "Yes," she answered with a wavering smile.

"Really?" he pursued, still with such pressing energy in his voice that Angeline was almost afraid to respond. She simply offered him a nod.

"You look wonderful, you know," he whispered, reaching up to run his fingers through the soft tendrils that his sister had created in her hair. "Like the loveliest of Boston's ladies with your hair up like this."

"Thank you," Angeline replied, still with a lump in her throat at his suddenly intense air. She couldn't imagine what he wanted of her. Perhaps he simply wished to make love again. But maybe it was something more. Perhaps she

433

was about to find herself in a position where she would have to refuse him, and she felt such gratitude, so much love for him now that she wasn't sure she'd have the strength of will to do so. "Pudding . . . Pudding had to cut off about fourteen inches of my hair," she continued, hoping that some chatter might distract him from whatever it was he sought. "To make it look this way," she concluded, her heart beginning to race now as he bent down, swept the cascade of curls away from the side of her neck and started kissing her so passionately it took her breath away.

"What is it, Richard?" she asked, no longer trying to hide her trepidation.

He lowered one of the puffed sleeves of her gown and let his fervent kisses continue down the length of her shoulder. "Isn't it apparent?"

"No, no it isn't," she choked.

"I want to make love to you again," he answered, not bothering to lift his face from her perfumed neckline as he said it.

"And that's all?" she asked, her heart beating so hard at this point that she was certain he could hear it from where his head hovered so near her cleavage. "No. That's not all," he confessed, and before she could offer any objection, he swept her up into his arms and carried her off to the bed.

"Well, what then?" she asked, her voice cracking now with her uncertainty.

434

"I can't tell you. I won't tell you," he said firmly, "until I've had you once more. So please, just hold me now, Angeline. Hold me as if you were never going to see me again after tonight. Just as it was in Acadia," he directed, reaching down to where he'd laid her on the bed, and hurriedly, heatedly untying the ribbons that bound the tight front of her bodice. Once he'd finished this, he slid the garment downward, removing her underpinnings as well, as his large hands swept briskly to her feet. Then he stood at the side of the bed and stared desirously down at her naked form as he hurriedly shed his own clothes.

Angeline didn't know how to respond. Their intimacy was still so new to her that she hadn't yet grown accustomed to having him peruse her in such an undressed state, and she could no longer fight the impulse to reach over and cover herself with the draping edge of the bed's quilt.

"No," he declared, sweeping the bedcover off of her. "You're mine tonight, every inch of you, for my eyes to drink in like a fine champagne and my body to lose itself within."

This last sentence was followed by the removal of his breeches, and Angeline felt compelled to avert her eyes, to turn away from the sight of the fearsome evidence of his great arousal.

They had always made love in darkness or in the dimness of a single candle's flame flickering on one of the night tables. But the room was still filled with daylight now, at this late afternoon hour, and she couldn't avoid seeing what she had always only felt beneath the bed's linens before. It just looked so much larger, so much more swollen now with his obvious hunger for her. Even more dismaying was that she realized in those seconds, as he lowered himself down upon her, that he wasn't going to bother to put a sheath on for her, that he probably couldn't be stopped in this odd possessive state that had come over him.

"Richard . . . please," she whimpered, as he began pressing his burning kisses to her neck and breasts once more. "Please put something . . . something on," she pleaded awkwardly, "if you're going to —"

Her words broke off as he placed a silencing finger upon her lips. "I know I promised you," he whispered. "I know I said that I would always wear one with you. But just this once, just for tonight, please let me know you in the natural way. Please let my body lay claim to you in a way that my words of proposal can't seem to. Just this once," he said again in a whisper so ardent that she couldn't seem to refuse.

She would command her body to resist his, she told herself in those fevered seconds as she felt him part her thighs and slip deeply inside of her with even more practiced agility than he'd previously displayed. She would keep her body from really being penetrated by him, from allowing his seed to be implanted therein. But as soon as he began to move within her, stroking the most sensitive reaches of her with his accustomed expertness, she knew that she wouldn't be able to resist him, that her body would be as seduced by his as she always was by his words of love. She gave forth a pained groan and felt her arms reach up to embrace his broad shoulders as their bodies seemed to meld in those seconds.

"Promise me you'll stay with me, Angeline," she heard him say in a fervid murmur as his movement within her quickened and became more pronounced. "*Promise* me."

She was so enraptured now by his breathtaking motion that she couldn't seem to choke out a syllable.

"Please promise me," he said again, showering her shoulders and neck with wet, impassioned kisses as he continued his almost manic thrusts.

"*Oui* . . . yes," she stammered, thinking that perhaps he would stop and withdraw from her if she gave him her word on this. She realized in that instant, however, that it was too late, that his body would no longer respond to his commands, let alone to hers, and he began surging in and out of her with a ferocious energy that she'd never before seen in him.

Seconds later she, too, was drawn into the heart-stirring climax of the act, and she was so moved by the experience that she actually felt tears coming to her eyes as he gradually came to a stop within her.

"I'm sorry," she heard him whisper after a moment, not raising his head to look down at her now. It was as though he was simply too ashamed of what he had done to risk looking her in the eye.

"What is it?" she asked softly in response. "What made you do this?"

He eased off of her, then lay hugging her to him, almost like a frightened child. "It's the news I have for you tonight. I fear it will cause you to leave me, and I don't think I can bear that. Yet, I know I must tell you. I love you too much not to."

"For heaven's sake, what is it?" she asked again, not even trying to hide her anxiousness.

"It's . . . it's Elise," he replied. "I've freed her from Canfield's neighbor."

"But that's good news," Angeline declared. "She can come and stay here in the inn with me. Then I'll have a companion to help fill my days when you're away."

He shook his head sadly, and she found herself quite frightened by his somber expression. "No. She can't," he answered simply. "She won't," he amended, "because I haven't told you all there is to tell."

Angeline sat up and stared down at him worriedly. "What is it, Richard? She *is* well, isn't she? Tell me she hasn't been hurt or killed!"

438

He shook his head and softly shushed her. "No. Of course not. She's just fine, as far as I know."

"Well, what is it, then?"

"It's your father, *mon amour*," he choked, as though this were one of the most painful things he had ever had to disclose to anyone. "I've finally received word from Lawrence's staff that your father is alive and living in the French-owned territory of Louisiana."

Angeline gasped with joy.

"Apparently a small number of your people in New Brunswick managed to get away from Lawrence's detachments, and they made their way down to Louisiana, where they are starting a settlement now."

"But that's wonderful news!" she exclaimed.

"Not for me," Richard said sadly, "because I also discovered that Elise's fiancé and another chap named Marcel are with your father in New Orleans, as well, and your cousin wishes to be sent down to join them directly."

Angeline furrowed her brow in perplexity. "But what is so awful about that? It is only natural that she should want to be reunited with her fiancé."

"But what about you?" he rejoined, reaching out and running his fingers through her tendrils once more with a strange sort of longing in his eyes. "Won't you want to go with her? Won't you want to return to your father and people, after being torn from them as you were?"

Angeline was silent for several seconds. "I . . . I don't know," she answered finally. "I guess I'm so surprised by the news that I haven't had time yet to think of what I want to do about it."

Richard's eyes locked upon hers once more. "The thing is, I can't go with you, love, if you choose to travel down there with your cousin now. My life is here in Boston. I can't leave my business responsibilities at this point. My father has simply proven himself too loyal to me, for me to leave him in the briers now."

Angeline sank even further into her stunned silence as she leaned back against the bed's carved headboard and drew the quilt up to cover her. "*Mais oui,*" she said softly. "I do understand now why you've acted so strangely since you returned from work. I understand about the lovemaking, about you wanting to lay claim to me, as you put it. You are afraid that I will decide to leave you and hurry down to be with my papa."

Richard looked at her sadly and nodded. "Yes, precisely . . . I guess I could hardly blame you, if you do."

Angeline's mind was filled now with happy images of the village her people would build in this new French territory down south. Without Acadia's bitter winters and the British harassing them as before, they could probably establish a community that was even more utopian than the one they'd known in Grand Pré.

"Can you never leave Boston?" she asked after a moment.

Again his eyes reflected great sadness as he answered her. "Perhaps . . . someday. But not for a few years yet. There's just too much work to be done with the business. And now that I've helped to have Margaret and Nathaniel ousted from the estate and our business affairs, I can't very well go to my father and tell him I'm leaving as well. It just wouldn't be fair, Angeline, and it seems to me he's tried to be more than fair with me lately. I'll simply have to stay here," he stated after a moment. "Stay here and pray that, by the time I can come down to be with you in New Orleans, you haven't married another."

He was right, Angeline silently acknowledged. With her people's numbers so depleted now, every maiden among them would be urged to marry and procreate, so that the Acadian nation could flourish once more.

"Well," Richard began again, slowly withdrawing his hands from her and getting up to redress. "I'll have to leave it up to you from here on, love. You are free, as I told you you were the day I came to collect you at Canfield's. And no matter what other promises I may have broken to you since that time," he added, turning back to her once more with an apologetic gaze, "I won't break that one. I shall not try to stop

441

you, if you choose to go back to your people."

With that, he walked around to her side of the bed and began gathering up the clothing he had shed minutes earlier. To his surprise Angeline responded only with an abrupt snapping sound that he knew she couldn't have produced with her mouth. His eyes sped upward from the floor to see that she had apparently picked up one of the fans that she had purchased from a local millinery, from where he had seen it resting on the adjacent night table earlier. The snapping sound he had heard had obviously been caused by her having opened the fan, because she held it before her now completely unfolded. She began waving it with an odd sort of sportiveness that he hadn't seen from her before.

"Are you hot?" he asked with an amazed rise to his voice. He felt quite chilly, himself, now that he had abandoned the warmth of the bed.

She shook her head and smiled slightly. "No, silly. I simply wish to communicate with you."

He raised a questioning brow at her and continued to stand, considerately clutching his clothing to the lower half of his torso.

To his further surprise, she reached out quite ceremoniously and touched the open fan as she continued to flutter it before her. The message came to Richard's mind in a heartening flash. "*I always long to be near you.*"

"Do you really know what you're saying with

that thing?" he asked cautiously, afraid now of getting his hopes up over what could simply have been a mindless gesture on her part.

She nodded. "But of course I do. As you told me once, a lady's fan is like a sword, and she must, therefore, handle it as expertly. Don't you agree?"

"Yes. I suppose so," Richard replied with a smile. But before he could reach her and embrace her once more, she was on to sending him another message, and he froze and stood awaiting it more breathlessly than he ever had the fan talk of any other woman.

This time she simply shut the fan very slowly, stick by stick, with the grace of a swan.

Again the words flashed into Richard's mind like lightning. *"I promise to marry you."*

"And I you," he answered in a reverent whisper, rushing to take her into his arms.

Epilogue

Five days later, Richard and Angeline were married by a Puritan vicar in a church near the Brenton family estate. Angeline's cousin, Elise, graciously agreed to delay her journey to New Orleans so that she could act as maid of honor in the ceremony. Peter Tyler, rolling his eyes all the while and continuing to maintain that Richard had "taken leave of his senses," served as Richard's best man.

A few months after the wedding, Richard and Angeline traveled down to visit Angeline's father in the newly established Acadian settlement in New Orleans. Monsieur DuBay, though initially reluctant, finally gave the couple his blessings on their union.

Having long since acknowledged how risky it was for Angeline to continue to reside in Boston, where her gift as a healer might, one day, lead to accusations that she was practicing witchcraft, Richard believed that New Orleans would ultimately prove to be the safest place for her. So, in 1757, two and a half years after they were married, Richard made arrangements with his father to open a branch of the family shipping business in Louisiana. After apprenticing a suitable replacement as his father's business partner in Boston, Richard took Angeline back to New Orleans, where they began life anew among the Acadians—who would later come to be called the *Cajuns*.

In the spring of 1758, Angeline, with her cousin, Elise, acting as midwife, gave birth to the next heir of the Brenton estates in both Boston and Louisiana. All went smoothly with the birth, and the girl-child was christened Caroline Elise Brenton. Richard expressed concern that a female heir might find herself too heavily burdened with the running of *two* branches of the family estate and business. His sisters, Amelia and Louisa, however, were quick to assure him that, if little Caroline proved to be half the matriarch and mistress that her mother was, things were sure to go very well for her.

And thus began the next generation, a generation that would find its destiny in the Age of Enlightenment writings of such French philosophers as Jean Jacques Rousseau and Voltaire—as their ideas finally gave rise to the Revolutionary

War. Richard and Angeline would later be quite pleased to note that this was to be a war in which the Cajuns of Louisiana would win some very significant battles.

HISTORICAL ROMANCES BY VICTORIA THOMPSON

BOLD TEXAS EMBRACE   (2835, $4.50)

Art teacher Catherine Eaton could hardly believe how stubborn Sam Connors was! Even though the rancher's young stepbrother was an exceptionally talented painter, Sam forbade Catherine to instruct him, fearing that art would make a sissy out of him. Spunky and determined, the blond schoolmarm confronted the muleheaded cowboy . . . only to find that he was as handsome as he was hard-headed and as desirable as he was dictatorial. Before long she had nearly forgotten what she'd come for, as Sam's brash, breathless embrace drove from her mind all thought of anything save wanting him . . .

TEXAS BLONDE   (2183, $3.95)

When dashing Josh Logan rescued her from death by exposure, petite Felicity Morrow realized she'd never survive rugged frontier life without a man by her side. And when she gazed at the Texas rancher's lean hard frame and strong rippling muscles, the determined beauty decided he was the one for her. To reach her goal, feisty Felicity pretended to be meek and mild: the only kind of gal Josh proclaimed he'd wed. But after she'd won his hand, the blue-eyed temptress swore she'd quit playing his game—and still win his heart!

ANGEL HEART   (2426, $3.95)

Ever since Angelica's father died, Harlan Snyder had been angling to get his hands on her ranch, the Diamond R. And now, just when she had an important government contract to fulfill, she couldn't find a single cowhand to hire on—all because of Snyder's threats. It was only a matter of time before she lost the ranch. . . . That is, until the legendary gunfighter Kid Collins turned up on her doorstep, badly wounded. Angelica assessed his firmly muscled physique and stared into his startling blue eyes. Beneath all that blood and dirt he was the handsomest man she had ever seen, and the one person who could help her beat Snyder at his own game—if the price were not too high. . . .